Praise for Jan Moran's Novels

The Chocolatier

"A delicious novel that makes you long for chocolate."
– *Ciao Tutti*

"Jan Moran is the new queen of the epic romance."
— Rebecca Forster, *USA Today* Bestselling Author

"The pacing is perfect, moving the reader along bit by bit, holding back just enough to maintain the mystery and suspense."
— Betty Taylor, Goodreads Reviewer

"A feel-good book in which the love between family members and the love for chocolate is central." — *About My Bookshelf*

"Wonderful, smoothly written. The love of chocolate drips from the page. Full of intrigue, love, secrets, and romance."
— *Lekker Lezen*

Seabreeze Inn and the Summer Beach Series

"As delightful as the title sounds. An enjoyable, lovely read that will lift your spirits and have you looking up famous artists and seeing if the town is real or fictional." — *Silver's Reviews*

"Quite simply a wonderful story that is a great read at any time of the year. Still, if you want a book that makes you feel like the sea breeze is streaming through your hair, this is for you."
— Laura Bradbury, Author of *A Vineyard for Two*

The Winemakers (St. Martin's Griffin)

"We were spellbound by the thread of deception weaving the book's characters into a tangled web."
– *The Mercury News*

"Jan Moran weaves knowledge of wine and winemaking into this intense family drama." – *Booklist*

"Jan Moran rivals Danielle Steel at her romantic best."
— Allegra Jordan, author of *The End of Innocence*

"Beautifully layered and utterly compelling." — Jane Porter, *New York Times* & *USA Today* Bestselling Author

"Readers will devour this page-turner as the mystery and passions spin out." – *Library Journal*

Scent of Triumph (St. Martin's Griffin)

"Heartbreaking, evocative, and inspiring, this book is a powerful journey." – Allison Pataki, *New York Times* Bestselling Author of *The Accidental Empress*

"A novel that gives fans of romantic sagas a compelling voice to follow." – *Booklist*

"Courageous heroine; star-crossed lovers; daunting saga; splendid sense of time and place, capturing the turmoil of the 1940s; an HEA...featuring a larger-than-life heroine."
– *Heroes and Heartbreakers*

"A sweeping saga of one woman's journey through WWII. A heartbreaking, evocative read!"
— Anita Hughes, Author of *Lake Como*

"A dedicated look into world of fashion; recommended."
— *Midwest Book Review*

"A gripping World War II story of poignant love and heart-wrenching loss. Perfumes are so beautifully described, you can almost smell them." — Gill Paul, *USA Today* Bestselling Author

The CHOCOLATIER

a novel

Books by Jan Moran

20th Century Historical

The Chocolatier

The Winemakers: A Novel of Wine and Secrets

Scent of Triumph: A Novel of Perfume and Passion

Contemporary

The Summer Beach Series:

Seabreeze Inn

Seabreeze Summer

Seabreeze Sunset

The Love, California Series:

Flawless

Beauty Mark

Runway

Essence

Style

Sparkle

Nonfiction

Vintage Perfumes

To hear about Jan's new books first and get special offers, join Jan's VIP Readers Club at www.JanMoran.com.

The CHOCOLATIER

a novel

JAN MORAN

Library of Congress Cataloging-in-Publication Data
Moran, Jan.
/ by Jan Moran

ISBN 978-1-951314-02-6 (softcover)
ISBN 978-1-951314-04-0 (hardcover)
ISBN 978-1-951314-05-7 (large print)
ISBN 978-1-951314-06-4 (epub ebook)

Also published in German by Goldmann Verlag / Random House and in Dutch by Karakter Uitgevers B.V.

Cover design by ZERO Media GmbH, adapted by Sleepy Fox Studio
Cover images copyright ArcAngel, FinePic Munich, Zero Media, and Deposit Photos.

Sunny Palms Press
9663 Santa Monica Blvd STE 1158
Beverly Hills, CA, USA
www.sunnypalmspress.com
www.JanMoran.com

For my sweet family, friends, and readers.

Chapter 1

San Francisco, 1953

ONE CHOCOLATE TRUFFLE had changed her destiny. Indeed, it *was* one of Celina's best—a silky cocoa powder-dusted truffle filled with raspberry-infused, dark chocolate ganache and enrobed with a *couverture*, a layer of rich chocolate that melted optimally with the warmth of the body.

After she had offered one to a weary, dark-haired soldier who had just returned from the European front, he introduced himself as Tony Savoia, an Italian immigrant whose family had owned and operated Cioccolata Savoia before war rationing had made sugar difficult to obtain. The truffle had restored light to his eyes. Though she knew little else of the charming, impetuous man who wooed her with murmurs of love, they married within a few months.

"That's right. Cioccolata Savoia in Naples, Italy," Celina said to the international operator, trying to keep the crack of emotion out of her voice. She repeated the foreign telephone number to the world-renowned chocolate company and hung up. The operator would call back when the connection was ready.

A telegram wouldn't do, not for this type of news.

Anxious to reach Tony's father, Celina had waited until midnight to place a call to his company. She perched on a little wooden chair in the narrow hallway of the tiny apartment near

Union Square, poised to answer quickly to keep the trilling ring from waking her young son. Turning up the collar of her flannel robe against the chill night air that bathed her neck, she clutched a piece of notepaper and gazed out the living room window at the city lights that lined the sloping hillside street as it fell toward the bay. The brightly lit sign of Ghirardelli, the chocolaterie that had been serving up chocolate for the past hundred years in San Francisco, illuminated the Golden Gate Strait. How many times had she gazed at that sign, a beacon of what she, too, might achieve with hard work? Yet now, her future seemed as foggy as the mist hovering over the city.

Months ago, Celina had written to her husband's family in Italy, notifying them as she felt she should, regardless of Tony's strained relationship with his parents. Just as he'd warned her, they had never replied. Had they even received her letter? She felt a duty to inform them, as well as reaching out on behalf of little Marco—her son and their grandchild—even though Tony had always forbidden contact with them. That had been his only rule.

She drew a trembling hand across her forehead. *Six months.* How could that be? Every day since then had been an exercise in suppressing her grief to get through the day. She felt adrift without her husband, without a real home or family. Through the open window, foghorns bleated in the distance as if to signal danger in the murky depths of her memories.

A second letter she'd sent to Tony's parents had also been returned to her just last week. *Invalid address. Undeliverable.* She'd even wondered if his parents were still living, though she knew his family's company had resumed operations in Italy after the war. Among connoisseurs of chocolate, Cioccolata Savoia was famous. From Torino to Amalfi, experts lauded the family's legendary chocolatiers for fusing the smooth, delicate flavor of *Criollo* chocolate with Sorrentino and Amalfitano lemons. Chocolate aficionados around the world had celebrated the reopening.

When the telephone jangled on the wall, Celina snatched the receiver. "Hello?"

The telephone line clicked.

"Who is this?" an angry male voice demanded. "Who is calling this time of night?"

She considered herself lucky to have a telephone line at all, though she had to share a party line. Hearing her son whimpering, she cupped her hand around her mouth and the receiver, shielding the noise.

"Mr. Albertson, this is Mrs. Savoia," she said, lowering her voice. "I'm sorry, but I have to place a call to Italy." His wife chatted on the phone so much that Celina could hardly get a call through when she needed to. "Please go back to bed."

"Can't do that during daylight hours? Some of us have to sleep."

Mr. Albertson muttered something else Celina chose to ignore. If Tony had been around, he would've leapt to her defense. At the moment, an argument wasn't worth it.

"Excuse me," the operator intoned. "I can connect you to Italy now."

Celina clutched the phone. "Mr. Albertson, please hang up, this is important." At the sound of the disconnection, she blew out a breath in relief.

"Hold, please. I have your party in Italy. Connecting now."

As the operator switched the call across transatlantic lines, Celina heard a series of clicks. Moments later, a tinny voice echoed toward her.

"Pronto? Cioccolata Savoia. Pronto?"

"Posso parlare con il Signor Savoia, per favore," Celina said, raising her voice as she read from the paper she held, asking to speak to her father-in-law. *"Sto chiamando dagli Stati Uniti." I'm calling from the United States.* She had visited the library and used an Italian dictionary to form the words she would need to say. She'd been practicing how to deliver such dreadful news in a

language with which she struggled. When she spoke Italian, Tony had often laughed—lovingly, at least—at her efforts.

"*Si, si. Un momento per favore.*"

Celina could hear crinkling and bustling, and she imagined that the secretary was rushing to find Tony's father. She drew in a breath to quell her nerves. This call wasn't one any parent wanted to receive.

"*Lui non è qui.*"

Pent up air surged from her lungs. *He wasn't there.* She was half-frustrated, half-relieved. This call wasn't one anyone wanted to make either.

"*Qual è il tuo numero di telefono, per favore?*"

Slowly, Celina recited her number. The woman said something else, but Celina couldn't make it out. *"Mi dispiace, non capisco."*

After saying good-bye, Celina returned the receiver to its hook and stared from the window.

Non capisco. She still didn't understand why Tony had to be taken from them, repeating the pattern of her childhood, yet ruminating on this regretful coincidence wouldn't bring him back. As a parent, her son depended on her. She no longer had the luxury of childhood, fretting about her turn-out in ballet class or practicing her piano scales as she had before her father had died and her mother had returned to work full time as a *chocolatière.* Now she knew how her mother had felt. Resolutely, she rose to prepare for bed.

She was in a deadened sleep when the telephone rang again.

Recognizing her party line ringtone, Celina whipped off the duvet and bounded toward the phone, her feet slapping the oak hardwood floor. Marco cried out as she passed his room, but she couldn't stop to comfort him.

"Hello?" Pushing her tangled hair from her forehead, she stood barefoot, shivering from the damp morning chill off the bay that seeped through her cotton gown. The moon illuminated the room, glancing off trees that lined the street outside and projecting alien shapes into her home. "*Pronto?*" She held her breath. Eerie shadows swirled before her like wispy wraiths twisting in a silent, moon shadow dance. Turning from the window, she hugged an arm around her midsection and rested her forehead on the wall. "Hello?"

The line crackled, and from half a globe away a man's deep voice reverberated through the connection. "This is Lauro Savoia. May I help you?"

"I called earlier." He spoke in accented English, but the smooth, rich tenor of his voice made Celina grapple for the wooden chair. Trying to dispel the nocturnal fog from her brain, she rubbed her eyes.

"*Mi dispiace,* it sounds like I woke you." He hesitated. "You are in New York, no?"

"San Francisco."

A small silence ensued. "*Sono le cinque di mattina.* Forgive me, it must be five in the morning. I will call back later. It is too early for business."

"This isn't a business call," she blurted out. Squeezing her eyes, she struggled for composure. "I'm calling about your son, Tony."

The line fell silent, and Celina thought she had lost the connection. "Are you still there?"

"*Sì*. I am Lauro Savoia. Do you mean Antonino? He is my brother..."

Brother? Tony had never mentioned any siblings, but maybe this was better. And he spoke English. "Yes, Antonino." *Tony* was her husband's nickname. But before she could go on, Lauro's voice rippled across the line.

"I cannot help you," he said. "Antonino went missing at the end of the war."

"No, that's not right. He was in America." Her words tumbled out. "We were married. We have a son. But something terrible happened, and I thought his family should know." Celina paused before delivering the words she knew would break his heart, just as they had devastated her when she'd received the telephone call that foggy evening.

"Hurry up, girl." On the other side of the glass case filled with handmade chocolates, a plump woman in a woolen overcoat snapped her fingers at her. "I haven't got all day."

Jarred from her thoughts, Celina blinked at the imperious cook who stood before her. Mrs. McCloskey, who worked for the Davis family's eldest son, tapped the tip of her umbrella on the French tiled floor of La Petite Maison du Chocolat, a jewel-box of a shop that catered to Nob Hill aristocrats. Chastising herself, Celina yanked her mind from its wretched recesses, where she tried to keep herself from going day after day. Nothing good would come from that.

"Yes, ma'am," Celina said, returning her attention to the tray of creamy fruit-filled chocolates that sat before her. Scents of raspberry and apricot teased her nose. With a deft hand, she nestled each silky delicacy with care into a cardboard box.

Celina had grown up with the aroma of chocolate wafting through her home. As a young woman, her mother had studied at a chocolaterie in Paris before the war, and she had taught Celina how to make handcrafted praliné or truffles, the molded or rounded chocolates filled with delectable centers, such as caramelized nut paste of *noisettes* or *amandes*. For hers, Celina often chose apricot, cherry, salted caramel, cream liqueurs—or any other filling that might catch her fancy. Lately, she had been experimenting with the delicate flavor of green tea she'd found in San Francisco's Chinatown.

She secured the lid on the box and unfurled a length of twine. Perhaps she'd bring a treat home to little Marco today, though not one of these chocolates. He'd surely like one of the miniature bunnies she'd made this morning. Without his father around, she indulged the six-year-old perhaps a little more than she should in an effort to bring a smile to his solemn face. His grief seemed even deeper than hers, though he had fewer words and ways to express it. Even now, she often heard his quiet sobs in the night. She would hurry in and stroke his back, reassuring him until he fell asleep again.

Reaching for scissors, Celina darted a glance across the busy commercial street to the apartments stacked above the shops. Theirs was a third-floor walkup, a far cry from the gaily painted Victorian home they'd lived in until last year, though she'd sold it for a good price. She couldn't bear waking in the same bedroom she'd shared with her husband. Returning to work at the chocolaterie where she'd met Tony was hard enough, but at least the job provided for them and kept her mind occupied.

Lifting her gaze, she caught a glimpse of her little boy through a window at a neighbor's apartment, where he stayed while she worked. Her heart full, she smiled at the sight of him, his head bent over a toy truck. It wasn't the comfortable life she'd once enjoyed when her days were filled with taking Marco to the park or the bay to watch boats, but it worked for them for now.

Whizzing past her field of vision, a wiry teenaged boy in a uniform and riding a red bicycle jumped the curb and wheeled to a stop at the entrance to her apartment building. She watched as he pushed up his Western Union hat at a rakish angle and pressed the buzzer.

Even now, years since the war had ended, the thought of a telegram still filled her with dread. So many of her uncles and cousins and childhood friends had never returned from foreign shores—their parents informed only by a telegram sent from the Secretary of War. *With deepest regret...* An involuntary shudder coursed through her. Tony had survived the war, only to lose his life on the Golden Gate Bridge. To this day, she couldn't understand why he'd gone out so late that night.

If only that man with a thick New York accent hadn't called. She had no idea who he was. It was almost ten in the evening when she had answered the telephone, and after Tony had spoken to the man, he told her he had to do something. When she asked what, he scowled, saying it was men's business. *Whatever that meant.*

Blinking back memories, she clipped the twine.

Mrs. McCloskey cleared her throat. "Those are the missus' favorites, so I'll need them on Tuesday and Friday until she gets on to another flavor."

"Of course," Celina said, shifting her attention back to her customer.

The woman crossed her arms across her ample bosom. "My missus turns her dainty nose up at my fine meals and then calls for tea and chocolates. I swear she lives on champagne and sweets. Trying to get into the clothes she wore afore the baby. Won't do no good, I tell her. Once you lose your teeny waistline, it ain't never coming back." She pointed the frightful, carved monkey head of an umbrella she'd probably bought in Chinatown toward Celina. "You'll see someday."

Celina swept a cordial smile onto her face but offered no reply. After Tony's death, her lingering baby weight had swiftly fallen off as she'd lost interest in food, cooking only to keep Marco fed and healthy—not that he'd had much appetite either. Though according to her boss, divulging such personal information to customers like Mrs. McCloskey was strictly *interdit*—verboten, forbidden. Pleasantries, *oui.* Personal details or gossip, *non.* Which was fine by her. She placed a finger on the rough twine, double knotting the bow for protection. Most people took her for younger than her years, but these days she felt every bit of her three decades and more.

Celina tucked the box into a bag with care. She truly loved her work. Except when her co-worker Marge was off, or the owner had an engagement, as Monsieur Jean-Jacques did today, she spent most days in the kitchen behind the shop creating new chocolate fantasies and beloved favorites for their clientele. Fine *Criollo* or *Porcelana* chocolate made from cacao beans sourced from Venezuela and the more robust *Trinitario* chocolate sourced from Peru had to be melted slowly to just the right temperature, poured into molds, and decorated by hand.

Some might think the attention to labor tedious, but it appealed to her artistic sense. And she loved seeing the pure delight on faces when people tasted her creations. To share chocolate was to share love; each bon-bon held a piece of her heart.

Besides playing with her son, this was one of the few activities in which she could lose herself. While she worked, images flickered through her mind, and she could hear her mother's admonitions as clearly as she had as a young girl. *Watch it closely, my love. The higher the fat content, the faster it melts.* Celina recalled her instruction about the white discoloration that sometimes developed on chocolate—unsightly, though harmless. *Careful, covering a cold center will create fat bloom. Too much moisture in the air, you'll risk sugar bloom.* Making truffles was as much a science as an art. Celina missed her mother more these last six months than in the decade since her death during the war.

"Here's your package, Mrs. McCloskey. Try not to jostle it." Celina plucked a dark chocolate *praliné* filled with buttercream she'd made just that morning from the case and placed it on a lacy paper doily. "And something special for you," she added, challenged to obtain the rare smile from Mrs. McCloskey.

The cook accepted the offering and popped it into her mouth. A strangled expression Celina took to be as close to pleasure as Mrs. McCloskey ever experienced crossed the woman's face. As the cook pushed her way out, the bell on the door tinkled. Celina pursed her lips. She'd win that woman over yet.

Through the window, Celina noticed the telegram boy pacing as he waited, impatient to be on his way, and she idly wondered who his message was for. Certainly not for her. After the war, she had no family left, save her little boy. Maybe it was for Lizzie LeClerc, the flamboyant young actress who lived across the hall from her and currently had a supporting role in a new stage play at the Geary Theater. If so, Celina was sure she'd hear all about it. At least Lizzie could make her laugh from time to time.

She picked up a cloth to clean smudges from the glass. The door tinkled again, and a young couple stopped to admire a display, exclaiming over the chocolate flights of fancy.

In honor of the beginning of summer, Celina had cut out large shapes of palm trees and sailboats from cardboard and painted them in vivid hues of pink, yellow, and blue to showcase her ornately embellished chocolate eggs fashioned after Richard Cadbury's original Victorian chocolate egg designs in England. *Coral rosebuds, trailing green vines, tiny bluebirds, palm trees, starfish, and sailboats.* Similar eggs had been popular at Easter, but these had themes of summer in San Francisco. She had even created a large, molded chocolate Golden Gate Bridge for one party.

Beyond them, she could see the Western Union boy talking to Lizzie. The platinum-blond actress was flirting with the boy and pointing across the street to the chocolaterie. Celina was curious, but she refocused her attention on the couple.

"Imagine these on the table for our party," the woman said, grasping her husband's hand. "The children would love them."

Tipping his hat at Celina, the man said, "Good day. We want to order a dozen of these."

"Can you create a special presentation?" the woman asked.

"I can put them in a picnic basket lined with checked cloth." When they agreed, Celina said, "I'll write up the order for you.

When would you like to pick them up?" While she took down their names, the door jangled open.

"Mrs. Savoia?" The Western Union boy clutched a thin envelope.

"That's right." Celina signed for the telegram and withdrew a couple of coins from her apron pocket for the boy, who then rushed out. After finishing the couple's order, she slid onto a stool beside the counter and picked up the telegram. She'd saved the condolence cards she'd received. The wording was always so similar. *Deepest sympathy. Our thoughts and prayers.* She'd received several late cards from people who had just learned of his death. Bracing herself, she opened the thin envelope.

As she scanned the few typewritten lines stretched across the page, her lips parted in surprise.

> *We send you our deepest regrets. Parents anxious to meet you. Please come to our home in Amalfi with your son. You are family and welcome here. Will arrange air tickets to Italy. Details to follow. - Lauro Savoia*

Tears sprang to her eyes, and Celina crushed the telegram to her chest with joy. Never had she imagined such a response. And now, they'd invited her to Italy to visit. On an airplane, no less. Her heart thudded with excitement. What did she have to stay for here? *Nothing.* Dabbing her cheeks, she made her decision. She and Marco would go.

Springing from the stool, her mind began to buzz with thoughts of packing and traveling. She wondered how soon they could be off. Pressing her hand to her chest, she broke into a broad smile. Not since Tony had died had she felt such excitement. That's what she and Marco needed now—a change of scenery, even the chance for happiness again someday. Her son deserved that.

She stopped and caught a glimpse of herself in the mirror, frowning at the gaunt woman whose wavy blond hair was scraped into a bun. Her face was pale and devoid of makeup. Maybe Lizzie could help her freshen her look before she left.

And then a darker thought assailed her as she recalled what Tony had said about his parents. *Cold as fish. Full of themselves. Can't trust them.* Although she'd tried to get him to talk more about them, he had stubbornly refused. Were they as mysterious as her husband had been? *Only today and tomorrow matter*, he'd often said.

Tracing the scars on his skin, she'd understood why some stories were difficult to share. He'd seldom spoken of his U.S. Army service, mainly because he'd worked in military intelligence and his activities were classified as secret, he said. But family was different. Family was forever, or so she'd desperately wanted to believe. As it turned out, their forever had been cut short.

Should I be worried? She reread the telegram. *You are family and welcome here.* It was sent by Lauro Savoia, the brother Tony had never mentioned. *Why hadn't he?* Who was Lauro and what had happened between them?

The thin paper wavered in her hand as trepidation seeped into her mind.

Celina stepped back from the small mirror she'd balanced on the bureau, bobbing up and down to take in the full effect. She'd put on a dark navy wool suit to travel in, along with sensible heels. Next to the mirror were the tickets the Savoia family had sent her, and tomorrow morning, she and Marco would board a transatlantic flight bound for Rome.

Even now, she could hardly believe they were going. Squinting at her reflection, she turned to the side to see her profile. The skirt hung on her. She poked a safety pin through the fabric to take in the fullness.

It will have to do. She drew in a nervous breath. Soon she would meet Tony's parents and his brother, reopening tender scabs over wounds of grief she felt would never fully heal. She was worried about Marco and concerned about how reliving the funeral would affect him.

Pressing a hand against her pounding heart, she tried to focus on the positive aspect of the journey—Marco would meet his only living grandparents. She hoped they would be kind to him, though she couldn't help wondering how they would feel about meeting them so long after they should have.

Footsteps tapped behind her, and Lizzie plopped onto the cotton quilt, lacing her fingers behind her platinum waves. Deep, matte red lipstick outlined full pouty lips. "You're going to Italy looking like *that*?"

"What's wrong with it?"

"Nothing, if you're going to a funeral."

Celina shot her neighbor a look across her shoulder and sighed.

Lizzie clamped a hand over her mouth. "Oh, I'm so sorry, was that …?

Smoothing a hand over a sleeve, she said, "Actually, I got married in this suit, too. With a white embroidered eyelet blouse and a bouquet of red roses." So many memories were woven into this cloth.

"You're kidding, right?"

Celina slid a look of consternation toward her neighbor. Lizzie was just twenty-one years old and had been raised on a farm in Iowa. What a difference the decade between them made sometimes. "Rationing was in effect then. It was considered unpatriotic to wear reams of silk, not that we could get it anyway."

"A flour sack would have been a happier prospect."

Celina made a face, concealing her emotions. Shrugging out of the fitted jacket, she hung it in the narrow closet next to a light gray suit, then eased the slim skirt over her full slip. She ran her hand over the dark worsted wool, lowering her eyes to blink back hot tears that threatened to slip over her lashes. The last time she'd worn this suit she'd watched the love of her life being lowered into the cold January earth. After that, she'd never wanted to wear it again, but now she would have to go through the mourning process again in honor to his parents.

Lizzie sat up, hugging her knees through black tights. She'd just come from theater practice and wore a leotard with a dance skirt topped with a black leather jacket. "Don't you have anything in there that'll razz their berries?"

"This isn't a holiday," Celina said, feeling a little dowdy in comparison. Still, she couldn't help but smile through her sadness at Lizzie, imagining what it would be like to be that carefree age again. Actors, artists, musicians—Lizzie's flat was a haven to free-thinkers who had different outlooks on life and unique ways of expressing themselves.

"You should at least try to have some fun after... Why, where I grew up, we had old-fashioned wakes that went on until sunrise. And the drama between all the kin was more than you can imagine." As if struck by inspiration, Lizzie pushed off the bed. "I'll be right back."

Celina watched her rush out. Lizzie was like the younger sister she'd never had. Her friend had never known Tony or his extravagant laughter and generous smile, so Lizzie couldn't possibly understand the depth of her loss.

Marge was the only one Celina could confide in, after all, Marge had liked Tony from the beginning when they'd met at La Petite Maison du Chocolat, but even a good friend grew tired of misery. Grief was a perpetual yoke to the past, and she was worn out, too.

Stepping out of her shoes and sliding an embroidered robe she'd bought in Chinatown over her slip, she padded down the hallway to check on Marco, who was being awfully quiet in his room. He loved to draw, and she had implored Tony to buy him art supplies for Christmas. His Santa Claus gift was a shiny bicycle, and on Christmas Day Tony had helped Marco onto the bike, trotting alongside him on the lane in front of their old home.

She still recalled everything about those last happy days. After basting the turkey, mashing the potatoes, and making individual chocolate pot de crème for their holiday supper, she'd changed into the emerald green silk dress Tony had surprised her with and stood in the doorway watching, just as she was now, never imagining it would be one of the last times she'd see the two of them together and full of joy.

Marco looked up from the small pine desk Tony had made for him. She crossed the room and peered over his shoulder. He'd been drawing the three of them again. Daddy was in every picture, and it broke her heart each time he showed her his artwork.

She paused, swallowing a sudden surge of emotion. Every day she pushed aside her feelings in an effort to function, superficially, like everyone else. "That's really nice, honey."

Sucking in his lower lip in doubt, he looked up at her. "Daddy's eyes were blue, weren't they?"

"Like yours."

"I'm forgetting what he looked like."

Another stab to the heart. She hugged Marco and rocked him, and he wrapped his arms tightly around her neck. "You don't have to have a picture to remember his love for you."

Though visual mementos would have helped, that much she knew. How she wished she'd insisted on taking photos with Tony. But he'd always ducked away from cameras.

How could such a self-possessed man be so sensitive to photographs of himself? Tony's scars were part of who he was, not what she saw when she looked at him.

"Get a load of these," Lizzie hollered as she burst through the hallway. "And look who I found coming up the stairs."

Celina kissed Marco's cheek and released him to continue his drawing. As she stepped into the hallway, she saw Marge huffing toward her.

"I swear, that girl has enough energy for the two of us," Marge said.

Pushing her wispy, gray-shot brown hair from her forehead, Marge plopped a weathered brown leather suitcase onto the bed and opened it. She still wore a dark blue cotton dress, her uniform at La Petite Maison du Chocolat, but she'd removed the crisp white apron.

"You might as well have this suitcase," Marge said. "It needs to get out and travel, do what it's meant to do. Lord knows I ain't going anywhere any time soon."

"Thank you," Celina said, embracing the older woman who had been like a mother to her. "We'll only be gone a couple of weeks."

"Just bring me back something Italian, like a handsome man." Marge sighed. "But chocolates will do."

"Promise I will."

Lizzie crowded into the small bedroom, and in her arms was a riot of colorful satins and silks. "The party has arrived."

"Gracious," Celina exclaimed. "What on earth is all this?

"The costume mistress was cleaning out the old costumes." Lizzie flung a white feather boa into the air. "Get a load of these. Bound to be something here you can wear to liven things up. It's *Italy*, after all."

"Lizzie, I can't possibly..." Celina began, but she had to admit some of the dresses were stunning.

A flaming red flapper dress, a sleek black dress with full, satin purple sleeves and a matching flounce, a summery cotton frock with a cheerful red poppy print, and a musketeer's gold-trimmed jacket tumbled out of the pile of clothing. A mound of scarves fluttered onto the bed.

Marge fingered the frayed, tasseled edge of a silk jacquard scarf in shades of amethyst and emerald green. "This is lovely. It's easily mended."

"Perfect for her." Lizzie tossed it around Celina's shoulders. The fringe added drama, sweeping almost to the floor. "*Voila*!"

"That's a showstopper," Marge said, her eyes growing wide as Lizzie swept Celina's hair high onto her head.

"You're a star," Lizzie said. "Start acting like one."

"Listen to you. You'll be a director in no time." Glancing at herself in the mirror, Celina burst out laughing at the sight of herself in a Chinese robe and a scarf that could only be called theatrical.

Marge and Lizzie joined in, and soon the three friends were chuckling together.

It was the first time Celina could recall laughing since last New Year's.

"I haven't room in that suitcase for much," she said as Lizzie folded a couple of garments and whipped the scarf from her neck. "Where would I wear that?"

"You could take the train and go sightseeing with Marco," Marge said. "Italian women are very stylish."

"The men, too," Lizzie added, pursing her lips. "Maybe you'll come home with a handsome fella."

"I've got first dibs on the fella," Marge said.

"Wow, you have to take this." Lizzie reached into the closet for an emerald green silk dress.

"But not the boa." Celina plucked the feathery mound from the open suitcase.

"Why, this color is beautiful," Marge said, running her hand over the rich silk fabric with reverence. "You must take it. I'll fold it for you."

Celina grew quiet, watching as Marge carefully folded the dress Tony had given her, and she'd worn only that one day. She didn't protest.

It's what Tony would have wanted. He would have liked her wearing his last gift to her to meet his parents.

Or would he?

She couldn't help the uneasy feeling that threaded through her, stretching her nerves taut with apprehension.

Chapter 2

San Francisco, 1945

"HERE COMES YOUR Italian man," Marge said, turning up the radio to sing to the latest Andrews Sisters' harmony, which she did whenever Monsieur Jean-Jacques was away. The older woman had been working at La Petite Maison du Chocolat since Monsieur had opened it ten years ago, and after Celina's mother died, she'd taken it upon herself to match Celina with every handsome man who passed through the door.

With the shop's location near Union Square, there were plenty of men, but Celina knew that most of the young men who still wore their sailor whites or dress uniforms were just passing through, waiting to take trains home to loved ones.

Celina glanced up from behind the glass case, where she was arranging freshly made chocolates on lacy paper doilies. Business had been brisk due to returning troops from the Pacific theater pouring in through the San Francisco harbor. Boxes containing decorative gift tins were stacked to the ceiling in the back of the shop, waiting to be filled with gifts of chocolates for reunited lovers and families.

The scents of chocolate and other rich ingredients filled the air. Vanilla, sugar...raspberry, apricots...almonds, pistachios, pecans...cinnamon, nutmeg, cardamom, cayenne. Celina breathed in. She loved the aromas of her artistry.

This job was everything she had ever dreamed of, and it would have made her mother proud. Stella Romano had taught her daughter everything she'd learned about making exquisitely flavored and formed chocolates while studying in Paris before she'd married. Celina had all of her old recipes, and she'd also crafted many new versions.

"Celina, you wait on them," Marge whispered, tucking strands of gray-shot brown hair into her bun. "That tall one is terribly attractive. Distinguished. A professor, maybe."

Marge liked to guess people's vocations. "He comes for the chocolates."

"Oh, please. Every day?" Marge rolled her eyes as if Celina were naive.

Celina waved her off. Most people were naive compared to Marge, who used to work as a waitress at an all-night diner near the docks. She'd often start a story, saying, *I got one that'll roast your ears.*

"Bet he asks you out today. Look here, he's brought a friend for courage."

He didn't strike her as the kind of man who needed anyone's moral support to ask a girl to dinner. Or coffee. She wouldn't say no to either, though she didn't even know his name. Once he'd spent an entire hour in the shop, asking her about her favorite fillings and flavors, how she tempered the chocolate, and all sorts of details most people didn't give a hoot about.

She guessed he'd been a chef or teacher, maybe a pastry chef, or even a fellow chocolatier before the war, but he never offered any information about himself. Still, the way he looked at her was almost eerie. Intimate, but not sexual, as if he'd known her before. Or maybe he was an artist analyzing her features.

The bell on the shop door jingled as Marge disappeared behind a pair of short swinging doors into the kitchen, where Celina spent most of her time. Two weeks ago when the man had started asking questions about Celina's truffles, Marge had seized on a matchmaking opportunity and brought her out of the kitchen to meet him.

Since then, this courtly man with the kind eyes had been visiting the chocolaterie almost every day. Celina smiled at him. Maybe today was the day. "Good afternoon."

"*Buongiorno,*" he said, his deep voice filling the shop and reverberating off the tiled walls and floors, reminding her of a magnificent singer she'd once heard at the opera house with her mother. The man turned to his friend. "This young woman makes the finest chocolates in all of San Francisco. She has the soul of a true *chocolatière* and knows to use only the finest chocolate."

Celina felt her face warm. One day he'd quizzed her on her knowledge of ingredients, and they'd discussed the merits of different varieties of cocoa beans from Central and South America. His favorites were from Venezuela, but he also loved those from Ecuador, and he spoke with reverence about cacao from a particular part of Peru.

"I've been experimenting with a new raspberry truffle recipe." She plucked two perfectly hand-rolled truffles from the case, placed them on a white doily on a small silver tray, and offered them to the two men. "Would you like to try one?"

"Raspberry, yes?" the tall man asked, hesitating. "Not strawberry?"

"That's right," Celina said.

The man's stocky friend quickly accepted her offering. "*Grazie.*" A warm, engaging grin creased his face, though it didn't quite reach his weary eyes. Despite the angry red scars that ran from temple to jawline, he'd been handsome, and there was still something intriguing about him. She returned his quick smile. Many men and women had returned with physically lingering signs of service to their country.

As the man's friend tasted a morsel, his dark-lashed eyes lit with delight, and he seemed to transform in front of her as if her chocolate held a magical ingredient. Slinging an arm around the taller man, he grinned. "You were right, Doc. Best truffle I've ever had. And the prettiest chocolate maker."

"I'm not a chocolate maker, I'm a *chocolatière*."

A grin played on the stocky man's face. "What's the difference?"

"Chocolate makers process cacao into chocolate through fermentation," Celina said. "Chocolatiers are the artisans who use the processed chocolate to create molded and hand-formed sweets." As she spoke, Celina glanced shyly at the taller man. *Doc.* The nickname suited him. He certainly had the gentle manner of a physician. She wondered if he'd been called for duty, or if he practiced medicine here in the city. Both, perhaps.

"Smart young lady." The stocky man laughed with admiration. "You sure showed me."

Celina couldn't help but smile along with his infectious laughter.

"Don't test her, Tony," Doc said, admonishing his friend with a chuckle. "She knows what she's doing."

Doc tasted the truffle, thoughtfully measuring the texture and flavor. Celina held her breath, waiting for his opinion. He was so knowledgeable about her craft, and she trusted his judgment. Finally, he brought his fingers together and touched his lips. "Magnificent. This is your masterpiece." He smiled. "So far. But you will achieve so much more."

Celina's cheeks burned, though she tried to hide her great pleasure. "Thank you. I'm working on another recipe today. Perhaps you'd like to try it tomorrow."

"I cannot stay here." Doc shook his head, and his eyes were filled with sorrow. He took her hand in his—the first time he'd ever done that. "I'm leaving San Francisco in the morning."

His touch was magnetic, and Celina felt a chill course through her, almost like a vision. Blinking, she reminded herself that like so many other people who streamed through the shop, he was also on his way elsewhere. Nothing more than a tourist.

No, he was not the man who would change her life as Marge imagined. How silly to think he could. She cleared the thickness she felt in her throat. "I'm glad you found our chocolaterie. It's been a real pleasure meeting you."

"I'll be coming back," Tony said with a broad grin, vying for her attention. "I'll buy a box of your best." Looking hungrily at the chocolates in the glass case, he asked her to select her finest assortment, and Doc asked for the same to take with him.

While Celina wrapped up the selections, adding satin ribbons and finishing each with a deft bow, Doc's friend leaned on the glass top, watching her every movement. Glancing at him, she saw that he wore a silver medallion around his neck of St. Christopher, the patron saint of travelers.

"Sorry for testing you," Tony said in a rich, gravelly voice. "I have a real appreciation for chocolate, too."

"Really now?" she asked as Marge bustled from the kitchen with more gift tins. She must have overheard the conversation because now she was inspecting Tony. Celina stifled a laugh. She'd even applied pink lipstick and smoothed her hair. Marge didn't waste any time zeroing in on another potential suitor for her.

"Absolutely," Tony replied, trying to catch her eye while she packaged their chocolates. "I recognize and appreciate quality."

Marge quickly cut in. "Then you'll come back tomorrow to sample Celina's new truffle recipe, won't you?"

After the two men had gone, Celina smacked Marge's shoulder with a towel, playfully chastising her. "You're awfully bold."

"And why not? You're young, talented, and beautiful, and there are scads of men flowing through here." Leaning on the counter, Marge folded her hands under her chin and gazed after them. "Take it from me. Doc's leaving. When one door closes, yank open another door. Blink, and ten years pass."

"I don't know if Tony is my type."

"I bet he's a lot of fun. Don't you remember how to have fun? Ah, if I were twenty years younger, you wouldn't stand a chance with him," she said, fluttering her lashes. "That man has a kind face, I can tell. That's what counts. Handsome, too. Look past the scars, sweetheart. Most young women won't."

"Scars don't bother me."

With a wink, Marge elbowed her in the ribs. "Makes him look dangerous. Sexy, even. Shows he can handle himself and survive."

Celina felt her face warm. Resting an elbow on the case next to Marge, she cupped her chin in thought. "I think every scar and every wrinkle tells a story. But I don't know if he's my type."

Still, there was something about his lively dark eyes and the intense way he looked at her, just like she remembered her father looking at her mother. Despite her disappointment over Doc's departure, she found herself hoping she might see Tony again.

Chapter 3

Naples, 1953

"*Napoli Centrale*," a train attendant called out as the train slowed to a stop in the bustling city. Weary from the arduous journey that had taken them from the airport in Rome to the southwestern region of Italy, Celina slid her leather handbag over the sleeve of her light gray traveling suit and adjusted a chic crimson scarf Lizzie had given her. With care, she hooked a bag containing a box of chocolates over her arm. She'd made her best truffles for Tony's parents.

She gripped Marco's shoulder, determined in her mission, and stepped off the train. Passing through the crowded station, the smell of roasted espresso and sweet *sfogliatelle* teased her nose, accompanied by the whirring clatter of grinding beans. The flow of the crowd carried them outside onto the sidewalk, where she glanced around, looking for the person who would be meeting them.

With a gloved hand, she secured her hat against an early summer breeze, hardly believing they were here. She'd taken leave from her job and sublet the apartment to a pair of actress friends of Lizzie's who were hoping to find theater parts in San Francisco.

Just two weeks ago, she could never have imagined this. The flight over the Atlantic Ocean had been scary at times due to frightening turbulence, but the stewardess attending them had put Marco at ease by giving him a small replica of the Boeing 377 Stratocruiser airplane they flew. He'd been enamored with it until he fell asleep after a dinner served on fine china with real silverware. Only then had Celina allowed herself a glass of wine to take the edge off her anxiety.

Screwing his face against the sunshine, Marco stumbled on a cracked cobblestone and let out a wail. He clutched a worn gray monkey Celina had stitched together from knitted socks. The crimson heels formed a wide mouth in a perpetual grin.

"You're all right," Celina said, kneeling to hug him and brush off his dusty trousers. "Be sure to hold onto Rocky. He'd be so sad if you lost him."

She'd woken him from a deadened sleep. Despite the clacking rails and her thrill over the awe-inspiring countryside from Vesuvius to the shoreline rushing past, she'd also been lulled to sleep by the rhythmic movement. After the turbulence of the air flight, she was relieved to touch her feet to solid ground once again.

Their fellow passengers bustled past and melodic strains of the Italian language rose around them, flowing forth with the energy of the tumbling sea. "*Ciao! Come stai?*" People hugged and pressed their cheeks to each other, trading multiple kisses. "*Benissimo! Che piacere!*"

Celina kissed Marco's cheek. "Listen. Hear it? There's happiness in the air."

Marco stopped crying, and the edges of his mouth curved upward.

To Celina's relief, a tentative smile grew on Marco's face. Gazing around with saucer-round eyes, Marco was enchanted. She had to admit she was, too. From the fresh sea air to the warmth of expressions bubbling around them, Naples was already sunlight to her soul.

Then, biting her lip, she thought of Tony, and how she'd always wanted to visit Italy with her husband. He'd never wanted to see his family again—yet they *were* family, and she couldn't imagine how he could turn his back on them. As a spirited teenager, she'd sometimes argued with her parents, but she would never have thought of breaking off relations with them. Tony seldom spoke of his parents, and he'd always found an excuse not to visit Italy—any part of the country.

Taking in the beauty of her surroundings, Celina regretted that they'd missed experiencing the land of her husband's birth together.

If only she'd been more insistent, perhaps Tony would have relented. How would she explain this to his parents? She swallowed against a lump that rose in her throat. She would do the best she could, though apologies would hardly absolve her of fault to a family robbed of their son and the chance to see him one last time.

Yet, maybe they were the ones who should be apologizing. Had the kind words in the telegram been a veneer over a scarred and ugly past? During the trip, it seemed the closer they got, the more nervous she'd become. Would his parents blame her? If she learned a dark family secret, would she wish she'd never come?

A train attendant placed their leather bags beside them.

"*Grazie*," Celina said. She'd learned a spattering of Italian from Tony, but they'd mostly spoken English, although now she was glad that Tony had started teaching Marco a few phrases.

At least Tony's parents would have the joy of seeing their grandchild. Despite what had transpired between Tony and his parents, she knew this was the right thing to do. She couldn't help but wonder if Tony would have acted differently if he had known his time would be cut short.

Neither of them could have foreseen the events of that foggy evening that stole Tony's life. Or that the last words they'd uttered to each other would have been so sharp—his so full of vitriol, and hers so full of accusation. She had lain awake at night in regret, but no amount of midnight prayers begging for forgiveness could erase the last words they'd spoken in anger. She'd wanted him to stay in and kiss her at midnight of the New Year, not charge out into the night after a mysterious telephone call.

Now that seemed such a trivial matter.

She let out a small sigh. Her mother had always told her that even the best marriages were complicated. Now she understood. Or at least, she was trying to.

After his death, she'd committed herself to remember only his generosity, his gregarious nature, and the good times they'd shared, but the truth was that when he had been in one of his dark moods, his fury frightened her, and his scathing comments sliced off slivers of her confidence and burrowed into the marrow of her bones.

As the distance in years from the war increased, his darkness had lifted, but she'd always felt he was concealing a part of himself that he could trust with no other soul. Not even his wife. She assumed this secrecy had to do with his military service, so she let it be. She wasn't the only person whose spouse shielded loved ones from nightmarish memories. Maybe if he had unburdened himself… She swept away the questioning thoughts that could drive her mad if she let them.

Blinking, Celina shaded her eyes from the sun, growing worried that no one might meet them, yet she had to keep her wits about her. As thoughtful as Tony's parents' gesture seemed, this visit could be a disaster. At least she would know she had tried to do the right thing. And someday, Marco would understand that she had not kept him from his father's family.

Celina knelt and wrapped her arms around Marco. When Tony was feeling good and in fine form, few could outshine his charm or his devotion to his little family. She'd never doubted his love for her or Marco.

Was his family like that?

To one side, a well-dressed man stood staring at her.

"*Scusami*, Signora Savoia?"

Angling her face toward the voice, Celina rose and tented her hand against her forehead. The sun framed the man who stood before her. "I'm Celina Savoia."

"*Buonasera.*" He furrowed his brow and stared at her for a moment as if he recognized her. Then, remembering his manners, he quickly removed his hat, revealing sleekly groomed, ebony hair. "I am Lauro." He glanced at the small boy who clutched her hand. "Your son?"

"And Tony's. This is Marco. Your nephew." She turned slightly from the sun to see Lauro more clearly, and as she did, she was startled, though not at his resemblance to Tony, but rather, at the lack thereof.

Wearing a fitted, dark charcoal suit, Lauro was as broad-shouldered as Tony, but there the likeness stopped. He was taller, and where Tony had a proud face, high forehead, and thick features, Lauro had a classically chiseled profile and well-proportioned features. Strong cheekbones balanced an aquiline nose and a full lower lip that undoubtedly drew women's attention.

Lauro was undeniably attractive, but more than that, he stood comfortably in his space, exuding quiet self-assurance. Tony's usual stance had been with his chest thrust out in forced confidence, daring to take on the world—or defend it. She could only surmise that they took after different branches of their family tree.

Celina smiled and held out her hand in greeting.

Though Lauro took her proffered hand, he also leaned in respectfully, kissing first one cheek and then the other in a traditional Italian greeting Celina knew well. The warmth emanating from his neck and his spicy, sandalwood scent drew her in. She was surprised to find that his closeness was pleasant. He was proper enough, though sadness rimmed his olive green eyes and he seemed aloof.

Based on Lauro's telegram, this was not what she had expected. She would have thought that he'd be more like Tony, who was glib and outgoing. Lauro displayed more restraint. Perhaps this was what Tony had meant when he'd described his family as cold.

After pulling back, Lauro squatted on his haunches and peered into Marco's face as though searching for physical traces of his brother. "*Ciao*."

Embarrassed, Marco turned to hide his face in the folds of Celina's light woolen skirt. Celina slid her hand over her son's back. "He's not usually like this, but he's tired. It was a long trip."

Looking up, Lauro stared at her again, unsmiling. "Your luggage?" He motioned to her suitcases. When she nodded, he hoisted them with ease and started toward a shiny Alfa Romeo sedan gleaming with chrome parked at the curb.

Celina took Marco's hand and hurried after Lauro. He wasn't unattractive, and his gaze seemed to reach her soul, summoning emotions long buried and not exactly welcome now.

After placing the bags in the rear, he opened the door for her. Celina tucked Marco between them, and they started off.

As they wound through the city, Marco pressed his hands against the window in curiosity. Celina followed his gaze toward a plaza, in the middle of which stood a stone fountain trickling with water. Marco laughed, pointing toward a couple of boys who were splashing each other as they passed the fountain and chasing each other in fun. Nearby, children clamored at a gelato shop, women peered into a boutique's fashionable window, and men sat on benches talking and chuckling.

Lauro turned onto another street and Celina stared in awe at the delphinium blue ocean that spread out before them. Sunlight kissed the crystalline waves, throwing diamond sparkles across boats moored in the harbor.

Soon they were traversing a road that hugged the mountains and crossed inlets, suspended in air. Celina marveled at the views, though she edged away from the sheer drop-off over the ocean.

"This is the corniche road that runs from Sorrento to Amalfi," Lauro said. Nodding toward the ocean, he added, "*Il Mar Tirreno*. A beautiful sea that flows into *il Mar Mediterraneo*."

Celina had read about the Tyrrhenian Sea, which stretched out like an endless sapphire sparkling in the sun. Gazing above the winding road, Celina could see rock-terraced gardens.

Lauro followed her gaze. "Lemon gardens. Amalfi grows the finest lemons in the world."

As incredible as the scenery was, she wasn't a tourist here for the views.

"I suppose you want to hear all about Tony," Celina began, picking at a seam in her glove.

"It can wait until you meet our parents. They're quite anxious to talk to you. To learn more about what happened. Although my brother disappeared in '45, this is all quite sudden for us."

"All of this. You mean Marco and me."

Lauro darted a scowling glance toward her. "I will never understand why he didn't contact us. Or why you never wrote to us. Didn't he speak of us?"

Well, there it is. Celina cleared her throat. "I'll tell you everything I know."

Lauro glanced down at Marco and drew his eyebrows together.

Celina caught the quizzical look in Lauro's expression. Quickly deducing his thoughts, she was appalled. "Except for having his father's temperament, Marco takes after my side of the family. He quite favors my father."

"And is he still living?"

"My father, also named Marco—Marco Romano—died of a heart attack when I was a teenager."

"I'm sorry to hear that." He patted the top of Marco's head. "And your mother?"

Celina shook her head. "A couple of years later, she became ill."

Even now, she found it difficult to talk about her mother. So great was Stella Romano's grief over the death of her husband that the summer before Celina was to start college, her mother's body had revolted against the thought of living without him. When Stella discovered a lump in her breast, her doctor had immediately ordered a procedure to remove the cancerous tumor.

Celina postponed college for a year to help her mother. However, during that year another, more aggressive tumor was found, and Celina put off school indefinitely to care for her. Lacking the will to live without her husband, Stella withered away, even losing her appetite for the chocolates Celina made for her that she had always loved.

Celina touched a gloved finger to the corner of her eye. It still pained her to think of how her mother had wasted away at the end. "She's no longer with us."

"Do you have other family?" Lauro's voice held only a small note of concern.

Celina shook her head. Her mother's labor and delivery with her had been so difficult that she could never have other children. Celina was the only child. With her arm wrapped protectively around Marco, she rubbed his arm. "It's just us now."

Lauro nodded thoughtfully. "So you're Italian. Your family—where are they from?"

"My father's family came from Italy a century ago. I don't think we have any family left here. My mother's ancestry was Italian, German, and French, but we're American."

"That explains it." He turned onto a small lane that led up an incline.

When they reached the rise, the hillside fell away and on either side of the car, glossy green leaves and sunny yellow fruit framed the azure ocean beyond. Celina sucked in a breath at the vast expanse of the sea met by an endless canopy of sky.

Celina turned back to Lauro. "That explains what?"

He cast another odd glance toward her. "Your blond hair."

Celina smiled wistfully and turned her face toward the passing landscape. Her mother had been a fair blond, and Celina had also inherited her gold-flecked hazel eyes. "How much longer until we arrive?"

"We're on our property now." Lauro gestured to citrus groves on both sides of the car. "It's not much farther." He paused. "My brother told you about our lemons, no?"

"He only mentioned the chocolate." And that, hardly at all. Tony hated to talk about it, so she knew little. She imagined Tony's family would find that odd. Lightly, she asked, "All this belongs to your family?"

"The land has been in the family for many, many years."

Celina gazed from the window, awed at her surroundings and amazed that Tony had never told her about any of this. *Why not?* It was stunning. Lemon groves climbed the mountain slopes around them. She began to feel left out, and then an awful thought occurred to her.

Maybe the fault had been with her.

Could Tony have been ashamed to return with an American? An American with an Italian surname who stumbled through their language like a wild child out of control. Guilt sparked through her. Why hadn't she tried harder to become fluent? Feeling color rise in her face, she pressed a hand to her cheek.

"He didn't talk much about Italy," she said, preparing herself for the onslaught of questions that were sure to follow.

Lauro shot a puzzled look at her. "The chocolate, the lemons, the olive oil—all this was his passion before the war. He was to follow our family's traditions and manage the businesses with our father, particularly the *fabbrica di cioccolato.* The chocolate factory is our most profitable business for export."

"So why didn't he?"

Lauro set his jaw and stared ahead. "He left for America."

"He worked hard to provide for us and secure our future," she said, yet now she was confused.

It wasn't like Tony to shirk responsibility. He was the most dependable person she'd ever known. She slid a glance toward Lauro. Whatever had happened between her husband and his family must have been tragic for him. Thinking back, perhaps Tony hadn't been angry; he'd been hurt. Clinging to this thought, Celina pressed Marco close to her side. A wave of unease spread through her. How would his parents greet her?

Lauro huffed and went on. "Our ancestors were quite industrious. They established several enterprises, and we've been working hard to expand them. People need jobs here." He sent a sideways look at her. "We could have used his help after the war. We are family, and this is what we do in Italy. He should have come home. That is, if my brother were of sound mind."

"Which he was," Celina shot back. "Tony was smart, and he worked hard to take care of us. We were his family, too."

His tone was accusatory. *If not for his American wife...* An uneasy feeling rippled down her spine. *Why would Tony have kept all this from me?* Was his upbringing so horrible? Had he fought with his parents?

Lauro let out a dry laugh. "*You* call him Tony."

Celina didn't appreciate the intimation in his voice. "That's what he called *himself*." Were his parents as angry as Lauro was?

"Antonino was his name, but he was usually Nino to us. I guess he became Tony in America for you."

"I didn't take him from your family. He was living in the U.S. when we met."

"You kept him there."

Celina was tempted to tell him that Tony had no desire to return, that he had nothing but disdain for his parents—but what good would come of that?

Gritting her teeth, she turned to Lauro. "I know you're grieving over him. We are, too." She spoke as gently as she could, but she wanted to scream. *Did you ask me here to interrogate me?*

But she couldn't. No, she *wouldn't.* She squared her shoulders. *She* had manners.

By now she knew grief took many different forms. Some days her anger at Tony for leaving them burst from its vault. Some days her sadness stretched to infinity. And some days, depression descended like the devil's darkness.

But not today.

She took Marco's hand and stroked his soft skin, drawing on his innocence to will compassion into her soul. Marco looked up at her with his father's adoring eyes, and Celina smiled down at him. Tony lived on in his son's quick smile. The light and trust in his eyes always gave her the strength to carry on, and today would be no different than the other dark days she'd faced down.

Closing her eyes and turning her head from Lauro, she tried to summon empathy for Tony's family.

Lauro said nothing more until he turned the car into the entrance of a property at the top of a mountain that took Celina's breath away. When they reached the villa, he parked in front of a pair of imposing, carved wooden doors. "*Siamo arrivati.*"

Celina and Marco didn't move, enthralled by the view. Lemon and olive trees surrounded the expansive, sun-bleached yellow villa. Built on several levels, the house was topped with a tiled, pitched roof and situated to take advantage of the astounding view. Arched windows and walkways echoed the curved shoreline and hillside slopes. Riding stables flanked one side of the property, while a vegetable garden thrived in the sunshine on the other. Ruffled mounds of pink and blue hydrangeas spilled from urns near a long reflecting pool.

Beyond it all, the ocean swelled beneath them, its waves rolling ceaselessly onto the sandy shores below, the distant roar a constant symphony of nature. Celina sat, taking in the astounding beauty of the setting and wondering how Tony could have left it behind.

She grasped Marco's hand. "This is where your daddy was born." Even he was quiet, awed by the magnificent artistry of nature.

Perfunctorily, Lauro opened her door and held out his hand, his eyes lingering on her.

"*Grazie*," she said, ignoring his studied gaze as she slid out. His insinuating comments and token courtesies seemed at odds with the warm message contained in his telegram.

In a flashing moment, she regretted their journey, but she tried to shake the feeling, telling herself it was important for Tony's parents and little Marco. She would not let a surly-faced brother ruin that.

Now she dreaded meeting his parents. If they were anything like Lauro, she understood Tony's reticence to return to Italy. She sighed in resignation. A few days, a week perhaps. She could change their tickets and return early. Lizzie's friends would understand. Celina and Marco could sleep on Lizzie's sofa if they had to.

Barely touching Lauro's reluctantly outstretched hand, she stepped out, gravel crunching beneath her low-heeled T-strap shoes. She lifted Marco from the car and set him down, taking care that Rocky, the grinning stuffed monkey, accompanied them, too.

Following Lauro, they had not yet reached the entryway when the door was flung open. A modern-looking woman in her early fifties lifted her hand in a tentative wave. She wore a charcoal black dress, and her dark hair was pulled back from her face in a thick bun.

A tall, distinguished man appeared beside her, protectively sliding his arm around her shoulders.

Tony's parents. Celina had pictured an older, domineering couple. A wave of guilt surged through her. They hardly looked like the monsters Tony had portrayed them to be, but who knew what went on in some families? Lauro was certainly handsome, but his manner could only be described as ugly. She was his brother's widow. If nothing else, that deserved some modicum of respect. Celina clutched Marco's hand and pulled him close beside her to shield him. He ducked behind her skirt.

"My parents," Lauro said with a curt nod, introducing them.

Celina nodded, and Marco peeked from behind her skirt.

As soon as Sara Savoia saw Marco, she pressed a hand against her heart. "*Cuore mio*," she cried. She held out her hands to them in greeting, and a smile grew on her face.

Celina stepped forward.

To her surprise, Sara gripped her hands with genuine warmth, and her husband Carmine, a silver-haired man with an imperious air, was nevertheless polite and engaging.

Celina was partly relieved, though still guarded. At once she knew who must have dictated the telegram Lauro sent. Only a grandmother would want to see her grandchild so desperately.

"And this is Marco, Tony's son," Celina said, her voice catching on a note of regret. She wished now that she'd at least sent baby photos. Tony had been adamantly against that, too.

"*Che tesoro, che dolce.*" Her face shimmering with a mixture of sorrow and joy, Sara hitched her slim skirt and sank to the little boy's level. "*Ciao, Marco. Sono tua nonna.*" When Marco darted a look of confusion to Celina, Sara quickly added, "I am your grandmother." She held her arms open to him.

Marco hesitated.

"We have a gift for you." Bending over, Carmine Savoia held out a wooden toy train engine. "It was your papa's." He raised his eyes, which were now brimming with emotion, to Celina. "It was Antonino's favorite toy when he was a boy."

Lauro cut in. "He called himself *Tony* in America."

Blinking back the sadness etched on his face, Carmine said, "That was probably easier for the Americans."

Marco looked up at his mother, a question looming in his round blue eyes. "That was Daddy's?"

Celina brushed aside Lauro's snide comment. She nodded her permission and gently nudged her son forward. She'd told him they were going to meet his grandparents, and he'd been excited. He'd never had the pleasure of knowing any of his grandparents, but he sensed they were a special breed from watching his friends with their loving, pampering grandparents.

With a shy smile, Marco stepped toward Sara, and she took his hand. Tears gleamed in her eyes. As Carmine gave Marco the toy, the older man blinked heavily.

Sara gazed up at her with pure joy blooming on her face. "*Mille grazie*," she said, pressing a hand to her heart. "I cannot thank you enough for coming. Marco is our only grandchild." She hugged Marco to her, and his little arms swung willingly around her. As tears of gratitude spilled onto her cheeks, Sara closed her eyes and swayed with a blissful expression.

Sara's joy was palpable. Celina watched as the wonderment of discovering the love of his grandparents illuminated her son's sweet face. Her reticence dissolved, and she felt prickles of emotion behind her eyes.

She wondered what could have happened between Tony and these seemingly kind, caring people. *Couldn't the love of family have led them out of emotions wracked with anger and hurt?*

Standing beside her, Lauro coughed into his hand and turned away.

"I only wish we'd come sooner," Celina said, allowing the remorse she felt to shade her words. At that moment, she knew she had done the right thing by coming here, though due to Lauro's behavior, she'd had misgivings.

Seeing Sara with Marco, Celina realized that whatever had happened in this family that had forced Tony away, his mother had suffered over her son's disappearance. Being a mother, she empathized with Sara, yet she could only imagine the magnitude of her despair over losing a child. Sharing her son with Sara and giving the older woman the gift of time spent with her grandchild could hardly make up for her lack of contact. For this, she was genuinely sorry.

"I hope you can forgive me for not contacting you earlier to tell you about Marco," Celina said. To blame Tony now seemed insensitive to their memory of him.

"We *were* shocked by your call," Carmine said. "We'd held out hope for so many years. While this is not what we expected, we're glad you came."

Sara rested a hand on her husband's shoulder. "At least we know he experienced the joy of having a family before he died."

To his credit, Carmine didn't ask why she hadn't bothered to contact them before. Celina had no doubt they wondered and would ask her about this at some point. Now that Tony was gone, did it matter what had happened between them?

Lauro turned back to her. "As you might imagine, my parents have a lot of questions about my brother. They're wondering why he didn't come home. Why he returned to America."

There it was.

A flush crawled up Celina's neck. Clearly, Lauro was more vocal. "Tony said America was his home. He didn't tell me why he never returned." She looked helplessly from Lauro to his parents, fervently wishing Tony had left her with something that she could share with them. Tentacles of resentment slithered around at her heart, restraining the finer memories of her husband she tried to keep fixed in her mind.

If only her husband had at least written to his family. She couldn't understand why he hadn't—not even once to let them know he was alive. *Why had Tony cultivated this situation?* What's more, Tony's family seemed just as perplexed—and angry, she thought, casting a glance at Lauro—as she was at Tony's neglect. Even if Carmine and Sara were more restrained than Lauro, they must have those thoughts, too. Surely Tony could have imagined the pain his actions would cause.

"The stress of war affects men in different ways," Sara said to Lauro. Standing and turning to Celina, she said, "Let's go inside." Folding Celina's hand warmly in hers, she added, "You must be hungry and tired from your long journey."

Taking Marco by the hand, Celina followed Sara inside. She stepped into a cool, terracotta-tiled foyer, its walls splashed with hues of celestino blue, terra rossa, and pale yellow. Frescoed ceilings soared above, and the scent of yellow roses arranged in a vase on a round antique table filled the air. Beyond the foyer, tall windows framed the panoramic view as a spectacular backdrop to the expansive rooms, which were lavishly, though comfortably, decorated with Italian antiques and patterned textiles.

"This isn't the way Nino would have remembered his home," Sara said, following Celina's gaze. "We've only just finished redecorating this part of the house."

"My great-grandfather built Villa Savoia to gather the family for holidays by the sea," Carmine said. "His wife was born here, too. He started the chocolate business in Torino, but he loved the ocean breezes so much that he moved their business here."

"Come with me," Sara said. "I'll show you to your rooms so you can relax."

Celina and Marco followed Sara through an arched, brick-ceilinged hallway to a pair of connected guest rooms. Lauro trailed with their luggage.

"I hope you'll be comfortable here," Sara said, swinging open the rustic door to a view of the ocean beyond.

A breeze cooled Celina's face and lifted the sheer curtains by the windows. She turned to a four-poster bed nestled between marble-topped nightstands. An armoire stood on one side, and doors stood open to a balcony on the other. Lauro deposited the bags and left the room.

In awe at the sheer beauty of the setting, Celina stepped onto the balcony, which overlooked a terraced garden of fruit trees.

"It's so beautiful here." She breathed in, catching the scent of fruit trees below. "What type of fruit are you growing?"

"Mostly lemon," Sara said. "But also olive, grapefruit, orange, fig, and pomegranate. With our temperate climate, most everything thrives."

Celina peered over the balcony's edge. To one side, a cliff dropped to the sea, while on the other, a terrace sprawled along the hilltop perch. Flaming pink bougainvillea and snowy white jasmine curled around the corners of grapevine-covered archways that framed the shimmering ocean view.

Breathing in air that had a softer, sweeter quality than that of the San Francisco Bay, Celina admired the stunning view that had probably inspired artists for years.

How could Tony have left this magical seaside land?

Sara picked up a silver-framed photograph from a nightstand and flicked specks of dust from it. "You can probably guess who this is," she said, nostalgia thickening her voice.

"Tony?" Celina joined Sara in looking at a sepia-toned photo.

Two young boys stared solemnly into the camera.

Sara drew her fingers over the glass and nodded. "With Lauro." Smiling, she traced their faces. "We had such good times then. This is a wonderful place for boys to grow up." Sara shifted the photo so that Marco could see, and he peered at it with curiosity. "This was your papa, Marco. He grew up here." She tousled his hair and hugged him to her side. "You remind me so much of him."

Celina was touched by Sara's thoughtfulness in placing Tony's photo in their room and thanked her.

"I have more photos to share with you later." Sara indicated another framed photo on the other side of the bed that stood on a nightstand in the shadows. "That one was taken not long before he left. It was the last time we ever saw him. I thought you might like to have it by your bed while you're here."

Celina slid her hand softly over the other woman's. "It's usually by your bed, isn't it?"

Sara embraced her. "You're quite perceptive. And I'm so glad you came."

Carmine appeared behind them with a glass of white wine and a plate of homemade bread, olives, and slivers of parmesan cheese. "Thought you might like an *apertivo* while you relax."

"*Grazie*," Celina said, gratefully accepting the lightly chilled wine. Inhaling the bouquet, a memory sprang to mind. "I recognize this," she said, as Carmine and Sara exchanged pleased smiles. "It was one of Tony's favorites, and mine, too." He'd sought out a small wine purveyor in the Italian district of San Francisco to find it.

"It's our Falanghina wine, a specialty of Campania, our region," Carmine said with pride. "Light and refreshing on a warm day. Tonight we'll have the special Piedirosso wine we've been saving," he added with a meaningful glance at his wife.

Celina caught the look between them and wondered about the significance.

"And there's fresh *limonata* and biscotti for Marco," Sara added, motioning toward the table.

"I brought something for you, too," Celina said, reaching into the bag she carried. She withdrew a box of her best chocolates that she had taken special care to wrap. "Something I made, I thought you might like."

"Why, how thoughtful," Sara said, pressing her cheek to Celina's. "I'm sure we'll enjoy it. We'll let you freshen up now."

After Sara and Carmine left, Celina unpacked their clothes and changed Marco into a fresh, checked-cotton shirt and twill trousers. Tony's parents had kindly furnished the smaller room with toys that must have belonged to their sons, so Marco was busy investigating the trains and cars and wooden blocks.

While he played, Celina splashed her face with water and brushed her hair. Nibbling on the almond-flavored biscotti, she felt her energy return. As she sipped the wine, she changed from her traveling suit into a dress she'd just finished making from a new Vogue pattern and fabric she'd bought at the opening of Britex Fabrics on Geary Street. Made of navy polished cotton, the dress had a fashionable full skirt and fitted bodice. She slipped on the matching bolero jacket with three-quarter length sleeves and stepped into a pair of peep-toe pumps. Leaning toward the beveled mirror, she nestled her cherished locket into the neckline of the dress.

As she sipped her wine, she studied the photo that Sara had shown her. Peering closer, she found she could hardly tell the boys apart. Tony and Lauro favored each other, and she guessed that Lauro was just a couple of years younger. Closer to her age, probably. If she didn't know better, she wouldn't have seen Tony's resemblance in this youngster. She smiled, thinking how the skinny young boy had grown into such a solid, stocky man. She replaced the photo and then walked around to see the other photo on the far nightstand.

"Mommy," Marco called out. "I'm hungry. When are we eating?"

"Soon," she replied. Marco had such an appetite, and he had already polished off the snack Carmine had thoughtfully left for them. Lifting the photo, she peered at the shadowy image.

"Mommy, can we go now?"

"Just a moment." Tracing the frame with her thumb, she thought about how thankful she was that she'd contacted Tony's family. She loved her husband, even though over the years their marriage had been emotionally complicated, but then, no more so than many others. The war had taken a toll on many men and women. Adjusting to civilian life had been hard on them—Tony included.

Celina pressed a finger to the corner of her eyes. The warmth of her husband's love seemed even stronger here in the home where he'd grown up. She sighed and brought the image closer, anxious to see the image of the man she'd known.

She flicked on a nearby lamp. Her beloved Tony, a man sometimes worried, but always loving, passionate, and well meaning. Her husband, the man who could charm—

She frowned and drew back. Sinking to the bed, she sipped her wine, shifted the frame, and squinted at the photo in frustration. For the life of her, she couldn't find the resemblance she'd expected. Trying to see it better, she shifted the photo's protective glass pane against the glare of the lamp until it came into stark view.

As an unfamiliar image of Tony stared back at her, a hollow, sinking feeling grew inside of her. His appearance had changed drastically, but then, he must have been so young when this photo was taken, she thought. She tried to calculate the years, guessing this might have been taken in 1940. Thirteen years ago. A man could change a lot in that amount of time.

Couldn't he? She blinked, intently focused on the black-and-white image. Without the scar that ranged along one temple and cheek, Tony looked so different that she might not have even known this was the same man. As a chill coursed through her, a sudden thought dazed her, and she gasped. The frame slipped from her hand, shattering on the terracotta floor.

"Mommy, are you okay?" Marco ran into the room.

"Stop, there's glass on the floor." Gathering her full skirt, she knelt to the floor.

Marco leaned against the doorjamb watching as Celina picked up shards of broken glass and put them into a waste bin.

"Did you hurt yourself?"

Flustered, Celina replied, "I'm not hurt."

"Then why are you crying, Mommy?"

"Am I?" She brushed moisture from her cheeks. Confusion roared through her mind, yet she steeled her emotions. "Mommy will be through in a minute. Go play until I'm ready."

Marco hesitated, then turned around and returned to the toys in the side room.

Her hands shaking, Celina wiggled a shard of glass, attempting to dislodge it from the frame. "Ow," she cried, jerking her hand back.

Blood dripped from her forefinger onto the photo. "Oh, no," she murmured, grabbing the inside hem of her dress and dabbing blood from the image, although it left a small, discolored spot on her husband's neck. Pressing her throbbing finger between her lips, she rocked back and forth in agitation. *What had she done?*

Her heart raced as words formed in her mind. For a split second, she'd thought that this man couldn't possibly be Tony. But that was crazy, wasn't it? She pushed the picture aside and took a drink of wine to quell her nerves.

Of course that's Tony. Her eyes flicked across the photo again. It was how he looked before his injuries.

How silly of me, she thought, chastising herself. Just when she thought she had reined in her grief, she often lost control again. She shot another glance at the photo. *Besides, who else could it be?*

Chapter 4

"You haven't told us how you and Antonino met." With a smile of understanding, Sara passed Celina another fresh napkin for Marco, who was relishing chocolate cake from the tip of his nose to the bottom of his chin, as only a six-year-old can do.

Carmine chuckled at Marco, while Sara clasped her graceful hands and waited with expectation. Lauro hadn't changed; he was still quiet and sullen.

They had just finished supper on the terrace overlooking the ocean. An intermittent breeze filtered the mild evening air, ushering in the scent of jasmine like a sweet *digestivo* of nature. Candles flickered, illuminating the focused interest on faces of those gathered around the rustic wooden table, over which an azure blue and carnelian red cloth had been draped.

Awaiting her story, they sipped a rich, ruby-colored Piedirosso, the last wine that Tony had harvested in nearby vineyards with the family. Carmine told her they'd been saving it for his return. It was a fine wine and paired well with the dark chocolate they'd put out. A thought nagged her while she fortified herself. The terraced lemon gardens, the chocolate, the olive oil. Everything they made and exported to countries around the world. Why hadn't Tony ever mentioned any of this?

With Sara staring at her expectantly, Celina replied, "I was working in San Francisco, and he came into the shop."

Celina dabbed a smear of chocolate from Marco's chin with a napkin. Though usually finicky, tonight he'd eaten with gusto once he'd begun, devouring the antipasto, ziti, and salad, and he was now working his way through a slice of Torta Caprese, a dark chocolate almond cake with a moist center. The little boy stifled a yawn. It was late for him, and the time change had disrupted his usual schedule. Out of habit, Celina smoothed the chestnut-colored cowlick on his crown and then turned back to Sara.

"A friend of Tony's brought him to the shop one day, insisting that he try his favorite chocolaterie in San Francisco."

"*Cioccolato*?" Sara tilted her head with interest. "Professionally? *This* is what you do?"

"I tried one of the truffles she gave us," Carmine said. "It was excellent."

"I hope you left some for me," Sara said.

Carmine nudged his wife. "You'll have to find where I hid them first."

Celina realized she hadn't told them much about herself. They'd been sharing stories about Tony—or Nino, as his mother called him—for the benefit of Marco, who seemed intrigued at his father's escapades as a boy. The tricks he and Lauro had played on each other, the sunrise harvests, the fun they'd had galloping through the countryside. Much to her relief, Sara, Carmine, and Lauro all spoke English well, due to their long-standing business relationships in England.

"My mother trained me as a *chocolatière*," Celina said. "She learned the trade in Paris."

"She is French?" Sara seemed to take an avid interest in everything.

"American, with Italian and French heritage, and a little German. She visited Paris, fell in love with it, and apprenticed there."

"And this friend Nino was with," Lauro interjected. "Who was it?"

"Just another soldier back from the war." Celina kept her reply light, though his comment stung her. Lauro had been challenging her throughout supper—on Tony, where they'd lived, what he did, everything. She paused, checking her annoyance in consideration of his grief. "Why?"

Lauro shot her a frown. "So we can find the truth about why he never contacted us again."

"Don't be rude," Sara said. "We can talk about that later," she added, darting her eyes in Marco's direction.

Celina didn't like the tone of Lauro's voice. He seemed bent on accusing her of something—she had no idea what—but she only had one truth to tell. "I'll get Marco ready for bed. We can talk afterward."

Excusing themselves, Celina took Marco to their suite. Kneeling before her son, she unbuttoned his shirt. "It's been a long journey for you, my young man. And you met a new part of your family."

"I like them a lot," he said, rubbing his eyes. "They miss Daddy, too. I wish he could still be here. Can we ever visit him in heaven?"

Celina's heart clenched. "Someday we'll all be together again."

"When?"

"Not for a long time. You have an awful lot of growing up and living to do first." She managed a smile and tapped his nose.

"I wish I could talk to him again."

"I know, sweetie. Me, too."

He fidgeted for a moment. "I feel bad. I forgot what his voice sounds like."

"Just remember what his love felt like." Aching at his comments, Celina cradled him in her arms and kissed his cheek. The one thing he yearned for was the one thing she was incapable of providing. Drawing on her reservoir of emotional strength, which had run as low as a trickle, she blinked back her emotion and kissed him on his forehead. "You look sleepy. This bed will feel so good, won't it?"

Marco was so exhausted and full from supper that he didn't fuss at all. She'd hardly managed to put his pajamas on him and brush his teeth before he nodded off. Hefting his deadened weight, she carried him to bed. Marco was long and gangly for his age and already quite a big boy for her to carry, though Tony used to flip him over his shoulder like a flour sack, sending the little boy into a riot of laughter.

She tucked Marco into her bed, positioning Rocky next to him. Marco flopped an arm across the smiling stuffed monkey. Stroking his back, she thought about leaving him alone in a strange room without her. What if he woke and she wasn't there?

As if in answer to her thought, a tap sounded at the door. Celina covered Marco with the downy duvet and rose to open the door to a portly woman. Her gray hair was wound into a bun, and her face was wreathed with a smile.

"*Buonasera, signora,*" the woman said. "*Mi chiamo Matilde.*"

With a few words, Celina quickly ascertained that Sara had sent her housekeeper to stay with Marco so she'd feel comfortable leaving him alone. The family had many more questions of her, and she was anxious to share everything she knew, too.

"*Grazie,*" Celina said.

Matilde eased into a chair and tucked a skein of blue yarn onto her lap while Celina finished tucking him in.

Celina was impressed with Sara's seemingly effortless household organization. Had she developed that skill out of necessity? In the last decade during the war, many women in the states had stepped into men's jobs, working in factories and running farms.

Celina recalled her part-time work for the San Francisco library, raising money to send thousands of books to military personnel overseas. After the final armistice, most women had returned to their roles as housewives and mothers. Celina didn't have the luxury of choice now, but then, she had always enjoyed working.

If only other women didn't make her feel so guilty about it. One new neighbor had even derided her for working and called her son an eight-hour orphan until Lizzie had set her straight about Tony's death.

Soon Matilde's knitting needles were clicking softly to Marco's rhythmic slumber. Celina bent to kiss him again and then tiptoed from the room.

The family was still on the terrace, and even before Celina stepped outside to join them, she could hear Lauro thundering on in some sort of diatribe. Not that she could follow such rapid-fire Italian, but when she heard her name uttered, she caught the gist of his displeasure.

Hesitating at the doorway, she felt her doubts rushing back at her in a force equal to his anger. A chill licked through her veins. Trembling, she pressed her fingers against her temples.

Tony was right. This is why he'd tried to shield me. A thought dawned on her. Maybe the problem hadn't been his parents, but his brother. She was stepping back into the shadows when Sara spied her.

Lauro's mother made a sharp hand gesture toward him. Abruptly, he stopped speaking.

Carmine waved for her to join them. "*Perdonalo, scusaci,*" he said, rising from his chair to pull hers out for her. As she joined them and sat down, he added, "It's a tragedy to lose a brother. Please forgive our son."

Lauro crossed his arms and fell against the back of his chair.

Celina perched on the edge of her chair, poised to take flight should Lauro explode like Vesuvius—as Tony sometimes had. What a shame, Lauro might have been handsome if not for his attitude. No wonder he didn't have a wife. She'd had enough of that ugly behavior from Tony, mostly right after they'd married—and mainly attributed to his military service—but she would not stand for it from a man she hardly knew. *Any* man now, in fact. She tilted her chin up at him. "Go on. I might as well hear it."

"My son is in pain." Sara folded one of Celina's hands between hers. Her eyes sought conciliation in Celina's. "He doesn't understand our desire for you to join our family."

"I don't understand what you mean," Celina said.

Sara's eyes gleamed. "If you want, we would love for you to stay here and truly become part of us."

This offer deeply touched Celina. "Why, that's so generous of you—"

Lauro cut her off with a snorting sound. "How do we know she is who she says she is?"

Feeling her chest tighten, Celina rose from her chair and marched back to her room.

Chapter 5

Santa Monica, 1945

"Isn't the sunshine wonderful?" Celina tossed her head back in the convertible, letting the breeze blow through her hair, which she'd secured with a paisley print scarf tied just so at the nape of her neck as her mother had taught her to do.

Beyond the glistening beach, the ocean roared onto the shoreline. Pelican and cormorants dove into the white-tipped waves for fish, while smaller shorebirds skittered across the sand in peripatetic paths.

"Feels good to have a full tank of gas and be out on the open road again," Tony said. With one arm stretched across the back of the bench seat, he drove along the Pacific Coast road, his other hand resting on the Chevrolet's large steering wheel, the engine rumbling beneath the long hood. "I knew you'd love this trip," he added, stroking her shoulder over her white cotton eyelet blouse.

"Oh, I do," she said, smiling at his light touch. The warmth of his fingers sent a thrill through her. After Doc had left, Tony had come to see her at the shop the next day and asked her out for a malt at the diner around the corner. And after that, he stopped by to see her every day. A month later, when he'd asked her to go to Santa Monica with him, she hadn't intended on going, but Marge had pushed her.

"He's your boyfriend now," Marge had insisted, although she made Tony swear he'd pay for a separate room for her.

My boyfriend, Celina thought, turning the phrase over in her mind. She supposed it was true; she had grown quite fond of Tony. He'd found a job in construction that paid him in cash, so he started work at dawn. After a long day, he cleaned up and met her almost every day after work to take her out for supper at an Italian restaurant in North Beach or a restaurant at the docks to get fresh-caught seafood. They feasted on crab sautéed in garlic and olive oil, hot clam chowder and fresh sourdough bread, and raw oysters shucked right off the boats at the pier.

As they shared meals, she laughed at his frequent barrage of silly jokes, and he wanted to know everything about her. He had great ambition, too, and often talked about starting a firm to build houses on the city's outskirts where new families were settling. He seemed like an educated man, and when she pressed him, he said he'd studied to be a pharmacist, but that he'd lost his enthusiasm for that type of work.

All week, Celina had worked long hours to make the inventory they'd need while she was gone. Now, as they drove, she studied Tony's profile, the side that had fewer scars than the other, and ticked off a mental list. *Good-looking, kind, considerate. A good provider.* Her heart thumped. *Her boyfriend.* He had promised Marge he'd be a gentleman on the trip, and Celina trusted him. But was he *the one*?

Celina circled her forefinger against a suddenly throbbing temple. Marge had pressed her, saying it was time Celina thought about getting married and starting a family. *Did she love Tony? How would she know?* She wished her mother were still living to give her the advice she so desperately missed and needed.

Once they had cleared the foggy chill of the San Francisco bay and the sun had peeked from the clouds, Tony had pulled over in Carmel to fold down the beige ragtop.

"This baby is a Special DeLuxe, 1942," he said, proudly running his hand along the shiny paint. "Ensign Blue. What a beauty." Gasoline rationing had been lifted, and Tony told her he had waited in a long line yesterday to get the tank of his car filled for the trip.

They'd been driving since sunrise, and Celina loved everything she'd seen along the way, from the windblown cypress trees of the Monterrey peninsula to the wild craggy cliffs that eventually gave way to smooth sandy beaches. Her stomach rumbled, and she placed a hand across the top of her powder pink skirt. They'd stopped at a small seaside restaurant and eaten shrimp scampi at wooden picnic tables under sprawling mimosa trees, but that had been hours ago.

"Almost there." She ran her finger along the folded paper map she held. They had driven through the village of Malibu and were almost to Santa Monica. He'd put her in charge of directions, but she hadn't the heart to tell him she had never read a road map before. She had grown up in the city. As a girl, she and her parents had usually walked or taken the cable cars or taxis wherever they needed to go. Her dad had an old Ford pick-up truck he sometimes drove and liked to tinker with, but her mother had sold it after he died, saying it was more trouble than it was worth. Still, she'd managed to be a reasonably good navigator and had only gotten them lost once.

"Would you look at that mansion?" Tony pointed to a sprawling, white beachfront estate. "That's Ocean Beach. Belongs to Marion Davies. Hearst, the millionaire newspaper magnate, built it for her. And our inn is just down the beach. We might even see some movie stars."

"I've heard about that place," Celina said. "Marge follows Marion Davies in the Hollywood magazines, but I've never seen any of her films."

"Must be lots of big parties there."

She could hardly believe she was here with Tony. She shivered a little from a tingly feeling that had started to creep into her, unlike anything she'd ever known before.

Their little inn was nothing like Ocean Beach. The Sunset Poppy Inn was a neat, white clapboard house that had been converted to a guesthouse. Yellow daisies, pink hydrangea, and purple lantana bloomed along the bleached stone walkway, and a brass wind chime tinkled in the sea breeze. Stepping inside, Celina couldn't help but smile. Wherever she looked, colorful paintings and crisp cotton floral prints jostled for attention.

Tony stepped to the reception desk, which was painted with orange poppies. "I have a reservation for Savoia," he began, clasping Celina's hand.

The thin, middle-aged woman behind the desk folded her hands over the registration book and looked them over, her eyes falling on Celina's left hand. "Perhaps," she replied haughtily. "For you and your wife?"

"I called about two rooms," Tony added quickly, coloring slightly.

Celina gazed around the room. A painting of a skull with flowers caused her to suck in her breath.

Ignoring Tony, the spirited, gray-haired woman focused on Celina. "A Mexican artist by the name of Frida Kahlo painted the picture you're admiring. I'm an artist, and I collect paintings by other female artists." She indicated another vivid painting of a vase of lilacs. "Mary Cassatt painted that. One of her few still lifes." The woman lifted her chin and eyed her through narrowed eyes. "And what do you do? You have a profession, I hope."

"I'm a *chocolatière*." From the corner of her eye, Celina could see Tony, who stood by wearing a bemused expression. From what she knew of his quick wit and outgoing manner, he was accustomed to being the center of attention. Not that she minded, because she was more thoughtful. "My mother studied as a *chocolatière* in Paris and Brussels. She taught me, and I work in a chocolaterie in San Francisco."

As if a ray of sun had warmed her face, the woman's stern expression broke into an approving smile. "Then you're an artist of food. Welcome." Having determined they were worthy of her attention, she opened her registry book.

"I bought this cottage after my husband left me," the woman said as they signed their names in the book. "It's my home, and I only entertain interesting people." She paused, reading their signatures. "Savoia. Any relation to the Savoia chocolatiers in Italy?"

Tony hesitated, as if he were being discreet, then he puffed out his chest. "Yeah, sure we are. My folks own it. But I don't talk about it much."

Celina gazed up at him. "I can hardly even dream of working on that scale."

"Celina's not that ambitious," Tony said.

Celina snapped her head around. "Why would you think that?"

"Don't most women your age want to get married and have babies?" Tony gave her a knowing smile.

"Maybe the ones *you* date." When Celina saw his face fall in disappointment, she added, "I didn't say I never want children. Just not right away. I really love what I do."

The woman was watching the exchange between them. "No reason you can't do both, dear." She slid two keys across the reception desk. "Sounds like you two have a lot to talk about."

"We sure do." Tony grinned sheepishly at the woman and paid for their rooms in cash.

Tony opened the door for Celina. Retrieving their small bags, he hefted them both in one hand as easily as if they were empty.

Her suitcase certainly wasn't. She couldn't decide what to wear, so she'd crammed in several dresses and shoes. She hooked her makeup case over her wrist, and Tony caught her other hand. They started down a garden path to their rooms.

Tony cleared his throat, something she'd noticed was a nervous habit he had. She found it endearing. How could such a powerfully built man have anything to be nervous about?

"Hope you're having a good time," he said.

"The best," she replied.

"I wanted this trip to be special."

"It already is, Tony. I'm with you."

"You'll tell me if there's anything you want." He gazed down at her, his dark brows drawn together with concern.

She laughed lightly. "Promise."

Sand crunched beneath her beige espadrilles as they walked, and she breathed in the briny smell of the ocean. The beach was different than those in San Francisco. Golden sand stretched out for miles, just like in the movies that were filmed here, and the sun warmed her face and shoulders. San Francisco could be cool and overcast even in the summer.

Celina liked the feel of her hand in his. Hers felt small and narrow in his large, roughened hand, yet he clasped hers with a gentleness that surprised her. His touch radiated care and assurance.

Not since her mother had died had she felt such a sense of belonging with someone, and it was surprisingly comforting. Standing next to him, connected to the vitality that surged through him, she felt that all was right with the world. Her mother would've liked him, she decided. Marge certainly did.

Celina glanced up at Tony with a shy smile. He responded by sliding his arm around her shoulder and hugging her next to him. His heartbeat was strong and quick, and so, she realized, was hers.

They came to her room first. It was a tiny single room splashed with shades of marine blue and white paint. Blue poppies arched over the bed, and daises loomed around the dresser mirror. "I love it," she breathed.

"You get settled and freshen up. I mean, not that you need to," he added quickly. "I'm going to change my threads."

After she had unpacked her few things in her cozy room and changed into a polished cotton dress with a sweetheart neckline, Celina heard a tap on the door. She crossed the pine floor past the bed draped with a chenille coverlet and hand-painted floral pillows.

Tony's surprise was evident on his face. "Wow, you look beautiful, even more gorgeous than usual. Like a real Hollywood movie star."

His comment pleased her. She'd stayed up late to finish sewing her new dress, trying it on half a dozen times to make sure it fit just so. The lightweight, ivory cotton fabric caught the highlights in her hair and skimmed her hips in a flattering manner. Experimenting with a Butterick pattern, she'd substituted handmade lace her grandmother had made for the fitted sleeves, shortened the hem, and added a belt.

Weight had slipped off after her mother died, and she'd lost the appetite to gain it back, even working around chocolate every day. Marge insisted her newly svelte figure suited her, making her look like a fashion model. To prove her point, Marge had taken her to Woolworth's to buy some cosmetics.

Celina felt her face grow warm at Tony's compliment. She caught a glance of herself in the small beveled mirror by the door. Red lipstick and pink cream rouge brought color to her face, and the cake mascara she'd carefully applied with a little brush framed her tawny eyes.

"You look really nice, too," Celina said.

"Except for these, right?" He drew a finger along one angry red scar on his face.

"Why, no, not at all." His attitude surprised her. He was a handsome man, there was no denying that, and the more time she spent around him, the less she noticed his scars. Maybe he was as nervous as she was.

Tony beamed and leaned against the doorjamb. He'd changed into a pressed shirt and slicked back his hair. Cologne wafted from his neck, reminding her of her father.

"I thought we would eat at the pier," he said.

"I'd like that."

They held hands on the short walk down the beach, where a long wooden pier loomed, lined with tourist shops and food stands. A roller coaster rose behind them. Cars full of riders hurled around the track, and screams of joy could be heard above the surf.

Celina was glad they were going there. There would be plenty to do there if she ran out of conversation. They'd played the radio on the way from San Francisco. When they could find a station, that is. Except for tiny San Luis Obispo, there hadn't been many music stations after Carmel on the long coastal route until they came to Santa Barbara.

Catching her hand again, Tony led the way. The warmth of his sure clasp sparked through her, calming her quivering insides. As they strolled toward the pier, they saw a band setting up to play music.

"Do you like to dance?" Celina realized how little she knew about him.

With a grimace, he tapped a knee. "I did, but now..."

"Oh," she cried. "I didn't know, I'm so sorry." How could she have been so thoughtless?

He screwed up his face. "I don't want pity from people, especially not you. Lots of guys worse off than me."

She bit her lip. Now what should she say? Feeling self-conscious, she angled her face toward the swift surf.

With a finger on her chin, he turned her face back to him. Seeing her concern, he swiftly changed his expression. "Hey blondie, it's okay. I'm over feeling sorry for myself."

Those words were easier to say than to feel, Celina knew, though she nodded her agreement. Most of the returning troops put up a good front, but she knew better.

Friends had expressed their condolences after her mother died, but after a few weeks, their lives went on. They forgot about her, or maybe they felt uncomfortable around her, reminded of their mortality. After Dad died, her mother had once said that Americans weren't good at grief. She squeezed Tony's hand. "I understand."

His broad smile lit a slender fuse of hope in her.

"This is my second chance at life," he said, running his hand up her arm to rest on her shoulder. "Maybe for both of us."

She heard a yearning in his voice. "Is your family in San Francisco?"

Tony shook his head.

"Where then?"

He gazed at her as though choosing his response with care. "Italy."

"Do you ever see them?"

Lowering his eyes, he said, "No, it's complicated."

"When was the last time you saw them?" She couldn't imagine being estranged from her family.

"Sweetheart, that's the one subject I don't like to talk about. There's no changing the past." Scowling, he quickened his pace.

Celina kept up with him, and by the time they reached the pier, his dark mood had passed.

Tony spied a hot dog vendor's cart. "Would you look at that? Just like we had in New York. Want one?"

"Sure. You lived in New York?"

He hooked his arm in hers. "Yeah, for a while." Tony's eyes lit up at the sight of a carousel. "Hey, look at that. Let's do that next. Come on, let's go."

As they strolled along the pier, watching people and listening to music, vendors called out to them. Tony was like a big kid, giving her a leg up on a carousel horse, slathering mustard on hot dogs, and engaging everyone around them with jokes and laughter. Celina couldn't remember when she'd had such a fun, carefree evening.

"Get your fresh hand-churned ice cream, right here," a vendor called out.

"What's your favorite flavor?" Tony asked.

"Guess."

Laughing, Tony smacked himself on the forehead. "Chocolate, right?"

Celina shook her head and pressed her hand against her mouth, giggling as he reeled through the flavors.

"Not chocolate, then, and surely not vanilla. Banana, cherry, peach, strawberry—"

"That's it!"

"No kidding? Mine, too. Two cones with double scoops of strawberry," he said to the vendor.

Later that evening, after they had danced to the band and ridden the carousel again, he steered them toward a Ferris wheel trimmed in lights. It was late, and there weren't many patrons. Tony said something she couldn't hear to the old man running the ride, and then he shook the man's hand.

They climbed into a compartment, and Celina held onto Tony. At the top, the amusement ride stopped, and their little chamber dangled in the air. Enjoying the breeze off the ocean, Celina tipped her head back, gazing up at the stars overhead and feeling loved. Every time she looked up at the stars, she thought of her mother, because her mother's name, *Stella*, meant *star* in Italian.

"What a beautiful evening," she said, nestling in the crook of Tony's arm. "I could stay up here forever, just like this."

"It doesn't have to end." Tony took her hand and kissed it.

"What do you mean?"

"Tonight. You and me. It could be like this forever, I promise." Tony tilted her chin and feathered a tentative kiss on her lips.

She'd wondered what his kiss would feel like. His lips were soft and warm, and she responded, letting him know it was okay. When he deepened his kiss, Celina felt a strange sort of energy shoot through her limbs as if she were electrified. Heat gathered in her midsection, and she felt her body responding in a way she'd never experienced.

After a few long moments, Tony regretfully pulled away. "I could gobble you up," he said nuzzling her neck. "I've never felt this way about any other girl, Celina."

His voice sounded funny—thick and emotional. She ran her hands along his broad chest. "That means a lot to me, Tony."

"I don't think you understand how much you mean to me. Celina, I'm in love with you, I knew I was the first time I saw you. Maybe it was your smile, maybe it was that chocolate truffle, but whatever it was sure walloped me. I've never been in love before. But this is right, I just know it."

Smiling, Celina pressed a finger against his lips. "That's so sweet, and I care for you, too." She felt her cheeks blaze. This must be love. This is what all the songs and movies were about. "I, I guess I love you, too, Tony."

"Oh baby," Tony cried, peppering her face with kisses. "This is what I've been dreaming of. You and me, baby." He kissed her again and fumbled in his pocket. "I've been carrying this around, afraid to ask you."

He held up a delicate, silvery band with a small diamond that glinted in the Ferris lights. "I know you can have your pick of any guy, but I'll make you proud, I promise. I'll love you until the day I die."

Celina stared at the slim band and the stone that winked in the light at her. Tony's eyes were moist and pleading, and held such a pure look of adoration. How could she let him down? That was love, wasn't it? Wanting to do your very best by a person, wanting the best in the world for them. That's how she felt about him.

He was so close to her that she could feel his heartbeat, matching hers in intensity. Being so close to someone, feeling so protected and loved, it was the sweetest feeling she'd ever had. A feeling she never wanted to let go. It was like coming home.

She raised her eyes to his. "I'd like that, Tony." She held out a wavering hand.

"Um, wrong one," he said.

She laughed and switched hands, and then Tony slid the ring onto her finger. As she gazed at it in awe, the happiness of belonging, of togetherness, washed through her with force. She raised her lips to meet his, and their passion sealed their promise, though she could tell that Tony restrained himself.

"We'll get married as soon as you want," he said in a husky voice when they finally parted. "Very soon, I hope, but it's up to you. Is there anyone you want me to talk to?"

"Talk to?"

"Ask for your hand. Make it official."

"My parents are gone, Tony."

"An uncle or grandpa?"

Celina smiled. "You're the only man in my life, Tony Savoia." At that, the Ferris wheel shuddered, and they were soon spinning through the air again, the ocean breeze cooling their hot skin, but not their newfound passion for each other.

"Since neither one of us has any family, we'll have to start our own." Tony hugged her close to him. "Imagine, you'll be my *wife*. I'm the luckiest guy alive. Now it's you and me against the world."

Filled with happiness and hope for their future, she kissed him again, and as she did, she felt the tears on his cheeks mingling with hers. Now everything was going to be all right in her world—*their* world—forever and ever.

When the Ferris wheel came to a stop, they stepped off. Spying a Photomaton, Tony grabbed her hand and raced toward it, laughing. "I need a picture of you."

"What for?"

"The guys are never going to believe me." He fished in his pocket for coins and pulled back the booth's curtain. "In you go."

Laughing, she posed for a shot, her left hand over her heart. *Snap*. On a whim, she yanked Tony's hand, pulling him inside with her. "Come on, your turn."

He protested, burying his face behind her hair. She smiled for the camera. *Snap.*

"I want one of you, too." She tried to push his face toward the camera, but he resisted. *Snap.*

"Aw, come on." She ducked to the side, exposing him.

"Don't!" he cried out with sudden rage, whirling around.

Snap.

Blustering with anger, Tony jerked away from her and stormed from the photo booth. "I don't take photographs."

Celina sat in the booth, stunned. How could he have morphed so in a split second?

Two teenage girls pushed back the curtain. "Are you finished?"

Moving in shock, Celina stepped out. Tony stood with his back to her, running his hands through his hair.

She walked to him and touched his shoulder.

He clasped her hand in his, which was trembling from his outburst. "Look, I'm sorry. You didn't know."

"But why?"

"Isn't it obvious?"

"I think you're awfully handsome."

"Never liked photographs anyway. Don't force me again, okay?"

Celina nodded, still disturbed by his behavior.

But in the next instant, he swept her into his arms and planted a kiss on her mouth. "Hey, weren't we celebrating?"

Before they moved on, he snatched the black-and-white photo strip from the Photomaton. "This first one of you is good."

"The second one isn't bad. At least I can see the back of your head pretty good." The last two were blurry messes.

Tony tore the first photo from the strip and slid it into his wallet. He tossed the remaining three into a waste bin by the photo booth.

Tony spied the men's bathroom. "Wait here for me?"

"Sure."

As soon as he disappeared, she lifted out the discarded photos. After separating the one she wanted, she tucked it into her purse.

Upon emerging, Tony bought a couple of beers from a vendor, and they danced to the band and a Bing Crosby-like crooner. Afterward, they strolled along the beach, talking until almost sunrise, the Photomaton incident nearly forgotten.

After Tony kissed her goodnight, she lay in bed replaying the events of the evening, from Tony's proposal at the top of the Ferris wheel to the fun they'd had dancing. She recalled how livid he'd become over taking photos, and this disturbed her.

Yet, if their places were reversed, she imagined she'd feel the same way.

Yawning, she slid her hand with its new ring under the pillow and burrowed under the covers. Outside the ceaseless roar of the waves drew her toward sleep, yet her mind was still troubled about his reaction. Shifting in bed, she thought about how she'd never seen him angry before.

Was this an isolated incident, or should she be concerned?

Chapter 6

Amalfi, 1953

Celina left the dinner table and whipped through the bedroom door, surprising the housekeeper who'd just settled in to watch over Marco.

Alarmed, the older woman lowered her knitting.

"It's okay, Matilde." Celina bustled toward Marge's brown suitcase, which rested on a bench at the foot of the bed.

Matilde's face crinkled with warmth, and she lifted her yarn.

Celina smiled and nodded toward Marco. "*Grazie*."

Returning to her task, Celina opened her suitcase and shuffled through their belongings, fuming with anger as she did. Lauro Savoia was maddening. He'd ruined a nice family dinner. Never had she thought she'd have to prove who she was. *How demeaning.* She pulled out a folder and pursed her lips.

Surely this would do.

When Celina returned to the dinner table, she pushed a brown folder with a sheaf of documents toward Lauro. "If it's proof you want, there it is."

The folder held her marriage license and birth certificates and passports for herself and Marco. She'd traveled with all the essential documents she'd thought they might need.

"That really wasn't necessary—" Sara began.

"Actually, it is," Lauro cut in. Stretching his neck and shifting in his chair, he reached for the documents and began to inspect them.

Celina slid a hand into her pocket and withdrew a sturdy chain with a notched metal tag debossed with Tony's name and serial number—the identification tag he'd worn in the Army. Handing it to Carmine, she said, "He would have wanted you to have this." She paused. "I kept the other one for Marco."

With his lips pressed into a solemn line, Carmine accepted the well-worn dog tag. He brought the metal tag to his lips and kissed it, while tears gathered in his eyes.

Watching him, Celina realized Carmine—and Lauro—were both as passionate and emotional as her husband had been. They were family, of course.

Sara ran her fingers over the metal tag with reverence. "He was such a handsome young man when he left. Did you bring any photos with you?"

This is what Celina had been dreading.

She slid her hand over her gold locket, cupping in it her palm. "I have one here." After lifting it over her head, Celina found a tiny groove on the side of the locket that had once belonged to her mother and opened it. One of her most cherished possessions was inside.

"After the gasoline rations had been lifted in the States, Tony and I took a motoring holiday to Santa Monica. There was a Photomaton on the pier. He was clowning around..." Celina's voice tapered off as she recalled her cajoling efforts to get him to face the camera. Now she wished she'd been more insistent. His face was mostly buried behind her hair.

Sara peered at the photo, her lips turning up in a sad smile. "I can't see him very well, but it looks like you two were having a good time." She hesitated. "What's that on his face?"

Closing her eyes and sighing, Celina recalled the angry, jagged crease that coursed from hairline to jawline. "A scar. It faded more over time."

Sara drew her eyebrows together and caught her lip between her teeth. Carmine placed his hand over Sara's, but she steeled herself and went on. "Had he been injured?"

"In the war." Celina tried to choose her words with care. "That's what he told me."

His mother pressed a hand to her mouth. "He never told us..." Carmine encircled his wife's shoulders and drew her close to him.

"Do you have any other photos?" Lauro asked.

"That's the only one I have." Celina lowered her eyes. After a while, she had seldom noticed his facial scars. With his gregarious and generous nature, Tony endeared himself to people, forcing them to look beyond ugly reminders of the past and laugh along with him. Now she was glad he'd laughed so much in life. He did everything to excess—especially love. If there was one thing she was certain of, Tony had loved her and Marco with the fullness of his heart. "He didn't like to have his picture taken."

"I don't remember that," Lauro said, folding his arms.

"Have you ever torn up a photo of yourself you didn't like?" Celina asked, straining to keep her voice level. "He felt that way about all of them."

Nodding in agreement, Sara showed her son the photo.

Lauro peered at it. "I can't tell if that's him. You don't have any others?"

"That's what I said." Was he listening to her at all? Celina flicked an apologetic look toward Sara and Carmine. "He didn't like to take photos because of his scars."

"Did he have more than...this one on his face?" Sara asked, her voice barely above a whisper. She touched his photo again before returning the locket to her.

"A couple on his arms." Celina lifted the gold chain over her head and let the locket nestle in her décolletage again. And his torso and legs, but in seeing their reaction, she couldn't get those words out. Lowering her gaze to adjust the chain, she blinked away the hot tears gathering in her eyes.

"With his personality, most people forgot all about his physical imperfections. And the scars faded over time. He was still attractive, and everyone loved him." The scars really hadn't faded much, but Sara looked so stricken.

Sara smiled with relief and touched her hand. "Then you never saw him—his face—as he was in the photo in your room."

"No." Celina wouldn't mention the multiple surgeries he'd told her about, or the painful reconstruction and having to learn how to eat and speak again before leaving the hospital—or how drastically different he'd said he looked. There would be time for that later, if ever. Why intensify their pain?

At least they weren't asking about the accident. Having to identify her husband's body was the most horrific, gut-wrenching task she'd ever had to do. If not for her neighbor who'd looked after Marco that night, and another neighbor who'd taken her to the morgue, she didn't know what she would've done. Without family, she'd been suddenly and painfully adrift.

Swallowing against her thickened throat, she cupped her chin in her hand, taking in the faces around the table. She couldn't imagine having the extent of injuries that Tony had and not wanting to reach out to your family for comfort and support. Even one of them.

If only she'd been able to reach out to them during the long days following his death. Her neighbors had families and jobs. Seeing their faces full of pity, she'd even hated to go outside to hang the laundry. She'd only step outside to collect the milk bottles on the porch before hurrying back inside to the sanctuary of her darkened house and bedcovers. But that was no way for

Marco to live. So she'd let their home go, along with all the plans they'd had for the future there.

"How was he injured?" Carmine asked, his voice gentle.

Celina shook her head. "He wouldn't talk about it." Glancing at Sara's troubled expression, she doubted she would have shared such details now, even if she had known.

Carmine kissed his wife's cheek and hugged her to him. When he pulled away, he asked, "Who'd like more wine?" He motioned to Lauro. "Would you bring another bottle from the cellar? You know the one."

Without a word, Lauro got up.

Sara and Carmine turned to her after he left the room. "Please don't judge Lauro by what you see tonight," Sara said.

"I don't know what's happened to his manners," Carmine added, shaking his head. "That's not how I raised my sons. Antonino was never like that."

Sara shook her head. "Both our boys are passionate—or, *were*," she added. Taking a handkerchief from her pocket, she blotted errant tears on her cheeks. "Like their father sometimes."

How well Celina understood. "Tony *was* passionate."

"Lauro suffered a double loss," Sara said. "His brother *and* the woman he loved."

Celina saw a strained look pass between them. "His wife?"

"He wanted to marry her," Sara said. "He doesn't like to talk about it."

"Lauro has never gotten over her," Carmine said, his eyes darting toward the doorway where Lauro had gone. "That's why he's the way he is sometimes."

Celina wondered what had happened to Isabella. What had caused them to break off their engagement? Whatever the reason, Lauro had suffered, too.

"It's good to remember Antonino," Sara said, indicating closure. She drew a breath of resolve. "But it's up to us to create the future for our family. For Marco."

Sara smoothed her hand over Carmine's shoulder. "God works miracles when we least expect it. Nino is lost to us, but in his place, he blessed us with a grandson." With her eyes shimmering through her tears, she held her arms out to Celina. "And his beautiful mother. You are part of our family now. We mean that."

"Thank you," Celina murmured, sinking into Sara's embrace. "And in my husband's place, God gave me a family."

This wasn't how she'd envisioned her life unfolding a year ago, or even a month ago. After the losses of her parents and her husband, if there was one thing life seemed intent on teaching her, it was to be prepared for the unexpected. This time the unexpected seemed far more pleasant—a relief, really. Celina hoped she wasn't wrong. Tony's words still rang in her mind, but people could change, couldn't they?

Or would whatever had occurred between them affect her, too?

Sara smiled. "You know, I could use some help around here."

"Let her decide, *cara.*" Carmine gave his wife a sweet nudge.

"Oh, do stay here with us, Celina, at least for a while. We want to get to know you better."

Celina knew Lauro wouldn't like it. "An extra week, perhaps."

Sara brightened. "There's so much to be done, not only here, but in all of Italy. The country is growing, and the economy is improving." She swept her arm out, gesturing to their surrounding property, bountiful with citrus trees laden with blossoms and fruit, the hills that cradled them, and the azure sea beyond.

"I would be happy to help," Celina said, though she was sure that they would be helping her far more.

"That's a start." Sara beamed. "I understand, but just imagine, isn't this a beautiful place for your son to grow up? Marco will be near his grandparents, and he'll have lots of cousins to play with, too. You won't have to worry about anything."

Sara had a point. With Tony's extended family surrounding them, Marco would no longer be an eight-hour orphan staying with a neighbor. He would have a family vested in his life. People who would grow to love him as one of their own. Didn't her son deserve that?

With thoughts racing through her mind, Celina bit her lip. Suddenly, their life in San Francisco seemed so lonely in comparison. But what was she giving up? The country she knew. The familiarity of a culture she knew and understood. And she'd have to improve her Italian.

Dizzying questions swirled in her mind. Could she grow to love Italy? What kind of opportunities would Marco have here? Would he want to return to the United States when he grew older? Would *she*?

Celina passed a hand across her forehead. The future was too much to think about. And if the past had taught her anything, it was that the future often made a mockery of even the best-laid plans. *If only Tony...* She pushed the thought away. She had to set a course for them, and school was a few weeks away yet. Looking from Sara's eager face to Carmine's, Celina committed to as much as she could. "We can stay until the end of summer."

"Excellent," Sara exclaimed. "You're going to fall in love with Italy, I can just feel it."

Lauro returned with a bottle of wine, and Celina couldn't help but notice that his eyes were rimmed with red as if he'd been crying. *Maybe he has a heart after all.*

After removing the cork, he tilted the bottle, and they both watched the velvety red wine swirl into her glass.

"Grazie," she said, raising her gaze to his.

Lauro's eyes, full of passion, lingered on hers for a moment, then he looked away abruptly to fill his mother's glass.

"Did you and Nino have a home in San Francisco?" Sara asked.

Celina nodded, noticing the way Lauro poured the wine, the flick of his wrist, the way he raised the bottle. Maybe there was a family resemblance in some of their mannerisms after all.

Turning her attention back to Sara, she said, "We owned a home, but I couldn't imagine living there without him. I sold it and found a little flat for us to rent right across from the chocolaterie. I went back to work recently."

Sara nodded. "You like to stay busy."

"I love what I do. Someday I want a little home for us again." She swirled the wine and lifted it to her nose, inhaling its warm earthiness. As she sipped, she saw Sara and Carmine exchange a glance.

Lauro placed the bottle on the table and sat across from her, his narrowed eyes assessing everything about her. "Marco must be in school, no?"

Shifting under his intense scrutiny yet meeting his gaze, Celina lifted her chin and replied, "He'll start in the fall."

Lauro nodded to himself, his lips curving with satisfaction.

He's happy about that, she decided. *He'll only have to put up with us for the summer.*

"We have a good school in the village," Sara said. "He'll have the summer to learn Italian." Her face lit. "Tomorrow I'll introduce you to my niece Adele and her husband Werner, who's from Germany. They met during the war and fell in love. They were separated for a long time, but love always finds a way. He promised he'd return to her and he did. They married several years ago and have children Marco's age, so I think you'll have a lot in common."

"I'd like that."

As Lauro scowled, Celina let the thought of a future in Italy thread through her mind, measuring and examining it as if it were a length of exotic cloth ready to be fashioned into a new style of coat she could try on to consider. *A new life for us.* Even with a few loose threads, it had some appeal.

Yet how would it be, she wondered, with the memory of Tony in his mother's quick smile and his father's rich laughter. Though she wasn't selfish, she was still young; she still had needs. Would she ever be able to move on with her life and marry again, even if she wanted to?

Or would she forever be cast in the role of the widow Savoia in a small village in Italy?

Chapter 7

"This wine that we will enjoy today was harvested by the hand of my brother, the man whose life we honor today." Standing on the bougainvillea-shaded patio at a long, hand-hewn table worn smooth by the kiss of salted air and years of use, Lauro eased a cork from a well-aged Piedirosso, releasing the musky scent of aged fruit into the air.

"Antonino Savoia had the finest taste of anyone I've ever known." He poured the robust wine into waiting glasses of family and friends who had gathered on the patio at his family's estate after the memorial service for Nino, which had been held at the Duomo in the village. Always appreciative of exceptional artistry, Nino had often sketched the cathedral's old Byzantine tower.

As the wine swirled into the glasses, Lauro shared his memories of the brother he'd loved, and even, for a while, hated.

"Nino told me this was the finest Piedirosso vintage from Campania he'd ever tasted," Lauro said. "He told me that after the wine had a chance to age, it would complement our chocolate. I think all of us can agree that when it came to chocolate, wine, olive oil, and lemons, Nino had a savant-like knowledge, as if he'd inherited the cumulative learnings of our ancestors on this land."

Around the table, Nino's beloved family and friends murmured their approval and brought the glasses to their noses and lips.

Nino had grown up refining his palate on the agricultural specialties of the region. The vineyard that produced this wine adjoined their property and was owned by a widowed cousin. He'd always made time to help her with the harvest.

And yet, he'd wanted something different for his life.

Taking a sip, Lauro nodded to himself. "The wine needs to air to smooth the edges, but Nino was correct. Dark chocolate, indeed." He slid a glass toward Celina.

"To Nino," he said, lifting his glass.

At the other end of the table, his father's silver-shot hair gleamed in the slanting sun as he raised his glass.

"To our beloved son, husband, brother, father, nephew, and cousin," Carmine said in a thick voice. He touched his wife's glass and Celina's, before acknowledging each person there and what they had meant to his son.

When his father's voice faltered, Lauro continued. "We are all the better from having known Nino. He was the best brother and the finest friend we all knew. More than that, my brother's encyclopedic knowledge and quiet persistence elevated our craft." During his summer breaks from school, he'd introduced daring, unique new flavor combinations with chocolate and improved processes for hand- and machine-molded chocolates. He'd even bred a finer strain of lemon to marry with chocolate and use in limoncello.

And still, it wasn't enough for him.

Around the table, family members responded. "To Nino."

Lauro tilted his head heavenward toward the endless skies where he imagined Nino's soul floated freely, watching the family gathering.

This mourning felt surreal; it seemed he ought to *feel* the loss of his brother's soul more, and be certain of its departure from terra firma, shouldn't he? He'd heard people say they had known the moment their loved one had died, no matter where they were in the world, and yet, he'd detected nothing. No sudden void, no devastation, not even a twinge. He and Nino had once been so close, but that was before Isabella. This was even more mystifying because he still felt his brother's presence.

Now he felt only sadness because the hope of Nino returning was gone. As Lauro had come to regret their parting words, he'd clung to that hope for years.

After Isabella and Nino had left him, Lauro had felt his reason for being wither. Besides his parents, the two people he had shared everything with were suddenly gone. Now, he managed the *fabbrica di cioccolato* for his father, and he was devoted to his parents as he should be, but his life seemed hollow without a family of his own making, as his other friends were doing. Still, he clung to hope that someday that might change.

Glancing at the faces around the table, at the family and friends he'd known all his life—save two new faces—he could only imagine that Nino's soul surrounded them. A cacophony of whistles and warbles erupted from the old trees shading the veranda. Even the sparrows and warblers seemed to sing Nino's praises.

"What's that?" Celina shaded her eyes against the sun, smiling. "Oh, robins. Look, Marco, how pretty they are."

"*Pettirosso*," Lauro said, nodding toward the carnelian red birds that shimmered in the sun under spring green canopies. "He needs to learn Italian."

"He is."

Celina's retort held a defensive edge. Wasn't she even a little embarrassed that Nino's son could barely speak their language?

Reaching for bread from the basket in front of him, Lauro tore off a piece, dipped it in olive oil, and offered it to Marco. "*Pane e olio*?" Marco took it and nibbled, his eyes registering his delight.

"What do you say?" Celina prompted him.

"Thank you," Marco said between bites.

"*Grazie*," Lauro replied, correcting him.

Marco grinned. "*Gra-zee.*"

While the cousins and aunts and uncles reminisced about Nino, Lauro slipped off his dark jacket and helped himself to an antipasto platter brimming with olives and artichokes, as well as a basket of fresh-baked bread that his mother had placed on the table. Tending to last-minute details, he'd only had time for a steady diet of *caffè* today, and it had put him on edge.

As he ate, he watched little Marco. Crouched on his knees near his mother's chair, the boy played in a world of his own, his nimble fingers prying the small wheels from one railway car and switching them to another. Adult conversation swirled around him on the patio, but he seemed intent on renovating the train cars—just as Lauro had recalled doing when he was a boy. Testing the new set of wheels on the stone floor, Marco emitted little engine sounds to accompany the clacking wheels.

He could have had a son that age. The thought struck him with regret.

Was this really his nephew? The boy looked nothing like Nino and barely like his mother. Unlike his parents, who saw what they wanted to see, he had a hard time buying the idea that Marco was a blood relative. Fortunately, the boy and his disturbing mother would soon return to the United States, and life would return to normal.

"Maria, Gino, have you met your new cousin?" Adele, Lauro's cousin, sent her children to meet Marco. Curious about the new boy, the two children scooted next to him.

Adele was the firecracker of the family. As children, she'd been the adventurous one, always the first to take her horse into the lead or tackle the steepest snowy incline when their parents had taken their families skiing at their *nonno's* chalet in the Alps just north of Torino. Not that he hadn't quickly gained the lead as he grew older and stronger, but Adele was smart and kept him alert.

She had new ideas about a woman's place in the home, too. Adele had opened a fashion boutique near the cathedral catering to tourists who visited Amalfi and locals along the Sorrentino coast.

Adele's husband, who was seated next to her with his arm draped around her, seemed proud of her accomplishments, too. Werner was a man who was confident enough to allow his wife the freedom to do what she wanted. He called their marriage a partnership, which sounded quite modern to Lauro, and he liked that. Maybe someday he'd have a relationship like the one they enjoyed.

"Marco seems like a sweet soul, so much like Nino," Adele said, smiling at the boy's easy interaction with her son and daughter.

A sweet soul like Nino. That much was true, Lauro allowed grudgingly, his gaze trained on the boy. Why would Nino have kept his young family from them? "There the resemblance ends," he muttered.

Frowning, Adele poked his side. "What's the matter with you? Of course Marco looks like his father."

At the sound of his name, Marco stood and flung his arms around his mother. "I like Daddy's home," he said, an innocent smile lighting his face.

"Glad you're having fun, sweetheart." Celina smoothed her son's light brown hair. She cast a glance in Lauro's direction.

Had she heard his comment? Not that he cared much if she had.

"We're playing," Marco replied, skipping over the toys to return to his new playmates.

Adele smiled. "Marco, did you know that I used to play with your papa like that?"

The boy shared a shy smile again and turned his face to Lauro.

Second cousins, Lauro thought, watching young Maria and Gino playing with the new boy. Marco had light brown hair but so did many of their extended family in the north. As he studied Marco's face, he noticed the boy *did* take after his mother.

Lauro stole a glance at Celina. Her dark lashes and brows were a striking contrast to golden hazel eyes that seemed to glow with mystery.

Averting his gaze, he reached for more olives. *Distracting, that's what she is.* Nino must have fallen hard for those mesmerizing eyes. He'd always liked beautiful women.

The children turned their attention back to the carved wooden toys that he and Nino had played with as children. While the children played, Adele and Celina worked out that the children were stair steps in age, with Maria a year older than Marco and Gino a year younger.

"They get along so well," Adele said to Celina, her face lighting with motherly pride. "We'll have to spend more time together."

"I could take Marco fishing with the kids," Werner added.

"He'd like that." A faint smile lifted Celina's full lips.

Adele inclined her head. "Sara tells me you and Marco are welcome to stay here. I hope you will."

"We're trying to convince her," Sara said, leaning in toward the conversation. "Marco is so much like his father," she added. "And my uncle Enzo." She trailed her hand along Marco's shoulder as he scooted past her on his hands and knees, guiding a trio of train cars beside him.

Lauro watched as his mother stared happily after Marco. Sara had hardly left the boy's side since he'd arrived. Seeing how she gravitated toward her new-found grandson—if that's *really* who he was—and showered him with love, he felt crushing guilt for not marrying and giving his parents grandchildren before now. Yet even after all these years, Isabella's laughter still rang in his ears. He swallowed against the lump in his throat that had plagued him all day.

While Sara watched her grandson play with Adele's children, her face softened. "Marco is our precious gift from heaven."

Lauro swirled his wine, listening. He wasn't entirely sure *where* Marco was from. To him, Marco looked like the scrappy young American he was, though his heritage could be Italian. He was puzzled, though. He couldn't see the Savoia family resemblance or that of his mother's family.

His father held out his arms to Marco. *"Vieni qui, figlio,"* Carmine said. When the boy didn't respond, Carmine repeated his request in English. "Come here, son. I have something for you."

Marco's face lit with a shy smile, and he hurried to his grandfather.

Lauro narrowed his eyes, disturbed that the boy didn't know their language. Leaning forward, he caught Celina's eye. "Why doesn't your son speak Italian?"

His mother shot him a look. "Marco knows some Italian," Sara said in the boy's defense. Turning to Celina, she added, "I believe he understands more than he speaks, no?"

"I think so," Celina said, casting her gaze toward her son.

Lauro tapped his fingers on the table. "I'm surprised Nino didn't make sure his son spoke his family language."

"He tried, of course," Celina said with a slight shrug of a slender shoulder under a closely fitted dark jacket. "But we wanted to make sure he knew his letters and had a head start on reading and writing in English before he began school." Staring again at the white handkerchief she'd been twisting during church, she added, "We thought we'd have plenty of time. I haven't kept up his studies as I should have. There's just been so much to do since..." Her voice trailed off.

Sara quickly covered Celina's hand with her own. "We understand. I'm sure Marco will learn Italian just as quickly as Nino learned his languages. He is his father's son, after all."

Celina nodded. "Tony spoke English well. Almost as if he'd been born to it."

"And French," Sara said with pride. "Better than mine."

When Celina looked nonplussed, Lauro asked, "How many languages did your Tony speak again? I've forgotten."

Celina seemed uncertain of his question. "Well, besides English and Italian, he'd learned a little Japanese in the war."

"That's Nino for you." His father let out a hearty laugh. "Always the modest one of the family. Top of his German class, too, he was."

Sara's expression softened. "He spoke Spanish beautifully as well, didn't he?"

"So do I, but we spoke English at home," Celina said, as her neck and face flushed. "I'm afraid I was to blame."

The conversation veered into another direction, and Lauro leaned back, bent on observing Celina's interactions with his parents and other family members who had returned with them after the priest's service at the church.

Lauro could hardly believe how much their lives had changed in the past few weeks—and not for the better. From the moment he'd received that strange telephone call from America and told his parents about Celina Savoia—or whoever she really was—his family's life has been altered beyond what he could have imagined.

His mother had prepared the house as if royalty were expected. Bedrooms were aired and painted, old toys were unboxed, and childhood photographs were framed and placed throughout the house. Sara had donned the traditional black clothing in memory of Nino, but her heart was full of anticipation for their newly discovered grandchild.

The thought of a grandson also filled his father with pride. While getting a close shave at the barber, Lauro had overheard him telling his friends at the *barbiere* his father had patronized for years that he had a new grandson. With reluctance, Lauro admitted to himself that the idea seemed to reinvigorate his father. Carmine had even suspended a swing from one of their tallest, stoutest trees on the property. He was never too tired to swing little Marco high into the air, filling them both with forgotten joy.

Lauro had taken over most of the daily responsibility at the factory, but since Celina arrived, his father had hardly been in the office.

As far as he was concerned, Celina was not a good influence on his family's productivity.

Still, despite his parent's delight, Lauro couldn't see Nino in the boy. And he certainly couldn't excuse Nino's silence all these years.

With Nino gone, the first grandchild should have been *his* child. Lauro shouldered the duty to carry on the family line now, and he had promised himself that one day he would fulfill that responsibility. If only Isabella hadn't been so fiery and reactive, though that was one of the many things he'd loved about her. To this day, he hadn't been brave enough to replace her in his heart. And, unlike Nino, he was not one to shirk his duty.

The children's quick laughter bubbled through his thoughts. As if feeling his attention on him, Marco looked up at Lauro and grinned, the sunny innocence of the boy's expression dislodging the tightness he'd felt in his chest since this morning.

Immediately, Lauro felt guilty for his attitude. Whatever Celina had done in alienating Nino from his family—or had in mind now—the fact remained that this boy had lost his father. If Marco was actually his nephew, shouldn't he be relieved that Nino had removed the burden of having children from his life?

Sipping his wine, Lauro studied Celina. He had to admit she was attractive, and he could see why his mother embraced her. Celina's voice had a unique pitch, a velvety smooth quality that was mesmerizing, and she spoke in a forthright manner that reflected her American upbringing. His mother liked people who expressed themselves. *Like Isabella.* Yet for someone who said they worked with chocolate, Celina was curiously lean. Svelte, he supposed, was the fashionable word, like a Parisienne. Or an athletic American. Her legs were nicely toned.

Not that he should notice. He averted his gaze and sipped his wine.

Sara rapped the table in front of him. "Aren't you going to offer our guest something to eat?" She angled her head toward the antipasto platter.

Sheepishly, Lauro slid the platter and bread basket toward Celina.

Sara shook her head at him. "Would it kill you to serve her? She's your sister-in-law."

Feeling his mother's eyes on him, he scooped a few olives and artichokes onto a small plate for her. "There's more if you want it."

Inclining her head, Celina took it from him. "*Grazie.*"

Those lips turned up again. Was she laughing at him? His mother had admonished him like a child.

Her call had irritated the family's still gaping wounds. After the war, he and his parents had held out hope that Nino would soon come home. He'd sent a short letter years ago, telling them he had become an American citizen and was shipping out with the army to the Pacific region. They'd contacted the military in the United States, but their records had been incorrect. They told his father that Nino had been released. If that were true, he would have contacted his family. Perhaps he'd been injured, or imprisoned, or was in the care of a kind Samaritan somewhere. Something was terribly wrong, they were sure of it.

Miraculous stories of survival were circulating, and if anyone was deserving of a miracle, it was Lauro. Hadn't he once considered the priesthood? Hadn't he taken up the causes of those in need, from managing the harvest of a widowed neighbor to taking up arms on behalf of his adopted country?

Still, Nino was an independent thinker. None of them had imagined that he'd actually move to America or join the army. Nino had changed, that was true. Lauro stroked his chin. Had he really known his brother after all?

Lauro glanced around the long table of the family who'd endured so much together. Here they were, sending to rest the soul of the brother he'd looked up to his entire life. His parents had insisted on putting up the death announcement posters in town, as was the custom. As a result, a basket in the entryway held condolence telegrams, and flowers and food covered every surface in the kitchen and dining room.

He noticed that though Celina had accepted his plate of antipasto, she didn't touch it.

Their friends and family were curious about Celina, too. Most of them seemed to accept her and dote on Marco, especially his mother's sisters and Adele.

Celina was dressed in what Lauro supposed was a modest enough outfit for a funeral, but she could have worn anything and heads would turn. When she thought no one was watching her, she moved gracefully, deliberately, as if in time to a slow tempo adagio. Or a brisk allegro, as when he'd spied her playing outside with her son. Her sylph-like figure gave her an advantage over many, yet she carried her height with confidence.

For the past few days, she'd worn scarves around her thick, coppery blond hair, which fell in waves to her shoulders, but not today. Twisted at the nape of her neck, her hair was brushed back from her face, revealing strong cheekbones and an angular jawline that gave her a look of determination in contrast to the sometimes faraway look in her eyes.

Without a doubt, Nino had excellent taste. Lauro brought his wine to his lips and gulped.

If indeed, she truly *had* been married to his brother.

Sure, Celina had all the right documents. He'd examined them with care. But couldn't she have had those created? Document forgery had been elevated to an art form during the war.

Lauro couldn't help wondering, what did she want of them? Support for her son, probably. She seemed cultured—as if she came from a family of some standing, but many in America had lost assets in the stock market crash or during the war.

Or she was a damned fine actress. How close was San Francisco to Hollywood?

Too close. Even though she didn't seem like the type.

Why had she waited six months to call about Nino's death? She said she had sent letters, but they'd received nothing.

However, sometimes letters were lost in international mail.

As he sat staring at Celina, she seemed to feel his gaze on her. She looked up, her gold-flecked, ambery eyes as luminous and chilling as those of a tiger eyeing its prey. He shifted under her sudden scrutiny.

"Yes?" She stared, unblinking.

"Don't you have to return to work?" At once, Lauro realized the brusque tone of his voice. From the corner of his eye, he saw his mother purse her lips in admonishment. "Or to your home in San Francisco?"

"I took a leave from my job. But I miss being busy."

"We can keep you busy," Carmine said. Standing behind him, his father clamped a hand on his shoulder. "Lauro, you should take Celina to see the *fabbrica di cioccolato*."

That was easily the last thing he'd want to do with her. "I can't imagine she'd be interested. Our process is quite different from what is done in America."

"Actually, I'd like to see it."

Of course you would, he thought to himself.

She beamed at Sara and Carmine. "I'd like to see more of the area, too."

"Why, yes, you should." Sara clapped her hands. "Lauro, why don't you take a couple of horses and show her the groves?"

And that was the *second* to the last thing he'd want to do with her. Both his parents were looking at him with pleased expectation. As was Celina, with those great, luminous eyes.

"I don't have much time," he began.

"Don't be silly, of course you do," Sara said. "Celina isn't only our guest, she's our new family. You must take her out tomorrow. And be nice."

Lauro nodded his assent, though he couldn't help but feel he was venturing into dangerous territory.

Chapter 8

STARTING TOWARD THE barn, Celina turned to wave at Marco, who stood in the doorway of the villa clutching his *nonna* Sara's hand. Her son was eager to spend the day with his new cousins, Adele's children, Maria and Gino, who were coming over. While she and Lauro were riding, Sara planned to take all the children through the orchard and gardens to pick fruits and vegetables. Celina smiled. She hadn't seen her son this happy in a long, long time.

After she'd sold their home in San Francisco, Marco had mourned the loss of his neighborhood playmates, and she'd often wondered if she'd done the right thing. For a boy to lose his father *and* his friends was difficult. The fault was hers; she couldn't bear to stay in the house surrounded by the memory of Tony and the love she'd lost.

Celina watched as Sara knelt and Marco flung his arms around her neck and kissed her cheek. *My dear Tony's mother.* Surely he would have changed his mind about visiting if he'd known how happy his son and mother would be. *If only he could see this now.* Wouldn't he have changed his mind?

She swallowed against the sudden constriction in her throat and pressed a knuckle to her lips, stifling the intense feeling of loss that still assailed her, often when she least expected it. If nothing else, the sight of Marco with his *nonna* made the journey worthwhile.

This morning, Sara hadn't forgotten the promise she'd extracted from Lauro yesterday at the memorial.

Though Lauro had balked at the idea, Sara insisted. "My sons grew up on horses. Are you a horsewoman?"

"Tony and I used to ride at a friend's ranch." Which was true. Her husband had been a good rider, although she'd had no idea that he'd learned as a child. But then, she hadn't thought to ask him.

Or had she? Like Marco, she worried that her memory of him was fading. Yet, at other times she still felt his presence, though not as much since she'd sold their home. Alarmed, she'd started writing recollections in a journal so that Marco could read it when he was a little older. Once she'd started writing, her memories poured back, and she couldn't write fast enough. Soon she'd need another journal.

Continuing to the stables, the tall leather boots Sara had given her to wear crunched on the gravel path. The riding pants her mother-in-law had loaned her fit just right, too. "Wish I could fit in them," Sara had lamented, but Celina told her she still looked fit and trim.

This morning, Celina had brushed her hair back and secured it with a silver clip, though the light morning breeze tugged free a few wisps around her face. She didn't care much about how she looked today, but she was determined to enjoy herself, even if Lauro was still in a sour mood.

"Hello?" she called out, wondering where Lauro was. From the stables, two large dogs bounded toward her. She stiffened until she heard their welcoming yaps. Long ears flapped gleefully against their white-and-orange spotted fur.

"What a welcome," she said, chuckling. They jumped in front of her, delighted at the sight of a new acquaintance. "Lousy guard dogs, aren't you?"

From behind the stables a sharp whistle cut through the air. "Rubino, Bellina! *Giu*!"

"Rubino and Bellina, eh?" Celina laughed.

Trotting astride a sleek black horse, Lauro appeared in the clearing. He swung from his mount and strode toward her. At his command, the dogs ceased jumping and began to circle her, sniffing at her boots. "*Seduto!*"

Celina bent to scratch their heads, "*Seduto, seduto.*" Minding her, the pair of hounds sat at her feet. "They're so friendly."

"Not always," Lauro said. "But they like you."

"What sort of breed are they?" As the smaller one nuzzled her, she ran her hands over its silky ears. "And who is this?"

"That's Bellina. She's a Bracco, an Italian pointer. Her mate here is Rubino."

Celina watched as Lauro dropped to one knee to pat the flanks of the large male dog. He seemed to relax with the dogs around.

"Rubino and Bellina," she said. "What pretty names. They sound like a pair of Shakespearean lovers."

Lauro threw a swift glance in her direction. "In a way, they are. They're named after a pair of dogs that one of our ancestors owned. *Il marchese*."

Rubino pawed Lauro for more attention.

"Are these their descendants?"

"Perhaps. That was more than four hundred years ago, but the Marquis of Mantua, Ludovico Gonzaga, had such a special bond with them that when Rubino died, he buried him in a casket and erected a tomb in his honor. He did the same for Rubino's mate, Bellina, who died giving birth."

"That's certainly devotion, isn't it?" Celina watched Lauro's tense expression dissipate. While scrubbing his hands along Rubino's neck and relaying the story, he looked as if a heavy cloud had parted in response to a persistent ray of sun.

"You can still see the tombs on the palace grounds. The Gonzagas bred Braccos for years, and these two are probably direct descendants. My family brought them when they moved to this region from Piemonte."

"Why did they move?"

"My great-grandmother is from Amalfi. After marrying, she grew homesick and suffered from hay fever in the north. The fresh sea air and the juice of lemons helped her. Together they expanded her family's lemon production by terracing many of the lemon gardens you see now. The groves, where we'll ride, came later."

"And the chocolate factory?"

"Also moved from Piemonte, though we still have a factory in Torino."

Celina ran her hands along the dogs' coats. This was the most Lauro had said to her since she'd arrived, and though he still wore a slight scowl, he seemed cordial enough. "There's so much history here," she said. "Four hundred years ago, America was just a vast, mostly unsettled land. At least, unsettled by Europeans." After she stopped, Bellina dragged her head across Celina's shins, begging for more attention. "I'd like to see more of Italy while I'm here."

Lauro paused. "You're still leaving at the end of summer, no?"

Celina noticed the tightening in his voice again, and the light in his eyes dimmed. "Marco is starting first grade, and I have to return to work." That seemed to placate him, and the shadow lifted from his face. "Shall we go?"

Lauro drew up. With a gesture and command, he sent the dogs racing back to the stable.

Celina followed him to the old stone building, which housed about a dozen horses. The scents of hay, leather, and manure mingled with that of the ocean and hung in the air, giving the stable a fresh, earthy aroma. A groomsman was checking the saddle on a gleaming chestnut mare, while other horses neighed in adjoining stalls.

"*Lei è docile,*" the groomsman said, stroking the horse's neck.

Lauro turned to her. "I didn't know how well you rode."

She ran a hand down the mare's strong neck and met her inquisitive gaze. The horse pricked her ears. "She'll be fine."

Lauro gave her a leg up, and they started off. Following Lauro, she picked her way up a steep trail that stretched toward the summit of a hill.

"You can get a good view from the top," Lauro said over his shoulder. He'd hardly said a word to her since they'd left the stables, although he'd been murmuring to his horse in Italian the entire way.

Or maybe he was cursing her under his breath.

She sighed. Unlike his parents, he couldn't make it any plainer that her presence was not appreciated.

Celina clicked her tongue, urging her horse onward. When they reached the crest, she reined her horse in. From this vantage point, she felt as though she were on top of the world. Far below them, the sea hurled itself against ancient rocks worn smooth with time, while on the other side, groves stretched languidly in the summer sun.

She breathed in the scent of lemon blossoms, inspired by how their citrus sweetness mingled with fresh ocean air. Closing her eyes, she ran the tip of her tongue over her lips, tasting a faint saltiness in the moisture laden breeze. She imagined how dark, rich chocolate filled with the brightness of a lemon filling and dusted with chunky sea salt might taste. Delicious, she decided.

With a start, she realized how much she missed her work in the kitchen, surrounded by the ingredients she used to create chocolate fantasies that brought smiles of delight to others. She snapped her eyes open, just in time to catch Lauro staring at her with an odd expression of interest.

"What are you doing?" His voice held a faint edge.

She doubted he cared to know about her, let alone her deepest thoughts. Wordlessly, she urged her horse forward to avoid his direct gaze. With his emotional gauge running cold to at best, lukewarm, he was easily the most vexing man she'd ever met.

Her horse paused in the shade of an olive tree. Slender, silvery green leaves sprouted from an old gnarled trunk, shading a bounty of smooth green olives hanging from the branches.

Celina recalled something Tony had once told her. Tony had been particular about his olive oil. Surely that was a safe topic of discussion, although by now, she didn't much care. Marco and his grandparents were getting on well, and that's all that mattered to her.

"Do you make your olive oil from these?" she asked.

"We grow most of the food that is consumed at the villa." Lauro jerked a thumb toward the property that spread beneath them. "Olive oil, vegetables." Turning in his saddle, he gestured toward another barn and added, "Eggs and milk, too. Fruit trees there. And over there, *nocciola*. We use those in our chocolate."

She smiled to herself. At least he was civil when he talked about food.

"Hazelnuts. So you make a paste, *gianduja*." Celina said, referring to the chocolate and hazelnut blend that Italy was known for. "For *gianduiotto*."

"You know about that?"

She raised her eyebrows at him. "I'm a *chocolatière*, too." Did he think she didn't know her craft? Still, she had never seen an actual hazelnut tree. Though she wouldn't tell him that.

"So you say."

There it was again, the challenge in his voice. Reining her horse in, she ignored his comment.

"As I recall, during Napoléon's regency, cocoa became hard to come by," she said. "So in Torino, an enterprising chocolatier named Prochet ground up hazelnuts from Langhe to extend his supply. In the mid-eighteen-hundreds, Caffarel created Gianduiotto. Soon, the *gianduiotto* proved so popular that it became a hallmark of Italian chocolate-making." Lauro was staring at her with such surprise that she couldn't resist a satisfied smirk. "So yeah, I've heard of it. I'm going to take a closer look."

A corner of his mouth lifted in what some might have taken for a grin, but by now, she knew better.

Without answering, Lauro clucked his tongue, and his horse started off.

Curious, Celina cantered past him, eager to inspect the trees. Broad, leafy canopies arched over multiple trunks, filtering sunlight that danced around them like fairies on the path. She stopped beside a tree and reached up to bend a branch toward her. A bract of green, fringed leaves encapsulated the hazelnuts.

Inhaling the scents of nature surrounding her, she paused, wondering why her husband had shunned such a beautiful place where she'd found acceptance, welcome, and love. She shifted on her saddle and peered behind her.

From everyone but Lauro, that is.

Celina heard his horse trot behind her. Turning away, she tented her hand and gazed toward neighboring hills beribboned with grapevines arching across mounded earth in neat, graceful lines. Was Lauro the reason Tony had stayed away? Her horse tossed its head. "What do you know, pal?" she murmured to the mare, who only snorted in response. She ran her hand along its silky neck.

Lauro brought his horse to a halt next to her. He held a large, wrinkle-skinned lemon. "These are *sfusato amalfitano*, and they're unique to our area." He brought out a pocket knife and peeled off a slice. Handing it to her, he added, "Go ahead, they're sweet."

Celina hesitated. After Lauro bit into the fruit, she tentatively tasted it. She was surprised; it was much sweeter than the lemons grown in California. "It's good," she said, peeling back sections to finish it.

After they finished, Lauro tossed the peels aside and shifted in his saddle. "We should keep going. I'm sure you want to be on your way."

Celina glanced at him. "Your words, not mine. I'm enjoying the ride and the view."

When he shrugged in response, Celina turned toward him. She'd had enough of his attitude. Since she'd decided to stay here until it was time for Marco to start school, it was time to clear the tension between them. She pursed her lips and lifted her chin toward him. "You don't like me, and that's okay. But I deserve to know why."

Lauro stared at her as to gauge her reaction before he spoke.

"Well?" she said, growing irritated. "Does it have to do with Tony?"

"*Nino* did what he wanted," Lauro shot back, throwing off any semblance of polite behavior. "He often had a faraway look in his eyes, even as a child. He was never fully present, always lost in thought."

"That was Tony, not me."

Ignoring her comment, Lauro pressed on. "When Nino left Italy for America, you have no idea how much it hurt my mother. He chose to live his life how he wanted, but we live ours. And I don't have to welcome his...*eccentricities.*"

"So a wife and child are eccentricities in Italy, are they?"

"You know what I mean. You're an American."

"Of Italian descent."

Lauro expelled a breath of exasperation.

"So that's why I'm not welcome here? The telegram you sent said something entirely different." The resentment she'd felt toward Lauro coiled within her. "Whatever was between you and Tony, I had a duty to inform my husband's family. Your parents have certainly welcomed us."

Lauro leaned forward. "Who sent that telegram? Who collected you from the train station? I've done everything to make you welcome."

"Except be nice to me. Your only brother's widow." She paused as her resentment and hurt transformed into anger.

Throwing up a hand and shaking it toward her, Lauro burst out, "In suggesting you stay at the villa, my parents made a polite gesture to you." His eyes flashed under dark, lowered brows. "But you are not part of this family. Don't accept their offer."

Celina laughed. "Is that a threat?"

Spreading his hands, Lauro leaned back. "I don't threaten women."

"I might not be part of your family, but Tony's son is." Her horse stepped back, seeming agitated by their exchange. "Your mother told me it's been years since she's seen Carmine's face light up as it does when he's with Marco."

His face reddening with frustration, Lauro spat on the ground. "That's just it. What if you're using your son to get to my parents?"

"Oh, no. No you don't." Swinging her horse around to face him, Celina advanced toward him. "You will *not* sully their relationship. Your brother's little boy—who just lost his father and has been grieving over him for *months*—has a right to have a relationship with his grandparents. Just as they have a right to assuage their grief over their son and transfer some of that love in their hearts to his son. If you don't like it, you can get the hell away from us."

For a moment, he looked as though she'd struck him. He muttered, "Spoken like a true *American*." His lips curled as if the word itself were distasteful to him.

Nudging his horse closer to hers, he pulled himself up and glared at her. "What is it you want from us? Support for your son? For you? The chocolate factory? Maybe you think you'll inherit all this," he added with a wave of his hand.

"Absolutely nothing." Celina huffed in his face, indignant that he would even imagine that. *The idiocy of this man.* Lauro was nothing like Tony, who might not have been as cultured as his brother, but her husband's heart was so big it had burst with love. He had died not from the accident, but from the heart attack he suffered just before impact. How dare Tony's little brother accuse her of such a thing. "Surely you can't think that."

"You're transparent," Lauro muttered as he shook his head. "*Non capisci una fava.*"

Celina lifted her chin to him. "*Tu sei una fava,*" she shot back. *He* was the one who didn't know anything.

"No one calls me stupid." Lauro grabbed her horse's rein and yanking it toward him, brought his face close to hers.

"Then prove you aren't. You can't possibly believe that's why I'm here." He was so close she could feel his breath on her lips. She was appalled to think that he'd been sharing these thoughts with his parents. Staring at him with a mixture of contempt and sadness, she held his piercing gaze, which seemed to bore through to her soul.

In a flash, Lauro's hand slid behind her neck, and his lips hovered near hers, their warm breath mingling, so close he could have kissed her. Instead, he bit his lip, containing whatever emotions were raging through him. His eyes darkened, and his expression was one of anguished lust—as if he were fighting his attraction to her.

Tearing loose with a cry, she leveled her hand against his cheek, the sting shocking her as much as him. "Don't you dare take liberties with me."

She swung her horse around and pressed her legs into its body. What had possessed him to think he had the right to put his hands on her like that? Tears of anger burned across her cheeks and whipped into her hair as she rode.

While her horse gained speed, she glanced back to see Lauro, his head bowed, gingerly rubbing his face.

Chapter 9

Amalfi, 1939

"Maybe we'll be married in the spring," Lauro said to Signore and Signora Ferrara, friends of his parents. He searched the crowded salon for Isabella.

The Savoia family and close friends had gathered for the traditional Christmas Eve feast of the seven fishes at his parent's villa. Savory aromas of sautéed fish, clams, and oysters wafted from the kitchen. After fasting all day, which was their custom until after midnight mass, Lauro was starving.

"That's a surprise," Signora Ferrara said. "You've proposed?"

"Not formally," Lauro confided, feeling nervous. "But her father just gave me permission to ask her."

Candlelight flickered in the grand salon, and outside, the haunting harmonic sound of the local shepherds, the *zampognari*, playing their bagpipes floated to them. Lauro spotted Isabella with Adele across the room, whispering and laughing at some secret or gossip, he imagined. He caught her gaze, and she flashed a brilliant smile at him.

Lauro touched his fingertips to his lips in response. Never had he been happier in his life.

His family and Isabella's had just returned from mass services at the cathedral. To his great relief, Isabella's father had approved of his request to ask her to marry him, though he'd made him wait more than two weeks for his answer.

Isabella's father, Rocco Guardino, was a powerful, wealthy industrialist, and his company was responsible for building and improving roads and bridges throughout Italy. Built like a bull, he was admired and feared, Lauro suspected, in equal measures. After calling him into his cavernous study early this morning, her father had made him promise he'd take care of Isabella and protect her with his life until the day he died, which he intended to do, of course. But Signore Guardino had never once smiled during the entire meeting.

Lauro wiggled the ring in his pocket he'd been carrying around with him for what seemed like an eternity. But now, he was elated. Isabella Guardino would soon be his bride—if she accepted his formal proposal. He'd been hinting, and she'd been coy, but she had yet to give him a direct answer until her father approved.

"Isabella is quite spirited," Signore Ferrara said, drawing Lauro's attention back.

Signora Ferrara added, "By next Christmas, the two of you might have a little *bambino*."

"Maybe not that soon," Lauro said, gulping the French champagne Signore Guardino had provided in lavish quantities for the special evening.

He felt his face flush and glanced at Isabella again, hardly believing his good fortune. Sensing his gaze on her, she turned, her vivid, laughing blue eyes meeting his, her tawny blond hair framing rosy cheeks flushed with excitement. She blew him a kiss and sashayed toward him, her holly red dress swirling around her shapely legs.

Lauro smiled as the Ferraras moved on. *Babies*. They were both young, and he wasn't sure if he was ready for babies yet, but he did want a family. He just wanted to have Isabella all to himself first.

Turning around, Lauro spied his father in conversation with Isabella's father in the corner. Their parents knew each other socially as well as through business, for Cioccolata Savoia had also grown into a major export company over the last couple of decades, enhancing the Savoia family wealth along with it. First Germany and Austria, then England and Russia. Next, North America.

As the company grew, so did the line of mothers anxious to introduce their daughters to Lauro and Nino. After the wedding, that would be in the past, at least for him. Nino would still have to contend with the matchmakers. So far, Nino had dodged the question, insisting that he needed to spend more time at university than Lauro had. Although Nino had graduated with a degree in biology, he decided he wanted to continue to pursue medicine, so he was working in the family business until medical school began next year.

"You're the older brother," Lauro had told Nino in the summer, as soon as he was sure he wanted to marry Isabella. "You should be getting married first."

"I have essential work to do before I consider marriage," Nino had replied, though his pained expression seemed to imply something else. "Does your girl know who our family is?"

"Why shouldn't she?"

Nino shrugged. "I want a woman to marry me for who I am, not for who my family is or what we have."

Lauro didn't understand. "But that's who we are."

Nino shook his head. "Maybe you, brother."

"What are you saying?"

"Only if you've found the woman of your dreams, and you're certain, then don't let her get away. Marriage is forever for us."

Lauro had replayed that conversation many times, but it didn't hold any meaning for him. He was twenty-one, he had completed his university studies, and he was ready to embark on adulthood with a beautiful woman by his side. He would grow old with Isabella and never tire of her the way some men tired of their wives. Those men were married to women who weren't like his Isabella.

Isabella's family had a villa in nearby Positano, as well as a grand home in Rome. Everything Rocco Guardino did was large scale and designed to impress—or intimidate.

Originally, Lauro had meant to propose on New Year's Eve, but once he'd made up his mind, he couldn't fathom waiting that long. Isabella Guardino was the only woman for him.

How such an exquisite creature would agree to marry him was still beyond his grasp, but he'd fallen for her the moment he'd seen her. He'd met her just a few months ago at a summer party in Positano. Isabella and her cousin were seated at the next table.

Eavesdropping, he had heard her confide in the other girl that her boyfriend in Rome had broken up with her, which he still failed to understand. But she had been devastated. To him, Isabella was like a spark that lit the dimmest room, and everywhere they went people gravitated toward her.

The next day, Lauro had invited her to sail to Capri with friends, and within a week he'd known this was the woman he would marry. He'd worked hard to coax tentative smiles from her troubled face. Maybe she hadn't gotten over her last boyfriend, but Lauro saw that she was passionate and sensitive.

He felt his chest tighten at the memory of their stolen kisses on Capri when her older brother—her chaperone—had been lusting after a girl he'd met in a café. The despair he'd seen in her eyes when they'd first met was soon washed away on ocean waves, and her laughter peeled out as if from the heavens. By the end of the week, he was thrilled to have brought happiness to her suntanned face. How could he not have fallen in love with her?

Now, when Isabella reached him, she brushed her cheek against his, taunting him with lowered eyelids and the tip of her tongue that moistened her full lips. He slid his arm around her waist.

"*Bella*," he whispered, playfully pinching her hip. "You're a merciless tease."

"Who's teasing?" Isabella made a small moue with puckered lips and ran her finger along his smooth jawline.

Lauro groaned. "Maybe we should move up the wedding date."

"You haven't even proposed yet." She laughed. "Besides, it wouldn't look good to Mama and Papa if we did. *Pazienza, amore mio*."

Lauro brought her hand to his lips and kissed it. "Your papa worries too much."

Isabella lifted a coupe de champagne from a young man balancing a tray of chilled drinks and sipped from it, never taking her eyes from him. With effervescent bubbles clinging to her lips, she stole a quick kiss and handed him the glass.

"Mmm, champagne kisses." Lauro took the crystal glass and nuzzled her neck. His patience was being stretched thinner with every passing day. "Think of the fun we're going to have, my love."

Signore Guardino was called away, so Lauro's father joined them. Carmine slung an arm around his son. "You two look like you have a secret."

"Never from you." Isabella laughed and pressed her cheek against his father's.

Lauro tickled her. "Ask my father. He'll tell you I'm not the patient one in the family. And neither are you." They both laughed, but Lauro respected her wishes. The last thing he wanted was to get on the wrong side of her father before the wedding.

"No, that would be your brother," Carmine said, before turning his attention to Isabella. "In our family, Lauro has never been known for his patience."

"Papa, don't spoil my chance here." Lauro jabbed his father in the side.

Isabella's laughter bubbled through her as she took Lauro's hand and guided it around her waist. "I can hardly wait to spend more holidays together like this. You should come to my parents' home next year. My father always invites the best chefs for a lavish gourmet meal. Last year we had a formal dinner for more than a hundred people."

Lauro noticed that his father let her comment slide over him. He knew his father cherished their Christmas Eve, which revolved around family. Throughout the evening, they had more family stopping by—some staying for dinner, others on their way to the homes of other family and friends. He spied his younger cousins, lively and boisterous, clowning around and popping sweet *struffoli* balls into each other's mouths. How could he miss this? They would deal with that after they were married.

Carmine looked over the festive gathering with expectation. "Speaking of your brother, someone said he'd arrived. Have you seen him?"

"Not yet," Lauro replied. Since Nino had returned to Rome last year for advanced studies, they hadn't seen much of him. Lauro had already finished his university classes. Nino continued to work on behalf of Cioccolata Savoia in Rome, tasked with managing their accounts in Rome and introducing buyers in shops, restaurants, and hotels to their chocolates. Lauro had stayed in Naples to work in their main factory.

"Who is this mystery brother of yours?" Isabella asked. "Everyone speaks of him, but I think he's a ghost."

"More like a god," Lauro said. "Always the most popular and top of his class." When Lauro was younger, he'd sometimes been jealous of Nino's talents, but after he stepped out of his brother's long shadow, he'd gained confidence and skills. Now he was marrying before Nino, and this was the only thing he'd ever accomplished before his older brother.

"I have *two* talented sons," Carmine said, taking Isabella's hand. "Aren't I the luckiest man? Someday soon I hope to have beautiful daughters-in-law, and soon, *bambini*, no?"

Isabella fluttered her lashes, feigning shyness, but she was anything but shy. She was the most tempting, passionate woman he'd ever met, and he could never get enough of her intoxicating perfume. He longed to wake in the morning next to her and thread his fingers through her silky, golden hair. She fairly vibrated with energy, and even without touching her, she could send pulsing waves over him from across a room. She was like a high-powered radio transmitter, and he was her helpless, willing receiver.

She'd once complained about her last boyfriend being too studious and quiet for her taste, though he knew she'd been devastated when he left her. Her father had insisted on a marriage for her, but Isabella had rebelled.

Although Lauro had been a good student, his interests were far different from Nino's and much broader than what the university could offer. He wanted to work with new machinery and connect with retail shops all over the world—especially in America, where one could make a fortune overnight. Their chocolates would be world-famous. Someday, he would make Isabella and her father proud of his efforts.

Lauro looked up. Signore Guardino was approaching them. Quickly, Lauro put a respectable distance between Isabella and himself, though he ached for the warmth of her touch again.

"Don't step away from me," Isabella whined in protest, pulling him back toward her and sloshing his champagne.

"Isabella, your father is coming this way," he said, lowering his voice and maintaining his torturous distance.

Making a face, she lifted the champagne from his hand. "Here, I'll finish that for you." After a swift swallow, she tucked the glass behind her back.

Lauro felt his scalp sweating again as it had that day when her father had spoken to him about Lauro's request of Isabella's hand in marriage.

With a quick motion, she slid her hand around the back of him and pinched his buttock.

"You're going to be the death of me," he whispered, fighting the overwhelming involuntary physical reaction that threatened to give him away just as her father joined them.

Signore Guardino greeted Lauro by bestowing kisses on his cheeks. Smelling of garlic and grappa, the older man had been swilling champagne like water.

"Carmine, Lauro, are you enjoying yourselves?" Success emanated from the precision cut of the stately man's hair to the gold ring he wore on his smallest finger. The dangerous demeanor he'd long cultivated kept people at a respectable distance.

Speaking to Lauro's father, Signore Guardino said, "Your son tells me he is working in your business. He's your assistant?"

"He's learning about the manufacturing process," Carmine said. Pride was evident in his voice.

"I hope you'll give him the opportunity to be his own man, too."

"Of course. He'll soon be in charge of our chocolate operations here and in Torino," Carmine quickly replied, shooting a look at Lauro.

Lauro nodded solemnly, although this was the first he'd heard of this plan. His father had always planned for Nino to succeed him at Cioccolata Savoia. He wondered what had changed his mind.

Isabella's father drew up to his full height, half a head above Lauro. "When you travel, you will take Isabella with you. She does not like to be left alone."

"Papa!" Isabella protested against his command. "You're assuming we're going to be married."

Signore Guardino trained his eyes on his daughter, and she quickly averted her gaze.

Lauro took note. "Yes, sir." To Isabella, he added, "We'll be doing a lot of traveling, *amore mio*." He saw a fleeting look of pride in Signore Guardino's face. He'd have to do a lot more to earn the man's respect, but this was a start.

He would certainly oversee the chocolate factories if that's what his father wanted. Lauro was excited to expand the distribution of Savoia chocolate. Signore Guardino would understand this. Lauro cleared his throat.

"I want to expand our distribution around the world," Lauro said, his voice ringing with boldness. "The United States is an enormous market, and I'm confident that our chocolates are unique—far better than Hershey's. One day soon, I'll go to New York, and Macy's and Gimbels will fight over our chocolates. We'll make a fortune."

Isabella's father took Lauro's face between his hands and clapped his cheeks. "You do that," he said, his words a command rather than encouragement, before moving on to another guest.

Lauro rubbed his stinging cheek.

"That's a compliment from Papa." Isabella snaked her hand into Lauro's again and kissed his reddened face. "I need to talk to Adele before her boyfriend arrives."

He was glad that Isabella and Adele had become such good friends. "Adele has a boyfriend?"

"Werner Graf. His family is from Germany. They bought the old Rosso villa a few years ago for their summer home." Isabella hurried to Adele.

Lauro watched her go, aching with love for her.

His father chuckled. "The way you look, that's how I felt about your mother when we met," Carmine said. "And I still do." He gazed after his wife, who was talking to Isabella's mother, a brittle-looking society woman. "She looks like she needs a glass of champagne. I'm happy for you, son, but our holidays will never be dull again."

"Not that they ever were."

Carmine glanced at his watch. "Wonder what's keeping Nino?"

"I'll look for him, Papa."

Lauro wedged through the crowd of extended family and close friends and stepped outside.

Nino's sleek red convertible, a Lancia Astura Spider, was parked outside. Lauro called out for his brother.

Nino stepped from the shadow of an olive tree near the edge of the cliff. He seemed deep in thought; his hands were jammed into his pockets, and a sea breeze ruffled his hair away from his serious face.

They greeted each other with an embrace. Lauro hadn't seen Nino in months. He'd been so involved with Isabella and going to work every day with his father.

"Good to see you, Nino." Lauro could hardly contain his enthusiasm. "Did Papa tell you about Isabella?"

Nino nodded, his face masked with concern. "Lauro, there's something we need to talk about."

"Later," he said, punching Nino's arm. "Papa is looking for you. Come on." Despite Nino's protests, he steered his brother into the villa.

"No, wait," Nino said, bracing himself against the arched door jamb.

Lauro peered at his brother. "Looks like you started celebrating early."

"It's not that, it's...Isabella."

"She's beautiful. I can't wait for you to meet her."

Nino winced as if in pain. "Lauro, I—"

The door burst open, and some of their younger cousins spilled out, laughing and pushing each other. Through the open door, Lauro could see Isabella chatting with Adele. He pulled Nino inside.

One of their aunts enveloped Nino in a hug, and other family members followed suit.

Isabella turned to cross the room to him. Lauro held out a hand to her. Behind him, Nino extricated himself from the aunts and uncles.

"Lauro, I can't stay—"

"But you have to meet Isabella—" He caught Nino's arm.

"This isn't the time…"

When Isabella was two paces away, her gleeful expression froze. Her face morphed into a look Lauro had never seen before—one of confusion, hurt, and anger.

Clamping a hand over her mouth, she shook her head, as wild-eyed as if she'd seen an apparition.

In the split second before Lauro caught her hand, a thought raced through his mind. *What's wrong?* Still clutching his brother's arm, he said, "Isabella, I want you to meet my brother, Nino."

Her eyes widened with a question. "*Riccardo*?"

"I can explain, *cara*," Nino began, lowering his voice and spreading his hands.

Cara. At that moment, with his brother's loving utterance of one simple, casual word of endearment, Lauro's world imploded.

"I waited." Isabella's lovely face contorted with anguish. "You never came."

"Isabella?" Lauro croaked her name through paralyzed lips, hoping she would fling herself into his arms again, but she only tugged away. The thought of Isabella with Nino was a gut punch that knocked the air from his lungs.

The conversation around them ceased, and the air that separated them stilled.

Isabella and Nino stared at each other with impenetrable intensity.

Nino swiped a hand across his brow. "You're better off with Lauro."

As if in a trance, Isabella stepped toward Nino and pressed a slender hand against his cheek. "I loved you," she whispered, cradling her soft belly with her other hand. "We created… together."

His sanity splintering, Lauro shoved Nino, desperate to break their bond.

Murmurs rose among their family and friends, surrounding them. Lauro's neck blazed with a toxic cocktail of shame and fury that coursed through his veins like grappa, singeing every nerve in his limbs until his flesh felt inflamed. Beyond Isabella, he saw her father's stern face twisting with barely concealed rage.

There was no doubt in Lauro's mind that Signore Guardino would kill Nino. Isabella was his most precious treasure.

As she was to Lauro.

Nino reached out to her, imploring her with a gaze that revealed everything between them. "Are you…?

Isabella shook her head, but her face was once again etched with injuries that Lauro had spent months kissing and smoothing away. Her vulnerability returned with such force that he knew she would never recover this time. Nino was too close.

Lauro thrust his brother aside, but his action did nothing to sever the transfixed connection between Isabella and Nino.

"Isabella, I beg of you," Lauro murmured, reduced to pleading with her. "Let's leave, right now." If he could tear her away from this moment, maybe time would reset itself, and the world would regain its balance.

But he was wrong. As if he, Lauro, her beloved, had ceased to exist, Isabella drew toward Nino like cold hands to a flame on a wintry eve. His heart pumping in desperation, blood roared through his brain, muffling most other sounds in the room—even the melodic strains of *Astro Del Ciel*—except for the three of them.

"Riccardo..."

She had never uttered his name with such passion. It was all Lauro could do to keep from doubling over in pain. He gripped her around the waist, pressing her to his chest, but she felt as cold as a corpse in a December tundra, staring over his shoulder at Nino.

He had lost her.

Lauro struggled with the sudden realization that he'd never really had her love, not like Nino had. And he never would. Could he live with that? He had to try...

"Isabella, I still love you," he murmured against her delicate earlobe. He didn't know how he could ever love another.

"I can't, Lauro..." With tears spilling onto her cheeks, she pulled away from him. Her face shimmered with the heat of passion beading on her forehead, as if she were awakening from a nightmare. Making an angry gesture toward Nino, she spun around, her scarlet dress swirling behind her, and stormed away from them.

Chapter 10

Amalfi, 1953

THE SUN WAS high in the sky, and Celina had shed her light jacket to feel its warmth on her shoulders. She had been riding for a couple of hours, exploring the countryside, trying to get the maddening exchange with Lauro out of her mind. He was easily the most insufferable man she knew. What made him think he had the right to touch her with such intimate implications? She slowed her mare and paused, glancing around the unfamiliar landscape.

She'd torn out of the orchard with no sense of direction, blinded by fury and consumed with Lauro's inexplicable action and what he'd charged her with. One grove had led to another, then another. She rubbed her knuckles across her horse's neck, anger over his action and her reaction tightening her chest. "Where are we, girl?"

Stopping by the stream she'd been following, she led her horse to the trickling water. She dismounted, and while her horse drank, she took in her surroundings. A smaller villa loomed behind her, shrouded by olive trees and lacy, pink bougainvillea flowers.

Squatting by the stream, she rinsed her hands in the cool water and ran them over her heated face and lips. How could Lauro have imagined that she would've given him permission to kiss her? Even though he stopped himself at the last possible moment. *He's crazy*, she thought, resting her haunches on her heels.

Most of the people she'd observed in Italy were more demonstrative than in the United States. Tony certainly had been. Here, kisses on the cheek were expected among family and friends. Her mother had been affectionate, so she was accustomed to it.

But a kiss on the lips still meant something else to her.

Tony. The last man she'd kissed. Occasionally she'd found herself wondering if there would ever be another. But she was in no hurry. Taking her time would be best for her son, too. Right now, she was better off alone. She wrapped her arms around her midsection, shivering from the coolness of the stream.

It's lonely, though. Glancing around, the trees seemed to close in on her. *Loneliness*. Why was she even thinking about this? She splashed cold water on her face again and again, as if the brisk coolness could clear her mind of all that had transpired today and in the past six months.

Suddenly, the vines behind her rustled, startling her. Had Lauro followed her? With every nerve in her body on high alert, she jerked around ready to fight.

"Celina?" Adele stepped toward her with a curious look on her face. "What are you doing here?"

Relieved to see Tony's cousin, she let out a small laugh. "Guess I got a little lost."

"You poor thing." Adele embraced her and pressed her cheeks to hers. "Come inside. I just made *limonata*. You look like you need to rest. We'll eat, too."

Relief coursed through her, and Celina realized how hungry she was. Guiding her horse, she walked alongside Adele.

"You can leave your horse here," Adele said, taking the reins and looping them over a wooden post. "At least Lauro gave you the gentle one." She ran her hand along the horse's neck, and the horse whinnied in greeting.

Inside, Adele led her to the kitchen, which was decorated with a cozy riot of cookware, flowers, and books. From a rack above a hulking stove hung copper pots rubbed until they shone. A tomato sauce simmered on the stove—a *gravy*, she corrected herself, as Tony had always done. The aroma brought back a memory of the first time he had ever cooked for her.

"Have a seat," Adele said, motioning toward a table in the center of the kitchen. "Werner has gone into town. It's too quiet when he's away. I'm glad you're here."

Gingerly, Celina eased onto the worn wooden chair. She rubbed a sore muscle in her hip and asked, "How far am I from the Villa Savoia?"

Adele laughed as she poured lemonade into tall frosted glasses she'd taken from the icebox. "Not too far by car, but you had a good ride." She garnished the glasses with sprigs of fresh basil and brought them to the table. She cocked her head and added, "I'm surprised you went off on your own."

Celina felt her face flush. If she confided Lauro's wretched behavior to Adele, would she believe her? She was beginning to think the Savoia family may indeed be more complicated than she'd imagined, and the last thing she wanted was to compromise her son's relationship with his grandparents. But maybe Adele knew about the rift between Tony and his family. "I started off with Lauro."

"And what happened? Did he leave you?" Adele asked, her voice registering dismay.

"No, I was so eager to explore that I took off, and we became separated." Part of that was true, anyway. She wanted to get to know Adele better before denigrating her cousin—though he deserved it. Adele and Lauro seemed as close as siblings. Their mothers were sisters, and all the children had grown up together.

"I can't imagine he let you get away."

"I hardly gave him a chance." Celina sipped her lemonade, thankful for the cool, icy drink. "But then, I don't think he cares much for me."

"What makes you say that?"

"He's always challenging me."

Adele stirred her *limonata* thoughtfully. "Lauro has been under a lot of pressure to help Carmine and Sara rebuild and expand the chocolate enterprise. They feel the responsibility to provide jobs in our community, but they lost nearly everything during the war, too. Except for their land and their spirit." She brightened. "Sara tells me you might stay. I hope so. Is that true?"

"Sara and Carmine have been so generous, but if I stay, I need to find work, too."

"You could work at the chocolate factory. I'm sure Lauro could use your help."

Anything but that. Celina shook her head. "Actually, I've always wanted to have my own chocolaterie. I have some savings I can use to get started." She still had the money she'd made on the house. It wasn't a lot, certainly not enough to start a shop in San Francisco, but right now, due to the exchange rate, her money might go farther here in Italy.

She'd promised herself she wouldn't touch her little nest egg except for something that would help secure their future. From working at the chocolaterie in San Francisco she'd learned a lot about how to run a business, and she certainly knew her craft. Celina was as ready as she ever would be to start a business. She glanced out the window, taking in the stunning view of nature's bounty against a mountainous backdrop.

Why not here? She could dream, anyway. Clasping her hands, Celina leaned toward Adele. "Do you know of a good area for a chocolaterie?"

"Then you'd stay?" Adele brushed her dark hair from her face, excitement glittering in her eyes.

"I don't know. Maybe. It's so pretty here." The idea began to take root in her mind.

"There's a vacant space next to my fashion boutique in Amalfi in the Piazza del Duomo, the main street near the cathedral. It would be so much fun to have you there."

The Duomo. That was the lovely Sant'Andrea cathedral in the heart of the village that rose sixty steps above the piazza. She'd been enthralled by the Byzantine façade and the soaring interior.

It was a perfect location. "Do you think it's expensive?"

Adele shook her head. "I don't think so. The shop needs work. Oh, Sara would be so happy if you stayed. Imagine what Nino would have thought, too. I'm sure he would have been so pleased to know that you and his son are here."

"Really?" Celina quickly glanced up. She doubted that, but Adele's expression seemed so genuine. Had she known about the disagreement Tony had with his family? "How was Tony—Nino—when you knew him?"

A far-away look settled over Adele. "He was such a good soul."

Celina nodded. "Did he seem different to you?"

"Different?" Adele intoned.

"From Lauro and his parents, I mean."

"Nino was always..." Adele's voice trailed off as she seemed to search for the right word. "Distracted, I guess. I'm not surprised he left. He inherited the wanderlust of our ancestors, ancient mariners who sailed the world in search of silk and spices. Amalfi was a crucial trading port, dating back centuries into antiquity." She laughed softly. "How Nino loved to sail. Oh, the fun we had, sailing to Capri with our families, skiing in the Alps."

Celina grew quiet while Adele reminisced about their childhood. She hadn't known any of this. Tony had never told her about skiing or sailing. But then, one of his legs often bothered him. Shrapnel, he'd told her. That was why he never danced. No wonder he hadn't mentioned skiing. He'd probably lost the ability. Her heart clenched at the thought. Since she'd been here, discovering Tony's old life, she realized how much he'd left behind and how much he'd been through since. He'd been forced to become a different person.

"Do you sail?" Adele was smiling at her.

Pulling herself back to the present, Celina sipped her lemonade. "No, but Tony loved to watch the sailboats in the San Francisco bay. We'd have picnics on the shore on Sundays."

Adele looked surprised. "He didn't sail anymore?"

"His leg had been injured. His balance wasn't as good as it could have been." Would that have mattered? When Adele looked confused, Celina added, "We didn't have the money for a sailboat. We'd been saving to buy our house, and after we bought it, we put a lot of money into making it a home."

Adele sighed. "I guess we all grew up." She leaned on the table and cupped her chin in her hand. "He was a good man, but you know that. I feel so sorry for you."

Celina blinked back emotion. "We loved each other a great deal."

Stretching her hand across the table, Adele smoothed her hand over Celina's. "We all miss him."

"So do we." Celina took another drink, swallowing hard against the lump that had formed in her throat.

She peered at Adele, whose dark eyes were filled with compassion and framed with long, inky lashes. What a beautiful woman she was, inside and out. Celina had to understand what had happened here with Tony. If not, whatever it was could shade her son's relationship with his grandparents and other family members.

"Adele, do you know anything about an argument my husband had with his family?"

Parting her lips as if to speak, Adele caught herself and shook her head. "Would it matter now?"

"It might to my son."

Casting her gaze down, Adele seemed to consider this but only shook her head again.

"Did it have to do with Lauro?"

Adele drew in a breath. "Celina, really, that was such a long time ago." She half-rose from her chair.

Celina gripped Adele's hand. The woman knew something, and it would haunt Celina until she found out.

"Sara and Carmine couldn't have been more welcoming to Marco and me, but Lauro is a mystery. As a mother, my main concern is for my son. You understand, yes?"

"Of course," Adele said softly.

"Whatever concerned Tony—Nino, might also affect his son. If we were to stay here, would my son hear of this from someone else? Would it hurt him? If so, please tell me so that I can be prepared."

Adele raked her teeth over her lower lip, hesitating.

"My son has suffered enough from being blindsided by tragedy." Celina moved closer. "As for me, you won't hurt my feelings. Nothing can possibly hurt any more than I have already suffered."

"I think you are stronger than you look, yes?"

Celina nodded, willing her on.

Adele shifted with unease in her chair. "It was so many years ago, but I don't think Lauro and Nino ever forgave each other."

What had Sara said? *Lauro is still grieving.* Clutching Adele's hand, she asked, "Did the argument have to do with Isabella?"

Adele's gaze darted away. "Then you know."

"Sara only mentioned her name."

As she watched Adele pick at a loose thread on her dress, a question she hated to even think of formed in her mind, yet she had to ask. If she were to stay here, she had to know what was behind Lauro's treatment of her.

Celina drew a breath and tried to imagine her husband as a young man, long before they'd met. *Tony, Lauro, Isabella…*

A thought crept into Celina's mind. "Was my husband in love with Isabella?"

Chapter 11

With her head tilted back, Celina swiveled, awestruck at the starry kaleidoscope on the soaring ceiling above her in the vacant shop. Moved by the hand-painted stars, she imagined how much her mother would have liked this place. *Stella.* How she wished she could see it. Dust motes danced around her in tempered rhythm to an enthralling adagio drifting from the café next door.

"What was this place?"

"Most recently, a shop for baby clothes," Adele said, gingerly bypassing an intricate spider's web laced from a chandelier to a display rack. "The last tenants, a young couple, were successful here. They outgrew the space and moved into a larger shop." She pushed open curtains, allowing sunshine to wash over abandoned glass cases.

"Why has it been closed up so long?"

"The landlord is lazy about renting it, and he's particular. He can afford to be. But I had a spare key."

Celina stooped to rescue a stuffed brown bear wedged under one of the cases. "Hello, you," she said, dusting it off and setting it on a shelf. Earlier this morning, Adele had picked her up at the villa, excited to show her the vacancy next to her fashion boutique. Sara had begged her to leave Marco with her, saying that she wanted to show him some of his father's old toys and games.

"It's interesting," Celina said. "But I will need a kitchen."

"There's one downstairs. I haven't seen it, but I'm afraid it's not going to be as modern as what you're used to in San Francisco."

"We have a lot of old buildings there, too." She sniffed the air. Maybe not this old, though.

"Needs a good cleaning," Adele said, stifling a sneeze from the dust. "But a lot of people walk by this location."

"The café next door...is it busy?" La Petite Maison du Chocolat in San Francisco was near a popular restaurant, and the shop had received a lot of foot traffic from it.

"Always. Between locals and tourists, people often wait to get a table."

That was encouraging, Celina thought. She might even be able to supply chocolates to the café. Walking across the floor, her heel caught on a cracked tile.

Adele caught her arm. "The place needs some work, too."

"How is the landlord about making repairs?"

"He can't be bothered." Adele shrugged. "Werner did all the work for me before I moved in, and he takes care of the property for me."

"I *have* to be concerned about the condition," Celina said, frowning. She liked Adele, but her new friend had no idea what it was like to be a woman on her own.

Celina set her jaw. "I can handle the cleaning and painting." She tapped on the broken tile. "And the tile work. Maybe even the electrical."

"My husband could recommend some friends of his to help."

She cast a wary glance toward Adele. "That would be a big help, but no mashers allowed."

"I'll screen them myself."

Celina glanced up at the starry ceiling and imagined display cases filled with heavenly chocolates in the shapes of stars and moons, and seashells and dolphins, circling her truffles dusted with sea salt and filled with the fruits of the region. She'd clean the gilded crystal chandelier, polish the tile floor, and maybe paint a mural on the walls—of San Francisco or a reflection of the mountains that cradled this area. How many times had she and Tony watched the stars twinkle over the bay?

"This space could be stunning," Celina said.

"What would you call it?"

Celina raised her gaze to the starry ceiling. "My mother's name was Stella, so Stella di Cioccolato." She mused over the idea, imagining her mother's happy, loving embrace.

"You can do a lot with that name. I see chocolate stars in your future."

Celina imagined a glittery silver and gold starred theme, maybe blanketed with an inky blue background. Or something more modern, like silver stars and pink polka dots. Her mind was whirring with dizzying possibilities.

Celina spied a staircase behind a low wall. "Let's see the kitchen."

The stone stairs were sturdy enough and had been built for the ages. Adele flicked on the lights at the bottom.

A thick layer of dust covered everything, but all the equipment was there. Stovetop, ovens, sink, countertops. The equipment was old but serviceable. There was room to bring in the specialized equipment she'd need, too. High windows would let in light, once she removed the boards covering them. She'd be spending a lot of time here. She'd have to install a bell on the door or hire extra help for the front, not unlike the set up at La Petite Maison du Chocolat. She wondered what the going wages were here.

"What do you think?" Adele seemed even more excited than she was.

Celina could hardly believe she was actually considering this. "I think it would do."

They climbed the steps, and as they were turning off the lights, a couple passing by stopped and looked into the open door. Recognizing Adele, they broke into a rapid conversation, laughing and gesturing.

Celina smiled and nodded, but she could hardly follow the conversation beyond a few words. A knot formed in her stomach. She didn't fully understand the language or the customs.

Was opening a chocolate boutique in Italy a crazy idea?

Absolutely.

Yet, Tony's parents would love for her and Marco to stay, even if Lauro would be a perennial problem. When her memories of Tony didn't mesh with those of his brother, Lauro had decided she was a fraud, ignoring the fact that war and time changed people.

Still, what did she have to lose in San Francisco? Lizzie was angling for a starring role on Broadway or maybe films in Hollywood, and Marge was intent on retiring to the country someday. Celina was only thirty. Didn't she have the right to recreate her life?

Maybe it was time for a little crazy.

She ran her hands over lacy grapevines and sweet cherubs rendered in plaster relief on the walls, remnants of another tenant, no doubt, and covered with layers of paint. She wondered how many shops had occupied this old building, and how many entrepreneurs had expressed their passion through artistry and grown their business here.

What would it hurt to dream? It was tempting.

More than anything else, Celina yearned to the depths of her soul to belong somewhere with her son. To have a home. She had noticed that people who had families often took them for granted, as though they would always be there in the bright light of morning. Once, she had, too. Did others realize what might await them on the far side of midnight? Or knowing the alternative, did they consciously choose life? Perhaps some did.

She *must.*

It was the only way she had managed to rise every morning these past six months. And now, a glorious, shiny second chance glittered within her reach.

Adele held a hand out to her. "I want you to meet my friends."

Although they could not share a language, Adele had told them about her potential plans.

"*Cioccolato,*" the pair said, exchanging a look of delight.

Chocolate was a universal language.

Adele traded cheek kisses with her friends before they left, and Celina followed suit. "*Ciao, ciao,*" Celina said.

"They're happy to know you and hope you stay," Adele said, translating the conversation.

For the first time in many months, Celina felt desire supplant despair. She wondered how long it would take for her to become fluent in Italian. Perhaps people would forgive her bumbling efforts. She couldn't help but smile to herself. If they didn't, they'd miss her chocolate.

"Let's get out of this dust," Adele said.

After they locked up, they made their way over to Adele's boutique. Lining the walls were hand-tailored dresses with full skirts and wasp waists, lightweight sweaters with pencil-slim skirts, and colorful beachwear.

Surrounded with color, shades of marine blue, sunny yellow, and peony pink lifted Celina's spirit. Thinking of Lizzie and Marge, she imagined what fun they would have here.

Adele eyed Celina's subdued gray skirt and white blouse. "As long as you're trying on a new life, you might as well look the part, too." She reached for a coral linen sundress and matching woven sandals. "These are about your size. Try them on." She led her to the rear of the shop and parted curtains in one corner to reveal a dressing area.

A bell on the door tinkled, announcing a visitor. "Just a moment. But I want to see that on you." Adele swept the curtain back and hurried away.

Celina shrugged out of her clothes. The linen felt cool against her skin, and the skirt skimmed her hips and swirled around her calves. She peered into the small mirror on the wall and brushed her hair from her face. The coral hue illuminated her face, and it was certainly an improvement over what she'd been wearing. Lizzie would definitely approve. When she had written to offer an extension to her sublet tenants in her apartment, they had agreed with enthusiasm. Could she really give up that life so easily?

Maybe I can. Celina stepped back, thoughtfully regarding herself in this new garb, and what it represented.

A different life sparkled before her—if she chose to accept it, embrace it, and claim it. She was old enough to know that no matter what accouterments of life shifted around her, she remained the same inside—though wiser, perhaps. Yet she couldn't deny the beauty of her surroundings, and the warmth and acceptance of most of Tony's family. She was also too old to expect perfection. She tossed her hair over her shoulder and pushed aside the curtain to step in front of a larger mirror to see the full effect.

"Stunning," Adele said, clapping her hands.

Celina looked up to catch Adele's gaze in the mirror behind her, but behind her stood Lauro, silently taking her in. She whirled around. She'd managed to avoid him after the horse riding incident, and Adele and Werner had kindly led her back to the Savoia villa later. Celina lifted her chin and readied herself for a confrontation.

Adele turned to him. "What do you think, Lauro?"

"She looks...beautiful," he said, clearly flustered.

A customer motioned to Adele. "*Scusi,*" she said, hurrying to help the other woman.

The last thing Celina wanted was a recurrence of the incident from their horseback riding.

Lauro locked on her eyes in the mirror. "I need to apologize."

Words she thought she'd never hear. Celina glanced over her shoulder. "I don't care what *you* need. But yes, you should."

Lauro's neck flushed, and he shifted from one foot to another. She'd made him uncomfortable. *Good.* Just as he'd made her feel violated. He was nothing like his brother. Placing her hands on her hips, she spun to face him.

Taking a few steps toward her, Lauro gazed at her, and she felt her skin blaze under the heat of his stare. He stopped in front of her.

"I did not mean you harm," he said, searching her eyes as if he could see into her very soul.

"Your actions…it wasn't right of you. Tony was your brother."

Lauro acknowledged this with a slight nod. "I'm truly sorry," he said, his voice deepening. "But your presence mesmerized me, your soul glows from within, illuminating all around you. You cannot blame me for falling into your beauty."

Her lips parted to rebuke him, but no sound came out. *Who spoke like that?* No one she knew, and few she'd ever met. Where was the surly man she'd come to know? She knew how to handle *him*. But this one? A poet? Not at all. She felt as if the North Star had shifted and the earth had tilted beneath her feet. A strange light was seeping through a fissure crack in her carefully protected world.

"You hate me," she said, clinging to the familiar status quo.

His brow crinkled with concern, and surprise registered on his face. "I might have had my reservations—"

"That's more like it." Dismissing him, she began to turn around.

"Wait," he said, swiftly sliding his hand over her forearm. "I've been…mistaken."

She bristled against his touch but found she couldn't bear to force his hand away. As if magnetized, she stood motionless, sensing energy flowing into her and filling her with a strange intensity that attracted as much as repelled her.

Why was he having this effect on her? She'd come to revile his attitude toward her. Steeling herself, she raised her eyes to his—questioning pools of agony and adoration shimmering with light. His breath labored, and his full lips twitched with barely contained passion.

Celina moistened her suddenly dry lips. "I must have your assurance that—"

"I can't," he cut in. "But I will try."

Why did such swift disappointment seize her chest? Feelings, long buried since Tony's death, pushed to the surface in search of sunlight. Desperately tamping them down, Celina tried to smooth the surface of her emotions, which were now ragged with rips in the fabric of her consciousness. This newfound awareness of Lauro was not what she wanted.

This would complicate everything.

She took a step back, forcing herself from the enchanted space that had captured them. The air around them seemed charged with strange electricity. She felt drunk with the realization that she felt attracted to Lauro. *No, not that.* She stumbled backward and let out a cry.

Lauro caught her before she could fall.

The feel of his muscular arms around her took her breath away and was almost more than she could bear.

Why in heaven's name did she have such a reaction to him?

"I...have to change," she mumbled, twisting herself from his arms and whipping the thin curtain around her. Slipping the coral straps from her shoulders, she shuddered against the strange, involuntary sensations that had gripped her. Resting her back against the brick-lined wall, she tried to regain her equilibrium.

After a few moments, she stepped back into her plain, sturdy clothing and took comfort in the solid familiarity cloaking her and separating her from whatever crazy, momentary dream might have crept into her mind. She stooped to peer into the old mirror. Her face was pink, her hair wild. She ran her hands over her cheeks and hair to calm the tell-tale signs.

Celina slid the curtain back.

Lauro was gone.

Thank goodness. After the heated connection they'd shared, the air felt cool on her skin, yet emptiness crept back into her heart. *This is better*, she insisted, chastising herself. This is real.

Yet, sometimes in the lonely hours before dawn, she still slid her hand across the sheet hoping to find Tony there. After she woke to realize she was alone, heaviness would settle into her soul. It was what she'd come to expect and now accepted. It was too soon to replace him in her heart.

Especially with Lauro.

Celina spied Adele in the front of the shop, where she was wrapping a parcel of new clothes her customer had decided on. Looping the coral dress and shoes over her arms, she made her way toward her new friend.

The customer left, and Adele turned toward her. "Lauro said he had to go."

Celina gave a nonchalant shrug and held out the dress. "Thanks for letting me try this on, but I guess it's not really my style."

Adele scooped the dress from her arms and began to fold it. "You're wrong. It's precisely your style for here." She paused. "Lauro liked it on you."

"His opinion doesn't matter to me." Even as Celina denied him, heat gathered in her chest, and she felt self-conscious.

"Doesn't it?" Adele slid the folded dress into a bag and handed it to her. "I insist. This is my gift to you. A new dress for a new woman."

Celina hesitated. Not wanting to appear rude, she accepted it. "Thank you, but I haven't changed," she said, still shocked by what had transpired with Lauro.

"No? Maybe it's time for a change." Adele's expression softened with compassion. "I don't mean to sound crass, but you weren't the one who died." Lifting her chin toward the door, she added, "Even as a boy, Nino was serious, studious, intense. He could never stay in one place, but then, you knew that. Lauro was the responsible brother, remaining true to only one woman. Although they were nearly mirror images when they were young, that's where it ended. Lauro is very different. Don't confuse them."

Mirror images? Even without his scars, Tony hadn't looked anything like Lauro. "I fail to see any resemblance."

"Lauro and Nino? Why, they even walked the same way." Adele raised her brow in surprise. "I could never tell them apart from a distance. And I'm not surprised that he likes you." Lowering her eyelids, she shot Celina an empathetic look. "I wouldn't blame you either."

"You're mistaken," Celina said, shocked at what Adele was implying. She pressed her lips into a tight line. "Lauro isn't fond of me."

The edges of Adele's lips quirked up. "I know my cousin."

Feeling flustered, Celina was anxious to change the subject. Yet somehow, she had to justify their differences, if only to herself. "Tony had so many scars…mainly physical, but also emotional. He'd changed, he was different."

"His scars…" Adele blinked with realization and pressed a hand against her mouth. "I'm sorry. Sara told me his appearance *had* changed."

"He had a lot of reconstructive surgery," Celina said quietly. More than she'd realized, until now. That *had* to be the explanation. The alternative would render her entire visit fruitless. She shook her head, dispelling the disturbing thought.

"Well then, Lauro looks a lot like Nino used to. He's a good man." Adele's expression softened. "You should know that he's been through a lot, too."

"In the war?"

"Actually, that seemed to be his refuge. No, before that. With Isabella."

She shouldn't be curious, but for some reason, the words tumbled out. "What happened?"

"It's…complicated." Adele glanced at her watch. "I have to go, but I'll tell you later."

Why should Lauro's story matter to her? Celina shook her head, trying to clear the fog from her brain, as much as in answer to Adele. Nothing good could come of such curiosity or thoughts.

Adele leaned across the counter in earnest. "But I saw Lauro's reaction. And I saw the wild look in your eyes when you arrived on my property on horseback. It was the same."

"It's not what you think." Was it? She caught a glimpse of herself in the mirror. Her hair was tousled, and she looked confused. No wonder Adele had made such an assumption.

"Accept love where you can find it," Adele said. "We don't find it often enough in this life."

"Impossible." Celina shuddered. She couldn't imagine what his parents would think if they suspected there was anything between them.

Which there wasn't, of course.

At that thought, a hollow feeling swelled in her heart.

She would talk to him, she resolved, to straighten out any misunderstanding. Celina straightened her shoulders.

Yes, that's exactly what she would do. As soon as possible.

Chapter 12

Celina was learning that in Amalfi, dining on the terrace under a starry canopy with the ocean crashing beneath them in accompaniment to operatic recordings was a typical summer evening. Tonight, a recording of tenor Enrique Caruso's "Vesti la Giubba" from *Pagliacci* by Leoncavallo played on the record player. The record had been played so many times the scratches had become part of the score, but it didn't diminish the astounding performance.

"There will never be another Caruso," Carmine said after the song ended and silence hung thick in the balmy evening air.

Celina sipped her red wine, savoring the earthy notes and trying not to let her eyes linger on Lauro, whose gaze was unnerving. "I saw Mario Lanza in a film called *The Great Caruso*. He's incredibly talented."

"And handsome," Sara said, fanning her face.

"Not too bad," Carmine said, sniffing in annoyance. "But not Caruso."

Sara flicked her hand dismissively. "I still think he's magnificent."

Celina was growing accustomed to the friendly bickering between them. Maybe that's what kept them interested in one another after all these years. "Caruso visited San Francisco, but after he survived the great earthquake in '06, he vowed never to return."

"The night before," Carmine began, gazing into the distance. "Caruso had appeared at the Mission Opera House and sang the part of Don José in Bizet's *Carmen*. And you're right, he never returned, God rest his soul. If only you could have seen him, Celina." He kissed his fingers for emphasis.

Celina smiled at her father-in-law. Carmine and Sara had made her and Marco feel at home, and she was beginning to feel like they were part of the family. Watching the flickering candles on the rough-hewn table before her, Celina breathed in the fresh sea breeze. A strap of the coral sundress Adele had given her slipped from her shoulder, and she quickly shifted it back in place.

Watching her movement, Lauro quickly averted his eyes and lifted the wine bottle. "Care for more?"

"A little."

He poured a splash of wine into her glass. "You like this vintage?"

"I do," she said, casually meeting his direct gaze. "It's a little smoky. What is it?"

"Taurasi, another one of our regional wines of Campania. It's from our Aglianico grapes, and blended with a little Sangiovese—*sanguis Jovis*, the blood of Jupiter in Latin." He lifted the glass to his nose to inhale, never taking his eyes from hers. "What chocolate would you serve with this?"

Celina touched her tongue to her lower lip in thought. "Hmm, dark chocolate…infused with smoky Lapsang Souchong tea."

"Chinese tea?" Lauro leaned toward her, intrigued.

"We have a lot of Chinese teas and herbs in San Francisco," Celina said. "I like to experiment with different flavors."

"Maybe you can introduce that here," Sara said, casting an inquiring glance toward her and Lauro.

When Celina didn't answer, Sara went on.

"Adele told me about your idea for a *cioccolateria*." Sara passed a basket of freshly baked olive bread to her. "It sounds exciting. I'm sure Lauro wouldn't mind helping you source the chocolate you'll need for your confections."

Lauro arched an eyebrow at her. "You're planning to stay here?"

"It's a consideration," Celina said, wondering why Sara was encouraging Lauro. "But I'm sure I can manage on my own. I'll write to the owner of the chocolaterie I worked in San Francisco for referrals. I plan on roasting the beans myself." She could also buy processed chocolate like the pastry chefs and most chocolatiers used, but she wanted to experiment with different roasts.

Celina tore a piece of bread and dipped it in olive oil for Marco, who was eagerly alternating between antipasto of mozzarella and prosciutto, and linguini with basil pesto and delicate green beans. She'd never seen him enjoy food so much as since they'd arrived. He was active all day, too, playing with Adele's children or following Sara as she looked after the gardens every morning. He loved to help pick fresh vegetables from the garden and fruit from the orchard.

"Nonsense," Carmine said. "It's no trouble for Lauro to help you."

"I can arrange *Trinitario* through our supplier," Lauro said.

"I prefer the delicate flavor profile in *Criollo* or *Porcelana*." She loved the Venezuela chocolate, which her mother had favored, too. It blended well with violet and bergamot, equally smooth flavors that created the lightest of delicacies. For most of her work, it was superior.

Lauro wore a serious expression she couldn't quite read. Celina reflected on what Adele had said about Tony at the boutique. *Serious, studious, intense.* That described Lauro more than Tony. But had her husband once been more like Lauro? If so, whatever had affected him must have been profound. Although many veterans had returned feeling withdrawn or fighting recurring nightmares, Tony had overcome his demons and more, evolving into a gregarious personality.

Carmine and Sara shared a fleeting look.

"Why don't we take care of Marco tomorrow," Sara said. "So you can visit our chocolate factory with Lauro." She glanced at Lauro as if to punctuate her sentence. "I insist."

From the tone of Sara's voice, Celina realized saying no wasn't an option. Lauro must have sensed that, too, because his face flushed, but he said nothing.

Marco tugged on her sleeve. "A chocolate factory? Mom, I want to go, too."

Sara and Carmine traded bemused expressions. Celina noticed that they seemed to communicate perfectly in a silent language of glances and touches, much the way she had with Tony.

Carmine ruffled Marco's hair. "Then we'll all go."

The boy beamed at his grandfather, and Celina couldn't say a word. To see the obvious attraction and budding love between Marco and his grandparents added weight to the decision she knew she must soon make. The weeks of summer had slipped from the calendar.

After they finished supper, Celina excused herself. "I have a surprise for dessert." She hurried to the kitchen, where she retrieved a tray of fresh strawberries she'd infused with orange liqueur and drizzled with dark chocolate. After arranging the berries on a platter, she returned to the table.

"I thought you might enjoy these," Celina said, serving a juicy red strawberry to each person at the table. "And a special one for my big boy, *sans liqueur*."

"These look and smell divine." Delight lit Sara's face for a moment before she frowned a little. "Marco can eat strawberries?"

"Can he ever," Celina said, laughing. "He loves them, just like his father. The two of them used to churn strawberry ice cream together in the summer. I had to be fast to get any at all."

Marco grinned and dug into his dessert.

"What a sweet memory." Sara lapsed into a thoughtful, melancholy gaze.

Celina watched her, wondering what was on her mind. Memories of summers past, perhaps. She didn't press it.

Sara shook herself and turned her attention back to Marco, who was devouring the large strawberry. "Marco, you're a fortunate young man to know how to make ice cream. We could pick some berries from the garden this week." Sara brought a bite of strawberry to her lips and tasted it. "That's heavenly."

"The chocolate is well flavored," Carmine remarked.

Across from her, Lauro met her gaze and nodded. "Exquisite."

"I'm glad you all like it." Celina smiled modestly. A new sense of excitement over what the future might hold was bubbling up inside of her.

When the conversation turned to plans for a cousin's wedding, Celina saw Marco stifling a yawn. She excused herself to put him to bed.

After helping Marco change into pajamas and brush his teeth, she tucked him into bed.

Even as his eyes were closing, he cried out, "Where's Rocky?"

Celina checked under his blanket and looked under the bed. Thankfully, the ever-grinning monkey was sprawled under the bed. She fished it out and tucked it next to Marco. With a satisfied sigh and the smile of an angel, he wrapped his arm around Rocky and closed his eyes.

Lightly stroking Marco's back, Celina watched over him for a few minutes to make sure he was asleep. Since they'd arrived, he'd been sleeping better here than he had in San Francisco. He'd often been agitated when she picked him up from Mrs. Jackson's, but even though she asked him what was wrong, he would never tell her. And when she asked Mrs. Jackson, the older woman just shrugged and said she had no idea what she meant. Celina assumed that Marco was still grieving his father, just as she was.

When Marco shifted and mumbled, Celina began humming a soft lullaby. As she did, she thought about how lucky they were to have been accepted by Tony's family.

She reflected on the time they'd spent here, satisfied that she'd decided to come. Marco had forged a relationship with his grandparents and cousins, and if nothing else ever came of this visit—though she hoped it would—she would be content that she had helped Marco discover the family she could never give him.

Sara, Carmine, Adele, and Werner looked upon her as family, too. Even Lauro had come around. *My new family*, she thought, her heart swelling with emotion. Although the circumstances of their arrival had been unusual at best, she was deeply comforted that they had welcomed her and Marco. *My family*. Silently, she rolled the words around on her tongue, smiling to herself.

Marco's breathing became steady, and Celina tucked the light summer blanket around his frame. Leaning over, she kissed his cheek. "I love you, my brave little boy." She tiptoed from the room and eased the door closed.

As Celina had learned was often customary, they finished dinner close to midnight. Two of Carmine's brothers she hadn't met stopped by, and they all laughed and traded stories. Sara had insisted that Matilde go to bed, so Celina helped Sara clear the dishes from the table and carry them into the kitchen.

"Your dessert was delicious," Sara said.

"Thank you. Chocolate-drizzled strawberries were one of Tony's favorites, too."

"Were they now?" Sara seemed to choose her words with care. "In families, my dear, what is not said is often more important than what is said."

Celina eased the plates she carried onto the tile counter. "I don't follow…"

"No, you might not." Sara furrowed her brow and brought her hands up to Celina's shoulders. "Whatever might happen, I want you to know right now that I love you and Marco, and I hope you will always think of us as your family."

"As I was tucking Marco in, I was thinking the same thing." Celina smiled. "But what do you mean by 'whatever might happen?'"

"Never mind that." Sara hugged Celina tightly. "You have given me the most precious gift—that of a grandson. We have big plans for Marco, my dear. You will never have to worry about college for him. Or anything else."

Surprised by her generosity, Celina pulled back. "I appreciate that, but that's not why we're here. And I wish that Tony had contacted you sooner. I feel so guilty about that. I often think about all the time we missed out on."

Sara waved a hand. "I don't care about any of that. Seeing Carmine's eyes light up when he sees Marco and knowing that he has accepted him as our Antonino's child—why, that's worth more to me than you can ever imagine. My husband's spirit is reinvigorated—mine, too. We needed that, Celina. So you see, we all get what we want."

Celina wasn't quite following what Sara was saying. "I only wanted you to know your grandson, and for Marco to know you. Really, I don't expect anything else."

"Of course not, dear. Just so we understand each other." Sara patted her cheek. "Whatever the reason, I'm glad you came, and you are welcome to stay as long as you wish. Which I hope will be forever." With that, Sara hugged her again.

Later that evening as Celina made her way back to her bedroom, she thought about the strange conversation, its undertones, and what Sara could have possibly meant. *Whatever might happen...always think of us as your family.*

What indeed, might happen? Celina couldn't imagine what she meant, or why she chose tonight to have this odd discussion.

Too tired to think about it anymore, Celina decided this must be another Savoia family secret of some sort. Would she ever piece them all together?

Chapter 13

THE NEXT DAY, Carmine and Sara drove Celina and Marco to the headquarters of Cioccolata Savoia, the main factory in Naples where Lauro worked. She enjoyed seeing the morning sun sparkle on the sea and light the mountains that rose around them.

"The old Bourbon palace was built two hundred years ago," Carmine said as they passed a massive, dusty red-colored structure under renovation. Framed with palm trees and flanked by park-like grounds, the two-story building had rows of long windows and seemed to stretch on forever. "It's being repurposed into a world-class art museum, which will showcase Italian art and our fine porcelain production. There is an entire room decorated in porcelain."

Celina had marveled over the exquisite, intricately painted Capodimonte porcelain at their home—lamps, teapots and teacups, urns.

"There should be one dedicated to chocolate, too," Sara said, laughing. "The Savoias supplied chocolate to the royal family for many years. That's why the factory is located nearby."

Carmine drove past the old palace and stopped at a similar, smaller building nestled among palm trees. Instead of a nondescript brick factory building, this petite palace could have been a grand old home on Nob Hill. A sea breeze cooled the elevated area, and workers on break were lounging and laughing under sunny skies. The pristine two-story building and its verdant, rolling grounds dotted with crimson-petal waterfalls of bougainvillea and voluptuous, pink-and-blue mounds of flowering hydrangeas looked nothing like the factories in San Francisco.

As Carmine eased the car to a stop in front of a wide stone entryway, a man in a trim suit hurried down the front stairs to greet them. He assisted Sara from the car, while Celina stepped out, pausing on the running board as she drank in the beauty of the grounds and structure. The man hurried to offer his hand to her. She stepped down.

"*Signora*," the man said, greeting Celina with warmth. "*Buongiorno*. I am Alberto. We have been preparing for your visit." He bestowed respectful kisses on Sara's cheeks and then leaned in to greet Celina in a similar manner.

Inhaling, Celina closed her eyes. The rich scent of chocolate wafted from the building, along with vanilla, fruits, nuts, and spices that jumbled together in an aroma that she instantly recognized and loved. This was the fragrance of her childhood, of her mother's kitchen when she came from school, of her first job at La Petite Maison du Chocolat, of the art she lost herself in—for love, for joy, for solitude, for healing. She smiled at the recognition and opened her eyes.

She had known that Savoia chocolates were sold outside of Italy, of course, but this operation was far more extensive than she had imagined. No wonder Lauro had doubts about her claim; the family had much to lose.

A sickening thought struck her. Had other women made claims like hers before? Although Tony had been alive then, no one here would have known that. Or, *had* Tony kept in touch with someone here? Maybe a distant member of the family or a friend…She had to find out more.

Blinking, she pulled herself back to the moment and helped Marco from the car. She turned to Carmine. "This is a long way to drive to work every day."

"I check in once a week," Carmine said. "This is Lauro's domain now. And it's only one of our businesses. We also have another factory that produces olive oil and other Italian staples. For Italy and for export." Hesitating, he added quietly. "We had always planned for Nino to run the *fabbrica di cioccolato*."

"But it was not what Nino wanted," Sara interjected, casting a gentle reprimand at her husband.

"He might have changed his mind someday." Carmine lifted a shoulder and let it drop. "Actually, we distribute a lot of food products to North America." His eyes lit up. "If you shopped the Italian grocers in San Francisco, you've seen our brands."

"Nino must have brought them home," Sara said. "He loved the apricot and fig preserves. It was my husband's great grandmother's recipe, in fact. Several generations of our family have enjoyed that recipe."

"And the next one is, too," Carmine said, rubbing Marco's shoulder.

Embarrassed, Celina simply smiled at Marco. Tony had never said a word about any of that. He'd never brought home a single chocolate from Cioccolata Savoia. *Why not?* She took in the pastoral oasis surrounded by the bustling city of Naples, his beaming family flanking her. Again she wondered what had happened here that had been so horrible that he'd sliced off his former life with such precision.

Not only that, he seemed to have changed or suppressed almost everything about himself, from the languages he spoke and the interests he had, to the foods he had once loved.

Whatever had happened had caused a deep rift in his psyche. Maybe he'd suffered a brain injury, too.

Glancing up, she saw that Carmine and Sara were staring at her with such pleasant, hopeful expectation, silently urging her to share a story of how Tony might have continued to enjoy their culinary specialties so far from home, never having forgotten his family. Even if he had never told them the story of his family, he might have relished his ancestor's recipe, a beloved taste of home that he would share with them. But she couldn't lie. She drew a slow breath.

"After his injuries—"

"Mom, watch this!" Marco took off across the lawn, spinning out-of-control cartwheels until he landed with a hard *thunk* on his back. He lay motionless in the grass.

Alarmed, Celina raced toward him. When she reached him, she saw that he was winded, but thankfully not hurt. Gathering him into her arms, she hugged him.

"Did you see that?" Marco grinned. Maria and Gino had been teaching him how to tumble and turn cartwheels.

"Sure did, silly." Celina kissed his cheek and brushed grass from his clothes, not caring about her white cotton gloves. Slightly winded yet relieved, she led him back to the steps, clutching his little hand.

"Stay with us, son," Carmine said. "You're going to see many sweet treats here that you can't touch, but if you are well behaved, I'll have a special box of chocolates for you when you finish your tour."

Carmine offered Sara his arm, and she slid a gloved hand into the crook of his elbow. "Here's Lauro now."

Celina tented her hand against the sun. Lauro stood at the top of the grand stone stairway watching them. He was dressed as he had been the first day she'd seen him, in an elegant dark suit cut to fit his broad torso and long legs. A warm sensation raced through her again, and she tried to ignore it. This was her husband's brother, for Pete's sake. What was she thinking?

That was just it. She *wasn't* thinking. This feeling emanated from some primal part of her, deep inside. Pursing her lips, she tamped it down. No, it would never do.

Celina took Marco's hand and started up the steps. As they neared the top, Marco skipped up the last steps, pulling Celina off balance.

"Oh," she cried, teetering backward. The cotton frock that Lizzie had given her caught the breeze and fluttered, exposing her thighs.

In a flash, Lauro was beside her, breaking her fall with one arm and sweeping Marco into the other.

"Are you okay?" he asked, smoothing the fluttery skirt of her dress over her knees.

Celina felt her face flush—as red as the poppies on her dress, she imagined. His thoughtful gesture surprised her.

"Marco's all right, too. Aren't you, buddy?" Lauro set the boy down and slung an arm around his shoulder.

"Thank you." That was all she could manage without making an even grander fool of herself. The strength of Lauro's embrace steadied her. The thought of Lizzie and her theatrical training and what she would have done in this situation made her smile.

"Beautiful dress," Lauro said. "You wear it well."

"Thank you." Was that all she could think of to say? "A friend gave it to me. An actress. I mean, it wasn't exactly hers, it was a costume from the theater, from San Francisco. The night I was packing. She came over, and she thought it might—" *Oh, dear God, why am I babbling?* Everyone was staring at them.

A smile flickered on Lauro's face. "I liked the one from Adele's boutique, too." He let her go and bent to Marco's level. "Ready for the tour, little man?"

"I'm not little," Marco said, indignant. "I'm six. I'm a big boy now."

"That's true," Lauro replied thoughtfully. "And I've seen that you take good care of your mother."

Marco beamed up at him, pleased that Lauro recognized his worth. Watching them, Celina's throat tightened. Tony used to say the same thing to him. Brothers were alike that way, she supposed.

Brothers. She straightened, reminding herself that this was Tony's brother. Marco's uncle. *Family.*

"I can't wait to see inside," she said, arranging a smile on her face to hide the strange nervousness that seemed to be plaguing her whenever she was near Lauro. If only he hadn't expressed his thoughts of her so, well, so eloquently at Adele's boutique. *Your soul glows from within, illuminating all around you. You cannot blame me for falling into your beauty.* Not that she had remembered what he said on purpose, but such lovely words were difficult to forget.

Sara came up behind her and touched her elbow. "I think you'll see a lot that pleases you," she said. "Come with me."

Holding Marco's hand, Lauro opened the door for them.

Celina walked inside. The delicious scent she'd detected outside intensified, and for the first time since she'd arrived, she felt as if she were home. She could almost feel her mother's reassuring presence.

Lauro led the way, talking about their process and specialties. Marco seemed engrossed, but only a fraction of what came out of Lauro's handsome, full lips actually registered in her brain. Instead, it was the melodic sound of his rich baritone and the nearness of him that resonated most with her.

As they walked into one room, the scent of roasting nuts permeated the air. Celina inhaled. "Hazelnuts. You're making *gianduiotto*."

"One of our main products," Lauro said with pride. He turned to Marco. "The roaster is over there, but careful, it's hot. One hundred twenty degrees."

Marco started to explore.

Lauro stepped in front of him. "That's centigrade, Marco. *Extremely* hot in Fahrenheit."

The boy snapped back and shuddered. Laughing, Lauro mussed his hair and went on.

"Then we crush the roasted nuts, add sugar, milk and the cocoa. It makes a paste, *gianduja*, which we mix with cocoa butter."

Carmine spoke up. "Every year, we add more machinery to further mechanize the process. This is the fastest growing part of the company."

An assistant held out a plate of *gianduiotto* to them. After removing her gloves and depositing them into her purse, she took samples for her and her son.

"Delicious," she said, admiring the flavor.

In another room, a woman ran a broad spatula across a wide plateau of dark chocolate ganache, smoothing the silky substance in graceful, expert swaths.

"Of course, we still make some chocolates by hand." Lauro directed his explanation toward Marco. "Once the ganache—the smoothest of chocolate—cools, it will be ready for the next step."

"Enrobing," Celina said automatically. "For truffles." Lifting her nose to the air, she detected the aroma of licorice. "Anisette, isn't it?"

With the edges of Lauro's lips twitching upward, he nodded. "You have a good nose."

"Have you tried Amaretto?" With her imagination piqued, the scent of bitter almonds, sweetened in liqueur, swirled in her mind.

"Yes, of course."

"Perhaps in a creamy caramel center."

Lauro met her faraway gaze and held it, two minds whirring with creativity.

"Dark or milk chocolate?" he asked.

"Dark…this time. With zest of orange as a finishing touch."

"A little apricot?"

"Oh, yes…"

She could taste it on her lips.

Marco, Carmine, and Sara looked between them, transfixed by their connection.

"And next," she continued in a dream-like state. "The tempering for the most exquisite dress, the couverature. Caraque chocolate—*Criollo*—cooled to twenty-nine degrees, then slowly warmed. Centigrade temperature, that is. To form crystals, just so…"

"Avoiding the white bloom," Lauro finished, mesmerized. "I should introduce you to our chef. I'm but a novice." His lips tugged upward again.

"He's too modest," Carmine said, breaking the spell by clapping Lauro on the back. "My son runs this operation better than I ever did."

Lauro led them into another room where a stainless steel mechanical marvel measured out the exact amount of chocolate to cover small orbs of ganache. A conveyor belt swooshed along carrying perfect truffles with fresh coats of glistening chocolate.

"That machine is called an enrober," Celina said to Marco, who was watching the process with wide eyes. "Watch how it drizzles the smooth tempered chocolate over the ganache heart of the truffles."

Marco turned to her with a pleading look. "Can I have one?"

"May I, you mean?"

Lauro chuckled. "Don't worry, we'll make an entire box of sweet treats for you soon."

"But you must not eat them all at once, or you'll make yourself sick," Carmine added. "They're awfully rich."

Pressing a finger to his lips to signal a secret, Lauro plucked one from the end of the production line, winking at the worker who was placing cooled ones onto a large stainless steel platter. "No telling the boss," he said, angling his head toward Carmine.

"Gee, thanks," Marco said, clapping his hand with glee. He shoved the entire truffle into his mouth. His expression was one of pure bliss. "Mmm, cherry," he mumbled through a mouthful of chocolate. "Mom brings these home from the shop when I'm good."

They all laughed. Celina didn't mention that it had been one of the ways she'd tried to keep his depression at bay after Tony's death. While chocolates wouldn't take away her son's grief, they provided a sweet respite as she spun tales about how each flavor was made, where it came from, and the stories behind them. Even if she had to make up a lot of stories. Smiling to herself, she recalled their quiet evenings after dinner and before bedtime—so different from the rambunctious play times he'd had with his father, who had tickled and laughed and tossed the boy into the air. Of course Marco missed him. She could never replace that part of Tony's bond with Marco.

Her heart twisted when she saw Marco slip his chocolately hand into Lauro's. "What else is there to see?" he asked, eager to explore.

She had observed that simple, trusting movement so many times when Tony had been alive, and it had always brought a smile to her face. Lauro threw a happy look over his shoulder.

Carmine joined them, and the three generations of Savoias walked ahead toward the next prep room while Celina and Sara followed.

Sara chuckled at the sight. "Reminds me of when Carmine used to bring Nino and Lauro here when they were boys. We have a home here in Naples, too. In Vomero. We used to spend a lot of time here in the summer so they could see their father more often."

"Your family is quite hard working."

"So are you, I think." Sara inclined her head. "Adele tells me you're thinking of opening a *cioccolateria* in Amalfi. Her boutique does a good business with the tourist trade. You would, too, I imagine." She paused and turned to Celina. "We'd love for you to stay."

Celina nibbled on her lip. "It's a big decision."

"Do you have any family in San Francisco?"

"No one."

"You seem to have a lonely life there. You'll have a lot of help here with Marco."

A lonely life. Her family had always been small. But here, with all the aunts and uncles and cousins, every gathering seemed to be bursting with people. After Marco went to bed, Sara and Adele often urged her to stay up with them and enjoy a glass of wine or amaretto or limoncello. They talked and laughed on the terrace on warm evenings, the stars twinkling above and the ocean caressing the shoreline beneath them.

What a seductive life this was.

She inhaled again, the aroma of chocolate teasing her nose.

Sara touched her shoulder. "If it's the cost of opening a shop that concerns you, I want you to know that we could help. After all, you're Nino's widow. It would be our pleasure, and that's the way he would want it."

"I appreciate that," Celina said, grateful for the offer, but hesitant to accept. "I wouldn't feel right about accepting money from you."

Sara looked perplexed. "I've heard that Americans have strange beliefs of independence. Here we believe in family helping each other."

"I wish I were part of your beautiful family."

"But you are, *tesoro*. And Marco, why, he's our only grandchild. If it makes you feel better, accept our help on his behalf."

Celina smoothed a hand over Sara's forearm. "You're too kind. I will definitely keep it in mind, then, on those terms. Still, I have some money from the sale of our home. I plan to use that." Even though it had been weeks ago, Lauro's accusation still rang in her ears.

Sara shook her head. "My husband would call you stubborn, but I think it's your pride, isn't it? And I mean that as a compliment."

"My mother taught me to think for myself and take care of myself. She had to after my father died. She had no way of knowing that we would share a similar fate."

"Marco is a lucky boy. He has a fine mother." Sara slid a glance toward her. "Many women would be looking for their next husband rather than thinking about opening a business."

Sara's comment sounded a lot like Marge's advice. "I haven't even thought about that." Which technically, was true. Whatever involuntary, physical feelings Lauro had aroused in her were just that—feelings, not thoughts. She'd sometimes had crushes on boys in high school. A week later, she'd forgotten them. "Besides, I'm in no hurry. I miss my husband. Can't imagine replacing him any time soon."

Ahead of them, Lauro turned around. He gave Celina a warm smile and gestured for her to join them. Watching the exchange, Sara pursed her lips in a satisfied smile. "I know it's selfish of me to want you and Marco to stay. Maybe you'll find someone here in Italy."

What did Sara mean by that? Her expression, her tone of voice… Had Lauro told his mother anything? She chewed her lip again. But what was there to say? Surely she had misread his attention. He was her brother-in-law. Flattery was practically the Italian way, after all.

Here, men were complimentary. They appreciated women and weren't afraid to express their appreciation for beauty. But their words and glances and touches didn't mean as much as they did in America, of that she was certain. She shouldn't take it the wrong way, nor should she read anything into Lauro's or Sara's actions or comments. She was merely in a different culture, that's all there was to it.

When they arrived at the last room, Lauro was explaining the final process to Marco. The room was filled with boxes covered with gold paper and vivid purple ribbons. Here and there were gift boxes in the shape of hearts or shells or jewelry boxes. Some were covered with fabric, while others looked hand-painted. Workers sat at long tables placing chocolates into boxes and wrapping each with a ribbon.

"Here, perfection is essential," Lauro said. "From the appearance of the chocolate to how it is placed in a gift box. Every chocolate is a gift—to family, friends, or yourself."

"How do you give a gift to yourself?" Marco asked.

"Isn't there something you've always wanted, but you've never told anyone? Or maybe you did, but they forgot. Since you know exactly what you want, you buy a gift for yourself."

"Or make one?"

"Yes, yes, of course."

"We like to make gifts," Marco said. "My mother says handmade gifts come from the heart."

"Your mother is wise. You should listen to her always." Lauro lifted his chin in her direction, a faint smile playing on his lips.

A warm sensation bloomed in Celina as she watched Lauro and Marco. Just beyond them, a quick movement caught her attention.

Behind Lauro, the women assembling the boxes were whispering, their slight frowns and furtive glances trained in her direction as they caught the look Lauro gave her.

Sara touched her elbow. "I think we should move on," she said softly, her gaze lingering in the direction of the workers.

Self-conscious, she ran her hand over her hair. She wondered how much the employees would talk.

As she was following Sara out, Marco raced to her, and she turned to grasp his hand.

"Celina, wait." Lauro caught up with her. "Don't mind them," he said, indicating the women who were watching her leave.

"Why are they staring?"

"You're an American. They've heard you're a *chocolatière*. And I've never brought a woman here, not since—" He cut himself off.

Isabella. Who was this woman who had broken his heart, and why was the memory of their affair following her wherever she went?

This was a small community that stretched back generations. Not like San Francisco, where people poured in from all over. She'd met few people who were actually born there. No, this was a different culture. Who your parents were mattered, and old transgressions were not often forgotten.

If she ever expected to fit in here, people would have to accept her for who she was. She could just imagine what they were saying. *Tony's widow—the shameless hussy has an eye for his brother now. What did she do to our poor Antonino? Lauro should watch out.* Annoyance seeped through her reserve. For them, but also for Lauro.

"Everything here seems to have happened ages ago, but no one forgets." Celina's words had a sharp edge, but she couldn't help it. "Although my husband should have kept in touch, at least he got on with his life."

Sara shot a look at her son and made a quick gesture.

"We should talk about Isabella," Lauro said to Celina. "And my brother. Come with me?"

"Alberto promised Marco a surprise," Sara said, holding her hand out to the little boy. "I think we should find him, don't you?"

Celina was torn between her exasperation and the physical attraction she had for Lauro that she was trying hard to deny.

Marco happily went with Sara and Carmine, leaving her alone with Lauro. He took her hand and led her down a corridor.

Maybe now she would get some answers about Tony.

Chapter 14

LAURO LED CELINA into a commercial kitchen and closed the door. "This is our test kitchen. We can talk here."

Celina took in the expanse of white porcelain and gleaming steel and nickel-plated equipment. Windows framed views of the ocean in the distance, and luminous white porcelain tile lined the counters, walls, and floors, giving Celina the sensation of floating inside of a seashell.

Even the cool air, redolent with the rich aroma of chocolate and sweet liqueur, seemed tinged with sea salt, yet this setting, so soothing in its familiarity to her work kitchen in San Francisco, did little to placate the growing frustration she felt surrounding the constant comparison to Lauro's old girlfriend, who was probably married with children by now.

Or was it the nearness of Lauro, of being alone with him, that made her uneasy, just as it had at Adele's boutique?

Shrugging off these thoughts, she turned and spied the source of the aroma. On a marble counter sat a small bowl of sea salt for finishing. Next to that was a tray of molded chocolates in assorted shapes. Sea salt sparkled atop each one.

"Our head chef and I have been testing nuanced fruit and liqueur flavor profiles," Lauro said.

Celina's nose twitched. "Balancing sweetness or bitterness with sea salt, which also stimulates the taste buds. A nice textural touch, too."

"That needs a steady hand. Too little, no result. Too much, disaster." Trailing a finger along her bare wrist, he added, "Much like love."

"I loved Tony very much," Celina murmured as heat rose on her neck. And she needed to know what had happened here.

He brushed her arm as he leaned past her, peering at the chocolates. A shiver raised the fine hair on the nape of her neck, and she felt her flush deepen. She imagined her cheeks were the color of the red poppies on her dress.

"I'm glad," he said, his voice imbued with compassion. "You were happy together?"

As he spoke, she blinked against a growing, long-dormant yearning that seemed to unfold in her like a seedling reaching for the sun.

Celina saw him waiting for her reply. "Very much, though we had our difficulties in the beginning. All of his injuries…they were traumatic for him."

"I'm glad you were there for him. We were both lucky to have loved him."

Lauro turned to choose two dark chocolates and handed one to her. "One early morning last week, I walked through a terraced garden over the ocean, peeling a blood orange. It was a Taroco orange, or *arancia rossa,* brought from Sicily many years ago, its skin thin with a hint of blush, its flesh the color of a setting sun, its sweetness beyond that of any other orange."

Pursing his lips in remembrance, he went on, his voice rich with reverence and wonder. "The salt air on my lips, combined with the sweet juice, inspired this new effort. Try it for me. I'd love to know what you think."

Celina brought the dark chocolate-enrobed delicacy to her nose and inhaled, reveling in the juxtaposition of aromas. Biting into it, a complexity of flavors melted across her tongue. The intense aroma of blood orange with its singular sweetness…a bitter edge of dark chocolate with hints of tropical earthiness…a tart explosion of sea salt that intensified every flavor. She licked her fingers, savoring the ganache that had melted, leaving traces on her skin. Smiling, she watched Lauro sweep his tongue over his lips to take in every morsel.

"It's magnificent," she said, a strange ache gathering in her chest as she watched him. "An intriguing dichotomy…"

"You are an artist, too, I think." Lauro perched on a stool and took her hand. Gazing at her slender hand in his, he ran his thumb along her fingers.

A subtle aroma of spiced sandalwood, tinged with sweet vanilla and a trace of chocolate, emanated from his skin. When mingled with his natural scent, the effect was purely masculine, like nothing Celina had ever experienced.

Barely able to contain herself, she slid her hand from his grasp. "Please, don't."

Surprise registered on his face. "I don't mean to anger you."

"It's just that…" She heard her voice quiver and hoped he hadn't noticed. How could she explain how he made her feel? This desire she hadn't expected, hadn't sought, but couldn't deny. Still, it didn't feel proper.

Not at all.

Yet if she were honest with herself, she had caught herself wondering what his lips would feel like on hers, or how his arms would feel locked around her.

"I understand. I am not Nino." Lauro stepped behind her and smoothed his hands over her shoulders, kneading the tightness in her neck. "Relax."

Tony used to do this. Celina fought to maintain her composure. At his touch, she realized how tense she'd felt for so long. After a while, she felt her muscles warming and loosening under his strong hands.

"You were going to tell me about Isabella."

"I will. But at the moment, you and these knots need more attention."

The heat from his hands coursed through her body, filling her with an indescribable sensation that should have concerned her, but instead, she sank into the feeling, and soon found herself welcoming the reprieve. Celina dragged her eyelids closed. *Just this once,* she promised herself. No one else was here, and she needed to feel something other than the oppressive cloak of mourning that had shrouded her shoulders since Tony's death. Every stroke peeled back the layers of misery, lifting her into another, brighter, dimension of life.

Love. It felt a lot like love.

Arching her neck to one side, she noticed how Lauro followed her movement. Slipping beneath the softly draped collar of her dress, his palms caressed her neck, his fingers threaded through her hair. It had been months since she'd been comforted like this, touched like this. His rhythmic breath was soft on her ear, and her muscles were as fluid as warm ganache.

As he shifted to the other side of her neck, more tension melted away. Taking his time, he pressed his thumbs at various points along the nape of her neck. "The line of your neck, your shoulders…exquisite," he murmured.

His melodic, baritone voice reverberated to the depths of her heart, warming the barren chamber left cold so many months ago. A moan of remembrance, of longing, escaped her lips.

"Your essence glows from your heart," he whispered, stroking her neck and transporting her to a realm where softness and strength entwined.

Warmth from the energy he'd released in her body welled up inside her and poured from her in waves. Once started, she never wanted this life force to stop again, for next time, it would still her heart. There was only one way to ensure that it never did.

She turned into his hand, pressing her lips first to his palm, then pulling him toward her, now arching against him, and at last finding the softness of his mouth. Testing the full lips that had held her gaze so many times, she tasted the lingering blood orange and chocolate on his lips, like nothing she had ever tasted before.

At once, his movements stilled, waiting for her to go on. She hesitated only a moment, feeling his heartbeat thudding in response, before pressing on and taking in the fullness of a kiss that enveloped them both in its soaring intensity.

Freed of the shackles of mourning that had restrained her expression, she framed his face in her hands, then threaded her arms around him. The weight of his body pressing against hers was glorious and left her astounded. This feeling, this desire, was unlike anything she'd ever experienced, and she sank into his embrace, deepening their kiss, never wanting to leave his arms.

Groaning with desire, Lauro lifted her to a marble counter.

The heat of her thighs sizzled through her thin dress onto the cool slab, fogging her brain and obscuring all reason. She yielded to her desire for this exquisite man, who stood before her wanting only to please her and soothe her.

She wanted all of him. She ran her hands over his bronzed face, exploring the fine breadth of his brow, the arched black eyebrows angled like raven's wings, the high cheekbones that balanced a profoundly dimpled chin. He was, she imagined, like an artist's rendering of a Roman god, but the light in his eyes outshone his beauty. It was as if her soul was reflected in his gaze.

"*Amore mio, anima mia.*" Murmuring her name between her kisses, Lauro uttered words she'd never thought she'd hear again. "*Quanto ti amo.*"

As they devoured each other, a power stronger than their will seized them, and it was as if destiny had reached beyond borders, beyond calamity, to join them in a joyous union neither could have ever imagined.

The click of an opening door sounded behind them, followed by a woman's soft exclamation. "*Mi dispiace, perdonami.*"

Celina pulled away from Lauro to put distance between them, but she realized it was fruitless. They'd been caught like a couple of students making out in school.

"You have a telephone call from London," the woman said. "It sounds urgent."

Lauro held fast to Celina's hand, reassuring her. "I'll be right there, Mariela."

Glancing over her shoulder, Celina caught the gaze of a young woman who was furtively attempting to close the door while also trying to catch a glimpse of who her boss was with. The woman smiled shyly at her.

After the door closed, Lauro let out a breath and kissed her forehead. "It's been a long time since I've been caught kissing a girl." He drew a handkerchief from his jacket and handed it to her. "I think you might need to freshen up."

"You, too." She wiped her red lipstick from his mouth and smoothed his hair back into place, while he adjusted his jacket. "I hope you don't think I'm always like that," she added. "I got carried away. Maybe we shouldn't…"

"I *was* surprised, but that doesn't mean this isn't real." Taking the handkerchief from her, he dabbed her lips, then kissed her lightly again. "I've never felt like this." He grinned. "I have burned inside for you. I've wanted to do that since the moment I met you."

"You certainly fooled me." While she was amused now at how he'd hidden such feelings behind a sullen exterior, his actions had caused her great anxiety. She lowered her eyes in a coy manner. "Any plans to make it up to me?"

"This is only the beginning." Lauro glowed with such pleasure, his face lit with love.

As she imagined the pleasures in their future, a smile danced on her lips.

"Come with me to my office while I take this call," Lauro said, offering her his hand. As he did, a shadow of concern crossed his face. "There's also something you should know about."

Chapter 15

Amalfi, 1939

"WAIT," LAURO CRIED, tearing loose from Nino's grip to follow Isabella across his parent's living room. Her scarlet dress slashed through the Christmas Eve crowd like an arrow intent on its target, which as near as he could tell, was the rear door.

"Let her go." Nino gripped his arm again.

Lauro whirled to face his brother. "*Bastardo*!"

"Maybe so. But we're not fighting over Isabella. Not here."

Nino tugged him toward the entry door through a throng of their uncles—their father's brothers—who had been standing nearby and had witnessed the entire debacle between him and Isabella.

Other friends and family members were watching them, and Lauro saw Isabella's protective mother toss her husband an angry look. His father was crossing the room toward Signora Guardino to calm her, while Sara was edging the room to find Isabella. *What was going on?*

Nino pushed the door open. "I've been trying to tell you."

Lauro plunged outside, sudden anger erupting toward his brother. "What did you do to Isabella?"

"It was before you met her."

"When?" Lauro spit out the word, barely able to contain his fury.

Holding his hands up as a shield, Nino stepped back, putting distance between them. "Last spring."

"Was there a baby?"

"She lost it. If I had known before, I would have married her."

Lauro closed his eyes in agony. The man who'd broken Isabella's heart was his own brother. A thought struck him, and he *had* to know. "Did you…force yourself on her?"

"I didn't have to. She's awfully persuasive—"

Filled with savage rage, Lauro lunged like a lion, blinded with the desire to obliterate the man who'd spoiled his one true love. His brother ceased to exist to him. Thudding against Nino, Lauro's impact sent them sprawling onto the gravel court, and he landed a solid blow against Nino's nose, which exploded with a spurt of blood.

Urged on by the satisfying blow, Lauro hit his brother again, while Nino crossed his arms against his face and curled under him, absorbing the impacts.

"Stop!"

Never before had he attacked his brother, but even the sound of his father's voice couldn't restrain his frenzied fists now.

Grappling for handholds, Carmine and two of his father's brothers, Guiseppe and Vito, tugged them apart and pulled him off Nino.

Lauro fell back onto the gravel, panting and sweating, wailing with outrage, his knuckles smeared with blood.

"How dare you do this?" Carmine held them apart, enraged at the sight of his bloodied sons. "And on Christmas, the holiest of days. What's gotten into you?"

"Nino ruined everything," Lauro shouted.

"How could he? Nino just arrived." Carmine stood between them. "He called me this morning, insisting I give you his position at *la fabbrica di cioccolato*. This is how you thank him?"

Their uncle Guiseppe pulled Nino to a seated position and pressed a handkerchief against his split nose and chin. Wincing with pain, Nino pushed him away. "It's my fault, Papa. I tried to explain."

The front door swung open and Isabella's imposing father, Signore Guardino, stepped out. His face was reddened with anger, though his venomous stare was ice cold. "Who are you, and what did you do to upset my daughter?"

Lauro groaned and covered his eyes. An anguished cry erupted from somewhere deep in his gut as searing pains of distress shot through him. *His beloved Isabella...*

Carmine hurried toward her father. Putting an arm around his shoulder, he conferred with him in a hushed tone.

Lauro would never know what his father had said to make Signore Guardino turn around, but he knew his father would pay for it. And so would he.

The door clicked shut, and Carmine spun around to face his sons. "You have about thirty seconds. One of you had better explain."

Nino coughed into his hand. Hanging his head, his voice was barely audible. "I dated Isabella in Rome."

Lauro's reaction was swift, but his uncle Vito held him back. "Why did she look so shocked to see you here?"

A sheepish expression filled Nino's face. "We met at a club. We agreed, no real names. It sounds crazy, I know...I called myself *Riccardo*."

Carmine dragged his hands over his face and cursed to himself.

Lauro's temper soared. Struggling to keep his voice down to a hoarse whisper in case Isabella's father could hear them, he gripped his father's shoulder, crying with pain. "He *ruined* her. He admitted it."

Carmine swung around to Nino. "Is this true?"

With regret etching his face, Nino nodded.

Lauro shot back at him. "Are you in love with her?"

"Does it matter? You're the one marrying her."

"It's *you* she loves. Why couldn't you have stayed away?"

A commotion sounded behind them, and Lauro turned to see Isabella and Adele rounding the corner of the villa.

Isabella's face was white with anguish and fury, and Adele was trying to calm her. Isabella yanked away from her and stalked toward them.

Nino struggled to his feet. "I never meant to hurt you—"

Isabella grasped his collar and pulled his face to hers. "I loved you." She spat into his face and finished with a slap that resounded through the still night air.

"Isabella," Lauro cried, scrambling to her.

She whirled around, her face a tortured mask of grief. "I can't marry you, Lauro, don't you see? I can't bear it. *Anyone* but him."

"No!" Lauro raced to her and enveloped her in his arms, shielding her from his brother with the force of his love. "We'll move, we'll go somewhere."

"I'll go," Nino interjected. "I'm leaving for America anyway."

"You don't know what you're saying," Carmine said, gesturing at Nino. "No one is leaving. We'll work this out."

With tears streaming down her flushed cheeks, Isabella clutched Lauro. She tore her hands through his hair and kissed him with such passionate fervor that Lauro felt his insides twist and melt to her will. *God, he loved her!*

"I don't care what happened, Issie, I love you."

She wailed and pressed her palms against her head. "But I don't, I can't, not with your brother so close. It's good-bye, Lauro."

Extricating herself from his embrace, she rushed toward the cars that lined the gravel court, her mussed blond hair and scarlet dress streaming behind her.

Stunned just long enough to let her get ahead of him, Lauro cried out and gave chase.

Isabella spied keys in the ignition of a low slung, red Alfa Romeo sportscar. Swinging into the car, she turned the key, revved the engine, and spun out, spraying gravel behind her.

Lauro and Nino raced behind her, but they were no match for the powerful coupe. Isabella sped out onto the road and quickly disappeared from view.

Sinking to his knees, Lauro doubled over in the dusty court, weeping as his heart shattered. In the distance, he could hear Isabella shifting gears through turns, tires squealing.

Winded, Nino knelt beside him, sharing his grief. "I'm sorry, Lauro."

"Don't touch me," he cried out, his nerves on fire. Only Isabella could comfort him now, and she was gone. Lauro spit dust from his mouth.

Nino pushed up and turned away.

Moments later, the sharp sound of grating machinery pierced the night silence. Tires squealed in a harrowing, hairpin curve beneath their perch and ended with a sickening crescendo of twisted metal and blood-curdling screams.

Silence.

Lauro scrambled himself to his feet and screamed into the night. "Isabella!"

Moments later, an explosion rocked the night, and flames illuminated the narrow road beneath them.

His heart leapt. He *had* to get to her.

Dio mio, did she make it?

Not this, Lauro prayed in desperation. *Please, dear God, not this.*

Nino cranked the ignition of his car. Flinging open the door, he called out to Lauro. "Get in!"

Chapter 16

Naples, 1953

After Lauro ushered Celina into his office, he took his call from London and quickly addressed the problem while Celina sat beside his desk, her heart still pounding from their stolen kisses in the chocolate test kitchen.

"With pleasure, my friend," Lauro said into the receiver, though he hardly took his eyes off Celina. "Your order should clear customs soon." As he spoke, a smile for her played on his lips.

While she waited, Celina glanced around the office, which was decorated with Italian antique furniture, framed awards, and old photos from the last century. A horse-drawn delivery carriage, a smaller building, a sign that read *Savoia e Figli*. Savoia and Sons.

Lauro's secretary, Mariela, had brought her an espresso and told her that Lauro's parents and Marco would meet them at a café for lunch later.

When Lauro had brought her into the executive suite, the young woman had been curious and excited to meet her. While Lauro took his call, Mariela had let it slip that she'd never seen Lauro with a girlfriend before. Celina guessed that Lauro kept his personal life separate from his work life.

"Twenty gift boxes per carton, that's right," Lauro said into the phone. "Two hundred per week now, five hundred for

Christmastime. Per store. Yes, of course we can." He winked at Celina.

When Lauro began quoting numbers, Celina did the mental arithmetic. She'd had no idea the volume that larger stores did. Or the sums of money involved. At La Petite Maison du Chocolat, Monsieur had never shared the finances, but she had a good idea of costs. Even a fraction of that sum could make a good living for her and Marco. The key would be to sell in the shop and distribute to larger stores, too. She wondered how much chocolate she could make in the kitchen beneath the shop. Busying herself with these thoughts, and watching Lauro on the telephone, she realized her future seemed brighter than it had in a long, long time.

Lauro listened to his client, but his eyes swept across her, and a smile tugged at his lips.

Celina blew him a kiss.

Very bright.

Lauro held up a finger, signaling that he was almost finished. "Excellent, *grazie*, my friend."

As she waited, Celina's gaze rested on a photo on Lauro's inlaid wood desk. Curious, she ran her fingers over the polished silver frame that held an old photograph of a dark-haired young woman staring defiantly into the camera, unflinching, unsmiling, as a wave crested behind her.

"*Mille grazie. Ciao.*" Lauro concluded his call and placed the receiver in its cradle. "Thanks for waiting. That was a new account in England. Business has been excellent this year."

"Who's this?" Celina asked, although she suspected she already knew the answer.

"Isabella." Lauro knelt beside her and smoothed his hands over hers. "We were both so young when the tragedy occurred, too young to know what's truly important. Now, I do."

At his reassuring touch, her heartbeat quickened. She averted her eyes from Isabella's unnerving stare. It felt as though the woman's spirit was in the room, eavesdropping on their conversation. She had to learn more about this mysterious woman.

A smooth wooden box was positioned in front of the photograph. Made of richly grained olive wood, the box was little larger than a deck of playing cards. Lauro reached for it and gave it to Celina.

"Go ahead, open it," he said.

Celina drew in a breath. The lid was difficult to pry off as if it had not been opened in many years, or it was loathe to reveal its secrets.

"Sorry," he said. "It's old. May I help?"

"I've got it." She found an indentation on the side. Sliding a fingernail over it, the lid clicked open.

Inside was a platinum and diamond ring nestled in a curl of black hair.

An engagement ring.

Celina sucked in a breath and turned to him.

"I never got the chance to give that to Isabella," Lauro said, his voice thickening with emotion. "I thought you should know that whatever you might hear, my intentions with her were honorable."

As difficult as Celina knew this was for Lauro, this is what she needed to hear from him. Especially as it concerned Tony, and in turn, her and Marco. She touched his face to reassure him. "What happened, Lauro?"

"It was Christmas Eve," Lauro began. "We had a terrible..."

"Argument?" Celina gently finished his thought.

"No, not that, not really," he said, seeming to search for the right words. "A terrible misunderstanding. When two people in love are not honest with each other, the results can be tragic. *Profondamente tragico.*" He stared past her at the photograph.

"I understand," she said, thinking about all that Tony had neglected to share with her. Or couldn't share, for whatever reason. "The secrets that your brother kept would have been tragic had we never met. But we did. Whatever happened, we can overcome it."

"I hope so. After Isabella's death, I couldn't blame Nino for leaving. At first, I was glad he was gone, because I thought that I was the only one who had the right to grieve. But many loved her. I learned that I had to share her memory."

"We are no strangers to that thief in the night." Celina circled the ring with her finger, then returned it to the box. Placing it on the desk, she turned back to him. "I'm sorry you had to go through that."

"I tried, I did my best, but I cannot change the situation."

She was sure he could feel her rapid pulse, now pounding in her ears and obliterating all sounds in the outside world past the confines of this masculine cocoon.

Here, right now, was her chance to discover the truth she'd been searching for. What had caused the rift between her husband and his family?

"Did Isabella's accident affect your relationship with your brother?"

"Her accident..." He stopped. "Her death became complicated. For both of us." Lauro shook his head, then lifted a strand of hair caught in her eyelashes and tucked it behind her ear. Letting his hand fall to her shoulder, he continued to trail it along her arm.

Celina waited, silently willing him on.

"I never thought I would meet another woman who made me feel like she did. Until you."

Celina closed her eyes. The moment she had felt his lips on hers, the scarred rift in her heart had cracked open just enough to let the pure light of love seep in, to remember what it had once felt like.

But he was still her husband's brother.

A brother she had never known. First, she needed to know more. "Lauro..."

He pressed a finger to her lips. "Please, let me speak first. Or I'll lose my will." He led her to a carved wooden bench and drew her beside him.

Nodding toward the photograph, he said, "You and Isabella are very different. She was impetuous, and so damned *alive* then." He let out a wry chuckle. "Life is ironic. Ah, how young I was. And now you—I can see why my brother fell in love with you. My brother and I...our taste in women... It was always exactly the same."

"What do you mean?"

"Isabella was in love with Antonino first, long before I met her. And it didn't end well."

She dreaded asking, but she had to know. "Why not?"

Lauro didn't answer. He only shook his head in sorrow.

"Whatever happened won't change the way I felt about Tony." She hoped.

Nodding, Lauro went on, measuring his words with care as if they were sharp, dangerous instruments. "Isabella and Nino conceived a child, though she lost it. Had he known, Nino would have married her."

Celina sucked in a breath. *A child!* She sat stunned as Lauro's revelation washed over her like an icy downpour.

He shook his head. "I'm so sorry to tell you. I know he must have loved you very much. How could he not? Look at you."

Tony and Isabella had conceived a child. She imagined the distress and dishonor this must have caused to their families—if it were known. She wondered, though it was becoming clear why he had left Italy. "You fought over Isabella?" she asked.

"It was my fault. I didn't know they had a relationship, or that they even knew each other. When he told me, I was jealous because I thought she loved him more than she did me."

"And did she? Did he love her?"

He stroked her cheek. "I'm sure he never loved her as much he loved you."

Celina was stunned. Did this change her life with Tony, or anything else? Not really. It had all happened so long ago. Tony had loved her, of that she was certain. She could choose to be the better person and rise above this. She *had* to.

What did it matter now anyway?

"I'm glad you told me," Celina said, and she meant it. At least she knew what had been plaguing Tony all these years and why he hadn't returned to Italy. Surely he would have, given time. Knowing how devoted he was to her and Marco, she could just imagine the shame he must have lived with. Her eyes welled at the thought.

"That's all in the past." Lauro dipped his head before her. "And you are the present. Your beauty, your essence, surrounds you like the most exquisite perfume and defies my mere mortal description, though I promise I will try."

Celina felt her face flush at his words. Even Tony, as aggressive and outspoken as he was, hadn't been so straightforward about his feelings with her. Although her husband had often told her he loved her, he hadn't had the poetic voice of his brother.

"So much is new to me," Celina said, her head swirling from the nearness of him and the secrets he'd revealed. "Have patience with me."

"Forgive me for speaking so boldly." Lauro must have picked up on her discomfort, and he shifted back with a heavy sigh, as if he were facing the reality of their situation. "Especially as your *cognato*, your brother-in-law. It's not entirely proper, and I know that. But I cannot hold this feeling inside any longer. I want you to know the truth about how I feel."

She struggled to process Lauro's revelations and her feelings for him. "When we first met, I thought you despised me."

"I had my doubts about who you were and what you wanted."

"What changed your mind?"

"It was my own awakening," he said. "Any woman with your knowledge and talent doesn't need us. You're an American, you're determined. You can make your way in the world without us, without our money. Everyone knows that in America anything is possible." He ran a finger along her jawline. "If anything, we need you and Marco. The hope of tomorrow. That is where our family is impoverished."

Celina was surprised to hear him reveal such thoughts and feelings. "There was a time I didn't think you wanted me to stay here."

"Frankly, I was afraid to believe you would." He clasped her hand in his. "Will you stay? You would do me and my family the greatest honor. Marco is their treasure."

Her heart leapt at his words, and she was almost afraid to believe this was actually happening. But it *was* real. She kissed him lightly on the lips. "I could never give Marco the gift of growing up surrounded by grandparents, cousins, aunts, and uncles. And now this."

She paused and glanced down at their entwined hands, which now felt so right. Her heart was bursting with the possibility of love again. Trying to keep her voice from quavering, she asked, "Where do we go from here?"

A grin spread across his face. "We still have much to learn about each other."

As enticing as he looked, something stirred in the back of her mind. "Of course, we have time."

Or do we? If she returned to San Francisco now, this relationship might never develop. If she stayed here, would they become as familiar as family and lose the spark they shared right now?

"All the time you need, I promise. And my parents will be so pleased if you stay. You and Marco can live at the villa."

"I need to adjust to all of this, and so will Marco." Suddenly, Celina realized this new version of reality could be much more complicated than she'd realized once they told his family what they meant to each other. It was more than that, though. They'd both lost their soulmates. As attracted as she was to Lauro, she still loved Tony, and Marco missed his father. Love couldn't be turned off like a spigot, or tucked away in a drawer with a sprig of lavender as a keepsake. Feeling she could confide her innermost thoughts in him, she asked, "How long did you carry the pain of Isabella's death?"

Lauro seemed taken aback by her question. "I don't think one ever gets over such a deep wound. I have felt married to her in my heart all these years. I vowed my life to her."

"But at some time, the anguish you felt must have subsided." Tony's death had left her reeling and forlorn.

He shook his head. "From the moment I met you, you have complicated my life, and now, my heart."

"*I* have complicated *your* life?" The thought was so absurd, she laughed. She's the one who was thinking of leaving all she and Marco had ever known behind.

Lauro looked perplexed, as if she were the one mistaken. "This feeling I have for you, it's also quite uncomfortable. You can understand, yes?"

"You've made me uncomfortable since the day I arrived."

Lauro leaned forward in earnest. "I thought you should know, but I *am* your *cognato*. Surely you agree that others shouldn't know about..." He motioned between them.

"Wait, you're ashamed of this?" Her chest felt constrained, as if the air had become too thick to breathe. "What did you want of me?" When he didn't answer, she knew. This knowledge hurt her more than she could have imagined, and she lashed out at him. "So I'm just someone to play with while you pine for Isabella."

Still he said nothing. She hated that she felt a measure of satisfaction from the hurt look on his face, and she knew she should stop right there, but inside, the pent-up side of her erupted, intent on searing his heart as he had hers. How dare he play with her emotions, which were still so raw from Tony's death—or was he the type who took advantage of widows? She curled her lip in a defensive sneer. "You're used to your brother's leftovers. Was kissing me your twisted way of getting even with him?"

He stared at her as shocked as if she'd slapped him. "*No, tesoro mio, no.* But you kissed me first. I couldn't help myself."

She blew out a puff of air. She *had* kissed him, but it wasn't as if she had misread the cues of their mutual desire. "Why are you doing this to me?" She held up her hand, shielding herself as her fragile heart shattered again. What a fool she was.

"So you could understand what I hold in my heart for you, and why I've been acting the way I have. Even so, we cannot dismiss the vows we each made. You see this, yes?"

"My husband is *gone.*" Celina jerked to her feet, unable to remain in his presence even a moment longer. "I feel sorry for you, but I understand you even less than before. If you are still so devoted to your memory of Isabella, then please don't make me feel anything for you. Don't look at me that way. Don't even touch my hand. And leave my son alone."

Drowning in anger-fueled despair, she bolted for the door. When she reached it, she hesitated, angling her gaze over her shoulder, a part of her praying he might call her name, willing him to speak the feelings of his heart again to prove her wrong.

Lauro's head was bowed and his hands covered his face. He drew a ragged breath as if to speak.

For a moment, hope sparked in her soul.

But he only shook his head.

Celina yanked open the door just as Lauro's secretary smiled with expectation, but Mariela's sunny expression quickly clouded with disappointment. Had she hoped that Celina would rescue her boss from a strange, unrequited love?

No, that would never happen.

Celina charged from his office and through the hallways, determined to get as far from him and Cioccolata Savoia as she could. She didn't need anyone to change her life. She could do that by herself.

And that's exactly what she was going to do.

Chapter 17

AFTER SLIDING OUT of a taxi, Celina hurried over cobblestone steps to meet Sara and Carmine and Marco. As she followed the directions to the café that Mariela had raced out the front door of Cioccolata Savoia to give her, she ignored the curious looks of sophisticated passersby and brushed angry tears from her cheeks, trying not to further soil the grass-stained white cotton gloves she'd pulled back on as she walked.

Though she didn't care about the strangers she passed on the elegant Via Chiaia, she hoped Sara and Carmine wouldn't notice her distress, if only because she didn't want to explain in front of Marco.

"That's enough," she said to herself with a swift spread of her hands, the way she'd seen Adele and Sara do. She had to admit, that felt better.

She was determined to put Lauro and everything that had happened today at Cioccolata Savoia behind her. Her mind was a swirling mess of emotions. She chastised herself for her moment of weakness in the test kitchen, but in her next breath, she found herself reliving it.

She blew out a breath of frustration.

There was no one to blame but herself. Indeed, she *had* instigated the kiss with Lauro. All he had done was massage her shoulders and arms and neck in a way that inflamed her senses. In a way no other man ever had, and she hadn't even known existed—unless she counted the way actors swooned over each other on celluloid film—which wasn't real anyway. *Oh, dear Lord!* Was she really so vulnerable?

Yes. Yes, she was.

Damn it.

That had to change. Starting now.

And yes, Lauro was at fault, too, even if he refused to admit it. How dare he play on her vulnerability and then make excuses to her?

Her T-strap heels clicked on the stones beneath her feet, each step a mark of her determination. Catching a glimpse of her anguished face in a boutique window, she slowed her pace and tried to gain control. She was on her own now, and she had to think of herself and her son, and what was best for them.

Her mind whirred with possibilities. She could stay in Amalfi, where she could live for less than in San Francisco, and open a shop on the main street near the Piazza del Duomo. After overhearing Lauro on the telephone with the London store buyer, she knew she could live here, make her chocolates, and sell her inventory abroad to make a good living. Sell to tourists, too. She could figure it out; she always had.

In listening to Lauro's call, what had surprised her most was the volume of demand at the large stores. After some quick mental calculations, she was sure that she could make a go of the business here in Italy, and she wouldn't need the Savoia family help.

Nearing the café on the corner, she slowed to catch her breath and paused in a doorway to smooth her hair and refresh her lipstick. Taking her pressed-powder compact from her purse, she pursed her lips. As she peered at herself in the tiny mirror, doubt chiseled at her budding confidence. Could she really manage what she imagined? Or was this merely an emotional reaction to Lauro? She swiped a swift slash of red across her swollen lips and snapped the cap back on her lipstick.

Stay in Amalfi, indeed.

Her wounded pride was filling her full of lofty ideas. She was too old for this nonsense.

No, they would go back to San Francisco right away, and Marco would start school. Surrounded by everything that was familiar, she would study the opportunity and make a decision based on logic, not on emotion.

And definitely *not* on Lauro Savoia.

Though he was correct on one point. He was her brother-in-law, for heaven's sake. What was she thinking? She started off again, marching toward her destination.

When Celina arrived at the Gran Caffè Gambrinus, she made her way through the well-dressed luncheon crowd dining beneath crystal chandeliers before spotting Carmine and Sara at a sunny table on the patio. A basket of bread and a carafe of wine sat in front of them. Marco was slurping a fizzy Italian fruit soda.

"Where is Lauro?" Sara asked, glancing behind her.

"He's not coming. He had a call from London." That much was true.

Carmine and Sara traded glances, and Sara looked concerned, but to her credit, she did not pursue the question. Celina was sure that Sara would ask her later.

"You seem winded," Sara said.

"I hurried because I didn't want to keep you waiting." She sat down and hugged Marco. "Did you sample any more chocolate?"

Marco grinned. "Nonna got a giant box and filled it with everything I wanted. Look, Mom, it has chocolate animals. Ducks, fish, bunnies." His face lit with delight.

"Only the best for our grandson," Sara said, looking as excited as Marco.

"What a beautiful gift, thank you," Celina said. After what she'd just been through with Lauro, watching the three of them enjoying each other's company calmed her.

"Sara has waited a long time to spoil a grandchild," Carmine said. "And I can't think of any young man more deserving than

Marco. He was a big hit with the staff. Even got to help make chocolates."

"Did you? I'm awfully proud of you."

Marco snuggled next to her and craned his face up, turning quite serious. "Mommy, can I ask you something?"

"Of course, what is it?"

The boy scrunched up his face. "I know school is starting, but I really like it here. Can we stay longer? I can start school here, Nonna says. She'll help me talk better Italian."

Sara smiled. "I don't mean to influence you—"

"Yes, you do," Carmine interjected, chuckling. He poured wine into a glass for Celina.

"We've grown to love Marco so much," Sara said.

"Mommy, please?"

Three expectant faces surrounded her, yet she maintained her poise. "It's a good thought, but I think we should go back to San Francisco and reconsider."

Marco's lower lip began to tremble. "I don't want to leave," he cried, clutching his grandmother.

Sara's eyes misted as she rubbed his little back and kissed the top of his head. "You'll be back, little one."

Carmine tapped the table in thought. "Adele told us you were looking at a shop in Amalfi next to hers. We thought you were planning to stay."

"Don't let anyone else in our family dissuade you from what you really want to do," Sara said.

Celina caught her meaning. "This is my own decision. It's rational and logical. I need to look at our lives and decide what's best. When I'm back, I can see more clearly."

Sara sighed. "Having family nearby is an advantage."

"Lot of opportunities here," Carmine said. "The economy is growing. Your *cioccolateria* would probably do quite well, and your money goes farther here than in America right now."

"Of course, San Francisco is an exciting place for a young woman," Sara allowed. "You probably have many friends there, yes?"

Celina shook her head, thinking about the question as she methodically loosened each glove finger before removing her soiled gloves. She wished she could say *yes, plenty of friends*, but her days were consumed by work, making dinner, and caring for Marco.

After her mother had died, she'd withdrawn to her work. It wasn't until Tony came along that she'd met many people outside of Marge and Monsieur at La Petite Maison du Chocolat. She'd just come to know a few families in their neighborhood, but after Tony died and she sold their home, they faded away. People had commitments, too, and she was a cracked, unmatched teacup at their social tea party.

"It's been a lovely vacation, but we have to return to our real world," Celina said, though now the thought saddened her. Her life in San Francisco was safe and predictable, but it was a dark charcoal sketch next to the fluid, watercolor life here in Italy.

"They must have a good life there," Carmine said to Sara. "We shouldn't push her."

Marco scrunched his face, which turned crimson red. "I don't have a good life," he cried. "I don't like Mrs. Jackson."

"Why would you say that?" Celina drew her brows together.

"Because I don't," he wailed. "She yells at me and makes me sit in a dark closet when I ask too many questions."

A chill snaked through Celina, and she sucked in an alarmed breath. "Why haven't you told me this before?"

"Because you told me I should mind her." Tears sprang from his eyes, and he balled up his little fists to rub them away.

"But that's not right, not at all." How dare that woman lock her son in a closet! The thought of it made her sick. How could she have overlooked his emotional distress? She felt guilty for having been mired in such blinding grief.

She hugged Marco and kissed away his tears. "I'm so sorry. I wish you'd told me as soon as it happened." She would certainly speak to Mrs. Jackson, but she'd have to make other arrangements for Marco.

"I don't want to go back to her, or San Francisco," Marco cried. "I know you can't help that Daddy died, but I want to stay here with my *nonna* and *nonno.*" He pleaded with them through tear-streaked cheeks. "I love them."

"But school—"

"I'll be good, Mommy, I can learn anything. You always tell me that."

"Maybe just for a year?" Sara ventured the thought. "Until you're both over the shock of losing Nino. Then you could go back—if that's what you want."

"You and Sara and Adele can go to the thermal spas in Ischia, where you can relax in natural hot springs and have massages and face packs—what do you call that?" He patted Marco's cheeks.

Sara smiled. "Facials. We could also go skiing in the winter. We have a chalet in the Alps, not too far from Torino. Then there's the opera, and so many museums and ancient sites we can visit."

"Don't forget sailing," Carmine added. "You'd love Capri. We like to sail there in the summer. Many excellent restaurants and activities for Marco, too."

They meant well, but the thought of Mrs. Jackson being mean to Marco, and the lonely life he led—even lonelier than hers—made her cringe with guilt. How could she deny her son's beseeching looks?

Sara nudged her husband. "And I haven't even taken Celina and Marco shopping yet."

"You make it sound wonderful," Celina said. "I wish we could stay."

Marco looked hopeful. "Mommy, please. Just for a year, like they said. Please?"

Carmine put his arm around Sara, and the three of them stared at her, willing her to change her mind.

They'd made strong arguments, but more than that, the air was lighter here, her cares farther away. Except for one, but she could ignore Lauro, couldn't she?

Was facing reality such a good idea if it meant missing out on once-in-a-lifetime adventures? She and Marco could share this, and hopefully, heal together, too.

Celina turned Marco's face up to hers. "Are you telling me the truth about Mrs. Jackson?"

He nodded. "I'm sorry I didn't tell you before. I didn't want you to be mad or worry about me."

"Oh, honey, that's a mother's job, and I wouldn't change it for anything." Celina held him and rocked him, though he was too old to hold on her lap like a baby anymore. Where had his toddler and baby years gone?

"He'll grow too fast," Sara said. "When he's older and has friends, you won't be able to visit often. I see that with my friends who have children in America."

At once, the thought of all the days and years stretching ahead of her was sobering. The sheer mundaneness of their existence was often mind-numbing. She woke as tired as when she'd gone to sleep, and she had little respite. Monsieur clucked his tongue and chastised her whenever she had to take off work with Marco. He'd already fired one woman, even though Marge said the woman had worked ahead and always had more than enough inventory. Plus, she knew that other chocolatiers made more money than she did, but they were men, of course. Although that shouldn't matter, because she considered herself more accomplished than most of them. But that's just the way it was if she worked for someone else.

Until she opened a shop of her on, she would never get ahead. How many years would it take for her to save the money she needed to open in a good location in San Francisco? She glanced at Marco. He'd probably be in high school.

Celina swept a hand across her face. Honestly, she was exhausted by it all. Why would she ever want to go back to San Francisco when she had so much here?

One year would stretch into another, whether it was here or in San Francisco. Although she loved her beautiful city by the sea, she hardly had time to enjoy it. Would she here? In Italy, people seemed to find time to enjoy life more. Life had a different rhythm.

As for opening a shop and running a business, it was an exciting, seductive thought. She thought about what the Savoia family had built up. She'd seen the photos of their modest beginnings in Lauro's office. Why couldn't she do the same? She was confident of her talent, and she knew she could find whatever answers she needed.

Yes, it was time for a little bit crazy. She was thirty years old and not getting any younger. If not now, when?

Celina smiled at the eager faces surrounding her. "Okay, one year."

Marco screamed with delight, and Sara kissed Celina on the cheek. "I promise you won't regret it."

Celina knew she would have only one regret, but it was two hours too late to worry about that one.

One glorious year. The thought took shape, blooming like a solitary flower in the dry landscape of her soul.

Now that she had finally discovered the reason Tony had never returned to Italy, she couldn't wait to move on with her life.

Chapter 18

LAURO SAT AT the dining room table across from Werner. They both watched Adele gliding down the terracotta steps of the couple's comfortable villa that was situated on a hilltop to take in the ocean view.

Werner is a lucky man, he thought. Adele had been quite an attractive young woman, and she had only grown more alluring since her marriage. Werner was devoted to her, and Lauro admired that.

Happy relationships like theirs were a mystery to him. In contentious relationships, it was generally easy to point out the shortcomings of partners, though here in Italy, most people remained committed to marriage by virtue of their religious vows.

Lauro had once vowed to devote himself to Isabella and her happiness. But that had been many years ago, and he had to admit that the memory of her had faded. Now, as a mature man, he saw their relationship as little more than infatuation. But he had made a commitment, even if she had pushed him away in anger at the end. That night had haunted him for years. Only by honoring her memory could he atone for his part in her tempestuous flight and ensuing death.

Savoring a fragrant amaretto after a light supper of *zuppa di cozze*—a dish of mussels with tomatoes, peppers, and parsley simmered in white wine that Adele and Werner had prepared together—Lauro wondered what it would be like to have a woman and children in his life now. His friends were far ahead of him. He missed having someone to come home to and cook with as Adele and Werner did. More than he'd ever thought he would.

For years, he'd closed himself to love and would not speak of Nino. His parents had questioned whether he was punishing himself. There was truth in that, he supposed. He hadn't forgotten the guilt he felt over what Nino had done to Isabella, and he felt he owed a duty of honor to her family. Unlike Nino, he was not one to run away. Even at the expense of his own pleasure.

Nino. Lauro drew a hand over his forehead and stared at the golden liqueur in his glass. As much as he was ashamed to admit it to himself and his parents, he was complicit in his brother's disappearance. He'd never told his parents about their argument, and his remorse intensified as the days stretched into years and Nino never so much as wrote.

Though Nino had started the catastrophic chain that would change all their lives, Lauro had finished it. And now, here was Nino's widow, complicating the even-keeled existence he'd managed to achieve in the wake of such tragedy.

Frowning against his memories, Lauro drained his amaretto as Adele returned to her chair next to her husband in the dining room.

"Are the children asleep?" Werner asked.

"They will be soon, they're reading." Adele smiled at Lauro. "Have you two solved all the world's problems while I was gone?"

"At least those in this household," Werner said, casting a glance at Lauro while he stroked his reddish mustache. "Lauro says he's sure there's a place for my youngest sister at the chocolate factory."

A smile played on Adele's lips. "Or she could work at Stella di Cioccolato."

Lauro looked puzzled. "Never heard of it. A new company?"

"It's opening in the space next to my boutique," Adele said.

"No, you don't mean…" A roar of confusion rushed through Lauro's mind. "She can't do that."

Werner glanced between them. "I wish my wife would fill me in. Who's moving next door to you?"

Lauro huffed with exasperation. "Antonino's widow, Celina. She's a *chocolatière*."

"Ah, the pretty American," Werner said. "So what's wrong with that?"

"You'd have to ask Lauro that question," Adele said. "I think she's lovely. And Sara and Carmine have the luxury of having their grandson close to them. Isn't that nice?"

Lauro furrowed his brow in consternation. "It is if you want an imposter nearby."

"Oh, for heaven's sake," Adele said. "You're not going to start that again, are you? I thought you two were finally getting along. What happened?"

Lauro jutted out his chin. Ever since she'd taken advantage of his weakness in the test kitchen, she'd taken up permanent residence in his head.

"Come on, with that look on your face, it must have been fairly horrible," Adele said, chiding him the way she had when they were children. "Did she put a frog in your bed? Tie your shoelaces together?"

"This isn't funny," Lauro said, scowling at her. Sometimes Adele pushed him too far.

"You know Adele teases those she loves," Werner said, observing his reaction. "Looks like Celina plans to stay. Maybe I can help you sort out the situation. What happened?"

Lauro threw up his hands. "If you have to know, she kissed me."

Puzzled, Adele and Werner stared at him, then laughter broke through their resolve. "How exactly did this terrible deed happen?" Adele asked. "Was she provoked?"

Lauro shrugged. "We were at the factory. She looked tense, so I rubbed her shoulders a little."

"That's often what we do to get them to kiss us," Werner said, winking at his wife. "So, was it disappointing?"

"Not at all. It was extremely pleasant."

"*Pleasant*? That's as bad as *nice*." Adele sighed. "What did you expect? She just lost her husband."

"No, no, no, you misunderstand me," Lauro said, feeling flustered at the interrogation. He wasn't easily unnerved, but this conversation was troubling. "Actually, it was absolutely incredible."

Werner sipped a digestif, studying him. "Then what's the problem?"

Exasperated, Lauro pushed back from the table. "Have you both forgotten about Isabella?"

Adele and Werner exchanged a guarded look.

He knew what they were thinking. They had been there that day, on Christmas Eve, when Signore Guardino had finally given him permission to ask Isabella to marry him.

But Lauro had never had the chance. He and Isabella weren't officially engaged. She'd been full of flirtation and innuendos, sure that he would ask for her hand in marriage if her father approved. Lauro ran his hand over his slightly stubbled chin.

"How long has it been?" Adele asked.

Didn't she remember the date? It was seared into his memory. "Thirteen years."

"Have you thought about letting Isabella go?" Adele stared at him with the same gentle compassion he'd once seen on her face when he'd broken his arm on a ski slope while racing her downhill. "She would have wanted you to live a full life."

"I made a vow." Lauro shot a look at Werner. "You vowed to wait a long time for Adele. Until after the war ended."

"That's true," Werner said, sliding his hand over Adele's.

"Then you two, of all people, should understand my dilemma." Lauro bit down on his lip after that last word. He hadn't wanted to admit that to himself, but there it was. Celina posed a severe dilemma for him.

"If you're going to keep walking by, you might as well come in and have a look around."

Lauro turned at the sound of Celina's voice and feigned surprise. He was curious, and he had been walking past her new *cioccolateria*, which fit snugly between Adele's boutique and a popular café. So he had walked past a couple of times, so what?

When he didn't answer right away, she shrugged and turned to go back inside.

"Anyone can walk on this sidewalk," he said, sharper than he'd intended. "You don't own that do you?"

She clamped her fists on her hips. "As a matter of fact, I'm putting tables and chairs right where you're standing."

"What for?"

"Why do you care?"

When he didn't move, she blew out a breath in consternation.

"If you're not going to move, then the least you can do is give me a hand."

"Don't you have workers for that?" Once again, his voice belied his frustration with the dilemma he found himself in.

"Not all of us have an army of employees."

The way she propped the door open and waited was a definite challenge and left him little choice but to accommodate her. And Adele was watching through her window. She'd certainly have something to say later. If nothing else, he prided himself on being a gentleman. Besides, it was only natural to be curious, and he wanted to see what she'd done with the inside of the old shop.

With her hair pulled up into a ponytail, Celina looked younger than her years, but she was marching around the *cioccolateria* with the air of a general. She looked better than she should in slim black pants that hugged her legs and stopped short, revealing slender ankles. She wore flat shoes and an oversized white shirt splattered with paint that gave her an artistic look.

Most men would find her attractive, so he could be excused for staring a little longer than he knew strictly proper.

Celina gave him a chilling glare and pointed to hand-wrought wicker tables and chairs. "Those, outside."

"Yes, sir."

She made a face, picked up a paintbrush and paint can, and climbed atop a step ladder like a nimble mountain lion. A love song blasted from a record player in the corner, and she began singing along with the music—and assiduously ignoring him.

Which he probably deserved. Admittedly, he had misled her with a shoulder massage—according to Werner—but he'd found her irresistible, and she had taken it even farther.

Glancing around, Lauro saw the transformation she'd made in the small space. Everything was clean—even the chandelier sparkled in the sunlight. New mirrors and the high ceiling dotted with celestial stars made the place appear much larger. The dusty old shop had come to life under her touch, and he was genuinely amazed. However, he didn't want her to think that he was easily impressed.

Gesturing toward the record player, he said, "Little loud, isn't it?"

She made a face. "Where have you been? That's Doris Day. It's her latest hit. My friend Lizzie in San Francisco sent me a package of records last week. Or you might like Eartha Kitt better. Have you heard her sing *C'est si bon*?"

"No, but I like *good* music..."

"You should watch out though." Celina tossed her ponytail over her shoulder. "That one's pretty sexy. Don't know if that's your style."

"My what?"

Celina ignored him and went back to singing a bouncy little tune.

Lauro shook his head. He deserved that, too, but what had changed about her?

Celina seemed to have transformed along with the space she'd renovated. She was more determined, more expressive. Definitely more American. He scratched his chin, unsure if that suited him. Not that what he thought about her mattered. But it had only been a few weeks since he'd seen her last. He'd managed to avoid going to his parents when he knew she was going to be there.

He stood rooted to the spot, watching her.

Now who was acting the fool? He'd always been decisive in business, but now he was venturing into an area of emotional quicksand.

From her perch on the step ladder where she was slapping paint onto a wall, she jerked a thumb toward the record player when the song ended. "See if there's something else you want to play."

Lauro flipped through the records. "Rosemary Clooney, Nat King Cole, Perry Como, Tony Bennett. Who are these people?"

"Those last two are Italian."

"By way of America, you mean. That's not Italian music."

"You'd like them, I bet."

"I doubt it."

She stopped with the paintbrush in mid-air. "What a grouch you've become. What happened to you? I'm the one who should be upset."

Lauro opened his mouth, but she'd caught him by surprise. Maybe she was right. He'd thought a lot about the last day he'd seen her at Cioccolata Savoia in the test kitchen and later in his office. He should've stopped himself; he should've explained himself earlier. Despite the vow he'd made to the memory of Isabella, he was a man, not a monk, and it had been a long time since he'd held a woman in his arms. Too long. "What is this *grouch*?"

"Look in the mirror." She motioned behind him.

An old beveled mirror had been scrubbed clean, and he leaned in. A scowling man stared back at him.

He looked bitter, angry, and old. So that's what a grouch was. *Deserved that, too, I guess.*

"I'm having fun here," Celina called out. "I would love some help with the tables and chairs, but if you're going to stand there and complain, or gawk at yourself in the mirror, I'd rather you get out and make room for someone who will help."

"Fine." Lauro grabbed a table in one hand and a chair in another and stepped out through the wide open doorway. After he'd set up the groupings outside, he went back in.

"Serving chocolates outside?"

"Ice cream in the summer. *Cioccolata calda* in the winter. And *bicerin*."

"*Bicerin*? That's only served in Torino."

"Why not? Is there a law?"

"Of course not, but this is Amalfi."

"The tourists will love it." She turned around. "And I told you I don't want that grouch in here."

"*Caffè napoletano*," Lauro muttered as he straightened a table. "And *cappuccino freddo* in the summer."

"What?"

"I should go. Let me know if you need more help in the kitchen."

Wincing at his choice of words, Lauro hurried from the shop before she could respond. Glancing over his shoulder, he saw her watching him. Her lovely lips parted in surprise. *Those lips…* How he yearned to take her in his arms again.

When he was out of sight, he smacked his forehead. He was a fool to let the past dictate his future.

What could he possibly do to make his actions up to her?

Chapter 19

"*Buongiorno*," Celina called out to the people she passed as she zoomed along the narrow road on her mint green Vespa, the sun warm on her shoulders and the salt-tinged sea breeze cool on her face. Citrus blossoms lined the road and sweetened the air, perfuming the hillside and filling her with inspiration.

What a sweet life, she thought, almost afraid of the happiness blooming inside of her. In the past weeks, she'd forged a truce between her head and her heart. She was thankful she'd decided to stay in Italy, though Lauro remained a thorn in her sunny garden. Marco had started school, and they were learning Italian together. If the year went well, she and her son would stay. If not, she could sell the chocolaterie or find someone to run it for her.

When she arrived at Stella di Cioccolato, she hopped off her scooter. She turned the key in her shop door, intent on completing the chocolate inventory she'd need for her grand opening party tomorrow. As she opened the door, the scent of chocolate wafted to her in welcome. She'd managed to track down sources for the most exceptional quality beans she could find. She inhaled the rich aroma. *Expensive, but worth it.*

After she'd turned on the lights, the door banged, and Werner's youngest sister bounded in. A strawberry blond of eighteen, Karin was thrilled to have a job as Celina's assistant.

"*Buongiorno, come stai?*" Celina grinned at the lanky young woman. She was glad to have her. Besides German, Karin also spoke Italian, English, and French, which would be helpful with tourists.

"Hey, great pronunciation," Karin said, sliding into a flat American accent while stashing her purse under the counter. "Once you learn Italian, I'll teach you German."

"By that time, you'll probably be in the diplomatic corps." With her sunny disposition, Karin would serve customers, but as a quick learner, she was also helping in the kitchen, carrying tubs of warm couverture from the tempering machine, or hand finishing truffles with toasted, finely crushed bitter almonds and pistachios, or artfully drizzled designs.

Karin rested her chin on her hands, a dreamy look in her eyes. "I'd rather go to Hollywood and be an actress like Marlene Dietrich. Do you know anyone there?"

"The closest I ever got was staying at an inn in Santa Monica on the beach next to the grand Marion Davies estate." That seemed like a lifetime ago now.

"Did you see any movie stars?"

Celina shook her head.

Karin rambled on. "Gregory Peck and Audrey Hepburn just filmed a movie in Rome. It's called *Roman Holiday.* Isn't that romantic? Gregory Peck is so handsome." Her eyes lit up. "Did you know that dreamy actor James Dean is in love with an Italian actress, Pier Angeli? Oh, he's even more handsome than Gregory Peck. Do all the men in California look like that?"

Celina laughed. She could hardly remember what it felt like to be that young and excited about life. But since she'd decided to remain in Italy, she felt like she was getting a second chance. Marco deserved that as well.

"Come help me with the truffles before we open," Celina said. "I'm starting with raspberry-infused truffles with dark chocolate ganache, and I'd like you to dip the candied ginger from yesterday."

Karin's eyes widened. "The raspberry truffles were your husband's favorites, weren't they?"

"I made them for him every Valentine's Day." The bubbly teenager asked a thousand questions and had a knack for drawing stories out of her.

Karin followed Celina downstairs, peppering her with questions all the way down the stone steps until they reached the kitchen.

After Celina and Karin had scrubbed the kitchen clean, with a little luck and a lot of telephone calls, Celina had cobbled together a kitchen of used equipment, copper pots, and cast iron molds, many of them antiques. She gazed around, satisfied with the work they'd done. It might not be as fancy or modern as the test kitchen at Cioccolata Savoia, but it was hers.

"We have a lot to do today," she told Karin, anxious to finish before the opening. Sara had agreed to look after Marco if Celina needed to work late in the kitchen.

As they worked in an assembly-line fashion, Karin chattered on, wanting to know everything about California, falling in love, and making chocolates. With her wide-eyed enthusiasm, Celina couldn't resist her questions. And in truth, Karin's enthusiasm had rubbed off on her.

While Celina had roasted and processed cacao beans for some of her most special truffles, for others she had obtained couverture, or blocks of processed chocolate that were ready to use.

She hefted a double boiler filled with water onto the stove and then melted a block of couverture in the double boiler, taking care to keep the water temperature at the precise temperature. Watching the silky chocolate, she made sure to add hot cream and liqueur at just the right moment to make ganache for the truffle's smooth centers.

However, in her haste, she lost the next batch when the water became too hot, which caused moisture to form inside the upper pot and separate the chocolate into a gooey, lumpy mess. Wiping perspiration from her face with a towel, she resolved to start over and pay closer attention.

While the dollops of ganache were cooling, Celina tempered more couverture to create the firm truffle coating. After that, she showed Karin how to dust the truffles they'd made with finely sifted cocoa powder.

"May I try one?" Karin asked, eyeing the truffles they'd made.

"I want you to sample everything. When customers ask you to recommend chocolates, you have to know what to suggest."

Karin bit into a truffle, and her eyes widened. "I can't believe how delicious these are. And I helped make them!"

Celina laughed. "We're just getting started with your education." She gestured to boxes that held presentation supplies. "Next, you'll need to place cooled truffles in pleated paper cups and nestle them in gold-foil wrapped gift boxes. I want an ample supply of inventory. Voluptuous."

Karin giggled. "Sounds seductive."

"And irresistible." Celina glanced at the clock on the wall and frowned. She was behind schedule, and her back and feet were already aching from the hours she'd been putting in.

"Tomorrow we'll give everyone who comes in a gift bag of truffles." Celina opened the door to a crowded cooling cabinet that kept trays of delicacies they'd made at an optimum temperature. Just for the night, she could put the overflow in the wine storage area she'd found, which was also cool and dark.

Celina surveyed her inventory. Candied lemon and orange slices dipped in chocolate, roasted coffee beans enrobed in dark chocolate, and coconut confections enveloped in milk chocolate. Petite Coeurs with a crème fraîche and raspberry liqueur filling, rum-spiked caramels covered in milk chocolate, bittersweet espresso truffles studded with crushed Sicilian pistachios.

For her seaside fantasy collection, the antique cast iron molds had yielded whimsical chocolate shells and seahorses. Within clam shells formed from chocolate were nestled pearls of white chocolate. Among the delicacies were her trademark stars: creamy milk chocolate, dark chocolate filled with peppermint-flavored crème fraîche, and white chocolate iced with candied lemon peel.

Every time she finished one creation, she had ideas for three more. Would she ever be ready?

Above them, a knock sounded on the rear door.

"Are you expecting more supplies?" Karin asked.

"Fresh strawberries," Celina said, brushing wisps of hair from her sweaty forehead. "I'll see to them."

Finding the best supplies in small quantities had been challenging. Thankfully, Marge had delivered on her urgent request. Monsieur connected Celina with the right cacao bean and cocoa suppliers from Venezuela and Ecuador. She promised them that her needs would soon increase. Another supplier sent Madagascar vanilla that was the most fragrant she'd ever found, and through Sara, she'd found nearby farmers to supply hazelnuts, pistachios, and other tree nuts. Every morning she'd been visiting the local markets to find the freshest, most unusual fruits, spices, liqueurs, and other flavorings. She had even found a berry farmer to supply the strawberries she needed for the *pièce de résistance.*

Ten minutes later, the scent of fresh strawberries filled the kitchen. "Can you clean and trim the stems on all of these, Karin?"

"What are you making?"

"I'm going to infuse these with orange liqueur and then drizzle white and dark chocolate over them." Celina took a pair of berries, rinsed them in the sink, and handed one to Karin to sample. Celina bit into the berry, assessing its quality. "Perfect level of sweetness and juice. We'll serve these with chilled prosecco."

Karin went right to work. "Think we'll be busy tomorrow?"

"We'd better be." Celina had invited shop owners around the piazza, restaurateurs, innkeepers, and a few friends she'd made through Sara. Amalfi was a small town, but word had traveled fast that an American *chocolatière* was in town. She was counting on the curiosity factor.

If she were lucky, she could build a local clientele and attract tourists. But her grand plan was to create unusual truffle flavors and whimsical molded chocolates for large department stores in the United States and England. That would require a lot more money than she had, but somehow she would figure it out.

As the sun set, Karin cleaned her workspace. "Are you sure you don't want me to stay longer?"

"Go have dinner. I'm almost finished." But Celina was far from through, and she continued working until midnight, anxious to perfect every detail.

The next morning, Celina zipped through the quiet village at sunrise on her Vespa. She had spent a lot more money than she had planned to outfit the shop and buy the best quality ingredients she could find, so the grand opening had to be successful. Based on her experience in San Francisco, she knew that offering people samples led to sales. Once people tasted her creations, few people could resist the lure of more.

Last night, she'd risked a few new flavors, including a truffle combination of basil, mint, and lemon in crème fraîche and enrobed in dark chocolate, and her delicately flavored Chinese tea line. For the less adventurous, she'd blended dark chocolate with a hint of blood orange and dusted the truffles with sea salt, which would enhance the sweet flavor profile. People were sure to like the strawberries, which had always been popular with the clientele at La Petite Maison du Chocolat.

Hurrying to her kitchen, she thought about the nearly insurmountable work she had to do today. Though she was exhausted, her mind was whirring with a hundred details, yet she couldn't shake the feeling that she'd forgotten something critical last night. Still, she was excited to open her doors to the public and see how people liked her artistry. The anticipation sent surges of energy through her.

"Hi boss," Karin said, breezing down the stairs.

"Thanks for coming in early." Celina was applying the finishing touches on a chocolate fantasy of birds and flowers that she was going to nestle in a spun sugar bird's nest.

Karin glanced around, her eyes widening. "Wow, you did so much last night."

"I was almost seeing double by the time I staggered out. But I was so excited I could hardly sleep."

As Karin tied her apron, she let out a squeal. "Oh, I love the chocolate stars."

"We'll pass those out when the guests arrive to celebrate the opening of Stella di Cioccolato. Could you pack the gift bags that we'll send home with guests?"

"Such a sweet name," Karin said. She retrieved the new bags printed with the shop logo. "I see you made chocolate palm trees, too."

"You have no idea what I went through to get those molds," Celina said, laughing. "The craftsman made them especially for me. I wanted something to remind me of California."

"People will love them here, too." Karin's eyes glinted.

"Go ahead, have one."

Karin slid a shaped palm tree imprinted with fronds off a cooling rack. "Mmm, delicious."

Celina and Karin fell into a smooth rhythm as they worked. Karin turned on the record player and picked out some music. With the records spinning tunes from Doris Day and Tony Bennett and the two women singing along, intoxicating aromas, laughter, and song filled the entire shop. They were oblivious to anything else.

"Anything I can do to help?"

"Oh!" Celina whirled around in surprise, bobbling the tray of truffles she carried. What was *he* doing here?

Lauro caught the tray in midair and eased it onto a countertop. "Careful with the inventory. These look as precious as gemstones."

Celina expelled a breath of relief at the salvaged truffles. "Do you always sneak up on your competitors like that?"

"Is that what you think I am?" He chuckled. "Guess that's so."

"Except I'm not a mass producer like Cioccolata Savoia." Celina held out a truffle, tempting him. "Try this one."

Lauro lifted the truffle and breathed in the aroma before sampling it. "That's different."

She waited, trying not to notice his full lips or the tiny bit of chocolate that he flicked with his tongue. "Different bad, or different good?"

"Very good. It has a smoky edge to it. Like the rich earth around Vesuvius, moist with morning dew." He brought his fingertips to his lips in a kiss of approval.

Celina smiled at his poetic description. "That's the Lapsang Souchong tea flavor."

"You've mentioned that before." He held her gaze for a moment and then quickly shifted his attention. He glanced around, taking in the cooling trays. "You have quite the inventory."

"A lot of it is for the tasting." Celina blew tendrils of hair from her damp forehead. "If people like it, they'll be back."

"You sound confident."

"I am," she said. Cioccolata Savoia might have legendary chocolates, but they couldn't compare to her handmade creations. "I use only the finest ingredients, along with innovative flavors. These are works of art."

Lauro stared at her, then slowly nodded. "You're going to intimidate the competition. They'll never admit it, though."

"I think you just did." Karin suppressed a giggle. "Aren't you the competition?"

"No, no, no, we can't compete with this," Lauro said, finishing the truffle.

Celina smiled.

"What time are you opening your doors?" Lauro asked.

Glancing at the clock, Celina let out a cry. "I have to get ready *now*."

"Anything I can do?"

Celina pointed to the bags Karin was preparing. "These all need to go upstairs, please. Arrange them artfully on the silver platters. Karin will pass out truffles one at a time so people can sample them as I tell the story behind them." She pressed her head between her palms. "I still have so much to do upstairs."

"Don't worry, Karin and I will make sure it looks stunning," Lauro said. "And the music?"

"I think everyone would like the Tony Bennett album," Celina said. "After all, he's Italian."

Lauro grinned and gamely filled his arms with bags. He seemed to be in a better mood today, and he was treating her cordially. Maybe *too* cordially. But nothing good could come of that, right? She shook her head, watching him. Lauro was so different from Tony. Even though Adele swore they were so much alike, she knew the man Tony had become better than any of them.

With a wistful smile, she thought of the importance of this day and how proud her husband would have been of her, although he had never wanted her to work while Marco was young because he said it was his responsibility to provide for them. Yet he often bragged about her skills to friends. She thought of her mother and was sure that Stella Romano would be just as proud, too.

Watching Lauro and Karin bustling around, Celina tried to calm her jittery nerves. She was glad for their help, though she'd been quite surprised to see Lauro here. She blew out a breath in an attempt to calm her nerves, but it seemed to have the opposite effect.

Today marked the beginning of a grand adventure. What was there to worry about? But she knew there was plenty of cause for concern.

She'd taken some risks with her chocolate creations.

In a few hours, her reputation as the American *chocolatière* in this small coastal town would be established—for better or worse. She worried that her taste was too different from that of the local residents who were steeped in tradition and accustomed to the finest and freshest fare that this exquisite spot in nature had to offer. They loved their *gianduiotto,* so she considered she start with that instead of her dark chocolate raspberry truffles. Or maybe the delicate violet-infused ganache.

Her head was aching now. Doubt that she was too far ahead of local trends crept into her mind. And she couldn't get rid of the feeling that she'd forgotten something.

Celina stepped into the small toilet area and splashed cold water on her face. Sweeping back her unruly hair, she piled it high on the crown of her head and clipped it. She pinched her cheeks for color and applied a bright red lipstick she'd bought in San Francisco. The color seemed to brighten her eyes. Adding a drop of water to her cake mascara, she swiped the brush over it and swept the darker shade over her lighter lashes.

After discarding her stained apron, she slipped on a new, starched white chef's jacket she'd embroidered with *Stella di Cioccolato* in inky blue over her heart.

When she stepped out into the kitchen, the light in Lauro's eyes told her all she needed to know.

She might look the part of a successful *chocolatière*—and she definitely knew her craft—but did she have the resources to build her little shop into the empire she dreamed it could become?

Setting her jaw, she straightened her shoulders. No matter what happened today, she knew she had the talent and the stamina, and she would figure out the rest.

Overhead, she heard footsteps and the sound of Karin welcoming their first guests.

Lauro stepped toward her and took her hands in his. "You're trembling."

"Just opening day nerves." Which were exacerbated by his touch. Hadn't she warned him against touching her? Yet she couldn't let go.

"I wish Nino could see you."

She lowered her eyes. Two brothers, so different, each claiming a piece of her heart. "I've been thinking about him today."

"So have I, *tesoro mio*." He kissed her hands. "So have I."

Chapter 20

"*Benvenuto a Stella di Cioccolato.*" Celina raised a glass of sparkling prosecco to guests who had crowded into her little shop. Around her, everyone was chattering and greeting friends, while outside, sunshine bathed people lingering at the tables Lauro had set up. Above it all, Frank Sinatra's latest hit spun on the record player, putting everyone in a cheerful mood.

Celina's heart thudded with excitement. Glancing out the window, she saw the beautiful Byzantine tile tower of the cathedral rising above terracotta-tiled roofs like a sentinel in the heart of the sun-dappled village. She sent up a little prayer. She'd worked so hard on this—her dream.

Over the past few busy weeks, she'd strolled the streets around Amalfi's Piazza del Duomo area, inviting her fellow business owners to her grand opening. Recalling her mother's advice on thoughtful niceties, she had delivered hand-written invitations on beautiful *bambagina*, the fine, thick writing paper that was hand-crafted right here in Amalfi.

She gazed around, amazed at the number of people. Almost everyone she had invited was here. The shopkeepers—the quiet woman who owned the bookstore, the stylish man who sold bespoke men's clothing, the sporty couple who sold yachting accessories—as well as the innkeepers and restaurateurs from Amalfi. Even a few from Ravello, the mountaintop village. She spied a fashion and food writer from a Naples newspaper that she'd met through Adele. People were dressed in sorbet shades of an Italian summer—whites, lemon yellows, marine blues, and rosy pinks. The shop was a flurry of color amid the chatter of anticipation.

So many people gathered in her tiny, starry-ceilinged shop. She had mirrored one wall to make the space seem larger and reflect her wares, so now it seemed twice as crowded. Her chest tightened as she thought what a small community this was. If anything went wrong, she would be doomed from the beginning. But no, she banished the thought—she *was* prepared.

Glancing around, Celina saw that Sara, Carmine, Adele, and Werner had joined Lauro, and they were all beaming at her in support. Sara rested her hand on Marco's shoulder, and he hopped from one foot to the other, looking eager to sample everything she'd made. These people were her family now.

Her family.

The thought triggered a sudden rush of emotion. Nothing in her life had ever been more important than family. How she wished her mother and father could be here, too, but perhaps, somehow, they were in spirit. This thought comforted her as she closed her eyes for a moment.

The memory of their love flooded through her, warming her with the sense of golden sunlight and casting showers of shimmering sparkles against the shade of her eyelids. The *feeling* of love never died. By transmuting her pain into love, she'd discovered that she could summon their love anytime she needed strength or comfort.

Thus fortified, Celina opened her eyes. She nodded to Karin, who changed the record to a slower, heartfelt Caruso song before picking up the first silver platter.

Celina tapped her wine glass. "*Benvenuto.*" This time the crowd quieted, and she went on. "Although I grew up in San Francisco, I feel like I've come home. Stella di Cioccolato is named in honor of my mother, Stella Romano, whose family came to America by way of Rome and Parma many years ago."

Polite applause and murmurs of approval sounded around the room.

Pausing, she ventured her explanation again in her fledgling Italian, which drew polite smiles and chuckles from the audience.

Lauro passed a hand over his face, and Celina could tell he was hiding his amusement. She should still be upset with him, but he'd been so helpful and supportive the last couple of days. His shoulders shook with a chuckle.

What *had* she said?

Stifling a giggle, Karin leaned close to her. "Most people in the hospitality and tourist trade here understand English. Please, let me help you with the Italian."

"Don't tell me I've embarrassed myself already."

Karina grinned. "It's okay. Chocolate makes people forget."

Looking out, Celina found her gaze naturally drawn to Lauro. He and Adele were still grinning, but she also saw pride in their eyes.

An encouraging nod from Lauro was enough to quell her embarrassment. So what if she made a silly mistake? Catching Lauro's attention, she raised a shoulder and let it fall. Despite their rocky history, having him there buoyed her confidence.

"Whatever I said, please know I'm working on my Italian." She smiled sheepishly. "Now, I'd like for you to join me in exploring the wonders of chocolate. We're embarking on a journey, and each delicacy you try today has a special meaning to me. Karin is passing around your first taste. We'll start our journey in Parma, where violets grow in profusion. I'll explain in a moment."

Karin offered a silver platter of chocolate squares that Lauro had arranged to their guests.

"First, a brief lesson in quality. I'd like for you to really look at the chocolate. Inspect it, observe the shine. This means the chocolate is well tempered and of good quality.

"Next, snap the chocolate in two. Fine quality dark chocolate will have a sharp snap, while milk chocolate will have a softer snap." She broke apart a chocolate square.

"Inhale, and sense the aroma." She passed the lightly scented chocolate under her nose, and the crowd did the same.

"Inspired by Parma, this chocolate is flavored with the ethereal essence of violets in honor of my mother, who loved their fresh, subtle aroma and often wore Violetta di Parma perfume. As a *chocolatière*, Stella naturally wore the essence of chocolate, which mingled with the delicate violet scent. This is the magical aroma I remember when she kissed me goodnight."

Sweet sighs rippled across the room. Celina saw the bookseller's eyes glisten with her wistful smile.

"Finally, we taste. Feel the softness on your tongue…close your eyes and let the chocolate melt in the warmth of your mouth…note the flavors that unfold on the tip of your tongue…taste the deeper, richer flavors that develop."

Murmurs of satisfaction flowed through the gathering.

Celina watched the crowd with relief. Nodding with enthusiasm, the writer withdrew a notepad from her handbag and scribbled a few notes.

"Karin is passing out slices of crisp apples so that you can cleanse your palate in between the stops on our journey."

Celina had arranged the tasting to flow from delicate to more intense flavor profiles. She had also grouped chocolates to move through different regions.

"We'll go to northern Italy now," she said. "Inspired by the traditions of Piedmont comes a handcrafted, milk chocolate *gianduiotto* truffle speckled with roasted hazelnuts. This is to honor my late husband's family, the Savoias."

When Sara and Carmine sampled the truffles and nodded their approval, Celina breathed a sigh of relief.

"Next, we'll sample the sweet lemon flavor of *sfusato amalfitano*, formed in the shape of lemons and dusted with sea salt to enhance the flavor." After explaining her inspiration for this local favorite and receiving approval, she gestured to Karin and moved on to the next one.

"This one is a twist on basil, mint, and limoncello. These flavors are enrobed in rich, dark Venezuelan chocolate. I import the cacao beans and roast them downstairs in my kitchen."

Surprise crossed a few faces, followed with growing delight.

Celina continued. "Next, you'll sample a truffle infused with blood orange and topped with roasted pistachios from Sicily, and sweetened with Madagascar vanilla."

The crowd's crunch of green apples punctuated waves of approval. They were eager for more. The writer continued taking notes, and the Savoias exclaimed among themselves over her creations. Marco grinned and wiggled his chocolately finger at her. The fact that her son was proud of his mother sent a warm feeling through her.

"Now, the truffle my husband credited with his falling in love with me." Celina smiled at the memory. "Dusted with silky cocoa powder, it has a raspberry-infused, dark chocolate ganache center enrobed with a dark chocolate *couverture.*"

Swoons of enchantment rippled through the crowd.

Emboldened, Celina moved on to her more daring combinations with confidence.

"The next pair is inspired by my hometown of San Francisco, where I often searched for rare spices and teas in Chinatown. My Chinese tea collection begins with a dark chocolate truffle infused with Lapsang Souchong tea. Cultivated in the Wuyi mountain region in China, the tea leaves are dried over pinewood fires, which give the leaves a smoky, aromatic flavor."

Finding Lauro in the crowd, Celina echoed his description. With a smile tugging at her lips, she added, "You might find it reminiscent of the rich earth around Vesuvius, moist with morning dew."

Bringing his hand to his lips, Lauro sent her a happy kiss across the crowd.

"Also from the Wuyi Mountains of northern Fujian comes oolong tea, which can be fruity, green, or sweet. This oolong is a sweet, roasted woody version. It's the last one on our flavor journey. Enjoy." This was her grand finale.

As guests bit into the star-shaped chocolates, their expressions morphed from pleasure to instant disgust.

With a sour expression on her face, the bookseller spat out the chocolate.

Something was terribly wrong.

After swallowing hard, the haberdasher frowned and wagged his hand.

Celina was stunned. Had a bad ingredient been the cause?

Karin took a bite of one of the truffles she'd been handing out. "Too bitter." She choked it out into a napkin, then began snatching the remaining ones back from guests.

At once, Celina knew what she'd been trying to remember. *Sugar.* She'd forgotten to add it to the last recipe she'd made. She'd been working rapidly, and she was tired. Without sugar, the chocolate and tea flavors were far too bitter.

Having tasted one of the offending truffles, Lauro cut through the crowd to her. "*Zucchero.* Celina, I think these needed sugar."

The newspaper writer shook her head, wiped her mouth, and made notes on her notepad. Another couple hurried toward the door. A man pressed a handkerchief to his mouth.

"It's too late," Celina said, watching the disaster unfold. In her rush, had she doomed her shop before it even had a chance to succeed?

"Never too late," Lauro insisted. "Say something now."

Blinking back hot tears of frustration, Celina grabbed a tray of strawberries. "I'm terribly sorry, but the oolong truffles lacked one of the most critical ingredients in the art of making chocolate—the sugar. I have to admit, I worked late into the night preparing everything for you and simply made a mistake. Please forgive me, but stay. Cleanse your palate with apples and water."

"And I'm opening more bottles of prosecco." Lauro laughed to break the tension.

While Lauro hurried to open the bottles for guests, Karin rushed around serving water and apple slices.

"I've saved the best for last," Celina said, trying to keep people from leaving. "Plus, I have a gift bag for each of you to take home. And I promise, no bitter sweets to surprise you."

Sara began clapping, and Adele and Carmine joined in. Soon guests were applauding and laughing about the mistake.

Celina knew she'd never live down this grand opening. Grinning sheepishly, she passed around her chocolate-drizzled strawberries to the guests who had recovered. Only one woman declined, but her husband took another one, promising that it was for later. She would have gladly given him the rest of the tray.

Celina brought out a special one infused with orange juice that she'd saved for Marco. Carmine proudly steered the boy to one of his brothers to introduce Marco to a great uncle, and Werner joined them.

Summoning her courage, Celina told the story of the strawberries she had prepared.

"These strawberries are infused with orange liqueur and drizzled with the finest dark chocolate to balance nature's summer sweetness. I call these *Antonino's* in honor of my late husband, a native of Amalfi whom most of you knew. These were his favorites."

Lauro lifted a glass. "To Nino."

Celina put a hand over her heart and raised her glass. Other guests followed suit, and then, as they sampled the berries, a wave of applause echoed in the shop. "*Brava, deliziose*," rang out.

Relieved and happy, Celina made her way toward Sara and Adele. She offered a strawberry to Adele, who held her hand up and demurred the offer.

Yet as a thought seemed to dawn on her, Adele frowned and swung around with a quizzical look. "Why would you tell that story about Nino? It can't be true." Her voice had a brittle edge that Celina had never heard from her before.

"Of course it is. Why would you say that?" Celina was nonplussed over Adele's challenging tone.

"Because I know it's a blatant lie," Adele said, her dark eye snapping with anger.

"It's the truth. Why are you so upset?"

With a grim expression, Sara quickly began speaking to Adele with quiet urgency in Italian. Adele shook her head and took a step back, staring at Celina with disgust as if seeing her for the first time.

Celina stepped toward her friend. "Adele, what's wrong?"

"If you don't know, then Lauro was right." Adele raised an accusatory finger to her. "Nino and I, we were both—"

"Shh, it's nothing," Sara hissed, clutching Adele's arm. Acting quickly, Sara forced Adele outside away from other people.

What on earth? Shaken, Celina left them and wove through the crowd. She needed to greet people to make up for her sugar blunder, yet watching Sara and Adele arguing outside was gravely distressing.

Nearby, Lauro was talking to the reporter, and everyone else seemed to be enjoying the strawberries. After chatting with people, Celina felt a gathering sense of foreboding. She had to know why Adele was so upset. She stepped outside.

Sara and Adele were still speaking in hushed, heated tones in front of Adele's shop.

Celina joined them. "What happened in there?" She had a right to know what had set off Adele. What did it have to do with her husband?

Sara held up her hand in warning.

Celina put her hands on her hips. "What is Lauro right about?"

"You," Adele said, spitting out the word. "You're an—"

"Don't." Sara cut her off. "There's a lot I could say to your mother that I haven't."

Adele folded her arms and whirled around.

"As for you, Celina," Sara began in a stern, measured tone. "You will go back inside and tell Werner that my niece is not feeling well. They must leave at once."

A chill coursed through Celina. This was a side of her mother-in-law she had never seen. "But—"

Sara halted her with a sharp slice of her hand. "We will never speak of this again. Is this understood?"

A chill crept through Celina, and she backed away from the two women. The secrets this family harbored cast a dark cloud over what should have been a day of celebration. First Lauro, now Adele and Sara. She wondered what else they were hiding from her.

Chapter 21

Amalfi, 1939

Nino pushed in the clutch and shifted gears, steering the Lancia sports car down the steep, tightly curved cliffside road. Lauro gripped the leather seat to steady himself. Though the brisk night air blew through the open windows, a cold sweat bathed his flushed skin.

"Why the hell couldn't you have left Isabella alone?" Lauro yelled.

Nino clenched his jaw as he leaned into a sharp turn. "You've got that backward."

"Conceited bastard," Lauro sneered. But it was probably true. Resisting Isabella's passion until their marriage took every shred of restraint he had.

Nino slowed as he wound around a hairpin corner. The acrid smell of burning rubber hung in the air. When they cleared the turn, Lauro's pulse quickened.

The headlights shone on a mangled car smashed against an outcropping of boulders. An older man sat on the pavement cradling a limp woman in his arms, sobbing over her.

"*Dio mio.*" Lauro pressed a hand against his chest at the sight of such a sobering calamity. "Do you think that woman's dead?"

Nino blew out a ragged breath. "I'll check on her."

A flash of red farther down the road caught his eye. "There's the car Isabella was driving." His throat tightened so with fear he could hardly speak.

The front edge of the car was dented, but it was nothing like the damage the other vehicle had sustained.

In the beam of headlights, Nino gestured toward a tragic silhouette standing like a lone sentinel near the edge of the cliff. "There she is."

Across the narrow road, Isabella hovered with her arms wrapped around her midsection. Her head was bowed, and her shoulders shook while the wind whipped her scarlet dress around her legs.

"*Grazie a Dio*, she's alive," Lauro said. Too many people had lost their lives over the sheer drops of these treacherous cliffs, which plummeted to a rocky shoreline. Most never made it to the dark waters beyond, falling victim to the craggy descent long before they reached a burial at sea.

On the hillside above them, a light in a villa blinked on, and a man called out. "Anyone hurt?"

Nino flicked his lights in response and yelled from the car window. "We need help. Someone's hurt."

Before Nino could ease to a stop, Lauro flung open the door and leaped out. "Isabella!" Panting with trepidation, he raced toward her, but she threw out her hands.

"No, Lauro, no," she cried out, stepping back toward the edge of the precipice.

Noticing just how close she was sent a chill through him. "I'm not angry, Isabella."

Sniffling, Isabella angled her chin toward the lifeless woman who lay in the old man's arms. "She's dead, isn't she?"

Glancing back, Lauro saw Nino hurry toward the couple. He knelt beside the woman and pressed his fingers against her neck, then lay his ear against her chest. He couldn't hear what Nino said to the old man, but his brother embraced the old man, whose weeping intensified.

"I'm sure she'll make it." Despite his belief otherwise, Lauro forced himself to appear calm. "See? Nino's tending to her." He nodded to the house above them. "A neighbor is calling for help right now."

Isabella shook her head, and her face contorted with a mixture of grief and shame. "I know I killed her," she sobbed, her voice cracking with hysteria. She wavered on the rocky ledge.

"No, no, no," Lauro said. "Please, come to me. Let me hold you, *amore mio*." He took a cautious step toward her. *Must reach her*. Three more paces, and he'd have her in the safety of his arms. Even on this chilly evening, sweat beaded on his brow.

She flung her hands up again. "I can't. I don't deserve your love. Not after this, not after your brother."

"Of course you do."

"No, I don't," she cried, her wail echoing off the mountains. "It was my fault. I crossed the center line. That poor, poor woman." She buckled over with grief, gasping for breath between guttural cries.

When she wasn't watching, Lauro slid a wary foot toward her. *Almost there.*

She turned into the stiff wind off the ocean, her sleek black hair streaming behind her like satin ribbons. One foot slid toward the edge.

"Isabella, I love you. Please don't think of that." He held out his arms to her. "Come back to me. Together, we can work out anything."

As she glanced down, the wind buffeted her slender frame.

"Isabella, please." The wind tossed his words back to him. *No, no, no!* Another step.

She whirled around, teetering on the edge, her scarlet dress billowing like a sail. "Stop. I'm not like you. I can't face it all," she cried. And then she leaned back into the wind, her hair whipping into a dark halo around her fine, anguished features.

With his arms outstretched, Lauro flung himself after her. "No!" Landing just short of her onto rocky ground, he caught the hem of her dress and grappled for her legs. For a moment, he had her.

Then the thin fabric ripped, and Isabella took flight like a wounded bird down the craggy cliff into the blackness beneath him.

"No!" Lauro screamed into the night, but she was gone. He collapsed at the edge of the cliff, his tears staining the thin scarlet fabric he clutched, his trousers torn and his knees bloody.

Minutes later, Carmine and Isabella's father rushed onto the scene.

"Where's my daughter?" Signore Guardino was frantic to find her.

Standing among the rocks at the edge of the sheer drop, Lauro shook his head and shifted his gaze down the cliff. While her father cursed and broke down, Lauro confided in his father that Isabella had stepped off the cliff of her own accord.

"She committed suicide, Papa." His breath came in short gasps, and he choked out his words. "I tried to catch her, but she stepped off the ledge."

Carmine wrapped his arms around him. "Don't tell anyone else that. Not even the police. I'll talk to her parents."

"But that's what happened."

"Shh." His father stroked his back with calming force, but his words were urgent. "Suicide is a mortal sin. If you want her to have a funeral mass and a proper burial, you must say she was thrown from the car. Give her parents that much."

"But the old man knows." Lauro nodded toward the couple. The older woman had regained consciousness. Nino sat with them, monitoring her heartbeat with his fingers wrapped around her frail wrist.

Carmine grimaced. "I'll speak to him. For Isabella's sake, we must never speak of this again. Understand?"

A short distance away, Isabella's father stood at the edge of the precipice. Signore Guardino's large frame dwarfed by the mountains around him. He stared into the void below, silently weeping.

With quiet resolve, Carmine approached Signore Guardino and embraced him. They spoke, although Lauro couldn't hear what was said.

Then his father strode across the road and knelt by the old man. After a few words, Carmine slid a card into the man's breast coat pocket. The old man nodded.

Lauro squeezed his eyes shut. In the end, his papa would pay dearly to protect Isabella's soul, but only Lauro's atonement for her mortal sin would help his beloved reach her heavenly repose.

Isabella was laid to rest the day after Christmas, and Lauro had been consumed with grief. At the funeral mass at the Duomo, he and his parents paid their respects to Isabella's memory and the Guardino family. For all Lauro knew, Isabella's broken mother believed her daughter had died in the accident and not by her own will. Only he and Nino had witnessed the truth of that night.

Nino had left before sunrise that day, neglecting the funeral mass and burial. For all Lauro cared, his brother could leave and never return. If not for him, he and Isabella would be engaged and planning their wedding.

After a restless night filled with despair, Lauro rose and dressed hastily. What he had to do today was crucial—*if* Nino was still here. Filled with rage over Nino's carelessness, he grabbed a pair of leather boots from beside the armoire.

Lauro gazed from the window across the jagged point where Isabella had died, vowing to pray for her soul to pay the penance for his brother's misdeed. He clutched his chest, feeling as if his heart had cracked. After stomping his heels into his boots, Lauro crumpled under a wave of grief. Never would he forget Isabella.

Never would he love another. He crossed himself, ending with a solemn kiss.

How long would it be until he could think of her without feeling such intense longing?

Lauro pushed from the chair, knocking it against the wall. He staggered into the bathroom where he splashed cold water onto his face. Isabella chose to plunge to her death because of Nino, and he would never forgive him for that. His brother would pay for what he'd done to her.

Hastening from his room, he called out for his parents, but there was no answer. He expelled a sigh of relief. During the holidays, a family breakfast and horse ride was a tradition in their extended family, but he'd ignored the early knocks on the door.

Had Nino done so, too?

Making his way through the villa, he spied Nino on the terrace, leaning against the stone wall that enclosed the patio area. His eyes were trained on the cliff beneath them.

Where Isabella fell. Clenching his jaw, Lauro stormed outside. At his footsteps, a seagull startled and lifted off, flapping its great white wings until it was soaring against the brilliant blue sky toward the sea.

Nino turned. His eyes were bloodshot. Had he been crying over her? Isabella was the love of *his* life, not his brother's.

"Thought you had gone riding with the rest of them," Nino said.

"As if nothing had happened?" Lauro gritted his teeth. "You should've paid your respects to her family."

"No one wanted to see me there. But I did send a condolence telegram." Nino spread his hands in apology. "I'm truly sorry. I know how much Isabella meant to you. I grieve for her, too."

Hearing his beloved's name on Nino's lips sent a flash of fury through him, and he advanced toward his brother. "*Bastante!* Don't ever say her name. You don't deserve to even speak of her. Never, you hear me?"

Nino bowed his head against the vitriolic gush.

His brother's passivity was infuriating, and Lauro sliced the air with his hand and cursed. "I thought you'd gone yesterday."

"You mean you'd hoped." Nino brushed sand from the rock wall. "Papa wants me to stay."

"I don't." A surge of anger shot through Lauro, and he could no longer contain himself. "All my life, I've lived in your shadow."

"I can't help it that I'm the older one, but you're closer than a brother, Lauro. You're my best friend. Surely we can get through this." Nino offered an open hand to him.

Lauro ignored his gesture. Nothing would ever be the same between them again. "You said you're leaving."

"A few months ago, I applied for medical school. In Rome, of course, but also to Johns Hopkins in Baltimore, and Harvard in Boston. This is what I really want to do."

"And leave your family? The business that will belong to you?" He let out a coarse laugh. "You'll be rich one day." His words came out more bitter than he'd intended. It wasn't about the money.

As the elder son, Nino had all the advantages. It didn't matter that Nino had little interest in the family business. Someday Nino would lead Cioccolata Savoia, and the family estate would pass to him. Every girl from every good family knew it; every mother had calculated the two brother's disparate worth. *The truth?* Even Signore Guardino would have preferred Nino to him for his darling Isabella.

Nino let out a sigh. "I wish you'd been born first. You have no idea what a burden it is to try to live up to so many expectations. You're the lucky one." His voice changed and became impassioned with possibility. "You can do anything you want with your life. Travel anywhere; marry anyone you want." He paused and shook his head. "Not me. Papa's counting on me to take his place someday. To step into *his* life. Maybe I should stay, but…" His voice trailed off.

"*Now* you develop a conscience. But you're right about one thing. I should be the one running the company." Lauro jerked his thumb toward his chest. "I've always loved it more than you did." *Just like Isabella.*

"You're right. Maybe I'm a self-centered bastard." Nino shifted his remorseful gaze toward the ocean. "I don't belong here. I want to live my own life and make a difference in others' lives."

"Just not your own family's life." Lauro closed the space between them. "Then go. If you stay, I promise I'll make your life hell. Not a day will go by that I won't remind you of what you did to Isabella."

"And I deserve that," Nino said quietly. "I don't know how I can ever repay her death to you, or to her family."

How could Nino be so calm? Fury swelled within Lauro. On impulse, he shoved Nino against the stone wall, clenching the lapels of his brother's jacket in his fists. "I could send you over this cliff right now. But I won't. You're already dead to me. Instead, you're going to leave before our parents come back. And don't bother sending letters or telegrams. I'll see to it that none of them reach our parents. You've hurt them enough already."

Nino gaped at him, speechless, but Lauro wasn't finished.

"Go, live your selfish life. And don't ever return." Lauro released him. "That's how you pay for Isabella's death."

Chapter 22

Amalfi, 1953

"Mommy, here's a good one." Standing on his tiptoes, Marco stretched toward a ripe grapefruit.

"I'll help you," Celina said, strolling toward him in the slanting afternoon sun. They were collecting grapefruit for breakfast and juice.

Many shops in Amalfi closed in the afternoon for a long lunch, so she did the same. She loved having time to meet Marco at school and walk home with him, which she couldn't have done at her old job in San Francisco.

In the weeks since the grand opening of Stella di Cioccolato, the sharp words exchanged between her, Adele, and Sara continued to worry her. One evening after supper, Celina had helped Sara clear the table and followed her into the kitchen to discuss this with her. When she broached the subject, Sara looked appalled.

"We will never talk of this," Sara said with a swift, adamant slice of her hand.

Celina swallowed against the lump in her throat. "I went to see Adele at her boutique."

Concern clouded Sara's face. "Did she say anything?"

"Only that she can't talk about it, and to leave her alone." As angry as Adele had been the day of the grand opening, she had turned equally cool toward her. Celina had been looking forward to working in the shop next to her good friend, but now that was over.

"That's best," Sara said with an implacable expression.

Celina couldn't understand what she had done. "Do you want Marco and me to leave?"

"Not at all, my dear. Carmine would be devastated. Let's carry on, happy as we are. Adele will get over it." She shrugged a shoulder. "Or not. It's her problem, not yours." Sara turned back to her task, ending the conversation.

Mystified, Celina wondered what it all meant. She missed her close relationships with Sara and Adele.

Yet as strange as that shift was, her relationship with Lauro had also changed.

Now, as Celina reached for the grapefruit for Marco, a flurry of leaves rustled behind her, and she whirled around.

Lauro raced to grab Marco around the waist, lifting the boy so he could pick the high fruit. "There you go, my little man."

Marco squealed with delight at the sight of Lauro.

As if trying to make up for his past actions toward her, Lauro had been lavishing attention on Marco, who was thrilled to spend time with his uncle.

"You nearly scared the life out of me," Celina said, scolding Lauro, but she was pleased to see him again. She'd caught herself wondering all day if she might see him again this evening.

Today, he looked exceptionally handsome. He was dressed casually in trousers and a cream sweater that set off his dark hair and olive green eyes.

"Just having fun," Lauro said, giving her a double kiss on the cheeks. This time, however, he lingered, adding a third cheek kiss and pressing his face against hers. "I've missed you, you know. And you smell like chocolate."

"I've been working in the kitchen." Warmth gathered in her chest beneath the lightweight sweater she wore. "And it's only been a day." Yet she'd missed his laughter and company.

While Marco scrambled up a tree, Lauro brushed his hand playfully along her arm. "A day without you is a day that the sun doesn't shine in my life." He grazed her bare neck with his lips.

"Don't be silly," she said with a laugh. "The sun shines almost every day here."

"See? Your magic is working."

Since Lauro worked in Naples at the factory, in the past she'd seldom seen him during the week. Now she noticed that he was joining his parents—and her and Marco—for dinner during the week and staying overnight.

Surely his mother had noticed, too. But Sara had kept up a wall of cordiality that was driving Celina crazy. As warm as Sara had once been to her, she was now a core of ice with a veneer of forced friendliness.

If Carmine was aware of the shift in their relationship, he gave no indication of it, treating her and Marco with the same affection as he always had.

She still had no idea what had brought on the chilly behavior toward her.

Lauro stood with her watching Marco. "I think you need to open a *cioccolateria* in Naples soon. Marco would have a lot more friends."

"Does the competition want to keep an eye on me, maybe steal my recipes?" She loved teasing him. "Besides, Marco likes his school in Amalfi."

"He's a smart boy. How is business at your shop?"

"Actually, better than I thought." She shook her head. "I'll never live down my opening day mistake. A lot of people make a point of asking for chocolates *con zucchero*."

He laughed. "With sugar. The fact that they're joking with you means they've accepted you. Actually, I've heard good reports about the American rock 'n roll *chocolatière*. The teenagers come in to hear Doris Day and Frank Sinatra."

"Not for the chocolates?"

He winked at her. "Better keep that record player spinning with the latest hits."

Marco abandoned the fruit and ran ahead, careening through the orchards, swinging from branches, turning cartwheels, and tossing fallen fruit like a juggler.

"Look at his energy," Lauro said, laughing at Marco's freewheeling antics. "It's good to see him happy."

"He is." Celina was so grateful for her son's new lightness of spirit. Over the last few weeks, he'd shed much of his sadness. "He likes school, and he's made many new friends. Math and art are his best subjects, but his Italian is shockingly good now." She laughed. "Better than mine."

"Children learn languages much easier. And math and art are universal subjects." Lauro nodded thoughtfully. "Italy agrees with him."

"It seems to."

Lauro took her hand and brushed his lips across her knuckles. "How about you?"

"Italy agrees with me very much." His gentle movement stirred her emotions.

Over the past couple of months, they had practiced restraint and had come to know each other more. Lauro was so different from Tony that she could hardly compare them. Yet she couldn't ignore her growing feelings for him.

She didn't mention Sara or Adele to him. Surely whatever imagined slight that was bothering Sara and Adele would soon blow ever. However, once she earned enough money from the shop, she planned to move into a cozy flat. She already had one in mind that had a fantastic view and was in walking distance both to Marco's school and the shop. It was time they had a home again.

"I'm glad you decided to stay." He held her hand as they strolled through the orchard after Marco. "Have I ever apologized for being such a jerk when I first heard about your shop?"

Celina laughed. "Come to think of it, you haven't. You're awfully slow at apologizing."

"Ah, right through the heart that time." Lauro clutched his chest and staggered back. Grasping her hand, he dropped to one knee. "I hereby apologize for hoping you'd leave, and I apologize for any and every jerky thing I might do in the future."

"So eloquent," Celina said, smothering her laughter. "You know that jerky is dried meat, right?"

"If we can get past this language barrier we have, we might have a chance."

He'd been dancing around the subject of the future for a few days. Celina pulled him to his feet and wrapped her arms around him. "What do you mean by that, Lauro Savoia?"

He pressed a hand to his heart. "Just what it sounded like."

Taking a step back, she held his hands at arm's length. "I don't want to hear that unless you're serious this time." Although if she were truthful with herself, that was what she longed to hear. Tony had been gone ten months now—a minute and an eternity.

Love didn't come around that often. Celina couldn't risk such heartache again.

But then, she feared she already had. She waited for his reply.

Losing two men in one year would be almost more than she could bear. She raised her chin to the chill ocean breeze, welcoming the sting on her forehead and cheeks.

Lauro chose his words with care. "You do have a right to know."

What he didn't say sliced through her heart. Foolishly, she had let herself care more for him than she'd realized.

They walked on, with only their footsteps and the distant roar of the ocean to alleviate the heavy silence between them.

Celina shaded her eyes, watching Marco dart after a rabbit.

At last, Lauro spoke. "Some time ago I had dinner with Adele and Werner."

She didn't ask how they were, nor did she mention that she and Adele hadn't spoken since her grand opening party. Adele was assiduously avoiding her. If they arrived at the same time to open their shops, Adele hurried in without even a glance in her direction. Her snub hurt a lot. Adele had always been on her side, and Celina had grown to admire and love her like family. But maybe there was another side to her, too, like so many of the Savoias.

Lauro squeezed her hand. "Adele said something that made me think. She said that Isabella would have wanted me to live a full life. At first, I thought those words were just empty reassurances. I grieved for Isabella, but now I know that grief should not be a way of life. Her memory is with me, as your husband's will always be with you. To honor them is to embrace life as they did."

Celina listened, appreciating that he was sharing his innermost thoughts.

He drew a hand across the panorama before them. "Isabella was like the brightest fireworks in the sky. She exploded onto the scene, scoffing at duty and responsibility. In many ways, I was too staid, too responsible for her. She was a free spirit who abhorred anything that tied her down. She and Nino were alike in that way."

He fell silent again.

Ahead of them, Celina saw Carmine step into the clearing beyond the orchard, and Marco raced to him. Hoisting Marco onto his hip, Carmine stared in their direction, as if noting their intimate posture.

Still clasping her hand, Lauro tucked their hands behind his back.

Carmine waved and ambled toward the villa with Marco.

"Marco loves his *nonno*." Eager to continue their conversation about Isabella, Celina tried to speak as gently as she could. "It was Tony she truly loved, wasn't it?"

"It takes a strong woman to ask that question."

"That was long before we met. It won't change my love for him."

Lauro gazed into the distance. "You can't imagine how devastated she was that night when she saw Nino at the party. She told me she couldn't marry me because of Nino. That's not easy for me to admit, because I thought I was in love with her. But also because I'm the one who usually bears the responsibility for making things right."

"You say that because he left."

Lauro nodded.

"But Tony *was* responsible," she said. "Have you ever thought that he left so that you could fulfill your dreams? That would have been the action of the man I knew." Although it pained her a little to say this, it was the truth.

Lauro took in her words. "In retrospect, I'm not sure if Isabella would have ever agreed to marry me. Her mother might have pressured her, but Isabella did what she wanted. And what she wanted was to burn as bright as she could, as quickly as she could. And she did that."

They came to a rock wall at the edge of the terraced cliff that overlooked the ocean. A wooden bench flanked by raised flower beds rested just inside of the low wall. Lauro guided her to it, and they sat down, watching as the sun slipped toward the horizon.

Lauro trailed his fingers along her arm. "Like Isabella, I've decided I want to live *now*—brightly, brilliantly—with the woman I love by my side. We have no guarantee of days—we both know that, don't we?"

Leaning into him, Celina nodded and gripped his hand. She could feel the intensity of his heart beating against hers.

"In life, the opportunity not chosen fuels regret—it takes bravery to change the status quo and follow a dream." She understood what it took to make a life-changing decision—she'd done that when she decided to stay here.

He circled his arms around her and kissed her forehead.

"Are you sure, Lauro? This isn't just a summer romance?"

"*Quanto ti amo*. Ours will be a romance for every season and all of eternity, *amore mio*. I respect that you're still grieving, but when the time is right, would you consider having me as your husband?"

His words reverberated in her soul. *Ti amo…I love you.* Celina pressed her hand first against her heart and then his, whispering the word he was waiting to hear. "Yes, oh yes." She meant them, perhaps more than ever before. "I never thought I could love again."

As the setting sun bathed them in burnished brilliance, Lauro bent his head to hers and framed her face in his hands. This time, he didn't wait for her to kiss him.

Celina responded to his lips, inviting him into her life. As they molded themselves to one another, there was no doubt in her mind that this was right for them, all of them—for her, for him, for Marco. They would be a family. Somehow, she felt that Tony would approve.

She let herself go in Lauro's arms, reveling in the softness of his full lips and the strength of his embrace. Their lives had magically aligned. A few months ago, she could never have imagined this outcome, but now they were perched on the brink of a new life together.

Throughout the evening supper, Sara was cordial enough, but Celina detected an undercurrent of coolness—not quite hostility, but something had changed. While Sara and Carmine seemed delighted to see Lauro again, she wondered if they were questioning why he'd been spending so much time here.

After Celina put Marco to bed, she returned to the terrace where they had dined. She passed the housekeeper in the hall.

"It's a beautiful evening," Matilde whispered to her. "Lauro enjoys your company. Such a nice young man. If you and Lauro would like to go out, I'll look in on Marco for you."

"That's kind of you, but we hadn't planned on going anywhere."

The older woman's eyes sparkled. "It's a pretty night for a walk. You're young. You should go."

Celina smiled. "*Grazie*."

The older woman nodded conspiratorially and hurried away.

Had they been that obvious?

She paused at the doors that opened out onto the terrace where Lauro and Carmine were discussing the business. When she walked outside, Lauro stopped in mid-sentence and stood up, holding his hand out to her. "Come, sit down. What would you like? A limoncello or amaretto?"

"Amaretto, *grazie*." Though he pulled a chair closer to him for her to sit down, she nudged it a little farther away out of respect for his parents. Would they approve of their relationship?

Sara had been gazing out over the harbor lights. Turning, she said lightly, "You two seem to be getting along much better. I'm so glad to see it."

Celina hardly knew how to respond.

Lauro grinned and touched her shoulder as he rose. "You were right, Mamma. Turns out Celina and I have a lot in common." He brought four glasses and a bottle of amaretto to the table and served everyone.

Sara held her glass aloft. "To Celina, and the success of your new business. Since you've arrived, it's been an interesting journey for all of us."

"And to you, Papa, for holding this family together through everything." Lauro chuckled. "I think you've found your match in Marco. And he adores you."

A fleeting expression crossed Carmine's face. Was it sadness or regret? Celina couldn't tell, but the older man's usual expressiveness seemed subdued.

"One moment, I need to speak to Matilde," Sara said, excusing herself.

Carmine watched his wife walk away. Once she was inside, he turned to Lauro.

"Son, I was watching you and Celina in the orchard this afternoon."

Celina braced herself.

Lauro smiled and shrugged. "Celina was telling me about how well the *cioccolateria* is doing. I'm proud of her."

Carmine nodded toward her. "I'm sure it is. You're a talented woman, Celina, and I like you. I wish Nino would have brought you here sooner so we could have known you better. As for Marco, he is such a gift, thank you. I'm so proud to be his grandfather. That's why it pains me to say this."

"Say what, Papa?"

Carmine passed a hand over his forehead. "Although you and Celina just met, by the laws of the church, you are family."

"Papa, we have a surprise for you and Mamma." Lauro turned to her. "I think we should tell them."

Yet Carmine seemed anything but excited over this potential news. Celina felt a chill course through her.

Lauro tightly clasped her hand under the table.

Tapping his fingers in a V-shape in front of him, Carmine continued. "We both love Marco, the son of your dear brother. Sara would do anything to keep him with us. *Capice*?"

Concern etched Lauro's forehead. "Celina wants to stay."

"Of course she does. Son, your mother is a romantic. I see that she has been encouraging a relationship between the two of you. And this is what has happened."

Celina grew worried as she listened to their exchange.

Lauro's face lit up. "We didn't plan on it, but we feel the same way about each other. I think Nino would have approved. I'll be there for his son forever."

"You can still do that, but this—" Carmine motioned between Lauro and Celina. "This cannot continue. You are family. It's absolutely forbidden in the church."

"That's an old, antiquated belief." Lauro leaned across the table. "It's not for today. Papa, we want to get married."

Carmine slammed the palm of his hand on the table. "Old or not, I will not have you go against the church and dishonor our family name."

"Dishonor?" Her heart racing, Celina squeezed Lauro's hand. "I don't understand."

"I do." Lauro kissed her hand and released it. He rose, smacked his forehead, and paced around the table. "Papa, you can't be serious."

"We are Catholics, and we must abide by the Code of Canon Law." Carmine turned a penetrating gaze on Celina. "You and Nino were married in the church. That forms a line of collateral affinity between our families. Intermarriage is strictly forbidden."

Lauro slammed his fist into his palm.

"I'm sorry," Carmine said to Celina. "As head of this family, it's my duty to tell you. Celina, you and Marco are part of our family, but you and Lauro must not act on your feelings for each other. If you do, it will not end well. Peace in the family is paramount."

"The family?" Lauro cried out. "What about my chance for a family of my own?"

Carmine scowled. "I will not have it any other way."

"But Papa, there must be a dispensation, something you can do."

Carmine rose from the table, his commanding presence signaling the end to the discussion. "Your mother asked the same question. The answer is still no." He left them, intercepting Sara on the way inside the house.

Stunned, Celina sucked in a breath. Her world had been ripped from beneath her feet once again, and she felt herself reeling from her father-in-law's ironclad mandate.

Lauro had a wild look in his eyes. "I've got to get out of here."

"Where are you going?"

"It doesn't matter." He spun around and charged out.

Celina followed him around the side of the villa to the gravel courtyard where his coupe was parked.

Celina reached for him. "I'm going with you."

"No," he cried, brushing her away. "I need to think."

Lauro revved the engine and spun out onto the narrow lane, sending a spray of gravel into the darkness.

As the car passed her, Celina grabbed the passenger door and flung it open, barely managing to swing herself inside.

"What are you doing?" he yelled.

"Not letting you drive like this. Now pull over."

"Get out." He slammed to a stop.

Celina didn't budge.

"Have it your way." He sped off, and as he executed the first hairpin turn, Lauro banged his fist on the steering wheel. "This is the 1950s, not the Middle Ages. They can't keep us apart. Please tell me you won't leave me."

They careened around the curve; Celina braced herself against the force. A tire nicked the narrow gravel shoulder of the road, and the powerful car fishtailed. Yanking on the wheel, Lauro straightened the wheels and jammed the accelerator.

Celina clutched the seat and gritted her teeth. "I don't *want* to leave you." She didn't want to inflame her father-in-law's anger either.

But what kind of love wasn't worth fighting for?

Certainly not the kind she wanted.

She shouted over the wind rushing through the windows and the tires squealing around the turns. "I went through hell when Tony died, and I'll be damned if anyone is going to tell me who I can love now. I don't care about the church, or what your family thinks." The smell of burning rubber assaulted her nose. "Lauro, please, please slow down."

He whipped the car around another curve. "I care. That's part of who we are. But I *will* find a way." He steered hard into another turn.

At once, headlights flared in front of them and tires screeched in the blackened night.

Celina screamed and flung her arms over her head.

Chapter 23

THE WORLD EXPLODED in a wrenching, deafening crash. An eerie, smoky silence ensued, interrupted only by a strange whirring sound.

Dazed, Celina lay on her back, her mind spinning, vaguely aware. The smell of dirt and grass filled her nostrils. Somehow, her feet seemed higher than her head. *How is that possible?*

She felt herself slipping into a sweet void.

Celina, wake up! A disembodied voice boomed in the dark.

Tony?

With great effort, she tried her eyes. *Open*.

Before her, blurry pinpricks of hillside light wavered. She blinked. Stars spun overhead like pinwheels, then slowed and sharpened into focus.

Where am I?

She lay splayed on a hillside, tossed like a Raggedy Ann doll onto a thorny cushion of shrubs and brush. Struggling to turn herself, she rolled to one side. Wretched pain exploded through her body in a blinding flash that robbed her breath. Staggering to her feet, she gasped for air.

Hurry. Tony's presence urged her forward. *Hurry, hurry, hurry.*

Suddenly, clarity seized her. The coupe lay twisted by a tree on the edge of the road.

Lauro.

She scooted down the hill and pounded across the pavement. Ahead on the road, another car was slowing down the incline.

"Help! Stop!"

Reaching the driver's side of the coupe, she flung open the door, heaving Lauro's limp body to extricate him from behind the steering wheel.

Smoke seeped from the car.

Using her body for leverage, she shoved him from the car. He toppled onto the asphalt, a dead weight on the road.

Headlights blinded her. People were yelling in rapid-fire Italian, but she couldn't follow what they were saying.

Smoke invaded her nose and lungs and stripped her of breath. Choking, she leapt from the car and flung herself over Lauro. Wrapping her arms and legs around him, she pushed off the ground to roll him away.

Behind her, the car ignited and then, in a flash, exploded in a shower of flames. Scorching heat lashed at her legs.

Moments later, strong arms reached out and pulled them into cool grass. At once, amid anxious cries, people were upon them, separating them, bearing down on Lauro.

"No, no, no." Celina grasped at Lauro. A stranger's arm curved around her shoulder in support.

She tried to sit up, but the scene around her appeared oddly speckled, wavering before her as everything shaded and went black.

Celina woke on a narrow iron bed in a white-washed room, her head pounding, and every fiber in her body screaming in agony. An antiseptic smell hung in the air, and she blinked against the scorching morning light.

A woman with an apron tied over a white shirtwaist dress hovered next to the bed. She pressed a cold hand to Celina's forehead.

Raising herself on one elbow, Celina tried to call out, but pain shot through her shoulder and she cried out, falling back onto the firm mattress. As murky events of the night before raced through her mind, terror flooded her, and she thrashed against the scratchy, starched pillow.

"No, no, you need rest." The nurse flicked a glass thermometer with practiced determination and inspected it. Satisfied, she held it aloft, poised to take Celina's temperature.

"Wait," Celina cried. "Lauro. Please, how is he?"

Hurried footsteps clicked on the stone floor, and Sara appeared in the doorway.

"*Grazie a Dio*, she's awake," Sara said, rushing toward the bed.

Carmine followed his wife. They wore the rumpled clothes of the night before, and neither one looked like they had slept.

Celina sought answers in Sara's tired face. A vein pulsed in her mother-in-law's forehead. Searching the older woman's weary eyes, Celina silently fought against what she couldn't bear to hear, yet desperately needed to know. "Is he…?"

Sara brought Celina's hand to her lips, kissing it and stroking it. "Oh, my poor, brave girl."

"Lauro is resting," Carmine said, a grave expression on his face.

Exhaling a ragged sigh of relief, Celina let tears trickle onto her cheeks. She brushed them aside, dampening her tangled hair. "How bad is he?"

"Only a few scrapes. A miracle." Sara smiled down at her. "He'll be sore for a while, but thanks to you, he's alive."

"That was a foolish reaction," Carmine said in a husky voice.

"*Bastante*!" Sara shot a stern look at her husband. "What did we agree on?"

Carmine slid a hand over his silver-shot hair and nodded with reluctance.

Sara turned back to her. "Celina, I'll never know how you managed to get Lauro out of that car."

"I, I did?" Bits of jagged memory floated in her mind like puzzle pieces, shifting slowly into place.

Tires screeching. A thundering impact. The blurry night...stars overhead. Then...a blast in the night.

"Oh, good Lord, I remember the fire." She pressed a hand to her mouth.

"You were thrown free of the car. But people in the other car saw you run back to him." With a loving touch, Sara smoothed Celina's hair from her forehead, just as her mother used to do. "My dear Celina, you saved my son's life." Her voice cracked. "That dreadful, horrible curve. That was exactly where Isabella had her accident."

Celina closed her eyes, recalling the rage and disappointment that had boiled through Lauro. The wine and amaretto they had been drinking. The argument he'd had with his father. Carmine's flat denial of their love for each other.

Her stomach roiled, churning against Carmine's decision, and she convulsed. Shielding her eyes from the brightness, she whispered, "Where is Marco?"

"Matilde is sitting with him," Sara said. "Don't worry, he's fine."

"Does he know I'm okay?"

"He was sleeping. Matilde is probably making breakfast for him right now. We'll let her know."

"I need to see him. And Lauro."

Carmine flexed his jaw and got up, crossing the floor. "You'll both come home today."

Home. But for how much longer? She could still feel the tension from the night before emanating from her father-in-law. And she could see it in his tightly drawn face.

Nothing had changed.
His mandate still stood.

Chapter 24

"*BUONGIORNO*," LAURO SAID, grazing her lips. "*Latte*?"

The pink blush of dawn streamed through her bedroom window. Celina stretched and wriggled her nose at the smell of coffee and Matilde's fresh, warm brioche. She was glad to be back at the villa, but she was still incredibly sore from the accident, even after three days. "How did you get in here?"

"You must have left the padlock off the door last night."

"You're not supposed to be in here. Your father—"

Lauro silenced her with a kiss. He wore a bandage across one cheek where he'd hit the pavement, and it gave him a rakish look. "I couldn't resist. You're gorgeous in the morning."

"Mmm, I could get used to this." A sleepy smile tugged at her lips as she breathed in a subtle scent of spiced sandalwood that clung to his white cotton shirt. She brought herself to a seated position and clasped her knees to her chest, acutely aware of her thin silk gown.

Lauro kissed her cheek. "I hope you do."

Remembering Carmine's decree, her smile slipped from her face. "What are we going to do?"

"I have some ideas." Bringing her hand to his lips, Lauro kissed her fingertips. "Why don't we escape and let the fresh air blow through our minds. Will you meet me at the marina in an hour? We can take out one of our boats."

The thought of being out on the ocean sounded like heaven because her life felt suspended in time. Karin was looking after the *cioccolateria* for her. Matilde had been walking Marco to and from school. Celina was beginning to think Matilde had seized on an excuse to take walks during the day. Not that she could blame her; it was such a mild, beautiful climate, and Marco adored her. Celina was grateful to have help. She gazed at Lauro, growing excited at the prospect of being alone with him. "I'd love to go out."

"Sailing or cruising?"

"I love sailing, but with this shoulder the way it is, I'm afraid I won't be of much help." She was still aching from the force of the impact and being thrown from the vehicle.

"Good point. We'll motor along the coastline in the yacht. See you soon."

Lauro kissed her and crept from her room.

Carmine had been watching their every move. She knew that if they violated his order, he had every right to ask her and Marco to leave their home. At supper, she and Lauro had kept a respectable distance from one another. She'd busied herself with Marco, yet she could feel the weight of Carmine's gaze on her throughout the evening.

And Lauro's.

At least Sara's cool attitude toward her had waned considerably. Sara had expressed her gratitude toward Celina for her efforts in saving Lauro in many ways and was treating her almost like a daughter again.

After finishing her latte and brioche, Celina shifted to the edge of her bed, breathing through the aches that slowed her movement. A hot bath would relax her muscles.

She padded into the tiled bathroom and turned on the porcelain hot and cold water taps, adjusting each one to just the right temperature. She poured in a scented mixture made from flower blossoms and olive oil that Sara had left for her and eased in.

Once ensconced in the large claw-foot tub, Celina closed her eyes and let her mind drift. She recalled the uncanny way she had heard Tony calling to her the night of the accident. *Wake up. Hurry.* His voice had been as clear as if he'd been standing over her, and she couldn't dispel the thought that she'd experienced divine intervention that evening. It was as if Tony hadn't wanted to see her lose another man she loved. Somehow, his spiritual will was so strong that it reached across the dimensions, enabling her to save Lauro.

She and Lauro were meant to be together, she was sure of it. But how? To stand between him and his father was a serious issue. Yet, somehow she and Lauro would stand united.

Over the past months as she'd watched Lauro and Marco together, she couldn't imagine a more perfect man to raise her son. And now, she knew in her heart that Tony approved. Surely the church would see the logic in this plan. A man raising his brother's son. Even if she had to plead their case in front of the Pope, she would.

She blinked through tears of gratitude, strengthened in her desire to form a family with the man she'd grown to love. Laughing at herself, she recalled the first time she'd met him in Naples and her distasteful impression of him.

Toweling dry, Celina thought how time and circumstances had shifted both of their perceptions. She brushed her hair into a simple twist and secured it with tortoiseshell combs, leaving wisps around her face.

A half-hour later, dressed in a soft yellow sundress with a lightweight sweater looped over her shoulders, Celina stood at the entry to the marina looking for Lauro. Assorted boats, including sleek Riva, Benetti, and Baglietto yachts, were moored along the wooden pier.

From the deck of a large yacht, Lauro waved, and Celina set off to join him.

They were soon underway. Lifting her face to the soft sea breeze, Celina basked in the sun. She glanced at Lauro, who wore a loose, white cotton shirt and casual pants. The sun glinted off his aviator sunglasses.

"You love being on the water." She hadn't seen him this relaxed since before the accident.

"I grew up on boats." He shook his thick hair in the wind. "Amalfi was a wealthy maritime republic dating to the 7th century. Every year, Amalfi still enters a regatta between the four old maritime republics of Italy, against Genoa, Pisa, and Venice. Nino and I used to row in it. We were fierce competitors."

"I can just imagine that." As they motored along the coast, she marveled at the villages that rose from the water's edge, clustered on cliffs. She pointed to an elevated road that hugged the cliffs. "Is that the corniche route we've taken to Naples?"

Lauro nodded. "The way people drive on that, I think the sea is safer."

She whirled around. "I can't believe you just said that. I've been thinking about the night of the accident. More than anyone, you know how treacherous these roads are. To have driven in the state you were in—angry, intoxicated—"

"I wasn't drunk."

"Even if you weren't, you were driving like a madman. Promise me you won't ever do that again. You endanger innocent people on the road." She folded her arms. "I've already had to identify the remains of one husband after an accident. And your mother told me that was where Isabella crashed."

Lauro rubbed his forehead, letting her words seep in. When he finally spoke, he said, "First, you should know that Isabella did have an accident there, but that's not how she died. She flung herself off the cliff, unable to face her future. But we never speak of it that way. She was given a funeral mass in the church and buried. Papa arranged it."

"Oh." Celina pieced this together, shocked that he'd kept this from her. Yet another Savoia secret. But this one she understood.

He went on. "Forgive me, I'm sorry about that night. Sometimes Papa makes me so angry I go crazy. What right does he have to dictate our lives?"

He doesn't, she wanted to scream. This was more complicated than that. Carmine had brought up valid issues as to why they couldn't marry in the church.

"We need to research dispensations," she said. Surely the church would understand and grant a dispensation after weighing the logic of their request. "Then we can make decisions. But storming off and driving like a maniac isn't going to solve anything."

"You're right, and I'll never do that again." Lauro gave a wry chuckle. "You sound like me. I'm usually the practical one. But I've had enough of doing what's expected of me. What about me? *My life?* When do I get a turn to do what I want? And what I want is you." He took her hand and pressed it against his heart. "I want to marry you. *Quanto ti amo.*"

Bringing his hands to her heart, she murmured, "Oh, my darling. I love you, too."

He kissed her and then motioned ahead. "Here's a good place to talk." After motoring into a private cove, Lauro cut the engine and dropped anchor.

Sheer cliffs rose on either side of them, and high above them fig and olive trees arched over the edges to provide dappled shade. The secret hideaway muted distant sounds of the outside world. Birds chirped above them, and waves lapped in a lazy rhythm against the hull.

"This is utterly magical." Celina breathed in, filling her lungs with calming fresh air.

"I thought we needed a respite." Lauro took off his sunglasses and held out his hand. "Come with me."

After opening a bottle of wine in the galley, Lauro and Celina settled on the deck on a large, cushioned lounge area. He took blankets and pillows from a storage bin, cocooning her in softness.

Feeling pampered, she smiled as he poured red wine, passed a glass to her, and touched it with his.

"Here's to figuring out our lives and regaining our sanity," he said, kissing her.

Celina sipped her wine. The boat's gentle rocking motion soothed the tension she'd held in her body since the accident. "When faced with an insurmountable problem, I always tell myself that there has to be a solution."

He trailed his hand along her arm. "We will find a way to do what makes us happy." Determination etched his face. "Are you as committed as I am?"

"I am, but your father—"

"If he doesn't change his mind," Lauro said, sounding resolved, "I'm prepared to leave Italy to live the way we want. I'm willing to go to San Francisco, or anywhere, with you. We can appeal to another bishop, maybe one in the States. *Amore mio*, I'll do anything to be with you."

She thought about the story he'd just told her of growing up on the water. "But this is your home. You love it here."

"I love you more." He curved his arms around her. "I have spent my life living up to my responsibilities. I've waited my entire life to *have* a life. Now, for us, this is the right thing to do."

"Then I'm the luckiest woman alive, my love." She nuzzled his neck, reveling in the sureness of his embrace.

Lauro ran his hands down the length of her back, and she shuddered against him, feeling the firmness of his physique through her thin dress.

Gently cradling her face, he tilted her chin and caressed her lips with his. "This is how I want every morning of the rest of our lives to begin…soon."

She melted into the reassuring circle of his arms and feathered her fingers along the exposed part of his collarbone beneath his shirt. As she did, she felt his body respond to her touch, as did hers. Her sweater slipped from her shoulders, and she lay against the pillows.

Bending his head, he dragged his lips across her neck, her shoulders, her chest. He held himself above her, passion flaring in his eyes. "How can what feels so right be forbidden?"

She ran her hands through his wavy hair. "I don't see how it can be when two people are in love." Shifting her leg against his, she felt desire building in both of them.

He kissed the length of her neck. "That day in the test kitchen, all I wanted was to show you how much I love you."

Celina ran her fingers along the edge of his shirt and slipped a button free. "Still need this?"

Lauro tossed his shirt aside, and Celina gazed up at him, taking in his well-toned chest and muscular arms. With his bronzed skin and gleaming olive eyes, he was even more beautiful than she had dared to imagine. She ran her hands over his chest, tentatively at first, kissing the bruises he'd sustained in the accident.

A craving for him grew deep within her. How she'd missed the physical touch and lovemaking in her marriage. Tony had been ripped from her so quickly, leaving her cold and lonely, broken and embittered at the unfairness of fate. Today, she needed to feel like a woman again, to love, and to be loved, now and forever, or as long as they might have together.

Lauro's hands were warm against her skin, and she hungered for more. She shrugged her shoulder free from a strap, inviting him in.

Gazing at her with glittering eyes, he whispered, "Are you sure this is what you want?"

"It's what we both want, isn't it?" After the cold dish fate had served her, surely her maker would understand her sweet appetite.

Between kisses and murmurs of love, Lauro took his time peeling off their clothing, pausing to stroke every curve and hollow of her body.

Celina stretched in the filtered sunlight, enjoying the freedom. A light breeze tickled their heated bodies. They came together naturally, twining themselves as one.

"*Amore mio, anima mia*," he murmured, making sweet love to her. He fanned out her hair like a halo and stroked her face. Caressing the length of her body, he whispered kisses over her blazing skin. "How I love dusting you with kisses under golden skies. *Quanto ti amo.* Forever my love, forever."

Reveling in his graceful, sensual touch and sweet, lyrical vow, Celina arched against him, clinging to him until they were both sated with love.

Afterward, they dove into the cool, vivid blue water, splashing like the happiest of dolphins in the secluded cove.

Celina had given her heart, wholly and fully, and herself, without reservation. And yet, as magical as their lovemaking had been, she couldn't help but notice that her neck prickled with prescience, a foreboding feeling that not all was right with her world.

She wondered where they would go from here—and what was to come?

Chapter 25

THE NEXT MORNING, still feeling the heat of Lauro's magnetic touch on her skin, Celina bathed and dressed. After walking Marco to school, she slipped on a lightweight, sleeveless ivory sweater and a flared navy skirt with casual espadrilles. She twisted a twill scarf and wrapped it around her neck, tying the brightly colored silk in a side knot.

Sara had asked her to join her on the terrace this morning for latte and brioche. Though the days and evenings were growing cooler now, the sun was still warm on Celina's shoulders as she strolled outside. Thankfully, Carmine had left, leaving the two of them alone.

"*Buongiorno*. I'm so glad you had time for me today." Sara welcomed her with a casually studied look. Celina wondered what her mother-in-law had on her mind.

Could Sara sense the joy in her heart or the apprehension in her thoughts? Though yesterday with Lauro, in their hidden cove, had been the most glorious day she could recall in such a long time, her pulse thudded with warning.

Her mother-in-law wore a slim taupe dress with a wide black belt. A silk paisley scarf tied at the nape of her neck secured her glossy hair. Gold earrings dangled from her ears, and she'd draped a colorful Murano glass and pearl necklace around her neck. Even in her daily dress, Sara Savoia's high standards were always evident.

"Since you're here today, I thought you could help me sort through some of Nino's old things," Sara said in a friendly manner. "You might want to keep a few mementos for Marco."

"Thanks, I'd like to help."

Celina was relieved that she was back in Sara's good grace. As she followed her through the villa, she thought about all she was thankful for. After Tony's death, when her life was the darkest she could imagine, reaching out to his family had changed her life. What began with a long-distance telephone call led her to a new family and rekindled her heart.

Since her mother was gone, Celina had welcomed the relationship with her mother-in-law. As with any relationship, occasional disagreements were normal, but she felt close to Sara. She would talk to her about the situation with Lauro and Carmine.

Her father-in-law was different. Carmine was the patriarch of the family, the oldest son of his father, who had been the oldest son in his family. Head of the family conglomerate, who employed his son and nephews in businesses his great-grandfather had founded. A man others in the family turned to for advice and assistance. A man unaccustomed to having his decisions challenged.

Could Sara help them, or would the cost to her be too high?

Sara led her into a bedroom Celina had never been in before and opened an armoire.

"For a long time I kept his room just the way it had been when Nino left, thinking that he would return soon." Sara smiled wistfully as she ran her hand over an old jacket. "Recently, Matilde and I found some items that she had packed away."

"Like the wooden train set." Celina smiled, feeling the tension between them dissolving.

"One of Nino's favorite toys when he was young. My father carved it for him. It makes us so happy to see Marco playing with it."

Sara brought out a box of painted blocks. "Marco would probably like these, too."

Celina picked up a worn blue block and rotated it. The initials *A.C.S.* were crudely carved into one side. "He'll be so excited to see these. Anything that belonged to his father he cherishes."

For weeks after Tony died, Marco had slept with a soft, worn flannel shirt that had been one of his father's favorites. Tony's scent clung to the fabric for months. Tracing the block's worn edges, she said, "Just knowing that his dad played with these blocks will make him feel closer to him."

Sara furrowed her brow and gave her a sad smile. "I can imagine how he feels. These toys are a substitute for a relationship that's gone. My grandmother once complained that if we live long enough, we lose most of those closest to us. She called it the curse of old age. I learned that unless one wants to be alone, one has to build new bridges in life."

Celina detected a deeper meaning in Sara's words. "I built a bridge clear to Italy."

"And I'll help you finish that bridge. Any way I can." She pressed her cheek against Celina's. "We are so blessed to have you and Marco. You have no idea what that means to us."

Celina sank into a brocade chair. Carmine adored Marco, but she wondered if his acceptance of her had waned. "Sara, do you think your husband will have a change of heart about Lauro and me?"

"Circumstances might soon change," Sara said, cryptically dismissing the question with a wave of her hand.

Before Celina could ask what she meant, Sara brought out a finely grained wooden box, set it on a desk, and lifted the lid. The slightly sweet scent of olive wood was still apparent. "This is some of Nino's old schoolwork from primary school. And drawings and watercolors."

"That must be why Marco likes to draw."

Sara gave her a sad smile.

Celina lifted a yellowed paper from the box. "His penmanship was—" She stopped. She was going to say *different*. But of course it was. He was a child then.

The letters were straight up and down, lacking the exaggerated right slant to his adult writing. Some letters even tilted a little to the left. The writing was smudged. As she studied it, a dull throbbing began in her head.

Flipping through the pages, she stopped at another piece of paper with strange writing that she couldn't make out. "What's this? It looks reversed."

Sara took the paper from her and smiled. "That's mirror writing. Sometimes he did that when he was a young boy."

"Why?" Celina raised a quizzical eyebrow.

"Some left-handed people can do that." Sara chuckled at a memory. "We always had to be careful where we placed him at the table. When Nino and Lauro were young, they often fought over bumping elbows."

While Celina studied the page, she felt Sara's eyes on her, almost as though she expected her to comment. A sinking feeling gathered in her chest. Tony often bragged that he was ambidextrous, although he wrote only with his right hand. Could he have switched because of an injury? Surely that was it.

She flipped to a typewritten page. "And this?"

"An essay from a summer study program he attended in London. Nino excelled at many things."

As Celina stared at the essay, an uneasy feeling crept over her. The text was so...*eloquent*. That was not a word she would've used to describe Tony, although he was smart. He knew a lot of Latin names of medicines she'd never heard of. "He liked science," she said. "And medicine."

Sara looked at her with a strange expression. "Why yes, he did. He studied biology in Rome, preparing for medical school."

That fit. Celina breathed easier.

However, the fact that she was relieved made her even more anxious. Wasn't she sure of who her husband had been? Surreptitiously, she pressed her fingers against a temple to conceal a throbbing vein.

Sara turned her attention to the wardrobe. "Would you like any of Tony's clothes?" She brought out a finely tailored pair of musty-smelling, light wool trousers.

Admiring the exquisite fabric, Celina reached out to run her hand down the long length of the legs. "He must not have had a chance to wear these."

"Why do you say that?"

Celina laughed. "Because I spent hours hemming his trousers. He was long in the torso, but he always complained about his comparatively short legs. I hope Marco inherits my family's longer legs."

"These fit him perfectly," Sara said softly.

Celina took them from her. She stretched a trouser leg along her arm from her fingertips to her chin, measuring. "No, that's impossible. These must have been Lauro's. They look about the right length for him."

"That's because they wore the same size."

"Maybe his injuries…"

Sara continued to stare at her as if she were waiting.

Waiting for what?

Celina's headache intensified. Feeling suddenly light-headed, she lowered herself onto the chair next to the desk. She stared at the trousers crumpled in her lap, then at the written pages in the box. Passing her hands over her face, she felt as if her carefully constructed world was crumbling.

Sara rested her hand on Celina's shoulder a moment before stepping into the hallway and calling for Matilde.

Celina couldn't hear them speaking in the hallway. Blinking, she had a wild, unbridled urge to find something that had belonged to Tony that would be familiar to her.

There, under the papers she'd looked at, was a worn, leather-bound journal embossed with her husband's name. *Antonino Cesarò Savoia.* With trepidation, she lifted it out and opened it.

The handwriting was in the same strange style, and the entries were written in Italian. Focusing her mind, she began to translate the first entry. In the past few months since committing to spending a year here, she'd been studying the language. Her reading comprehension was far better than her conversational skills. Dissecting the slightly smudged script, she began reading.

> *20 April 1937, Venezuela – Papa asked that I accompany him on his tour of South America this year. He knows how much I want to travel and see worlds different from our own. Here, farmers produce the most exquisite cacao varieties, Criollo and Porcelana. One day, armed with a machete, I helped harvest pods. Incredibly, some trees are more than one hundred years old. The beans ferment in wooden cases for only a few days to protect the delicate flavor. After the beans dry in the sun, they are inspected for quality, and then shipped to our factory in Naples. Tomorrow we will embark for Ecuador.*

Fascinated with the story, Celina flipped through the pages and ran her finger down to other handwritten entries. She had never seen live cacao trees, and could only imagine what an enthralling journey this must have been.

> *12 May 1937, Ecuador – Thus far, it has been fascinating to understand the farming and processing, to meet the farmers who produce our beans, and to learn more about Theobroma Cacao, the tree that produces what the indigenous people here call the "food of the gods." We met a fine man from Germany who facilitates this*

process by writing contracts with many of the local farmers and cooperatives to guarantee prices for their crops.

In the wild jungle, I have found myself strangely more at home than in Italy. After examining the cacao trees here, I talked to farmers about how they avoided and treated plant diseases. They also use many plants that are foreign to us for healing.

Celina could imagine the trip her husband had been on, but why hadn't he ever mentioned it? Particularly knowing how much it would have meant to her. She lifted the journal to continue reading.

30 May 1938, Peru – After a long, arduous journey, Papa led me to a community of cacao farmers in the Andean highlands of Peru where we found excellent, robust Trinitario trees growing on the mountain. What a magical, mercurial part of the world, with a mighty river and majestic mountains that rival the Alps. In the Marañón Canyon, a man could get lost from the world and never found.

Papa told me the story of a rare cacao tree that he fears has become extinct. About twenty years ago, aggressive hemibiotrophic fungi swept through this area, claiming the most delicate and flavorful cacao trees that produced the rare white beans and nearly destroying the cocoa production. Called la Escoba de Bruja, or Witches' Broom, the disease devastated the beans that gave us chocolate with delicate, complex floral aromas and mellow flavors. Alas, we found no sign of survivors.

As in Ecuador, I spent more time with the indigenous people learning about their healing methods than Papa preferred. I also shared ideas from our culture and found the people quite receptive. To me, medicine is more intriguing than cacao beans and chocolate, but as the oldest son, Papa expects me to learn the family business. He has allowed me to study biology because of our business interests, but my heart longs to practice medicine and explore the world, not be tied to a life toiling in commerce. Lauro is much better suited to the family business. If only Papa could see that.

Celina pressed her hand to her mouth. The words wavered and swam before her eyes, taunting her with their veracity. She scanned the journal pages, which included observations and drawings of local plants and the medicinal uses. But in scrutinizing the entries, one aspect of the writing mocked everything she had ever believed, and she could no longer discount it.

Sara's footsteps seemed muffled on the stone floor even before she reached the fine woven rug. She eased herself into another brocade chair next to Celina.

"I see you found Nino's journal," Sara said. "I hoped you would find it interesting."

Celina raked her teeth over her bottom lip and shook her head. "The handwriting..." Even her ability to speak faltered. The writing was a more mature version of his school boy's style with its slight left-leaning script.

It was nothing like her husband's handwriting.

Sara nodded and waited.

"This writing...those trousers..." Celina shook her head, piecing together the clues she'd tried to avoid for so long. "You said Tony spoke Spanish."

"Beautifully."

Blinking back hot tears of frustration, Celina went on. "My husband spoke Italian with some broken Spanish to the Mexicans in Santa Monica and San Francisco, saying the languages were close enough for them to understand him."

She was fluent in Spanish, having grown up in California, so she used to intervene, and they'd argue and laugh about it.

"Maybe he'd suffered some slight brain damage in the war," Celina said, grasping for an excuse, though his technical knowledge of drug terms hadn't dimmed.

Sara made no reply.

"His demeanor was so different than how you've described him." Sucking in a breath, Celina covered her mouth and squeezed her eyes shut.

It couldn't be.

Yet the facts remained. And they'd been there all along.

Chapter 26

As Celina fought the truth that the damning evidence before her confirmed, Sara rested a hand on her shoulder. Struggling to understand, Celina sank her face into her palms.

Matilde hurried into the bedroom and placed two glasses of a strong-smelling liqueur on the desk before leaving.

Sara slid a glass toward Celina. "I thought you might need some grappa."

Transfixed on the indisputable facts before her—the handwriting, the trousers—Celina stared at the clear, numbing liquid that rested in the glass. "That won't solve anything."

Sara leaned in and clasped Celina's hands. "We've been happy, haven't we? Why must we resolve anything?"

With anxiety jittering along her nerves like a thousand tiny insects, Celina sprang from the chair, and the trousers in her lap slumped onto the floor. "You've known?"

"That you were *not* married to my son?" Sara nodded. "Of course. I'm his mother. Though I didn't realize it for quite a while."

"When you did, why didn't you say anything?" Celina's heart pounded as she paced the room. "Why let this…this *charade* continue?"

"By then, we'd fallen in love with you and Marco." Sara's face softened with compassion. "Why not continue as we had been? We all had something to gain. Especially you."

Had Sara thought she was posing as their son's wife for material gain? Celina's knees buckled at this thought. Her words tumbled out, a jumbled mixture of incoherent thoughts.

"I never imagined, I thought...I had no idea. Oh, how did this happen?" Mortified and ashamed, Celina sank to her knees on the woven tapestry carpet and covered her face.

The family that she'd thought she'd found for her son, the life she was building for them here in Italy, the love she treasured with Lauro. All of it was nothing more than an imaginary life, a house constructed on quicksand, now sucked into a void of nothingness.

Nothing.

There were no relationships. No special bonds. No blood relations for Marco.

In terms of family, the woman who sat before her was a stranger.

Celina swung around. "What am I doing here?" she cried out. She was an unwitting accomplice in a dreadful crime. "Please, believe me, I had no idea. I thought my husband was truly your son. I never imagined that he wasn't." Aching to the core of her being, she spread her hands, frantically pleading for Sara's merciful understanding.

As if she could even expect that. She had set forth her husband as this woman's son and impersonated her daughter-in-law. The *real* Nino, for all she knew, still existed somewhere in the world. The enormity of her transgression was beyond her comprehension. Yet, she knew the stabbing pains in her head were nothing compared with what Sara must feel in her heart.

Sara reached for the grappa and drank it down.

"I've made a tragic mistake," Celina said. "My apologies will never be enough."

Pinching her skirt between her fingers, Sara eased to her knees to join Celina on the floor. Wrapping her arms around her, she clucked her tongue, soothing her.

"I didn't think you knew," Sara said, her voice catching. "I know women well. You are sincere, guileless, and unpretentious. You want to believe in the best in people. And you were probably too trusting of the man you married."

Celina pressed a hand to her head. *Who was*...who, *exactly?* Frowning, she tried to piece together the elements. Sara had figured it out, and she must have been privy to this knowledge for some time. "How long have you known? From the beginning?"

"We had our doubts then, of course."

Like Lauro. "Then why didn't you set me straight and send me packing?"

Sara ran a hand along Celina's burning face, taking care to avoid a bruise she'd sustained in the accident.

"You were so genuine. You're a lovely young woman, and Marco—why, Carmine fell in love with him the moment he saw him. Being with Marco has revived Carmine in a way nothing else could have. Your little boy has brought joy to our lives, to our family."

"Marco adores Carmine, too." *And Lauro.* Another wave of emotion crashed over her and a higher level of pain seared through her. "How will I explain this to my son? He'll be devastated."

"You don't have to. Not yet anyway." Sara helped Celina to her feet and into a chair. "Losing Nino nearly destroyed us. Lauro was shattered over Isabella, and Nino couldn't deal with it. He was always...different."

"Lauro told me what really happened to Isabella."

Sara sighed. "We don't speak of it. You're Catholic, you understand. Knowing Nino, I'm sure he thought that by leaving he was doing what was best for Lauro. He probably thought his presence would cause his brother endless pain. And Lauro could hardly bear to speak or hear about Nino for a long time. Though Lauro remained, we couldn't reach inside of him. It was as if we'd lost both our sons." She paused, pressing a hand to her chest.

As a mother, Celina understood. She would give her life for her son, and she couldn't imagine ever losing him.

Drawing herself up, Sara went on. "Nino had gone to America. He became an American and turned his back on his family and birthright. Then the war came, and he volunteered there. Some issues in life are too painful for young men to address. And I'm referring to *both* of my sons. They were strong and capable in so many ways, but not in matters of the heart."

As much as Celina ached, she understood the complexity of Sara's anguish. She touched her hand. "Please tell me more."

Furrowing her brow, Sara continued. "Their feud robbed us, too. Nino was gone. Lauro had vowed to remain true to the memory of Isabella out of remorse. We would never have the beautiful daughters-in-law or grandchildren that light an older person's life with hope. So your call was a miracle. You have lifted us in many ways. You gave closure to Carmine over Nino. The man I fell in love with has finally returned. And so I decided to believe you, too. Life was so much better that way."

"But you knew."

"I couldn't be sure. Not until the night you served strawberries."

Celina tilted her head, bewildered. She replayed the evening in her mind. "I talked about Tony and Marco and strawberry ice cream at dinner." She recalled what Sara had said to her in the kitchen. It hadn't made sense to her then. It still didn't.

"I don't understand," Celina said. "What was wrong with the strawberries?"

"My son was highly allergic to strawberries." A pensive look flitted across Sara's face. "Men might forget details like that in time, but mothers don't."

"The strawberries… Did Adele know?"

"Lauro can eat all the strawberries he wants, but Adele is allergic to them, too. At your opening party, she couldn't eat them, of course. When you said they were Antonino's favorite, she remembered the time they'd both attended a birthday party where they'd eaten strawberries and broken out with itchy hives. Their throats became tight and their tongues thickened. My sister and I raced them to a doctor."

Celina's cheeks burned with shame. "So Adele believed Lauro. He'd once said I was an imposter. As it turns out, he was right." Now she would have to tell him.

Her anguish ratcheted up, she reached for the grappa and swallowed it in one gulp, welcoming the burn in her throat. If only it could alleviate the pounding misery in her head. At best it might dull the edge of her pain. Temporarily.

"Adele wanted to confront you that day, but I forbade it." Sara's voice took on a stern edge. "We argued. I told her it was a matter for our family to address alone. She was not to discuss this with anyone, not even Werner."

Celina gnawed on her lower lip, tasting remnants of the strong liqueur. "And now we are."

"Yes." Sara closed the lid to the wooden box. "Your Tony sounds like a wonderful man who loved you and Marco. Though I wish you'd known my Nino, you must be thankful for having had a good man in your life."

A thought formed in Celina's mind. "You've known about this, so why today?" She waved her hand over the trousers and the wooden box of papers. "You wanted me to see this evidence and realize the truth."

"I didn't know for certain that you hadn't come to the same conclusion, but it was only a matter of time before you did." Sara leaned forward with urgency. "I've watched the way you and Lauro look at each other. I've known he was attracted to you from the day you arrived. He's never loved another woman as he loves you, even if he thought he was in love with Isabella." She shrugged. "They were so young, and she was a spoiled, impetuous girl who never would have made him happy, though I was heartbroken for her family."

"Carmine won't allow us to be together."

"That's why we had to talk today," Sara said, her voice taking on a conspiratorial edge. "You and Lauro are needlessly suffering. Don't you see?"

"I'm not following…"

"The Code of Canon Law is only applicable if you were married to *Nino*. Lauro's *brother*. Even if you don't know who your husband was, I think we can prove that he wasn't Nino."

Another stabbing pain streaked through Celina's head, and she turned up her palms. "Oh, for God's sake, who *was* I married to?"

Sara grabbed her hands. "It would help if you could find something that proved who he was, or if he had friends you could ask. But I think Adele would be willing to testify. Take advantage of her anger. Eventually, maybe she'll forgive you."

Celina gazed at Sara, astounded at the incredible acts she was asking her to undertake.

"You have to face reality. If you love Lauro, this is the only way to persuade his father. Then you can be married in the church."

"I don't know if we're ready." Celina shook off Sara's hands and stood up. "But when we are, we don't need anyone's permission to be married. We can go to the courthouse and have a civil marriage."

Sara rose, horrified at the suggestion. "That is not a sanctified marriage."

"Does it matter anymore?" Celina was overwhelmed and tired. All she wanted was to be with Lauro as they had been in their hidden cove. *Happy and free.*

"Don't do that to your children," Sara snapped.

"You're only concerned about your grandchildren," Celina shot back. "What about your son's happiness?"

"This is about honor and your relationship with the church, the community, and your family. Trust me; it's better this way. What happened was just a mistake. It was your husband's fault."

"Who will believe that? Everyone will think that I was an imposter. And as of right now, I am, because I know the truth."

"Please don't."

Celina whirled around. "And Lauro, what are the chances that he'll believe this story?" She stormed from the room, but as soon as she reached the doorway, she shrieked.

Lauro was standing just outside the door, his dark eyebrows drawn together. "What's going on?"

How much had he heard?

This was not how she wanted him to learn of this news, which had just slashed her heart and ego to shreds. She needed time. *Time to regain strength.* Feeling deeply ashamed and unable to face him, Celina pushed past him and raced outside.

Chapter 27

Celina rushed outside, her head aching from the onslaught of indisputable facts. As she raced from the villa, her espadrilles slipped against the rocky exterior gravel, rendering her unsteady.

She was drowning; her life had just capsized on the open sea, and she had no life preserver, nothing to lash herself to against the crashing waves of truth.

She had no idea know who she'd been married to, or who Marco's father was. Were there two men named Antonino Savoia? Possibly, but this Savoia family was not the family of her husband.

They were strangers.

Why had Tony told her they were relatives? To impress her? Or had he known that the real Antonino was missing? With her head throbbing in agony, she started down the hill, her shoes slapping against the pavement. Desperate for time to sort out her thoughts, she decided to walk to Marco's school to wait for him.

Overhead, clouds blocked the sun, and Celina shivered, brushing her bare arms. She hadn't taken the time to get a jacket, but she didn't care. She only wanted to distance herself from this disaster. Maybe she'd wake up and discover this had been a nightmare.

But no, she recognized the truth deep in her being. Once she reflected on the clues that had been there all along, she knew that Sara spoke the truth. Perhaps she had been scared to examine the little discrepancies, too afraid to acknowledge facts that didn't align in the *dolce* world she yearned to live in.

The chill air slapped her skin, awakening her nerves with a thousand excruciating pinpricks that heralded The Truth.

Had she been selfish? Perhaps, though not for the trimmings of wealth, but for the love and comfort of family. In the beginning, she had acted out of a sense of duty to Tony and his family. She had been motivated more for Marco than herself. Until Lauro had illuminated the dark wasteland of her heart.

Had love masked the persistence of facts right before her?

A whirlwind of questions, churning like autumn leaves, swirled through her mind. How would the truth affect the love Lauro professed for her? How would it affect every other person in the Savoia extended family, from Sara and Carmine to Adele, Werner, and Karin? Even the villagers of Amalfi, Marco's teachers, and friends, and patrons of her *cioccolateria*.

She would be branded a liar.

An imposter.

An opportunist.

This wasn't who she was.

Yet, a tiny, mean-spirited voice inside of her disagreed.

Had she been a willing accomplice in her husband's deception by ignoring the signs for convenience and continued acceptance?

And could she be forgiven for that?

Maybe, but nothing in her life would be as it had been before. This realization lit a thin fuse of fury in her.

Staggering under the weight of this revelation, she stumbled to the edge of the lane under a gnarled olive tree and sank to her knees, broken and sobbing. Above her, even the sparrows chattered their reproach. She had worked tirelessly to make a life for her son and herself. Never had she consciously meant to harm anyone or set herself out to be anything she thought she wasn't. How dare Adele or Carmine accuse her of such treachery?

The sputtering fuse of anger sizzled within her. She wiped her eyes.

Her husband *had* been a decent man, not a swindler or con artist, yet here she was, victimized by his actions. But she still had a choice. She could succumb to victimhood, or she could rise with strength and dignity, just as she had when he died, or when she decided to come to Italy, or open her shop. She curled her fingers and balled her fists.

Despite her misery, the fuse was lit, empowering her with fiery determination. She would follow it wherever it led.

Footsteps behind her, and she whirled around.

Lauro.

"*Amore mio*," he murmured. He knelt beside her and swept her into his arms.

Under the silvery gray boughs of the ancient olive tree, they held each other. In his tender embrace, she felt strength emanating from him, though for all Celina knew, this was the last time she would hold Lauro in her arms. Finally, she lifted her face to his.

"I'm so sor—"

"Shh," he said, pressing a finger against her lips. "You have nothing to apologize for. This doesn't change my love for you. You honestly thought your husband was my brother. I believe you."

At his words, relief coursed through her. *He believed her.* She was sure she could figure out everything else, but where to begin? "I never had a reason to doubt my husband's identity. He had his military identification and his dog tags. How would he have gotten those?"

"Maybe he stole them or bought them on the black market. Or they were counterfeit."

Celina bristled at this. "My husband wasn't a criminal. He was a fine, educated man." Even if he were a little rough around the edges.

"I didn't say he was, *cara*." He kissed her forehead. "During the war, many people had forged documents, for whatever reason. Often to protect themselves and their family."

"He told me he was part of the Savoia chocolate family." Or, had he only agreed when someone said it? She couldn't even recall now.

"Did you ever meet any of his family?"

"Only once. When we visited Santa Monica, he said he needed to visit his uncle." She pressed her temples, trying to recall the day. "He had just moved into a small bungalow not too far from the beach. Tony asked me to wait in the parlor while they spoke first. Then I met him."

"What was his name?"

"He introduced himself only as Art."

Lauro sighed. "That's not much help."

"But while I was waiting, the day's post was delivered through the slot in the door. I picked it up and put it on the sideboard for him. The letters were addressed to Arturo Romani. I remembered because his surname was so similar to mine."

He enveloped her in his arms. "We can start there."

"No, we can't. After Tony died, I tried to call him. His telephone number was listed in the telephone directory, but when I dialed the number, it had been disconnected. I mailed a letter, but I never received a reply."

Arturo had been such an old man, she'd assumed the worst—that he had passed away, too.

"We only visited him once. After that, Tony never had anything else to do with him. He said something about a falling out. I didn't press the issue." She'd learned not to press her husband for answers. When she would ask about his family, he often exploded. As long as she didn't broach the subject of family, Tony was generally happy.

Now, she knew better.

At that recollection, fresh tears burst through her new resolve. There *had* been earlier clues. And she'd ignored them to maintain a peaceful home life. But she'd had no idea that he wasn't who he said he was. Her anger against Tony—and herself—rushed back and she gripped Lauro's jacket lapels.

"Whatever happened in the past, I trust you," he said, rubbing her back. "I know you're not a fortune seeker out to defraud our family."

Outraged, she looked up at him. "That you mention that at all is proof that you thought of it."

"Those weren't my words, or even my mother's. But consider this, if your husband died, my brother could still be alive. Don't you see? We haven't lost anything. We're back to where we were before you came. And with both of us, we can double our efforts."

"I promise to do whatever it takes to help you find Nino." Even as Celina uttered these words, another thought occurred to her. If her last name wasn't Savoia, then what was it? Who had she been married to all these years? And who was Marco's father?

She gazed into Lauro's eyes and saw the commitment he had to her. Still, she had other issues to consider. "How will I ever explain this to Marco?"

"He's young. Will a few days matter, or do you have to go into detail right now?" Lauro wrapped his arms around her and swayed. "When you're ready to explain, I'll be there with you. I don't want him to feel abandoned. He's part of us going forward. We're going to be a family, Celina. I'm more determined than ever."

"Those are the kindest words I've ever heard."

"It's true. And the best news is that now my father can't use some outdated Catholic canon to forbid our marriage."

This thought eased Celina's mind a little. But she had an unsettling feeling that Carmine might have another, even stronger reason now.

Chapter 28

San Francisco, 1945

As soon as Tony cleared the troop ship, he knelt and kissed the ground. After a long tour in the Pacific theater that included the Philippines, all he wanted was to feel *terra firma* under his feet and have an authentic Italian supper. But first, he craved a well-deserved libation to celebrate his homecoming.

Unlike some of the guys, he had no perfumed sweetheart throwing herself into his waiting arms, no family cheering as he disembarked. Antonio Baldini was nearly alone in the world.

Other buddies had crowded into the first cheesy dive bar they found on the docks, but Tony wanted his first celebratory drink back on American soil to be special. Although he was proud of his service, he'd waited a long, long time for this moment.

While the Iowa and Nebraska farm boys on the corner were trying to figure out where to go, Tony shot out his arm and whistled for a Yellow Cab. "Just like back home in New York." He grinned and slid into the back seat. "Take me somewhere classy. Not the joints around here."

The taxi driver glanced in his rearview mirror and then did a double take when he saw Tony's scarred face. "Rough service, kid?"

"Don't feel much like a kid anymore," Tony said, drawing a hand over the ugly scars on his face. Sure, he was self-conscious sometimes. Who wouldn't be? But he was damned lucky to be alive. Instead of turning into a wallflower—not that he'd ever been that—and hoping no one would notice him, he was determined to make the most of the life he had left.

He had plans. Big plans. For sure he had the moxie, but at this moment, he had no idea how to make his plans happen—or keep himself out of danger. He'd joined the army in '41 right after Pearl Harbor to escape a risky situation that wasn't going to end well for him—one way or another.

Never again.

Before that, he'd poured his heart into going to college and making something of himself—what were the odds of anyone getting out of the tough neighborhood he'd been born in? But he'd done it.

For a while.

As the driver shifted into gear and eased into the dockside traffic, Tony stretched his legs in the back seat. "How about Nob Hill? I heard the Fairmont is pretty ritzy."

"For a young guy like you?" The cabbie shrugged. "It's had its day. Lot of old folks there now. Say, need some new threads? Got a cousin with a shop off Union Square. Fix you right up."

"Maybe later. Any swell places to get a glass of champagne?" Yeah, that's what he'd start with.

The driver pushed his flat wool driving cap back from his forehead. "Well, la-di-da," he said, chuckling. "Bubbly's pretty rare, what with the war in France. But we got good wines out of Napa and Sonoma valleys, just up the road. That or beer. I got a beer budget, know what I mean?"

Tony watched the city unfold before him, amazed at the gaily painted Victorian architecture and sparkling blue bays. The mighty Golden Gate Bridge soared above it all, connecting two rich bodies of land. *What a city.*

The cab driver turned onto Market Street. "How's the St. Francis Hotel? Fancy bar there. Lots of classy dames."

"That'll do." Tony eased back. That's exactly what he had in mind.

He'd keep a low profile here on the west coast until he figured out if it was safe to return to New York.

He had tried to leave his old gang behind. He'd juggled three soul-destroying jobs while studying to be a pharmacist. After graduation, he'd scraped together the money to open a new pharmacy with a partner near his old neighborhood. However, that money came at a big cost and the well-organized gang had a long memory.

One night, when he had tried to resist his old gang buddies who had turned up demanding drugs and cash, they'd cleaned him out and left him reminders—his permanently droopy eye and a slashed eyebrow. Soon he discovered that if he wanted to stay alive, he had to do what they wanted and supply them with drugs.

Tony hated his duplicity. Worse, his partner confronted him. Volunteering for the war effort provided a quick way out of a hot mess.

He wasn't anxious to return now. There had to be another way, another place, to build a life. He stared out the window. San Francisco looked pretty good.

After the taxi driver let him out, Tony strolled under the big clock at the St. Francis Hotel and into the lobby bar. Still wearing his officer's uniform, Tony hadn't even gotten to the bar when a man in a similar uniform offered to buy him a drink. Battle scars probably brought on pity. He'd gotten plenty more of those in his military service.

"What're you drinking?"

"I'm celebrating," Tony said. "Champagne."

"I like your style." The man spoke to the bartender.

Tony settled for a bubbly white wine from California, though he couldn't tell the difference. *Damn, this is good.*

"Just returned two weeks ago myself," the man said. Tall and well proportioned, he held himself with an aristocratic bearing and took a genuine interest in Tony.

Tony could tell this man had real class. "You're Italian, too, right? Tony's my name."

The man smiled. "Friends call me Doc."

"You a doctor?"

"I was in medical school when I decided to enlist and serve a greater, more pressing need. Were you in the Pacific?"

Tony nodded. "You?"

"Most recently. Do you have any plans for civilian life?"

"Besides a good Italian dinner tonight? Just the American Dream, my friend. Like every other guy coming home."

Tony had big goals, but he needed a safe place to work. If he couldn't make that happen back in New York, maybe he'd stay here. Meet a beautiful woman, get married, have some kids. Build a business, buy a home. A fresh start, that's what he wanted. But he'd heard the gangs had west coast operations now. Would he be safe anywhere?

Tony sipped his drink. "So how about you? Staying here?"

Doc shook his head. "It's time to move on."

"Awfully nice here. Where you headed?"

"I like to travel. I'm leaving for South America."

Tony let out a low whistle. "Brazil, Argentina? Beautiful women, I hear."

"You seem to have good taste." Doc chuckled and drained his glass. "I had something else in mind."

"No kidding? What?"

Ignoring his question, Doc stroked his chin. "I know a good restaurant in North Beach, Fior D'Italia on Mason, if you like the food of northern Italy. Should be able to get in tonight."

"As long as they serve *osso buco* and a good Barolo wine, count me in."

"Indeed they do," Doc said as he paid the bar tab. "On the way, I'll introduce you to the best chocolate maker—a *chocolatière*—in San Francisco. I want to visit one last time before I leave."

"So you're serious."

"Tomorrow morning. My passport's ready." He tapped his breast pocket. "I'll share my plans with you over dinner."

Chapter 29

Naples, 1953

When Celina entered the café, Lauro's heart leapt at the sight of her. The thought that his father might banish her once he heard the truth had kept him up all night with worry.

Celina lifted her hand and smiled when she saw him. She wore a white cotton shirt with a navy skirt, and a wide red belt cinched around a waist so slim he could span it with his hands. Navy peep-toe shoes teased him, and all he wanted to do was slip those off. At her neck, she had twisted a silk scarf and flipped up her collar. With her dark sunglasses pushed up over her thick blond hair, she could pass for a film star.

But Celina meant more than that to him. He blew out a breath, recalling how beautiful she had looked under dappled sunlight in their hidden cove, where she came to him as naturally as if they had always been meant for each other. Now, he *needed* her in his life. Surely his father would relent once he heard the news. But he had to be sure. Celina had been through a great deal in her life; he couldn't bear to see her hurt again.

Lauro stood to greet her and leaned in to kiss her. A light scent perfumed her hair and neck; he lingered beside her, a breath from her skin, inhaling her essence and aching with longing for her.

He felt his mother's eyes on them. Quickly, he greeted her and pulled out chairs for the two women.

"I thought this was the best place to meet," Lauro said, leaning across the table. He'd asked his mother and Celina to meet him in Naples for lunch to make sure they agreed on how to inform his father of Celina's revelation. Most of the shops in Amalfi closed at midday, and shopkeepers joined friends in the cafés or climbed the steps to prepare lunch or have a nap.

"I left early," Celina said. "Karin will take care of opening the shop after lunch. She's extremely responsible."

Sara nodded. "I told your father I was going shopping in Naples and joining my sister for lunch. The one he dislikes." She removed her white gloves and slid them into her sturdy handbag.

After a waiter took their order, Lauro began. "Papa is already against us, so first we need to show him how this shocking news is actually to our family's advantage. Because Nino might still be alive."

"I pray he is," Sara said. "We had lived with hope for such a long time that to finally mourn his death was a release. But if he might still be alive, then we have hope again."

Lauro exchanged looks with Celina. He'd thought about how this news would reopen wounds.

"This paves the way for Celina to become a real part of the family." Sara smoothed her hand across Celina's. "I'm being selfish. I don't want to lose you and Marco. You and Lauro love each other. You should be planning your future." She shot a look at her son. "That idea should come from Carmine, though. He's the head of the family, and he'll want to think it was his idea."

Celina arched an eyebrow. "How will we manage that?"

"I've been doing it all my life," Sara said.

"I have to agree," Lauro said with a chuckle.

His mother gave him a modest smile and met Celina's gaze. Lauro swung an admiring glance between them.

The two women who sat before him were the strongest, most resilient women he knew. People often said that men married women who reminded them of their mothers. In his case, it was true. His mother had been there for him when Isabella died and when Nino disappeared—and now, with his future in danger.

"Leave it to me to start the conversation," Sara said, touching her sleek brown chignon.

"About this plan," Lauro said. "I don't think Celina should be in the room when we tell him."

"I can bring it up with him in private," Sara replied. "If he's hurt by the news, and I imagine he will be, his pride will never allow him to show it in public. I fear what he might do."

"I know, but I want to be there, Mamma," Lauro said, draping an arm around Celina. "This is my future—our future—and I want to make sure he understands how this is an advantage to the family."

"He will," Sara said. "Your father takes his responsibilities seriously. He tries to puts the good of the family first."

Lauro noticed that Celina was frowning. "What's your thought?"

"I should be there," Celina said, looking directly at him with her clear tawny eyes. "As much as your father adores Marco, I'm the problem."

Lauro ran his hand along her forearm. "I think you're the solution."

Sara shook her head. "She's right. Your father has his mind set against Celina now. I'm praying for a miracle."

Supper at the Villa Savoia began on an even more subdued note than usual. Celina was sure that Carmine knew something was amiss, though he probably thought it had to do with his decree that she and Lauro cease their romantic relationship.

Nevertheless, Sara had prepared a lavish seafood dinner with *aragosta,* which was Carmine's favorite, along with Falanghina wine. Celina could tell he enjoyed it, and his dark mood began to lift. Perhaps women of Sara's generation had to resort to less direct methods, but she'd made up her mind that she would not have that kind of relationship with Lauro. Theirs would be a modern partnership of equals. Celina glanced at Carmine. Still, Sara's pampering and flattery seemed to work on her husband, and by the end of dinner, he was in an excellent mood.

After the meal, Carmine excused himself. Sara followed and stood by the dining room fireplace, looking regal in a vibrant dress of violet crepe wool and a strand of natural white pearls. Her dark hair was drawn from her face, framing a look of determination.

Smiling, Sara lifted her chin with confidence. "Lauro and Celina, would you excuse us for a moment? I want to speak to my husband."

Lauro sprang from his chair. "Mamma, I must speak to Papa, too."

Yet his mother would not be dissuaded. "Leave this to me. I know my husband."

While Lauro and Sara spoke, Celina fidgeted. Planning for this night, she had prepared an early meal for Marco and put him to bed before the later evening meal. She was as ready as she would ever be to face Carmine.

"Excuse me, but this is my mess," Celina said, standing up. "I'm the one who needs to break it to him."

Lauro and Sara exchanged concerned looks.

"Maybe you're right," Lauro said, slowly.

"And brave," Sara added.

Lauro shook his head. "*Amore mio,* you don't have to—"

"No. I do." Celina could never respect herself if she didn't confess to Carmine. She sat still while they waited.

When Carmine returned, he was chuckling to himself. "I stopped to check on Marco. I pulled up the boy's covers and told him good night, *'Buonanotte, ti volgio bene.'*" Carmine was beaming now. "Do you know what he did? With his eyes closed, still sleeping, he repeated after me. *'Buonanotte, ti volgio bene anche io.'* Perfect little accent, too."

They all laughed with him, but Celina was preparing herself.

Sara suggested they move into the living room, where Matilde had laid a fire for them in the arched stone fireplace to chase away the evening chill.

Sara began, "My dear, I know how concerned you are about Lauro and Celina, but Celina has something to share with you. We should all sit down."

Carmine stroked his chin and motioned for Celina, who remained standing, to go on.

"There's been a mistake." Celina spoke with a strong, clear voice, praying that he would listen without prejudice.

While she was aware that there were no words to adequately convey the enormity of this error, she also knew that this resurrected the hope that Nino was still alive. Tamping down the terror that threatened to seize her, she met Carmine's studied gaze. This powerful man—who protected his family at all costs—stood between her and the future she held so dear.

"I found..." She stumbled on her words, but as she thought of Marco, Lauro, and Sara, she found the strength to steady her voice. "Sara shared Nino's journal with me. I read his entries about a trip the two of you took to South America. Not until then did I grasp what happened. His handwriting revealed the secret my husband had kept from me."

Spreading his hands in front of him, Carmine surveyed the anxious group seated before him and spoke in a quiet, deliberate manner. "Which was what?"

Celina observed him carefully. Although Carmine's jovial mood was subdued, he was still pleasant. With nervous perspiration gathering around her torso, she pressed on.

"My husband was not the man I thought."

Carmine chuckled. "Few of us are. Ask my wife."

Sara smiled at him. "Go on," she said to Celina.

Glancing at Lauro for strength, Celina forged onward on the path she had cleared. She told Carmine about Tony's duplicity and her sincere belief that he was their son, Antonino.

"When I called you, my only thought was of my duty to tell you of your son's death. I didn't want anything from you then, and I still don't." A small chance that Carmine would understand still existed, but as Celina looked at him, that chance was rapidly dwindling.

Before Celina's eyes, Carmine's expression morphed—from that of the doting grandfather to the powerful head of the Savoia family. His smile dissipated.

"And that's all I know," Celina finished. "You have my most sincere, respectful regrets." With her heartbeat drumming in her ears, she sat down.

Lauro threaded his fingers through hers and gripped her hand in solidarity.

"I'm sure this was not Celina's fault," Sara said in a conciliatory manner.

Carmine glared at Celina.

The weight of his stare was staggering. Celina met his gaze, but she could hardly breathe, waiting for his response.

Carmine didn't scream, didn't pound the table, didn't break down. He glared at her with calm fury as she had never before witnessed.

At last, he spoke.

"*This* is what you bring me?" Carmine's measured words were chilling. "You have deceived me and those I love." He spread a hand toward the others. "My family. They are my most precious possessions in life. You brought deceit, anguish, and heartbreak to us. Because of you, we mourned the death of our dear Nino."

Celina shuddered, recalling the grief she'd felt over Tony's death. If only she could turn back time and spare them.

Carmine pressed his hands together and went on. "You did this for what, the money? Such temerity," he said, spitting out the word. "And now, with your husband gone not a year—not that I trust that now—you have the audacity to say you love Lauro. How utterly brazen of you. As the head of this family, tell me, what would you have me do?"

Lauro squeezed her hand, and Celina could feel his love behind this small movement.

More than anything, Celina wanted to be part of this family, to love and to be loved, to be accepted. To watch Marco grow surrounded by his family. To love Lauro, the man who believed in her. Nothing more, but this was everything to her.

Yet she would never have any of it.

Carmine will never allow it. Never permit her or Marco to be any part of the Savoia family. She could see it in his eyes—she was already dead to him.

She had caused this family immeasurable grief. As much misery as she felt now, churning inside of her. Riddled with guilt, she stole a glance at Lauro. He might think he loved her, but if he dishonored his father, it would eat away at him for the rest of his life. Maybe that was why Nino had never returned.

There was only one way to settle this with Carmine. And she couldn't do it here.

Celina let go of Lauro's hand and rose from her chair, summoning the last of her energy to face Carmine and do what she knew she must to follow the fuse that sizzled inside her.

"You won't have to do anything," she said, trying to maintain her dignity while everything inside of her shattered. "Marco and I will leave for San Francisco tomorrow."

Amid gasps from Lauro and Sara, she left the room, the crack of her heels echoing through the hallway like stabs to her already wounded heart.

By sunrise, Celina deposited the last of her luggage by the door. She had stayed up most of the night packing the clothing and personal items they had brought with them. The clothes from Adele she left in the bureau. She wanted no souvenirs, no reminders of her time here, save her precious memory of Lauro and their secret cove.

Last night, Lauro had followed her and tapped on her door, but she refused to answer.

She couldn't bear it.

Marco still slept. He would not be happy—indeed, he would be devastated, but he was young and resilient. And she'd nursed his fragile feelings through tragedy before. *We'll be okay*, she told herself, willing it to be so. They still had a life in San Francisco, or maybe somewhere else. She stepped onto the terrace to clear her mind with fresh ocean air.

At the click of the door, Lauro turned his face up to her. He stood in the garden just beneath her balcony. His face was drawn and tired.

She stepped back.

"Please, wait."

Under the dawning sky, she whispered to him. "What are you doing here?"

"I've been waiting all night. You can't go, Celina."

"You know I'm right." She could hardly bear to face him without breaking down.

Lauro spread his arm wide. "What do you expect me to do?"

"Just take us to the train station in Naples today."

"*Amore mio, no.* Please, don't. *Ti amo.*"

Celina hurried inside to wake Marco. In his sleepy state, she told him they needed to return to San Francisco. "Mommy has to do something very important."

Rubbing his eyes and clutching Rocky, his beloved sock monkey, he said, "When are we coming back?"

She couldn't answer him. She had no idea how long it would take her to find out what she needed to know.

If she ever hoped to return, it was her only chance.

Lauro drove them to Naples in Sara's sedan. Just as when they had arrived in Italy, they spoke little. Even Marco was subdued, gripping Rocky and gazing out over the ocean.

Lauro parked at the busy *Napoli Centrale* train station. Before getting out of the car, he covered her hand with his, brought it to his lips, and kissed her palm. "Won't you reconsider? You don't have to get on the train."

"Yes, I do," she said, her heart breaking. The feel of his lips had been almost more than she could bear.

After arranging tickets for them, Lauro carried their luggage and walked them to their train. She and Marco embraced Lauro for the last time on the departures platform.

His eyes rimmed with red, Lauro crushed Marco to his chest. "I will see you again, *dolce creatura*. Soon, I promise." He looped a canvas bag that held something bulky over the boy's shoulder.

"Mommy, we *are* coming back," Marco cried. "When?"

Celina shook her head at Lauro, who responded with a pleading look. She fished the key to Stella di Cioccolato from her pocket and pressed it in Lauro's hand. "The rent is paid for three months. Tell Karin she can run the shop. Or close it."

"You'll come back to it," Lauro said with conviction.

Celina couldn't answer. She didn't know if she would ever return.

He enveloped her with an embrace that nearly took her breath away. "I cannot live without you," he murmured.

Holding him, she tried to memorize the feeling of being in his arms. The steady rhythm of his heartbeat, the spicy scent of his skin. How his muscular arms held her with such strength and tenderness.

Consumed with guilt over the emotional devastation she had inflicted on Lauro and every member of the Savoia family, Celina pressed her hand against his heart. *Can I assuage their grief, can I make this right?*

She brushed her lips again his, blinking back threatening tears. "When I'm back in the States, I promise, my love, I will find out what happened to Nino. I will find him."

Lauro cradled her face between his palms. "Let me help you."

"If only you could, but no." She moistened her lips. "I promise I'll write if I find anything."

"Don't wait. Call, or send a telegram."

With an ache in her heart, she kissed Lauro for the last time, memorizing the feel of his lips on hers. Taking Marco's hand in hers, she stepped onto the train. She could have doubled over with grief, yet she kept her head high as she guided her son to a seat, unable to look back.

Sniffling, Marco wrapped his arms around her neck and clutched his sock monkey. Even the perpetual grin on Rocky's face seemed faded and forlorn.

A canvas bag dangled from Marco's shoulder. Opening it, Celina saw the wooden trains that had been Nino's. Her heart sank at the sight of them, but she knew Marco would be glad to have them.

She leaned her head back. *Even at the worst of it all, Lauro still thinks of Marco.* Tears lined her eyes.

As the train lurched and chugged from the station, Celina closed her eyes and thought about her promise to Lauro. Without question, her misguided actions had ravaged their hearts. Now, nothing would ever bring closure for Lauro and his family except to find Nino alive or present irrefutable proof of his demise.

Unless she did, she could never face Lauro or his family again.

Where would she even begin?

She gazed from the train, steeling herself for the journey ahead. Could she find out what had really happened to Antonino Savoia?

Chapter 30

San Francisco, 1953

"THANKS FOR LETTING us stay with you," Celina whispered to Lizzie. She unlaced Marco's shoes and removed them without waking him, and then she unfolded a chenille blanket over his exhausted, still-clothed frame. As soon as they'd walked into Lizzie's flat, he'd immediately snuggled onto the divan and fallen into a deep sleep.

"I wish I could've given you more notice," Celina said, following her friend into the kitchen. She'd called Lizzie from the airport in Rome just before they'd boarded the airplane. Since Lizzie's friends were still subletting her flat, she and Marco had nowhere to stay.

"Don't worry. I'm used to surprises. I'm an actress." Lizzie's hair was now a flaming shade of red. She opened the icebox, eased out a bottle of champagne onto the black-and-white hexagonal tile countertop, and popped the cork out with a loud bang.

Marco didn't budge.

"Tired little fella." Lizzie poured champagne into two ordinary drinking glasses and slid one in front of Celina. "I was saving this for a celebration—I don't even have decent barware—but you look like you need a drink now. Or *I* will after I hear your story. So spill it, sister." She brought out a baguette of sourdough bread and camembert cheese.

Celina unbuckled her T-straps and slipped off her shoes, relieved to sit down and relax. "Wish it were a celebration." She sipped the cold drink and broke off a piece of bread.

A knock sounded at the door, and Lizzie raced to answer it. "Shh," she said, holding her finger to her lips.

"I came as soon as I could close up the shop," Marge said, opening her arms to Celina. "Why, sakes alive, just look at you poor tired thing!"

After having kept up her steely resolve throughout the long journey from Italy, at the sight of her dear friend, Celina collapsed into the older woman's arms. Marge had known Tony and encouraged her to marry him. How long ago that seemed now. "I have so much to tell you that I hardly know where to begin."

"I thought you'd find yourself some sexy Italian man, and we'd never see you again," Marge said, settling onto a stool. Lizzie poured a glass of champagne for her.

Celina drew her hands over her face and shook her head as tears welled in her eyes, releasing her pent up emotions. "Worse."

"Oh, goodness gracious," Marge exclaimed, hugging her again. She took a handkerchief from her purse and handed it to Celina. "Unburden yourself, honey. Tell us all about it."

As she wiped her eyes, Celina told Marge and Lizzie about Lauro, the Savoias, and Stella di Cioccolato. And though it pained her to do so, she shared the worst of it—Tony's deception, Carmine's mandate, and her decision to leave Italy.

"I had to," Celina explained, her chest tightening as she recalled her last night there. "Not because Carmine would have asked me to, but because I couldn't stay in Amalfi knowing the suffering I had inflicted on them."

"Tony *lied* to you?" Marge's eyes were wide, and her red-painted lips formed an O.

Lizzie flipped her hair over her shoulder. "Men will tell you anything to get their way. I've sure learned that."

Marge sat back, dazed at Celina's saga. "Then who in heaven's name were you married to?"

"I'm almost afraid to find out," Celina said. Doubt crept into her mind. What if she made another mistake? What if her husband's family were con artists? She had to protect her son, too. "But I must track down the real Antonino Savoia. He might still be alive."

Lizzie raised an eyebrow. "Why would you do that?"

"For Lauro and his family. Am I right, honey?" Marge patted her shoulder with empathy. When Celina nodded, she added, "I know how you think. You're a good egg. That might be difficult, though."

"It's the only way I can hope to redeem myself in his father's eyes." *If even that.* On the flight back, Celina had been thinking about what to do. "First, to confirm it, I'll contact the military to get a copy of any records they can release. Technically, I'm Antonino Savoia's widow."

The two women nodded.

"And then, I'll contact Tony's friends and people he worked with. He might have confided in someone. I could also go to Santa Monica to see Tony's uncle. If he's not dead, that is." She told them about the visit that they'd made to Arturo Romani.

Marge let out a low whistle. "That's a lot to do. How would you go to Santa Monica?"

"We'll take the train to Union Station in Los Angeles and transfer." Celina had worked it all out. "There's a little inn on the beach in Santa Monica where Tony once took me. That's when we went to see his uncle. I'm sure I could find his house again. It wasn't too far from the beach. Just off California Avenue on one of the numbered streets. Third or fourth, maybe fifth. But I'll know it when I see it. I was navigating while Tony was driving." Surely she could find it again.

Lizzie grinned. "Here's to the lady with a plan." The three women clinked their glasses.

Celina prayed that her plan would work.

"Just remember, if you need your old job back I'm sure Monsieur would love to have you." Marge chuckled. "He hasn't found another chocolatier who suits him, and he's been complaining about your absence for months."

"But you'd have to find someone else to watch Marco," Lizzie said. "Old Mrs. Jackson died of a stroke a couple of weeks ago right in her apartment."

Celina sighed, dismayed at this news. She'd planned to confront Mrs. Jackson to ask why she'd been so mean to Marco but now she would never know. Still, she would have to think about school for him. At least he was ahead on his reading and arithmetic. Another week wouldn't matter. Soon the schools would be on break for Thanksgiving, followed by the Christmas and New Year's holidays. If she kept up with his studies, he wouldn't miss anything.

As she looked at Marge she could see herself, twenty years from now, still working for La Petite Maison du Chocolat. She shuddered at the thought. Since she'd opened the shop in Amalfi, she'd learned what she was capable of, and she loved it. Returning to her old position would signal defeat to her, but she would do it if she had to.

However, having access to the kitchen at La Petite Maison du Chocolat could help her set another part of her plan in motion.

"Could you watch Marco for a couple of days this week when the theatre is dark, Lizzie?"

Lizzie agreed, and Celina was delighted. Though Celina couldn't afford a shop in San Francisco, she could make chocolates and pastries to sell to restaurants. She could start in her kitchen or rent part of a kitchen somewhere. At Stella di Cioccolato, she'd learned how to be creative.

The next day, Celina called the Veteran's Administration office to obtain information on her husband and the real Antonino Savoia. She needed documents right away, so she scheduled an appointment as soon as she could. *The day after tomorrow.* She hated waiting even that long.

In the meantime, she sorted the mail Lizzie had been collecting for her, but it wasn't much, just a few receipts from the funeral home and condolence cards from acquaintances from their old neighborhood who'd heard about his death. She called them and asked if Tony had ever confided anything in them, but no one could remember anything that might prove helpful.

She made a point of turning on the radio to one of Marco's favorite afternoon shows to distract him while she spoke, but someday she would have to tell him the truth.

When Marco got cranky, Celina took him to the library, or they rode the cable car to the docks. Even though the weather was cool and breezy, they bundled up and watched the ships in the bay while they munched on lobster rolls and sipped creamy clam chowder. Every time Marco asked when they were returning to Italy, she tried to divert his attention. They were both feeling the pain of separation from people they had grown to love.

In her quest for clues that might help her understand her husband's motives, Celina retrieved a box of Tony's belongings that she'd left in her flat from her sublet tenants. Sorting through it, she found Arturo Romani's telephone number. Although it had been disconnected the last time she'd tried it, she dialed the number again.

The telephone trilled several times, and Celina was about to hang up when the call went through. An older man answered.

Celina gripped the receiver. "Hello? I'm calling for Mr. Romani. It's been a long time since I've spoken with him, but I'm Mrs. Savoia. We met—"

"I remember you. Art here. What do you want?"

She was shocked. "I thought that…I mean, I called before, but this number had been disconnected."

"Yeah, yeah, sometimes I forget to pay the bill. Like I said, what do you and Tony want?"

He didn't even know that Tony had died. "I'm terribly sorry, but your nephew passed away."

The old man cursed, and then he asked when and what had happened.

"New Year's Eve, last year. He had a heart attack. I tried to reach you for the funeral." She gave him the details, but Art only grunted and blew his nose. Maybe he had feelings after all. Or a bad cold.

Celina rummaged through the box next to the phone and pulled out an old set of dog tags that Tony said had belonged to a friend of his who died in the war. "I have something here that belongs to someone named Antonio Baldini. Do you know if he is a friend or relative of my husband's?"

There was a long silence on the line. "An old acquaintance."

"Is there any way I can contact him?"

The old man coughed. "He left years ago."

"Where did he go?"

"Peru, for all I know. No way to reach him, *capice*? Listen, real sorry to hear about Tony, but I got nothing to give you."

"I'm not asking for anything," she said. "I only want to know more about this person, Antonio Bal—"

"Don't call me again."

The line clicked, and the dial tone bleated in her ear. He had hung up on her. Celina put the receiver back in the cradle and thought about what he'd said.

Antonio Baldini. Maybe that was Tony's real name. But then she thought about what Art said about Peru. That struck her as too much of a coincidence. Of all the countries he could have mentioned, why Peru? Was that a slip of the tongue?

She massaged her temples, trying to recall Nino's journal entry. *Where a man could get lost...* She wished she could read the journal again. What else had he written?

Celina glanced at the clock. She was due at the Military Veteran's Administration offices in half an hour. Despite her telephone plea for information, they couldn't tell Celina anything about her husband's service except date of discharge. After tucking Tony's death certificate—for Antonino Savoia—into her purse, she hurried to the offices with Marco in tow.

In a clerk's bare-walled, linoleum-floored office, she presented the certificate, and an efficient-looking young man gave her an official copy of Antonino Savoia's honorable discharge and military record. Balancing it on her knees, she flipped through the sheaf of papers. He'd had an impressive military career with several exceptional honors. She thought about how much this would mean to his family.

One page had an old photograph clipped to it. The image of a strange young man in uniform stared back at her. Even though she'd been expecting this, she gasped.

"What's the matter?" Marco tugged on her skirt. "I'm bored."

"Oh, Mommy's just surprised."

The clerk leaned across the desk and peered through the half-glasses perched on his nose. "Did I give you the right file?"

"Yes, of course." She turned to Marco. "Daddy looks so young, that's all." Gazing at the photo, she chewed the inside of her mouth in thought.

Marco peered at the photograph. "That's not Daddy."

"It was before his injury, sweetie," she said, thinking quickly. "And he was very young then."

The clerk nodded in sympathy.

Marco kicked the legs of the chair. "Is that Lauro?"

"No, sweetie." But she saw the resemblance, too. How she missed him. Only the memory of their love and their magical hours in the hidden cove kept her going.

Celina ran her fingers over the grainy photo. The man looked a little familiar, but then, she'd met so many men in uniform at the shop, it could have been any of them. What was pertinent was that it was *not* Tony.

Another thought struck her. "My husband had a friend named Antonio Baldini, who was with him. I was wondering if I could see his file?"

"You're not family."

"No, but if he does have family, I can contact them."

The clerk stared at her, considering.

"Please. It would mean so much, after everything…"

"Okay lady. I'm not supposed to do this, but I understand."

He returned in a few moments and handed Celina another file. "That's a copy you can have."

When Celina opened it, a photo of Tony stared up at her. He had also been recognized for exemplary service. Only his uncle was listed under next of kin. She glanced at Marco, who was growing impatient. When her son was older, she would share this with him. She thanked the clerk, gathered the papers, and hurried from the building. Faced with the evidence, she could hardly breathe.

"On the way back, we have to stop at the post office and Western Union. Ice cream after that?" She wasn't above bribery to keep Marco placated.

Marco brightened and skipped beside her as she hurried toward the nearest post office. She needed to mail these documents to Lauro right away.

While she stood in line at the post office, she scribbled a note to Lauro saying that she was trying to find out where Nino might have gone after leaving San Francisco. At least he and his family could have that hope again.

After mailing Nino's military file, Celina hurried from the post office. For good measure, she also stopped by the Western Union telegraph office to compose a short telegram.

Sent Nino's military records with photo in the mail.

Marco tugged on her skirt. "You promised ice cream."

"We will, just a moment."

"Mommy, hurry up," he whined.

"Have patience." Feeling harried, she dashed off another line. *Investigating a lead to Peru.*

She paid for the telegram and then snapped her purse shut. "Let's go get that ice cream."

Over the next couple of weeks, Celina contacted Tony's few friends who had come to the funeral. As uncomfortable as it was, she told them the story and asked if they had any information that could help her.

No one knew the name Antonio Baldini. Or knew anything about Peru.

She had exhausted all leads, save one. She would have to confront Art Romani.

In the meantime, Monsieur Jean-Jacques asked if she could come in and make some of her specialties. She agreed, and as Lizzie had promised, she looked after Marco for a few days during the week when the theatre was closed for performances.

After completing her work for Monsieur, she made some of the specialties she'd developed at her shop in Amalfi, including her *gianduiotto,* raspberry truffles, and lemon-shaped *sfusato amalfitano* truffles dusted with sea salt. She tucked these into gold paper-covered boxes, along with her delicately flavored violet truffles, the blood orange and roasted pistachio truffles, and the basil, mint, and limoncello in dark chocolate. On the top layer, she nestled her chocolate stars.

Dressed in her best navy suit with a white blouse, a star-studded scarf, and pumps, Celina took her creations and rode the trolley to Union Square. She visited department store gift buyers she'd called to introduce a new line of chocolate truffles from Italy: Stella di Cioccolato.

After waiting for hours to visit buyers at The Emporium, City of Paris, and The White House, Celina was dismayed at their reactions. The buyers were reluctant to take a chance on a new vendor. Worse, they didn't even sample her truffles. Finally, at I. Magnin, she waited again.

As with the other buyers, the fashionable woman was reserved and reticent. "You haven't sold into any other stores yet?"

"Stella di Cioccolato is in Italy but new to San Francisco." Speaking quickly, she went on. "I'm not only a salesperson. I'm a *chocolatière*. I used to work at La Petite Maison du Chocolat."

Her interest slightly piqued, the woman said, "I love their chocolates. Did you actually make them?"

Celina nodded. "My mother was a *chocolatière* in Paris, and I learned everything from her. Here, I'd love for you to try just one." Celina offered her a raspberry-infused dark chocolate truffle.

The woman's attitude shifted in Celina's favor, and she nibbled at the offering. "Oh, that's delicious," she said, her eyes widening. "What else do you have?"

"I use Italian flavors in many of my truffles. These are my unique creations that your customers won't find anywhere else." Gaining confidence, Celina selected another one. "This truffle is made with limoncello, basil, and mint. It's as cool as a cocktail in Amalfi."

"Amalfi," the woman replied with a dreamy note in her voice. "I'd love to visit Italy."

Celina leaned forward. "I hope you do. It's the home of Stella di Cioccolato. You'd love it there."

"You live there?"

Did she still? "That's where my husband's family lives." Even that was a lie, she realized now. She forged on to close the sale. "My first available delivery is for Valentine's Day. Your customers will love to give Italian chocolates. How many would you like to start with?"

"Let's start with our largest stores in San Francisco and Los Angeles." The buyer immediately wrote an initial order.

Celina left the buyer's office thrilled. I. Magnin was one of the finest stores on the west coast. This was the break she had been hoping for. She knew that once I. Magnin offered Stella di Cioccolato truffles for sale, other stores would want them, too. One way or another, she would fulfill this order.

And this is only the beginning. Someday she would ship her truffles to the finest stores across the United States and Europe and beyond. Walking back to Lizzie's apartment, she envisioned every aspect of her glittering empire of the future. She was ready for the work she'd need to do. Next year, whether here or in Italy, she would ship her first order to the exclusive I. Magnin department store. Stella di Cioccolato was on its way.

If only she could sort out the rest of her life, too.

The next afternoon, Lizzie came home after an audition brimming with excitement. "I got the lead in a new theater production," she gushed. "Say good-bye to red hair, hello to platinum blond again. It's a traveling production that starts rehearsals right away, so you can stay here and have the run of the place. No more sleeping on the divan."

"Congratulations," Celina said. "It's a shame we finished off the champagne." Although her sublet tenants had extended the lease of her flat until the end of the year, they'd offered to find another place if she needed it sooner. But Lizzie was hardly ever here anyway.

Lizzie laughed and waved her hand. "More where that came from. Say, have you turned up anything?"

"Not much. I need to go to Santa Monica to speak to Tony's uncle. I think he knows more than he would tell me on the phone." Celina glanced at Marco, who was playing with Rocky and the trains Lauro had insisted he take with him. Now she knew that those had belonged to the real Antonino. It hurt her to even look at the toys because she thought of Lauro every time, but Marco wouldn't be separated from them.

"Think the crazy uncle will talk to you?"

"Can't hurt to try."

"Leave whatever you want here," Lizzie said. "When are you going?"

"Tomorrow." She had nothing to stay for, and she needed to find information fast. Soon she would have to start working again. She'd made a commitment to supply truffles, either from a kitchen here or in Italy.

The next morning, Celina packed a small overnight suitcase for her and Marco. Clutching his hand, she locked the door to Lizzie's flat and left the apartment building.

On their way out, Celina raised her hand and hailed a taxi. As she waited a few seconds for the cab, a telegraph boy on a bicycle swerved hard to avoid colliding with them and tumbled to the ground.

"Are you hurt?" Celina held out her hand to help the boy.

"No ma'am," he said, reddening with embarrassment. He picked up his hat and tugged it back on.

"Be careful on the sidewalk." Taking Marco's hand again, she slid into the taxi, shut the door, and gave the driver the address of the train station.

As the taxi pulled in front of the crowded train station, she couldn't help but wonder what Tony's uncle knew, if anything. And if he did, would he tell her?

The driver tapped the steering wheel while she juggled paying him, fidgeting with the suitcase, and tending to Marco.

"We're here," Marco yelled, anxious to go. In a split second, he slipped from her grasp and opened his door into the lane of passing traffic.

"Stop!" Celina snatched his collar and yanked him back in the cab, her heart pounding. "The other door. Please stay with Mommy."

With so much on her mind, she still had to watch over Marco. If anything happened to him, she would never forgive herself. Yet she couldn't forget that their tenuous future hinged on this trip and the good humor of a crotchety old man.

She wondered if Art would even see her.

Chapter 31

Santa Monica, 1953

"HOLD MY HAND and stay with me, Marco." Tired but determined, Celina clasped her son's hand and pushed her way through the crowd on the train platform. After arriving by train that morning at Union Station, they had transferred to the local train to Santa Monica. She prayed this expedition to visit Tony's cantankerous uncle, Arturo, would illuminate the mystery between her husband and Nino.

Marco tugged on her hand, but she held her grip. On the train trip from San Francisco, Marco had been whirling with energy and mischief, darting through the aisle while she chased him. But when he finally fell asleep, he had slept soundly to the clacking rhythm of the railcars. Celina knew this ordeal was a lot for a little boy to understand.

At last, they reached the beach. Even though the sun was warm on her shoulders, it was November, the off-season for beach-goers. A few people strolled the beach, and a group of teenagers with surfboards paddled out in the ocean in search of waves. Otherwise, the beach was fairly deserted.

"Race you, Mommy," Marco called as he broke loose from Celina and took off in the direction of the grand hotel on the beach.

"Wait, stop." Celina dropped the suitcase and ran after him. When she caught up to him, she scolded him. "That's not where we're going. You've got to stay with me. Come this way."

"Okay," Marco replied in a sullen little voice. "But I want to go there," he whined.

Squinting in the sunshine, the boy pointed to a sprawling white Georgian Revival mansion that Celina recalled had belonged to actress Marion Davies. Now signs proclaimed it a luxury hotel and private club.

"We're staying at another inn." Celina ruffled his hair and hugged him. She didn't know what she'd do if anything ever happened to him. Regardless of the outcome of this visit, her son was most important in her life. "It's where Daddy and I once stayed."

Celina lifted her face to the moist ocean air, aching with bittersweet memories. Though she had loved her husband and wanted to believe he'd meant well, she had to learn more about the reason for his deception.

As much as she loved Lauro, her first responsibility was to Marco. Providing her son with a stable, safe home was critical. He was becoming more active and inquisitive. In Italy, he had loved having cousins and grandparents and a variety of activities and places to explore. Here, it was just the two of them.

If she could locate Nino and redeem herself to Carmine, she and Marco might enjoy that life again. Though Lauro had pledged himself to her at any cost, if his father banished them, Lauro would suffer the separation. While not a guaranteed solution, finding Nino could be a step toward solving her problem with Carmine. It was a chance to set the past right for everyone.

With renewed resolve, Celina took Marco's hand and set off again. Still clutching Rocky and the canvas bag of wooden trains, Marco gamely stayed with her.

She led him along the path toward the Sunset Poppy Inn, which hadn't changed much since her last visit. Purple lantana and pink hydrangea still bloomed in profusion, and more brass wind chimes hung from the eaves of the white clapboard house.

Near the entry, she knelt on the sandy path to face Marco. Taking him by the shoulders, she asked, "Are you up for another adventure today, sweetie? I'm serious now. You will need to mind me at all times, understand?"

Marco turned his face up to hers. "I'll be good, I promise."

"We're going to see a very old, ornery man soon. I'm afraid it won't be much fun, but it's important for our future. Can you promise to behave and let us talk?"

"Does that mean I'll get ice cream?"

Celina couldn't help but smile. Ice cream had become his preferred exchange for good behavior. *What's one more time*? "It's a deal. Ice cream on the pier later."

She opened the door to the inn. Vivid paintings still graced the walls, and the reception desk still displayed its namesake poppies. But she could hardly recall the young, trusting girl she had been then, eager to fall in love and make a life with Tony.

Marco tugged her hand. "May I look at the pictures? I won't run away."

Celina relented. She liked to trust him; she only wanted him to be safe.

"A young art lover, I see." The proprietor emerged and took up her position at the reception desk.

"A reservation for Savoia, please." Celina gazed at the salon, which looked like an indoor garden of flower paintings, floral fabrics, and potted plants. "My husband proposed to me here in '45. It's still so lovely."

The woman ran her finger down the reservation list. "Here it is. Do you need a cot for the youngster?"

"It's just us now," she said as she signed the guest registry. "My husband passed away."

They chatted while Marco gazed transfixed at the woman's paintings by Cassatt, Kahlo, and others. Celina watched him, relieved that he was behaving himself.

After Celina settled Marco in the room, she called the proprietor and asked her to arrange a taxi to ferry them around Santa Monica. It wouldn't do to call Tony's uncle first to get the address. After hanging up on her, she doubted old Art would tell her where he lived. But she was sure she'd know the house when she saw it.

A half hour later, Celina and Marco were in a taxi exploring Santa Monica and searching for Tony's uncle's home.

The taxi driver had been crisscrossing the numbered streets in the village of Santa Monica for quite a while when he asked, "Are you sure it's around here, lady?"

Second, Third, Fourth, Fifth. Celina clutched the seat, racking her memory. "I know it's a neat white stucco house with palm trees and pink bougainvillea shrubs." Could the white stucco house have been painted? Maybe the palm trees were replaced, or the bougainvillea uprooted.

The driver tapped the meter. "I'll spend as long as want, but time is money, lady. Your money."

"I'm aware of that," she said, growing impatient with the process.

The cab driver drummed his fingers on the steering wheel. "Maybe it's south of California Avenue, ma'am."

"I remember seeing hills to the north." The sun was setting over the ocean. She was sure of it. But where was it?

The older man heaved a sigh. "Just saying, still could be south of here."

"No, I'm sure of it."

The driver glanced at her in the rearview mirror and shrugged.

Marco peered from the window on the other side. To him, this was a game. "That one, Mommy?"

She shook her head and pressed a hand against her temple. What else could she dredge up from her memory? "There might have been a birdbath."

The driver chortled. "The wife's gonna love this story."

Suddenly, Celina had a flash of insight. "Wait, I remember that large old house. Turn left here."

A neat row of bungalows punctuated by a sad-looking stucco house came into view.

"Mommy, a birdbath," Marco yelled. Bouncing on the seat, he pointed out the window.

"I see it. Slow down, please." *Could it be?*

The abandoned bird bath was little more than a parched stone bowl sitting lopsided on a pedestal. Two wind-whipped, skirted palm trees stood like bedraggled sentries at the sidewalk. Dirt dulled the white stucco, and rambling bougainvillea vines had overtaken the porch and obscured the front windows.

"Please, wait here," she said to the driver, stepping out. Marco scrambled from the car with her.

"I got all day," the driver mumbled. He turned the radio knob to a station and pulled his cap over his eyes.

Holding Marco's hand, Celina started up the steps. She didn't want to leave him in the cab, but she was nervous about who might answer the door. On a street of well-kept beach bungalows, this one was the eyesore.

"Stay close to me, sweetie." Drawing him to her side, she knocked on the door. Through a screen door, she could hear an announcer calling a horse race on the radio.

She knocked and waited.

"Who's there?"

"Mr. Romani, it's me, Celina. Tony's wife." A foul odor was blowing through the screen. Wrinkling her nose, she stepped back. Marco made a face.

"Got nothing to say."

She knocked again. "If you don't come to the door, I'll call the police and tell them I think you've died in there."

"Said all I had to say on the phone. Go away."

This is ridiculous. She jiggled the screen door handle. *Locked.*

A round of hacking coughing ensued. When he'd cleared his throat, he croaked, "I'll tell 'em you're trying to break in."

"Please, I just have a few questions. This means an awful lot to me and your nephew's son." For several minutes she stood arguing with him through the screen door until Marco tugged on her skirt.

"Mommy, he doesn't sound nice. And it stinks here. I want to go."

She wasn't getting anywhere with this unpleasant man. Frustrated, Celina called out again. "Have it your way. We're leaving."

"Good riddance," he replied, laughing.

Instead of leaving, she led Marco through a rusty gate to the rear of the house. Devoid of grass, the backyard was even more run down than the front.

"Shh," she told Marco. "Follow me." She crept toward an open window and stood on tiptoe to peer in.

The kitchen was a mess, but she could see straight through to the dining room and front parlor. There she could see Art, who was lying on a sofa and smoking, with the radio blaring nearby. His bald head faced away from them, and he seemed fully clothed. At least he wasn't in his boxer shorts. She blew out a breath.

"Come on," she whispered. Marco followed her.

She tried the rear screen door. *Open.*

Turning, she winked at Marco. "Bingo."

Marco clapped a hand over his mouth to stifle a laugh.

What would Art do when surprised? Celina hesitated, weighing the risk. *Could he have a gun?* She gathered her skirt and knelt by Marco.

"I want you to stay in the kitchen until I tell you to come out. It might not be safe for you. Do you understand?"

Marco nodded, his eyes as wide as walnuts.

Celina sighed. *And now I'm teaching my son how to break into homes.* It couldn't be helped though.

She eased open the screen door and held it for Marco, who crept in behind her. He wrinkled his nose against the stench, which was even worse inside. They tiptoed across the filthy floor, which was covered with tiny, black-and-white hexagonal tiles. Stained, red-checked wallpaper was peeling from the walls. She peered ahead.

Art hadn't moved.

She motioned for Marco to wait behind the dividing wall.

Through the doorway, Celina spied framed photographs on a mantle in the dining room. She had an idea. Opening her purse, she slid out Tony's war record and flipped to his picture.

Holding it in front of her like a shield, she crept through the dining room. When the wooden floor creaked, she froze. Art didn't move. The radio continued to blare the horse race.

She stepped closer.

"Yeah, that's right," Art hollered. "Home run."

At Art's outbreak, Celina's heart pounded, but she kept on going. She reached the archway between the dining room and the parlor.

She drew a breath and charged in. Thrusting Tony's war record toward his face, she demanded, "Who was Antonio Baldini?"

Shocked, Art fell from the couch, spilling a glass of whiskey on his shirt. The *Daily Racing Form* he'd been reading flew from his hand. "Good God, woman. What the hell are you doing in here?" Before she could answer, he let out a sizzling string of expletives. She was glad Marco was hiding in the kitchen.

"Get up and answer my questions. I have a right to know." As much as she hated to touch him, she held out her hand to help him up. He was fairly decrepit. She could defend herself against him if she had to.

Ignoring her offer, he pushed himself back onto the couch and retrieved his lit cigarette that had rolled between the cushions. He ground out the smoldering fabric and sat back to refill his glass. "Thought you gave up."

"I never give up." She held up young Tony's photo. "Antonio Baldini. Who was he?"

"Your husband."

"I know that now. Where was he from?"

Art mumbled something, then spat out, "New York."

"Does he have other family? Parents, siblings?"

Art drew on the cigarette and blew smoke toward her.

It was all Celina could do to keep from choking. "Look, I traveled from San Francisco, and I'm not leaving until I get some answers."

Art grumbled. "Only me. His mother was my sister."

"Where are his parents?"

"Both dead of influenza. Tony was an orphan, but he did real good for himself." An expression of pride crossed his face, and he raised his glass to her. "Smart boy. Went to pharmacy school. He loved that stuff, y'know."

Tony had told her he'd lost interest, but that hadn't been the case at all. *What a shame.*

At least she wouldn't have to contact another set of parents. She lowered her voice, keenly aware that Marco was in the kitchen, and hoping he couldn't hear above the announcer's voice still blaring on the radio. "So why did he steal Antonino Savoia's identity?"

"Why does anyone do anything?"

"Stop it. Answer me."

Art heaved a sigh and threw a look that sent shivers through her. "He'd just gotten back from Japan. Decided to stay in San Francisco, start over. The boys in New York—tough guys, y'know—were after him. So, he sensed what you call an opportunity. Smart, see?"

Celina hated to spend one more second here, but she needed more. "What did they want with Tony?"

Art shrugged. "Pills, I guess. Big money in that." He narrowed his eyes. "But you didn't hear that from me."

"Your secret's safe." She couldn't imagine the pressure her husband must have been under. "How did he know Antonino Savoia?"

"Does it matter?"

She was so angry she felt like throttling him. "On the phone you mentioned Peru."

"Yeah. That Savoia guy was running off to Peru. So Tony used his five-finger discount and got himself a brand new military identification card." He tapped his temple. "Smart boy."

Celina thought back to the night he died. "Did the men from New York ever find him again?"

Art waved her question away. "Not important."

"It is to me. The night he died, he got a phone call. I answered, and it was a man with a thick New York accent. It was New Year's Eve, but Tony said he had to go out. He didn't want to. Later that evening, he had a heart attack. He never came home."

"Yeah, yeah, okay, maybe they did find him. But they didn't get his whereabouts from me. Tony called me, see? He was worried. Asked me to mediate, but…" Art held up a hand and let it drop.

Celina swallowed against the heart-breaking sorrow she felt for her husband.

Art looked up at her. "That all?"

She swore she saw redness in his eyes. Maybe Art had some feelings for his nephew after all. "He's buried in San Francisco." She gave him the name of the cemetery. "And just so you know, Tony was a fine man and the best father to Marco. If you had ever seen them together, you would have been proud."

Art drew his fingers across his eyes. "Thanks for that." He sniffed, then waved his arm at her. "Now get outta here before I get upset with you."

She hurried toward the kitchen, where Marco was hovering by the door. She swept him into her arms and raced outside.

As they rode back in the taxi, Marco snuggled next to her while she closed her eyes in relief. She had gotten what she came for, but more than that, she had a clearer understanding of her husband.

Tony had stolen Nino's identity to protect himself and continued the deception to protect her and Marco. Even though he had lied to her, he hadn't meant to hurt her. He'd probably had little choice.

Celina thought about that last night when Tony had gone out. She could tell he was worried, but when she asked, he wouldn't say what was bothering him. In the end, the stress had overwhelmed his big heart.

She believed he was a good man. That was all that mattered. Though she wished he would have shared his past and his worries with her.

After the cabbie dropped them off at the Sunset Poppy Inn, Celina walked with Marco to their room. She felt utterly drained. Stopping at their door, she slipped the key into the lock.

Not far away, the proprietor was sweeping sand from the path. She waved at her. "Oh, Mrs. Savoia. Your family just arrived."

"Family?" She frowned. *Surely not Uncle Art.*

Marco looked up at her and shrugged.

Maybe Lizzie had decided to join them. She was just impetuous enough to do that.

As soon as she opened the door, Marco raced inside ahead of her and bounced onto the bed. She heard footsteps behind her.

"Celina."

Was she hearing things now? That sounded like… Celina touched her forehead. It couldn't be. She was just tired. She put her head down to go in.

"*Amore mio*."

She whirled around. "Lauro!"

He crossed the short distance to her and enveloped her with a kiss that flooded her with joy. Flinging her arms around him, she held him tightly—as if he were a mirage that might slip through her arms.

Lauro pulled back. "Celina, we have to talk. It's urgent."

Chapter 32

San Francisco, 1945

Tony was in heaven. The *osso buco* at Fior D'Italia was just as tender and flavorful as his mother's special recipe that he recalled. And the Barolo wine from Piemonte—exquisite. Even though he'd had a lot to drink, he was celebrating, wasn't he?

He patted his full stomach and leaned back in his chair. "Fine choice of restaurants, Doc. You were right."

"My father's family was from northern Italy. This reminds me of some of our traditional dishes, although the seafood on the Sorrento peninsula is magnificent. Thought I might as well share my best finds in San Francisco with you before I leave."

"What time do you board your ship in the morning?"

"I should be there by eight. Where are you staying?"

Tony stroked his chin. He figured he'd find a room. "Plenty of inns around."

"And most of them are sold out," Doc said. "I have a room you can take over when I leave. You can have the couch tonight."

"Gee, thanks, that's swell. Wish you were going to be around longer, but I sure appreciate the room."

"Wait until you see it. It's nothing fancy, but the location is good."

Tony wished he had friends or family like Doc, who spoke Italian so elegantly with the restaurant staff that Tony hated to say much. Tony was proud to be an American, though his family had come from Italy. When he was a teenager, his parents had died during an influenza epidemic, so he had no family except for his mother's uncle, who the last he heard had moved to Santa Monica, somewhere south of San Francisco near Los Angeles. No, Tony Baldini was on his own in the world.

Tony poured the remaining wine into Doc's glass. "So how long will you be gone?"

Doc sipped the wine and savored, a thoughtful expression on his face. "I won't be returning. I've spent enough time in America."

"What will you do there?"

Doc's eyes lit up. "There's a legend of exceptional quality cacao trees in Peru. I'll start there and try to find them."

"You know so much about chocolate. When you were talking at that shop, I thought your knowledge was pretty impressive."

"My family is in the industry." Doc gave a modest shrug.

"No kidding? In Italy?"

"Naples and Torino, but they've been closed for the past few years. I imagine my father will reopen the factories as soon as supplies become available." Doc heaved a great sigh. "That's in the past. I'm more interested in what I can do for farmers and their families in South America. The villages are a long way from medical facilities. There's a huge need there, so I can make a real difference in their lives. And I hope to gain a lot of knowledge in cultivating cacao and medicinal herbs."

Tony respected that. "So you're not coming back to settle down later?"

"If I wanted to do that, I would return to Italy. But sadly, I cannot."

"How come?"

"Even the best families sometimes have…disagreements."

An intriguing idea took root in Tony's mind. Though it would solve his problem, it wasn't exactly on the up-and-up. He resisted, yet it wouldn't hurt to ask a few questions, would it?

Tony cleared his throat. "Do you have family here in the states, Doc? A wife or children? Cousins?"

"No one. I'm a free man. I go where I please."

Tony smiled broadly. "That's a fine plan. Which pier are you leaving from?"

As Doc told him more about his plans, they finished the wine and moved on to dessert—*velluto di cioccolato* and *zabaglione*—and Doc went on to tell him about the research he'd done and his interest in medicine. Tony told him that he'd once been a pharmacist, but that he was thinking about starting a different business in San Francisco.

"The city is booming," Doc said. "I understand there is a real need for housing."

"I worked in construction when I was a teenager," Tony said. As he watched Doc, his idea grew into a plan. And the young *chocolatière* he'd met today might even be part of it.

"Say, about that pretty *chocolatière* you introduced me to today. Celina. Do you know if that sugar is rationed?"

Doc chuckled. "As far as I know, she's not dating anyone. She's a smart young woman. And she makes the finest raspberry truffles I've had in years."

After the two men left the restaurant, they hopped onto the cable car, which took them near the Victorian-styled house where Doc had rented a room.

They climbed the stairs to the second level. The house was quiet, and Tony assumed most of the guests were asleep.

"A widow owns this, and she rents out the rooms," Doc said, turning the skeleton key in his door. "Toilet and shower are down the hall. I'll have a shower tonight. Not much hot water in the morning unless you're first."

"You first," Tony said. "I'll go outside, have a cigarette. Great dinner, by the way. Thanks, again."

Tony left the room and started down the stairs to the first level. An electric charge of anticipation shot through him. He hadn't done anything like this in years.

After opening the front door and closing it, Tony remained inside. He paused and waited, hardly breathing. As soon as he heard the bathroom door click and the shower start, he hurried back to the room.

On the dresser were Doc's passport, military identification card, dog tags, and a wad of cash. The two boxes of chocolates from La Petite Maison du Chocolat that Celina had prepared for them sat beside everything.

Tony bit his lip. Should he risk it?

That ID card represented the path to freedom that he needed so much. Still, he felt bad about it.

In a flash, Tony palmed the identification card and dog tags. Feeling guilty, he jerked a Saint Christopher medallion from his neck, tossed it next to the cash, and scrammed out the door, his heart pounding. Once he might have been a tough kid, but this wasn't like him, not anymore.

Yet he needed a fresh start. A new name that no one from the old gangs could track down. A different place to call home. A new career. If the thugs found him again, he might not survive. He knew what they were capable of doing. No one would be safe—not him, not his wife, not his children.

Tony slid down the banister, raced out the front door, and swung onto the passing cable car. Later, he leapt off and spent the night in a deserted park, barely sleeping. He could hardly believe what he had done—and to such a genuinely nice guy—a true gentleman.

He felt like scum.

The next morning, Tony concealed himself near the pier where Doc's ship was departing. When he saw Doc pass through the line, he breathed a sigh of relief. All the man needed was his passport.

Tony needed Doc's old life.

He fished the military identification card out of his pocket. *What luck.* Tony's birth name was Antonio, which was close to Antonino.

Filling his lungs with fresh salt air, Tony felt lighter than he had in years. He rolled his new name around his mouth: *Antonino Cesarò Savoia.*

Chapter 33

Santa Monica, 1953

"How did you find us?" Celina was shocked at Lauro's presence at the Sunset Poppy Inn. She could hardly believe he was here, and she kept running her hands over his face and shoulders just to make sure.

"You're not the only detective," he said, kissing her cheek.

Sara appeared behind her son. "We came as soon as we could. I insisted on coming, too."

Soon they were talking excitedly over each other in English and Italian, and Celina could hardly follow their story. She stood listening, drinking in their presence with gratitude.

Lauro took her hand and brushed his lips over her fingertips, never letting go of her gaze. "Let's go for a walk on the beach, and we'll tell you everything." He looked past her into the room and called out. "Where's Marco?"

At the sound of Lauro's voice, Marco raced to the door and hurled himself into Lauro's arms. "*Zio*!"

Hugging him, Lauro laughed. "My big boy, how I missed you. *Come sta*?"

Marco held onto Lauro as if for dear life. Then, when he saw Sara, he screamed with joy and hugged her, too. "Nonna!"

If Celina needed any proof about how Marco felt about the Savoia family, this was it. Her son was hurting as much as she was.

Watching Lauro's and Sara's excitement, Celina recalled the telegram she'd sent. They all had hope again—hope that could light their path on the dark journey ahead. Even if they were successful, could she fully make amends? Carmine was the head of the family, and they all respected and abided by his word. Would locating Nino be enough to erase the damage she'd done?

Watching Sara hold Marco in her arms, Celina knew she *must* try to find Nino for her, even more than for herself or Lauro or Marco.

The four of them strolled toward the beach.

Marco broke loose and ran toward the waves, laughing and dodging the water. Shorebirds squawked overhead, chastising him for getting too close to their young, spindly-legged offspring. Sara trotted after him, waving the large birds away.

"You can't imagine how happy I was to read your telegram." Lauro put his arm around Celina as they walked. "As soon as we read the package you sent, I booked a flight."

Catching her breath, Sara joined them again. "The photo in the military file. That was our Nino. Carmine cried when he saw it."

Lauro squeezed Celina to his side. "You promised you would help us find Nino, and you are. At the train station, I told you I would help, so here I am."

"And I couldn't let him go alone." Sara's face shimmered with her faith in their mission.

Looking from one to another, Celina felt the intensity of their hope. They'd been traveling for more than a day, and they looked tired but optimistic. She prayed she wouldn't disappoint them.

"I haven't found much," Celina said. "But I'm hopeful."

"That's all we can ask for." Sara tented her eyes with her hand. "You mentioned Peru in your telegram. When I read that, I just knew." She pressed her hands against her heart.

"Wait, Mamma," Lauro said. "There's a lot more we need to know."

"You have no idea how much he loved visiting Peru," Sara said to Celina. "He always said, 'Mamma, I fell in love with the people there.' You read his entry in his journal."

Celina turned her face up to Lauro's. "And your father? What did he think?"

"Papa is going through a lot right now," Lauro said quietly.

Walking beside them with Marco, Sara nodded. "Carmine thinks it's too dangerous, but with Lauro, I'll feel safe enough."

"Mamma, stay with Celina while I look for Nino. Stay here, or in San Francisco." He turned to Celina. "But you have tenants in your flat. You could all stay in a hotel, no?"

Celina waved her hands. This was happening too fast. "Wait, how do you know that, how did you find us?"

Lauro chuckled. "First, I tried to call, but I spoke to your sublet tenants. They said you were staying next door, and they tried to find you, but you weren't home. I had your address in San Francisco from our first correspondence when I sent you tickets to visit us. So we went there. Didn't you get our telegram that we were coming?"

Celina shook her head, remembering the run-in she'd had with the telegraph boy. Maybe he'd had their telegram for her. Still, she didn't have much to go on and hoped they hadn't made this trip for nothing.

Lauro went on. "When we knocked on the door, we met two women who said they were subletting your flat. They introduced us to Lizzie, who remembered the inn you were checking into in Santa Monica. So we booked a private flight this morning, and here we are."

"I don't know how long we've been awake," Sara said. "But we couldn't wait. We are so close to finding our dear Nino."

Celina wished she could feel as certain as they did. She had only the story of an angry, drunk old man to go on. And Carmine had a point about the dangers in a remote area. Even if Art's story were true, what were the chances that Nino was still there, or still alive?

Although she was determined, she hated for Lauro and Sara to pin their hopes on such a weak lead.

Lauro must have read the doubt in her eyes. He turned to his mother. "Mamma, I know you believe we can find him, but I have to warn you, just like Papa did. The Andean highlands are a treacherous area. Anything could have happened. He probably moved on from there. I'll have to track him, and it will be an arduous journey. You know how restless Nino was. He could be anywhere."

"You can do this, Lauro, I know you can." Sara's eyes glistened with a mixture of steadfast love and courage. "Bring Nino home to us. One way or another. Your father needs this closure. It's been too long. Celina made us realize that."

At her words, Lauro was overcome with emotion. Hugging his mother, he said, "I'll do my best."

Celina had more to share with them, but she noted the fatigue in Sara's face. "Have you had anything to eat?"

"I don't remember when," Lauro said."

"There are several restaurants nearby. Nothing fancy, I'm afraid."

Marco threw sand in the air. "Then we can have ice cream."

Lauro laughed and threw Marco over his shoulder. "Why not? Let's go, sport." Turning serious, he said to Celina, "We have a lot to discuss."

"Four burgers with French fries and malts," Celina said to the waitress who was taking their order. Although she had suggested other restaurants, Lauro and Sara were determined to have American hamburgers, so she brought them to the diner on the pier. They exclaimed over the black-and-white checkerboard linoleum squares, the red vinyl booths, and the round, chrome-plated stools at the soda bar. A soda jerk was adding dollops of whipped cream to a pair of chocolate malts.

Marco swung his legs happily. "And two scoops of strawberry ice cream."

"After we eat. And if you still have room." Celina glanced outside at the balloon peddlers and jugglers. An upbeat, Rosemary Clooney song, *Botch-a-Me*, played on the jukebox, and Lauro and Sara started laughing at the silly lyrics.

This seemed like an odd place for a serious conversation, but Marco was entertained, and Lauro and Sara were having an authentic American experience. *Well, sort of.*

Despite all the activity, Sara stifled a yawn. "We'll sleep well after this. Won't we, Marco?"

"Can I sleep in Nonna's room?" Marco asked.

"Another time, your *nonna*—she's awfully tired." Celina stopped herself. Could she still call Sara that?

"I'll always be his *nonna*." Sara smiled at the boy's use of the word. "Let's keep positive thoughts about our future."

A clown sauntered into the dining area, and Marco bounced in his seat. When the clown began to twist colorful balloons into animal shapes, children gathered around him.

"Go on." Celina knew that would keep Marco busy so they could talk and make plans.

Marco jumped out and joined the other children.

Lauro laughed. "He'll be busy for a while." He leaned across the patterned Formica tabletop, searching Celina's face. "Now, please tell us everything you know."

"I'm afraid it isn't much." Celina told them about Tony's uncle and what he'd said about Nino traveling to Peru. She told them about how the identity mix-up had occurred, too, holding nothing back, even though it didn't cast Tony in a particularly good light. "This story aligns with Nino's journal. Now with what you've told me about him, I think it's a lead that should be examined. I only wish it were more specific or current."

"It's more than we've ever had." Lauro laced his fingers together.

"If we had his journal," Celina said. "We might find more clues."

Sara smiled. "I brought it with me. It's in my cosmetic carry-on in my room. I hand-carried it all the way from home." Sara's attention was drawn toward Marco, and as she watched him, a smile wreathed her face.

"We're prepared to find answers this time," Lauro said.

"So am I," Celina said. She saw Sara wiggle her fingers in a little wave at Marco, and he did the same. "I'm as committed as you are to finding Nino. I'm going, too."

Sara turned back to her. "What about Marco?"

"I'll take him with me." Although she felt bad enough about taking him into Art's house.

Lauro shook his head. "The trip is far too rough for him. He's only a little boy. Shouldn't he be in school?"

"I have to go."

"*Amore mio*, I—"

"It's critical that I do this. For all of you." Celina set her jaw, determined to go. Though her heart beat like crazy, it was the right thing to do.

Gazing at her with renewed respect, Lauro gripped her hands and nodded with a combination of reluctance and admiration.

Celina turned to Sara. "If I went with Lauro, would you look after Marco?"

"Well, I don't know." Frowning, Sara looked from one to another.

Celina understood her dilemma. "I'm not asking you to choose between Nino and Marco. But we should all consider who is best for this trip."

"I've never been, but Papa says it's rough land." Lauro gestured toward them. "That can be an unforgiving environment for either one of you."

Celina glared at him. "For anyone, I imagine. Not just women."

"I stand corrected," Lauro said, holding up his hands.

"Of course you should go," Celina replied to him. "But how will you get around?"

"I'll get a guide."

"Do you speak Spanish?"

Lauro shrugged. "Italian is close. I can make myself understood."

"It's not the same when you're trying to negotiate, which is what we'll have to do," Celina said. "Few people give up information willingly. What if Nino is gone, or doesn't want to be found? Being able to speak their language will be an advantage. My Italian might be poor, but I grew up speaking Spanish here in California. You'll need me."

"Good point." Lauro's eyes conveyed a mixture of acceptance, admiration, and love.

Sara studied her, then after a long moment, she nodded her assent. "I'll stay with Marco. Or take him back to Amalfi with me. You don't know how long you'll be gone, do you?"

Amalfi. Celina started to argue, but instead, she sat back, assessing the situation. As Sara would look after her son, she would search for Sara's son—and look out for Lauro. They were two mothers, each trusting the other with their most precious treasure. This was a dangerous undertaking. And if, *God forbid,* the worst happened, and she didn't return, Marco would have a loving home. She couldn't ask for anything more than that.

Gravely, Celina sought Sara's eyes. "I think Marco would like to go back to Amalfi with you."

Sara grasped her hands with a strength that surprised Celina. "We understand each other," Sara said, measuring her words. "*Mille grazie.* Having Marco around will help Carmine, too."

"Thank you. You do me a great favor." Celina appreciated Sara's reasoning. If they couldn't find Nino, or discovered his remains, then having Marco there would give Carmine a reason to live. Next to love, hope for the future was among the most powerful of emotions. Celina was well aware of how dispiriting and futile it was to merely exist without hope.

"And you do me a great service," Sara replied.

Looking deep into Sara's eyes, Celina saw that she still held out hope that Carmine would acquiesce in his decree against her. Sara had welcomed her into the family, championed her and supported her, even after she'd discovered that Celina's husband was not her son.

Celina loved and trusted this woman. Bowing her head, she kissed their clasped hands. "We'll look after each other's sons, won't we?"

Smiling at her through tear-misted eyes, Sara nodded. "With our lives."

"Then we have a decision," Lauro said, understanding the enormity of their choice. "Now, is there any reason we can't fly out of Los Angeles?"

Celina was already anxious to leave. "The sooner, the better."

Chapter 34

Marañón Canyon, Peru, 1953

"*TEN CUIDADO!*" VOICES rang out from the path above, and Celina pressed herself against a thick, broad-leafed banana tree.

"*Stai attento,*" she called to Lauro, who hurriedly limped for cover. She frowned with concern. He'd sustained a nasty gash on his leg two days ago when he had slipped on a muddy path.

Birds squawked overhead in the dense stand of trees, while furry guineas scurried through the undergrowth. Guides yelped and clanged wooden sticks against tree trunks. The noise startled the pair of llamas carrying their tents and packs.

A moment later, a powerful mountain puma shot past them. Celina prayed it wouldn't notice them in its headlong chase after the unfortunate creature.

A screech pierced the thin mountain air.

"*Vizcacha,*" Ernesto said, giving name to the newly deceased. With a bloodline that stretched to the ancient Incas, their wiry Quechua guide was dressed in brightly colored woven clothing and had an easy smile. His weathered face belied his relative youth. "*Está bien,*" he said, fanning himself with his hat. "*Son abundantes.*"

Celina nodded at this reassurance. So abundant, the poor furry creature wouldn't be missed. Unlike those of the human species.

In this high equatorial climate, perspiration beaded on her forehead, and she panted from exertion. Once the danger had passed, Celina tugged her boots higher around her knees and returned to the muddy path, trudging up the steep incline with renewed resolve. At least it grew relatively cooler at the higher elevation.

She paused on the path to wait for Lauro. "You're limping more today."

"It will heal." With Ernesto's help, they had cleaned the wound, covered it with medicinal herbs, and tried to close the gash with strips of cloth tied around his calf.

"Are you sure we should keep going?" she asked.

"I didn't come this far to quit because of an inconvenience."

Celina saw him wince as he tried to cover up the pain. A few days ago, after one of the frequent rain showers, the path had been muddy and the incline steep. Distracted by the rainbow wings of a scarlet macaw, she'd nearly stepped on a snake. He'd yanked her out of the way, but in the process, he had fallen, lost a boot, and cut his leg on a sharp rock outcropping.

Lauro breathed heavily beside her. "Wild cats, snakes. I wish you'd let me come by myself, then I wouldn't worry about you."

Celina scowled at his sharp retort. "You wouldn't have gotten this far without me."

"We'll see if we're on the right track, won't we?"

The journey's physical discomforts in these vast, treacherous Andean mountains had wrought tension between them. In this remote Peruvian outpost, they were surrounded by awe-inspiring mountains whose heavily vegetated slopes were dotted with wild cacao and coffee beans, the livelihoods of local farmers. Beyond the jungle climate rose high, arid rock formations. Majestic snow-capped peaks crowned above all.

At the beginning of their mountain trek, Lauro had hired Ernesto to help them track Nino. They based their plan on the notes and drawings in Nino's journal, translating the details among three languages and visiting adobe villages where he might have stopped.

Ernesto approached the village men and acted as an interpreter, translating between Spanish and Quechua languages for them. "An Italian man who spoke good Spanish. Very interested in medicine with a great knowledge of cacao. Do you recall seeing him?"

Although it had been years ago, people had long memories here. Replies were mixed, but the consensus was that Nino had been searching for the area he had visited with his father. He had been looking for cacao and other rare plants.

Celina spoke to the women, who were dressed in full *pollera* skirts hand-loomed of vivid colors paired with bright woven sweaters. "Have you seen him recently?"

The women darted looks at the men, but they offered little response. Celina suspected that they were concealing something. Finding one odd-looking woman alone with her weaving, Celina pleaded with her for information.

The woman reached out to run her weathered fingers over the trailing fringed ends of Celina's vibrant orange paisley, sheer cotton scarf that she'd rolled and tied around her hair. Indicating the beautifully crafted, striped woven shawl she wore, the woman removed it and held it out to Celina in trade.

Celina quickly removed her scarf and handed it to the woman, who rubbed it against her cheek and smiled in gratitude.

"When you find the *gran blanco*, you find your man," the woman said.

Rare white cacao beans. "Where? Aren't those extinct?" Celina recalled Nino's journal entry.

"*Es muy peligroso.*" She waved a hand toward the mountain, indicating dangerous forces there.

Indeed, Ernesto refused to take them into the highlands or up the mountain until they'd been blessed by a shaman in a native ritual.

By following the entries in Nino's journal and the local's guidance, Celina and Lauro traveled far into Marañón Canyon, which was northeast of the modern, multilayered city of Lima with its new buildings and Baroque churches, east of Chiclayo, and deep in the Andean highlands.

Yet once they pushed farther onward, local villagers had no new information for them. Most only shook their heads. Celina and Lauro had argued about which path to take, and in the end, Lauro had relented to her argument.

Now that the mountain cat was gone and the path deemed safe, their little group set out again with the llamas picking their way behind them.

Celina prayed they were on the right track. But where were the cacao trees the woman had described?

She strode ahead to talk to Ernesto. "I want to check any cacao trees we find at these higher elevations."

Ernesto stopped and eyed her with curiosity. "They are all the same."

He had already hacked open cacao pods from the lower elevation, revealing the expected purple seeds, or beans, nestled in milky white pulp.

Behind them, the wiry men Ernesto had met at the base of the mountain and hired to help also shook their heads with reticence.

Catching up with her, Lauro paused to catch his breath. "Do you really need to keep asking them to do that?"

"I'm looking for the *gran blanco*. You heard what that woman said."

"I'm not sure she was of sound mind.

"Well, I am, and I want to see those cacao pods," Celina said, putting her hands on her hips. "I'll hack them open myself if I have to."

"Papa said the white beans are extinct now."

"From Witches' Broom, I know." But maybe some had survived. Perhaps the strange little woman was telling the truth.

Or maybe she was deluding herself with hope, just as she had when she'd arrived in Italy. Still, Celina had seen a grain of truth in the woman's glassy eyes.

Lauro shrugged his assent, and they continued up the muddy path in silence.

Breathing heavily, her legs burning from the incline, Celina focused on one of the lean men ahead of her who traversed the narrow path as nimbly as a goat. She tried not to think about the enormity of what was riding on this trip, or what might be ahead.

As soon as the Pan American aeroplane had touched down on the Lima runway, she'd put on mental blinders to focus on her task ahead. Marco was safe with Sara, and through an international operator she had managed to get a call through to him from Lima before they'd set out. She'd studied Nino's journal on the flight and traced his path on a map. She was fairly sure this was the route he and Carmine had taken before the war.

She imagined Nino and his father had trekked this path with the same resolve they had. Probably not much had changed since then. Celina was exhausted and could scarcely manage the physical exertion, yet if Lauro could forge on despite his injury, she would, too. She refused to be left behind.

Celina studied the thick vegetation around her that was so foreign to her eyes. She brushed tiny, irritating flies from her face and ducked to dodge a flying insect the size of a tangerine. As she did, she caught sight of the strange-looking tree they were looking for shrouded under an arched canopy of banana trees heavy with fruit.

"Hold up," she cried out. Stepping across discarded, rotting pod shells toward the cacao trees, she wondered if these were the prized white cacao beans that produced the legendary chocolate that Aztec kings had consumed. Did these trees yield the smoothest, most flavorful, aromatic cocoa that had been the ultimate *lingua franca* between chocolate aficionados, chefs, and growers around the world?

She suspected that nothing less than this fabled cacao would have satisfied Nino's scientific ardor.

Was this the elusive strain? Ernesto told them that his family had harvested cacao in this vast area for generations. He had agreed with Lauro about the white *nacional* cacao beans. *Extinct.*

But were they? Celina inspected the tree, which looked much older than the ones they'd seen at the lower elevations. Pods jutted from the tree trunk and higher branches. She reached out with reverence and ran her hand over a thick, football-sized pod, its ribbed, mottled green-and-yellow skin encasing the source of her artistry.

The back of her neck bristled.

A surge of excitement and anticipation coursed through her, tingling in her fingertips. "I want to see these beans."

Lauro and Ernesto had followed her to the trees.

"They're the same as what you've seen, *Señorita.*" Ernesto shook his head. "We have to pitch camp before dark, so we shouldn't stop."

"*Señora,*" she corrected him. "And I have a feeling about this one."

Ruefully complying with her wishes, Ernesto sliced the pod from the trunk with the flash of his machete. He hacked it open, letting the discarded outer shell fall to the ground as fertilization.

Celina peered closer, and as the fleshy part of the pod fell away, she caught her breath. The milky white pulp interior was ringed with clumps of beans—not the usual purplish hue like the ones they'd seen at lower elevations or being harvested in long, low shacks near the villages. They'd watched workers scooping out the purple seeds onto wooden trays for the process of natural fermentation before packing the beans in burlap sacks to ship around the world.

Barely containing her excitement, she sniffed the beans, which yielded a distinct floral aroma. "It's *gran blanco.*"

Awestruck, Lauro ran his hand over the beans. "I thought these were extinct."

"*Sí,*" Ernesto insisted. "Mostly they are." He shot a look at his helpers.

"Well, not here." Not extinct at all, but Celina didn't want to argue the point. She glanced around. *Could Nino be nearby?*

"What a miracle." Lauro gripped Celina's hand.

She met Lauro's eyes and knew what he was thinking. *Find the white bean, find your man.*

He whipped around. "How many of these trees are there?" he demanded of Ernesto.

They'd talked about the importance of such a discovery late one night when they lay in their tent. Besides a possible trail to Nino, this meant a lot to scientists—and would be worth a lot of money to chocolate makers and chocolatiers.

Celina glanced around. Who else might know of this trove? Clearly, Ernesto and his men were reluctant to have this discovery made known.

"Ven aqui conmigo." Ernesto pulled Lauro away from their small group.

Celina started after them to translate, but Lauro put out his hand for her to halt. *Some conversations are better between men here* he'd told her one night in the tent, and she'd stormed out, only to encounter a swarm of insects that drove her back inside. The closer they were to the long Marañón River that formed the headwaters of the Amazon, the more insects.

"I'm not saying that's correct," Lauro had argued. "It's just the way it is in some places."

Like Italy, like Peru. She had turned over and gone to sleep in a huff.

Yet, she tried to understand, so she had developed a keen eye to know when to join a conversation, and when to stay out. Was this one of the red flags that Marge and Lizzie often discussed? Or was it the stress, the equatorial humidity, the cultural difference?

Watching them now, she saw Lauro pull money from his pocket and press it into Ernesto's hand.

Ernesto motioned to the two helpers he'd brought with him. After speaking in the Quechuan language, Runasimi, the people's language on the Andean Highlands, the two men shook their heads. Ernesto returned to Lauro and shoved the money back into his hands.

This cacao wasn't for sale. Not at any price. This was their private reserve, Celina realized. Safe from the ravages of the outside world.

Lauro limped back to her. "We're not to discuss the white cacao beans with anyone."

"So I gathered." Celina crossed her arms.

Gazing into her eyes, he traced her jawline with a finger. "You were right. I'm sorry I didn't trust your judgment."

She slid her arms around him and gave him a soft kiss. "Nino might be near." Echoing the odd woman's words, she added, "*Cuando encuentres el gran blanco, encontrarás a tu hombre.*"

Lauro looked up the vast mountainside. "Where, I wonder?" He stretched his leg. "I don't know how much longer we can survive up here."

She prayed the white cacao held the answer.

While the men set up camp for the night, Celina organized their belongings and set out lanterns to provide light against the encroaching twilight.

While the men slept under the stars, she and Lauro would sleep together in one tent for safety, although the tents were made of thin fabric and sound carried far. Lauro didn't want her to feel uncomfortable with intimacy here, so they practiced restraint. Instead of making love, at night they lay entwined in the other's arms, a comforting reminder of their magical cove. Feeling Lauro's arms around her and the steady sound of his breath as he slept made Celina feel closer to him than ever.

Carrying a lantern in one hand, she perched on a boulder, gazing out at the mountains that folded around them.

Lauro slid beside her. "It's beautiful isn't it?"

"And so remote…" As the rosy hues of dusk surrounded them, dense green hillsides appeared purple against a brilliant pink and orange sky. She ached at the vast beauty that seemed to stretch into infinity.

Leaning into the crook of his arm, she asked, "Why didn't your father bring you here on that trip with Nino?"

Lauro lifted her hair and pressed his hands along her shoulders, kneading her muscles as he had that day in the test kitchen.

"I was younger, and Nino was the one who was supposed to take over the chocolate factory. Papa wanted me to work in lemons. One of my cousins is running that company now."

"Someday, you'll take your father's place, won't you?" She rotated her neck, welcoming his massage.

"From one generation to another. Stewards of the business and the fruits of the land."

"That's quite a responsibility. Do you miss not having the chance to decide your future?"

"I did decide, *amore mio,*" Lauro said, kissing her shoulders. "My work means a great deal to me. I'm privileged to carry on the tradition."

"Nino didn't think so."

He brought her arms around her. "We're all different, aren't we?" With that, he brushed his lips over hers.

She couldn't help but respond. Hidden by dense growth as they were and secluded from sight, she wrapped her arms around his neck and drew him closer. She had missed the time they had spent together in Italy. Here, at this moment, the searing pain of leaving him at the train station in Naples was a dim memory.

Their future depended on this journey and what they found. If they returned without Nino—or conclusive proof of his demise—she dreaded Carmine's rejection. At that point, she had no doubt it would be final. She couldn't bear to take Lauro from his family because she knew how much he would suffer, as well as his parents. Was loving Lauro worth the potential of such great loss?

Yet she could not resist him. Their time together now might have to sustain her forever.

Deepening her kiss, Celina let the world around them fade with the day. Only this moment existed. As they melded together, the heat of his feverish skin was fiery against hers.

Nuzzling her neck, Lauro slid her onto his lap. "Remember our hideaway cove?"

"How could I ever forget?" She dipped her forehead to his and caressed his face.

"*Señor, Señora,*" Ernesto called. *"Muy importante."*

Lauro kissed her before reluctantly releasing her. She touched her lips, savoring his heat and the slight saltiness of his kiss.

Hoisting a lantern against the dwindling twilight, Ernesto was motioning for them to follow. His two helpers crowded at the small, partially hidden mouth of a cave waiting for them.

Lauro picked up another lantern and limped in after them, brushing cobwebs aside as they pressed on into the cave. An earthy, musty aroma assaulted their noses. Inside, the sounds of birds and wildlife were muted in the shadowy lair.

With her lantern held aloft, Celina stopped, awestruck at the interior. Rock walls soared above them and were splashed with painted drawings. Rudimentary scenes of fishing, fighting, and hunting covered the stone surfaces. More expert renderings of snakes and jaguars and llamas filled another wall. Symbols she didn't understand accompanied some of the drawings.

"*Dio mio,*" Lauro whispered, leaning in to inspect the markings. "From the Incas?"

"Maybe," Ernesto said. "This area has a long history of inhabitants."

Celina's lantern flickered against the walls, illuminating Lauro's profile. His expression was one of wonderment and reverence, mirroring what she felt welling up inside of her, too. Despite the hardships of this journey, miracles abounded. These drawings were from an older, possibly ancient civilization. Even today, on this mountainside, little had changed.

She leaned closer, inspecting the artwork. "This one looks like a dance. And in this one, women are harvesting food."

Holding hands, Celina and Lauro continued to explore. In front of one amazing scene, she stepped back to take in the fullness of the artwork. As she did, her boot scraped against something on the stone floor. A clattering sound echoed in the shadows.

"What's this?" Celina reached down for the object. "A fountain pen. How strange."

"People have been here before us."

"Maybe sketching these scenes." She used the hem of her shirt to wipe off the part of the pen. Bringing the lantern closer, she inspected it. "It's marked *Montegrappa*."

Lauro's lips parted in surprise. "Those are made in Italy. Let me see that." Taking the writing instrument from her, he brushed off the dust and dirt that had accumulated on it, revealing fine workmanship.

Sucking in a breath, he raised his eyes to her. "This pen is Nino's pen."

"Are you sure?"

He brushed off more dirt, revealing Nino's initials. *A.C.S.* "It was a birthday gift from our father."

Chapter 35

CRADLING THE FOUNTAIN pen to his chest like a treasure, Lauro embraced Celina and peppered her face with kisses. His heart hammered with joy. Without a doubt, the fountain pen had belonged to Nino.

"This is the proof we need," Celina exclaimed, her tawny eyes glowing like tiger's eye quartz in the golden lantern light of the cave. "We're on the right path."

Continuing on, they searched the cave, eager to find other evidence.

Lauro was desperate to believe they were drawing close to Nino. But *when* had his brother dropped this pen? On the trip here with their father, or years later, when he returned here on his own? Or more recently?

After searching for a while but finding no other clues, doubt edged into his mind. Had Nino been here at all? His brother often gave gifts to people. Could another guide or cacao farmer have dropped it?

Celina stopped and stood motionless, her hands over her heart. "Maybe it was the shaman's blessing. Right now I feel we are very close. I *know* Nino was here."

"Maybe," he allowed, not wanting to dash Celina's hopes or jinx his. Would they find Nino alive? Or would they find his remains? At the least, his parents needed closure to the loss of their oldest son. The worst of all would be to find nothing—no trace of Nino's subsequent journey here, or clues that would lead them elsewhere.

Nino was the brother he'd looked up to all his life. When he was young, he couldn't have imagined that he would go through the remainder of his life without the brother he so admired. For that reason, their final, grief-fueled argument haunted Lauro. He alone shouldered the guilt of banishing his brother. At times, the void in his heart was almost more than he could bear. And Nino—his brother hadn't argued with him. Instead, he had simply vanished into the night.

Now, the closer they became, the more vulnerable he felt as the old wounds of loss were reopened. If they found Nino, would he forgive him?

After leaving the cave, Ernesto and his men prepared supper over a fire for them. They had potatoes roasted over hot stones, along with fowl and grains, and ended with succulent mangos picked from nearby trees. Ernesto brewed *mate de coca*, insisting that it would help them handle the thin air of the high altitude.

After eating, the Quechua men folded their legs to sit and play the *zampoña*, a panflute whose music Lauro found hauntingly beautiful and elegant in its purity. Another played a string instrument with a light, quick touch.

He glanced at Celina, who also seemed enchanted with the ethereal music. The temperature was cooler at this altitude, so Celina had fastened a colorful *lliklla* over her shoulders that a village woman had given her in trade. With her fair hair spilling over the vivid colors of the hand-loomed fabric, Celina was spellbinding in the light of the flickering flames. He ached for her, and couldn't imagine returning to Italy without her. On this trip, despite their occasional quarrels and frustration, he realized how much he wanted her in his life, whether his father approved of her or not.

Ernesto brought out a similar woven cloth and draped it around Lauro's shoulders. Still, Lauro shivered in the night air, though his face was damp with perspiration. He stretched out his aching leg. At turns, he became blazing hot or teeth-chattering cold.

As they relaxed, Celina watched him, her brow puckered with worry. "Are you feeling worse?"

"My leg might be a little swollen." Lauro shrugged off the pain. "But your beauty is the salve to my aching soul."

"Forever my poet." She chuckled softly. "May I see it?"

He nodded, and she rolled up his torn pants leg. From the look on her face, he could tell she was concerned. She moved the lantern closer to inspect his injury. The gash had swollen and become inflamed.

Celina frowned. "It needs to be cleaned again." Using fresh water from a nearby mountain lake that Ernesto's men had brought, she flushed the wound. Looking worried, she brought Ernesto over to look at it.

"It will be fine by tomorrow." Lauro laughed at their concern. "It's not like I'm dying." But now, as he inspected his wound, which ran down his shin, he could see why Celina was anxious.

"Ernesto has some other medicinal plants he wants to use on your leg." Celina rinsed a cloth with cool water and applied it to his forehead.

When Ernesto returned, he brought with him an array of leaves and began to soak and swab the area with them. Another plant looked like some sort of cactus, while another oozed a dark red sap. He explained the uses to Celina, and she translated. "These are their traditional herbs. *Cordoncillo* for pain, and *Sangre de Grado* for healing. At first light, he is sending one of his men to fetch a healer for you."

"I don't need a shaman. We were blessed enough already, weren't we?"

"Ernesto says this man is more than a shaman. He's called the *doctor de milagros.*"

"*Miracoli.*" Lauro grinned. "We can always use more miracles."

Celina wrapped a fresh cloth around the wound and helped him into the shelter of the cave. "We're going to sleep here tonight," she said. Ernesto and his men had spread woven bedding over the stone floor.

As night fell and the sky lit with millions of heavenly bodies, the moon cast a gossamer glow over the mountains and highlands. Lauro wrapped his arms around Celina and drew her close to him for comfort. He turned his face toward the intermittent breeze wafting through the mouth of the cave.

Celina snuggled next him, spreading her fingers across his chest. "You're burning up with fever." She feathered kisses along his brow, cheeks, and lips.

Despite his agony, his body responded to her touch. *That will have to wait,* he told himself.

"Do you think you can sleep?"

"I don't know." Though he doubted it, with the fierce throbbing in his leg. In just a few hours, the intensity had ratcheted up tenfold.

She drew a few leaves from a small leather pouch Ernesto had given her. "Chew these, they'll take the edge off the pain and help you sleep."

He chewed the bitter leaves, and soon found himself drifting into a hazy dream state where he had trouble discerning what was real. Celina was there, bathing his face and limbs in cold water, and then they were in Amalfi, swimming in an aquamarine ocean surrounded by silvery dolphins.

Celina was singing to him in the most beautiful, angelic voice he'd ever heard…or was it sirens beckoning him to a rocky shore? A moment later, he was soaring over snowcaps that kissed the heavens and resonated with a sublime, crystalline sonata. As the sky lightened, the music morphed into a mournful dirge. Lauro re-entered his pain-filled world and screamed in agony.

Beside him, Celina pushed his damp hair from his forehead. "Ernesto should be back soon. Unless you start to get better, I'm taking you down the mountain. You need a doctor and probably penicillin." Her face was drawn into the gravest look he'd ever seen.

"No," Lauro croaked. "We're so close to Nino. You felt it."

"We can come back…" Her voice drifted off.

But Lauro knew that there would be no coming back here. He clutched her hand. "We won't. In my dream, I soared over the mountains. The Andes have triumphed."

"Don't say that," she snapped, blinking and rubbing her eyes with the heel of her palm.

He dozed a while—he couldn't say how long—and night shrouded them again. He heard Celina outside the cave, arguing with someone, though he couldn't imagine who.

Above it all, the symphony of nature thrilled him. Winds rustled the trees, the song of cicadas rose to a crescendo, and the distant river that never slept roared in his ears. The earth unleashed its fresh green perfume on the breeze to cover the stench of his wound.

That night, he brought Celina into his arms. In his mind, he extolled his love for her to the heavens. *We're soon free,* amore mio. Fully aroused, he devoured her lips, her beauty, her essence, and together they became as one, sailing through an endless night of brilliant constellations. He caressed the exquisite length of her body, savoring every hollow and curve to remember for eternity. With every brush of her fingers, the scent of her skin intoxicated him, and he lost himself in her silky hair.

"Lauro, Lauro," she murmured, calling him back. "Stay with me, my darling. I love you, *ti amo*. Please don't leave me."

Lauro smiled in peace. Her lips were soft as rose petals on his blazing forehead, and her tears splashed on his cheeks like a soft spring rain.

And then a dark, bearded man knelt over him—a *shaman* of last rites.

It was time.

Chapter 36

"Please, my love, keep fighting." Celina hovered over Lauro, cradling his head in her lap and willing him to live. Such fury blazed in her chest that she could hardly look at the tall, angular healer that Ernesto had finally induced to help them. To take Lauro down the mountain would have taken far too long. He needed medical attention now, so this healer was her only choice.

With barely a glance in her direction, the bearded man knelt before Lauro to inspect his infected wound and affected leg.

Yesterday, when the man who had gone to fetch the *curandero*—the one who cures—and returned alone, Celina had been livid.

"He does not treat white men," Ernesto had said, as if that explained everything. "He has trained a younger man, an apprentice. He will send—"

"No," she yelled, cutting him off. "Tell him that I will haul Lauro up that mountain by myself if I have to, but he *will* treat him."

Except that Lauro was so ill and delirious now that she feared he would never make it out of the Andes. Reaching into her reservoir of strength, Celina summoned the resolve that had enabled her to survive the untimely death of her husband and the demise of her parents. But this time, she vowed, was different.

"I will not allow these peaks to claim another Savoia." She refused Ernesto's excuses and sent him back up the mountain for the man he called the *doctor de milagros*.

All night she had wept tears of anger and anguish, thinking of Lauro's parents, and all the reasons he still had to live. *Why is this happening?* she demanded. Was it her fault? Or was this the ultimate revenge against her for the sorrow she had brought upon the Savoia family through her neglect of the truth?

When Lauro had turned to her during the night, his eyes glazed with fever and desire, she had comforted him, giving him the sacred part of herself. She wouldn't give up on Lauro without using every fiber of her being to fight for his survival. Just as Sara was caring for Marco and had vowed to protect him, so too would she care for Lauro.

Now, her mind reeling with distress, Celina watched while the dark-haired, bearded man used herbal medicine to drain and clean Lauro's wound. He worked as deftly as a doctor, with none of the rituals that the other shaman had sent them off with. Then, he brought out molded bread, scraping and applying a compress of mold directly to the ugly gash.

"What are you doing?" she cried, springing to Lauro's defense.

Without looking at her, the man spoke to Ernesto in the language of their people.

Ernesto replied to her in Spanish. "He says you need to leave."

"I will *not*. I have kept him alive this long, no thanks to that man." She whipped her head toward him. "Look at me and tell me what you're doing," she shouted in English, though she knew the man wouldn't understand her.

Without raising his eyes, the man calmly replied. "Trying to heal him. He is gravely ill." Though he spoke in English, his phrasing rang with a familiar rhythm.

His gentle words struck her with force. Her lips parted, but she could say nothing. With sudden insight, she shivered as a chill licked down her spine. This man was *not* a shaman. He was…something else, from somewhere else. Drawn here by her sheer force of will and guided by the hand of God.

Yielding to the man's direction, Celina gripped Lauro's hand. He was so delirious that his face was almost unrecognizable. With prayers on her lips, she willed her life force into him and let her tears bathe his face. Bending over him, she repeated her love for him and promised not to let him go.

When the healer finished his task, he gathered his materials. Pausing, he reached under the woven woolen shawl he wore and brought out a chain that held a silver medallion. After removing it from his neck, he turned toward Celina.

Taking her hand, he dropped the chain into her palm and then closed his hands over hers. "He needs higher powers now."

Weeping, Celina clung to the man's hands, feeling strength radiating through his touch. His soothing voice was like a memory she couldn't quite recall. The man's long, dark hair was threaded with silver strands, and his shaggy beard was unkempt, but there was something in his voice and mannerisms that dug into and irritated her memory, like a bit of sand in the gray flesh of an oyster.

Blinking, she stared through her tears at the medallion, which portrayed a man with a staff in one hand and a child on his shoulder. *Saint Christopher.* She kissed the worn silver, then lifting the cool cloth from Lauro's brow, she cradled his head and fastened the chain around his neck.

"Thank you," she murmured.

The man turned to Lauro. As he swept his hand across Lauro's face, he hesitated, taking in his features. Closing his eyes, he dipped his head reverently before him.

The healer leaned close to Lauro's ear and began murmuring to him, his words barely above a whisper.

Celina strained to hear. Although she could not make out his words, one element was unmistakable.

He spoke Italian.

The man smoothed his hand over Lauro's face and checked the pulse in his neck.

With his left hand.

Celina pressed her hand against her heart.

Her breath grew shallow, and she peered closer at the man who knelt by Lauro. His long hair partly concealed his profile, but she could make out the planes of his forehead, the curve of his cheekbones, the angle of his eyebrows.

Could it be? She hardly dared to hope.

She recalled Nino's entry in his journal. *My heart longs to practice medicine and explore the world.*

Who was this *doctor de milagros*? She contemplated this man, daring to imagine the nearly impossible.

Quietly observing him, Celina noted his attentive demeanor and elegance of movement. She tried to recall what Sara had said about her son.

Surely there were others who had been drawn to the wild, majestic beauty of this land to study its ancient mysteries of botanical treasures.

Yet, could it be?

If ever there was a time for a miracle, it was now. She reached a quivering hand toward the man and touched his sleeve.

"Are you Nino?" she asked, her voice barely above a whisper.

With a profound look of sadness in his eyes, the man heaved a sigh and bowed his head.

Celina held her breath, waiting.

His nod was nearly imperceptible.

Nino. She clamped her hand over her mouth to keep from crying out.

Now she saw the resemblance, though a dark beard shrouded the lower half of his face. And yet, there was something else about this doctor of miracles wedged in the distant corners of her memory.

"Your family has never stopped loving you," she said.

Nino met her gaze and a calm understanding passed between them. Returning his attention to Lauro, he stroked his brother's fevered forehead and continued to murmur to him as he performed his ministrations. With the utmost care, he lifted Lauro's head and managed to dispense a dark liquid through his brother's parched lips.

Her nerves spent, Celina felt her limbs go limp as relief flooded her body. Having been by Lauro's side longer than she could recall, she got up, her legs tingling and aching. The intensity of watching over him and fighting for help had weakened her. She stepped into the light of day, leaving Lauro with his brother.

Inhaling, she drew in the sweet scent of a rain shower looming nearby. As she stood at the mouth of the cave watching them, the similarities between them came into focus. Nino was far thinner, his skin darkened from his proximity to the sun at this altitude. But his grace of movement spoke of his ancestry.

Adele had been correct. *Two brothers, so alike.*

Overhead, smudged storm clouds blotted out the sun's warmth. Celina shivered. In the distance, broad-winged condors were dark etchings against a snowy mountain canvas. From somewhere on the mountain, the haunting melody of a flute serenaded them. She could almost feel Lauro's soul—beckoned by the pure, heavenly strain—separating from her and this world.

Alarmed, she hurried inside the cave and knelt next to Nino at Lauro's side. "Is he…?"

"Rest. I will stay with him."

Relief smoothed the frayed edges of her mind. Dazed from stress and lack of sleep, she collapsed nearby on a spread of woven blankets. As rain pelted the jungle, she yielded to the sweet tentacles of sleep.

Celina didn't know how long she'd been asleep when she woke, startled, to a strangled guttural cry. Whipping over, she started to scramble from the pallet to Lauro.

She rose to her knees and stopped, frozen at the sight before her.

Lauro was fully conscious now and clutching Nino. With tears gathering in their eyes, each brother held the other in a fervent embrace, rejoicing in their reunion and rocking from side to side. Nino wrapped his arms around Lauro in protection, stroking his hair and examining his eyes in the midst of it all.

Celina rushed to them, and Lauro swept her into their celebratory embrace.

"*Grazie a Dio*, we found him," Lauro cried. Debilitated though he was, he laughed with joy through tears that streamed across his cheeks.

Weak with gratitude, Celina kissed Lauro softly and turned to Nino. "Will he be okay?"

Chapter 37

"LAURO'S WOUND MUST be treated," Nino said, squatting while he washed his hands outside the cave after the rain had let up. "You need to take him to Lima."

Celina shaded her eyes from the sun that was peeking from behind clouds. "You have to come with us. We came to find you, and Lauro won't leave without you. "

Squinting up at her, Nino shook his head. "I don't go to Lima."

"Why not?"

He looked at her as if she were missing an obvious point. "I haven't left the Andes since I arrived."

"Lauro needs you. He could have died." Celina stared back him, incredulous at his lack of concern.

"He didn't though." Nino poured fresh mountain lake water over his hands.

"You brought him back from the edge of life. Not only with your medical attention but also with your love. That's what he needs."

"He has you, doesn't he?"

"We came here for *you*." How could he fail to understand the magnitude of what it had taken to find him? "And for your parents."

Nino grew quiet and gazed out over the mountains. "How are they?"

She wished she could lie and tell him that they were ill and needed him right away. But Lauro needed him, too. "They're in good health. They have missed you terribly, and there are holes in their hearts that only you can fill."

Nino sighed, acknowledging this fact. "There was a woman," he began.

Celina knelt beside him. "I know all about Isabella."

"Then you know that I was responsible."

"That's not true. She made her choice. Each of us is responsible for our own actions."

"All these years… I loved her, too, you know."

"You left right after the accident?"

"Is that what they called it?" Before she could answer, he nodded. "Of course, so she could have a proper burial."

With a faraway look in his eyes, he went on. "I was so destroyed that I couldn't face our families. I was the cause of it all, you see. The day after her funeral, a friend drove me to Naples, where I took a train to Rome. The next day, I caught a flight to New York."

"At least come for a visit." She touched his shoulder with compassion. "Your parents will welcome you with so much love."

Nino shook water from his hands and stood. "I can't leave my work here."

How was she ever going to convince him to go to Lima with Lauro or home to Italy? "What's more important than your brother? Than your family?"

"My research into ancient healing methods is extremely important," Nino argued. "Not only for the Andean dwellers but also for others who will benefit from my research. I'm not finished."

"Then share what you have now. Even if your work is not complete, imagine how many could benefit from what you have so far. You saved your brother's life with your skills." And Lauro needed him still.

Gazing out over the mountains, Nino considered her words. "In the Andes grow plants with healing powers unlike any others I've seen. I found my destiny here."

She grew more anxious. "By becoming a hermit and not sharing your findings with others? Ernesto told me you only treated the Quechua."

"I didn't want to be found. I felt safer that way, so I could dedicate myself to research and testing."

"You saved Lauro's life with your knowledge. Surely you can imagine that there are people out there who need what you know right now. You hold their future, their destiny, in your hands." She opened her palms to him. "You hold Lauro's fate, too. If you don't help your brother off this mountain, I fear he'll lose his will to live."

When Nino didn't reply, she said, "If you have the temerity to call yourself a doctor, then you will do what's best for your patient."

"I'm no doctor."

"Ernesto called you *el doctor de milagros*."

A corner of his mouth turned up. "His young daughter was gravely ill. I helped her, that's all."

"Then help your brother. Lauro risked death to find you. He still needs you." Anxiety tightened her chest like a vise. She tried again. "Your parents are good people. Please don't let them lose a second son."

Nino turned toward the mouth of the cave. Finally, he nodded. "I will go with him."

Relief coursed through her and left her weak with gratitude. "*Mille grazie*," she said, brushing her cheeks against his.

When Nino told her he had to trek back to his home to retrieve his research and materials, she prayed he would return.

Thankfully, he did.

Celina was so grateful that Nino agreed to come with them. The return journey was fraught with difficulties, and their pace was slow. Lauro leaned on Nino for physical support much of the way. After expressing their appreciation to Ernesto and his men and handsomely compensating them for their assistance, Celina, Lauro, and Nino set off for Lima. Once they arrived in the city, Nino guided them to a modern clinic.

After Lauro described his accident and Nino relayed details about his treatment and condition, the medical staff began their examination. They were visibly impressed with how Nino had cared for his brother.

Physicians cleaned and dressed Lauro's leg, and prescribed penicillin to ward off the possible return of the infection. "You saved his leg—and his life," one doctor told Nino.

As soon as they found a telephone, Lauro called his parents to tell them the good news and put Nino on the line to talk to them. She could hear their jubilation over the phone. His parents' joyous elation brought fresh tears to her eyes. Celina was so thankful they'd found Nino and that she'd fulfilled her promise. After a few minutes, Sara put Marco on the phone. Clutching the telephone receiver, Celina told him they'd be back soon and that she loved him very, very much.

To let Lauro rest, Celina contacted a travel agent who booked a return flight to Rome and found a hotel for them. Exhausted from their ordeal, Celina and Lauro checked in with Nino, and they all slept soundly. Upon rising, Celina savored a warm bath before she helped Lauro wash his hair and clean up without getting his bandages wet.

She dressed hastily in her lightweight gray suit and pumps, which now felt foreign after wearing mud boots and khaki pants for such a long time. Glancing at the clock on the dresser, she noticed they didn't have long before their flight. "Is Nino ready? Did he call while I was in the bath?"

"Can't reach him. Probably bathing, too. First bathtub he's seen in years." Lauro chuckled, but Celina could tell he was concerned.

Half an hour later, Celina knocked on his door. Growing worried, she checked with the front desk. To her dismay, he'd checked out early in the morning.

Nino had fulfilled his promise to help Lauro off the mountain and make the trip to Lima. He'd met with doctors and made sure Lauro received treatment. In his mind, he had executed his duty. Celina was furious that Nino had reneged on his promise to return with them. Didn't he care about the family that had risked so much to find him?

Celina marched back to their hotel room in a haze of anger and disappointment. How would Lauro take this, and how would it affect him?

As soon as she opened the door, Lauro looked up. "He's gone, isn't he?"

Celina nodded and went to him. "I don't know what happened. Nino assured me he would return with us. He'd even brought his research material."

Crestfallen, Lauro stared from the window. "Last time he left, it wasn't only because he couldn't bear to face our parents or me after Isabella died." He grimaced. "I sent him away. I was to blame, and I regret that."

"You were both angry and hurt, but that's all in the past."

He ran a hand through his still damp hair. "Maybe he's been here too long."

Celina drummed her fingers, anxiously wondering where he could have gone. "We haven't much time before the flight. Soon we'll have to go without him."

Furrowing his brow, he shoved his hands into his trouser pockets. "We can wait a little longer."

The clock beside the bed ticked, marking the minutes until finally, Celina ceded defeat. She picked up her purse in resignation and went to Lauro. Smoothing her arm around his shoulders, she felt the tension in his body.

"We should go." She spoke as gently as she could. "We'll leave word at the front desk. Maybe he'll meet us at the airport." Hoping against the odds, she clutched his hands in hers, knowing that his sorrow was even greater than hers.

"Well, we gave it all we had, didn't we?" Lauro said, blinking back his heartache. "I'll tell Papa how wonderful you were. I wouldn't be coming home if it weren't for you. Or Nino." He heaved a sigh and limped toward the door. "Let's go."

"Wait, I forgot my hairbrush." She had just stepped into the bathroom when a knock sounded at the door. *Please let it be Nino.*

Lauro let out a whoop and a whistle. "Celina, you're not going to believe this."

She snatched the brush and raced from the bathroom.

A different version of Nino stood before them—freshly shaven, hair trimmed, new suit. Lauro hugged him and led him inside.

"We were beginning to think you'd changed your mind," Lauro said, visibly relieved.

"I promised your wife I'd be on that plane," Nino said. "I couldn't go looking like I did."

Celina and Lauro exchanged glances. "We're not married."

Nino looked baffled. "At the front desk, you gave your name as Savoia. Are you related to our family?"

Celina shot Lauro a look. That question remained to be answered.

"She is," Lauro replied with confidence. He placed his hand on Nino's shoulder. "I have to say, you look really nice. A lot like the older brother I always admired."

A corner of Nino's mouth tugged up. "He changed a lot."

"We all did, brother."

Nino caught a glimpse of himself in the mirror. He looked slightly startled, as if encountering a stranger. Ill at ease, he loosened his tie, tugged his pants legs, and adjusted the lapel on his sports coat. "Haven't worn clothes like these in years."

Gazing at Nino in the mirror, Celina blinked at his familiarity. The clean-shaven face now fit the voice that had seemed vaguely familiar in the cave. As she stared at him, an old memory sparked to life. *Doc.* She gave him a warm smile. "Suits you, Doc. Even more than your old uniform."

Nino gave her a long look. "No one has called me that in years."

"You were in San Francisco after the war." Celina smiled. He'd never asked how they had located him. Nino was older and leaner than the man who had visited her, but now he looked much the same.

Nino narrowed his eyes in thought. "Have you ever made truffles?"

"At a little chocolaterie called La Petite Maison du Chocolat."

His eyes lit at the memory. "Raspberry infused, dark chocolate ganache. One of the best truffles I'd ever tasted."

Lauro was looking between them now, still mystified by their connection.

"The last day you visited the shop, you had a friend named Tony with you."

"I had just met him that day." Nino shook his head at the old memory. "Befriended him, showed him my favorite places, offered him a place to sleep."

Celina quirked an eyebrow. "He stole something from you, didn't he?"

"My military identification and dog tags," Nino said with surprise. "To his credit, he was a thief with a conscience. He didn't touch my cash or passport. And he left a Saint Christopher's necklace. That one," he added, pointing to the silver medallion that Lauro now wore.

Lauro clapped a hand to his forehead in amazement.

"How do you know about this?" Nino asked, furrowing his brow.

"He went by the name of Tony Savoia," Celina said. "And we married a few months after you left."

Nino rubbed his smooth chin. "So that's how you became a Savoia." Pointing between Lauro and Celina, he asked, "But how did you meet?"

"Tony died," Celina said. "Almost a year ago now. He never told me what he had done. While we were married, he refused to talk about his family, although once, early on, the connection with Cioccolata Savoia came up in discussion."

"I'm sorry to hear about your husband." Nino tapped his temple, recalling the night. "At dinner, he asked about you, and we talked a lot about chocolate. I must have told him about our family."

The final puzzle pieces were shifting into place in her mind. "My husband suffered a heart attack and died. So I contacted his family, or who I thought was his family, to let them know he'd died. And that he had a son." She glanced down, fidgeting with her fingernails. "I didn't know I had been living a lie."

At that, Lauro put his arm around her. "You didn't know, and it wasn't your fault."

Celina nodded and turned back to Nino. "It wasn't until your mother showed me your journal of your trip to South America that I realized Tony wasn't the son they had lost. Your handwriting was so different from my husband's. And he wasn't left-handed."

"That must have been a shock," Nino said, his voice rich with empathy.

"It was, but your mother had figured it out, too." She quickly told him about the strawberry allergy and the clues she pieced together from Tony's uncle with Nino's journal.

The corner of Nino's mouth twitched with a grin. "And then you and my brother fell in love."

Lauro kissed Celina and checked his watch. "We'll tell you about that on the way to the airport. We have to hurry now."

"Mommy!" As soon as Marco spied his mother at the Rome airport, he broke loose from Sara and Carmine and launched himself at Celina.

Having cleared customs, she raced toward him, catching him and whirling him around. At turns laughing and crying, Celina rocked her son tightly in her arms, reveling in his sweet little boy scent that she had missed so much and, at one point in the cave, feared she might never know again.

"How I've missed you, my sweet little prince." She peppered his face with kisses, marveling that his little heart was pounding even faster than hers.

Sara and Carmine hurried behind him, and Celina stood to hug Sara, whose eyes were rimmed with tears. "I cannot thank you enough for looking after Marco."

Sara was shaking so with nervous anticipation, Celina thought she might collapse in her arms. "Are both of my boys with you?"

With her arm around Sara to support her, Celina turned around. Sara stifled a cry.

Through the crowd, Lauro appeared, still limping from his excruciating ordeal and leaning on the lanky man beside him.

As Nino and Lauro approached their parents, Celina could feel love vibrating between them all. They were oblivious to the travelers who raced around them.

Nino wrapped his arms first around Sara, and then he greeted his father. Carmine—the powerful head of their family—broke down in Nino's embrace, his shoulders heaving with emotional relief.

Celina smiled through her tears. *A son, returned from the dead.* They had mourned Nino only a few months ago.

Hope.

As she watched the family reunite after enduring so many years of tragedy and uncertainty, Celina marveled over the power of hope.

Hope had driven her to contact the Savoias after Tony's death—the hope of connecting with a beloved family for her son's sake. Hope had driven her in California as she searched for clues to Tony's motives. And hope had sustained her and Lauro in the mountains, just when their circumstances could not have been more tenuous and dire.

Did she have the right to hope for a future with Lauro? On the mountain, Lauro had promised that if they made it down alive, nothing would keep them apart. He would defy his father's mandate to be with the woman he loved.

As she stood watching the family come together after so many years of tragic separation, she suddenly knew the answer—though it was not the one she wanted. In searching the depths of her heart, she knew that no matter how much Lauro loved her, she could not—in good conscience—come between Sara and her son. For if Carmine continued to impose his decree against her due to her deception—however innocent it had been—Sara would suffer a rift in her marriage. In banishing them from his life, Sara would lose her relationship with Lauro. The woman had endured the traumatic loss of one son; Celina would not inflict such pain on her again. In being separated from Marco for even a short time, and not knowing if she would return, she could imagine the heartbreak. Sara's would be multiplied by many years.

Celina couldn't do it. Her humanity wouldn't allow her to, not even to Carmine. No, if she had any decency left in her at all, she would march straight to the Pan American ticket agent and purchase two tickets for San Francisco. She knelt and hugged Marco, preparing herself to break this to her son, who would be devastated once again.

She heaved a great sigh. No matter which path she chose, someone would be hurt. But neither could she bear to return to the Savoia villa and see the family reunited, sharing food and wine and rejoicing, when she knew that she would have to break Lauro's heart—and hers and Marco's—by leaving.

Yet, glancing back she saw Lauro smile at her, a smile that rekindled the fuse of determination within her. She had come to love him more than she ever thought possible to love another. His smile held the hope for a better tomorrow.

She swung her gaze back to Sara and Carmine.

What parents, in looking at their children, have not felt hope encapsulated in the promise of their children? A hope often bound up in pride and duty.

Whatever the circumstances, one constant remained, and that was love.

Straightening her weary shoulders, she weighed her choices.

Today, she would choose love. Tomorrow, choices might be made for her, and she would have to accept those, but today, she would decide. And every day after that.

In the last year, she had earned the right to write the story of her future. Actually, she realized, the power had been within her reach all along.

Grasping Marco's hand, she took her place beside Lauro.

Lauro brought them into his embrace and kissed them both on the cheeks. "Without you and your willpower, neither one of us would be here greeting our parents."

Turning to his parents, Lauro motioned to his leg. "When Celina heard about the *doctor de milagros*, she was unwavering in her quest to find him." With a smile playing on his lips toward Nino, he added, "Even when he refused to see me, she was unrelenting."

"In fairness," Nino said. "I didn't know the injured was my brother."

Lauro chuckled. "That was fortunate, because then I *know* he wouldn't have seen me."

Everyone laughed. Celina was happy to see the brotherly bond between Lauro and Nino developing again.

Gazing at the small gathering, Nino went on. "And Mamma, had it not been for you, sharing my journal with Celina, I would not be standing here today, asking for your forgiveness. And Papa's, and Lauro's."

As the family embraced one another, Celina pressed her hand to her mouth, choking with joy. The fissures and wounds of the past seemed to heal right before her eyes.

Marco felt the love, too. He tugged on her skirt. "I love you, Mommy."

Celina knelt to hug her son. "I love you, too, sweetie. Forever and ever."

Watching them, Lauro smoothed his hand over her shoulder. "We all owe a debt to Celina. Her commitment to doing the right thing by contacting her husband's family put the final act of this saga in motion. She did that not for herself, but for her son and his family."

"To add to that," Nino said, "I knew Celina's husband in San Francisco. Although I didn't know him long, he was an intelligent man of principles." When Marco beamed up at him, he mussed his hair. "You can be very proud of your papa, son."

"Thank you," Celina said, grateful to Nino for sharing this with his family and Marco. Who would have thought that one chance meeting could have changed the course of so many lives for the better? *Tony would be proud.* She couldn't think of a more fitting tribute to him. "He would have appreciated that," she said. As well as the irony of it all. Tony had always liked a good story.

Sara grasped Celina's hands in hers. "You saved Lauro's life. And you brought Nino back to us. Had you never called us to tell us of your husband's death, we would not have the joy of welcoming Nino home." She kissed Celina on the cheeks. "Thank you for bringing my boys back to me."

Carmine stood next to his wife, stroking his chin as he registered this information. In his eyes, Celina saw the depth of his love for his family. At this moment, she also saw his pliant heart, void of pride.

Celina could bring them all together right now. If she had the courage to act, she could bring happiness to Marco, Lauro, and Sara. Even Carmine. If she let fear or pride hobble her, the chance would pass, the opportunity forever gone.

Reaching out to Carmine, Celina kissed his cheek. "*Stiamo tornando a casa anche noi.*" *We're coming home, too.*

With shoulders heaving with emotion, Carmine wrapped his arms around her. "*Grazie mille,*" he managed to say, before breaking down. When he'd recovered, he took her by the shoulders. "You are welcome in our family. I might be the last one to express that, but let me be the first to give you and Lauro my blessing for a long and happy life together."

Celina kissed Carmine's cheek, grateful for his acceptance, and understanding the selflessness it had taken for him to get there.

Love and courage. That was all it took to bridge a chasm of the heart.

As Lauro gathered her and Marco in his arms, Celina saw Sara fold her hands over her heart in gratitude.

"Let's go home," Lauro said.

Holding Lauro and Marco, Celina smiled. "We already are."

Epilogue

Amalfi, 1954

"Ready to get underway?" Celina stepped onto Lauro's sleek Italian yacht, thrilled at the journey ahead of them. Adele had helped her choose her outfit—a white strapless bandeau-top and shorts with a zebra-print swim cover-up. After depositing their favorite wine in the galley and dropping a shopping bag with new lingerie in the cabin, she joined Lauro on the bridge.

"I've been ready for this for months," Lauro said, kissing her. Positioned at the helm, he eased his new yacht from its mooring and slowly motored out of the Amalfi marina. He'd even christened the yacht after her: *La Dolce Celina*.

She secured her broad-brimmed hat and tipped her head back, gazing up at the clear summer sky and the mountains that climbed high above the village of Amalfi. She couldn't imagine a better day to begin their holiday—exploring the coastline of the Sorrento peninsula and the islands in the Tyrrhenian Sea. Later, they planned to venture farther to the south of France, Monaco, and the Greek islands, but first Lauro wanted to share the spectacular beauty of his home.

As Celina slipped off her cover-up, Lauro ran his hand over her bare shoulders. "You look stunning, Signora Savoia. Hmm, *C.S.* You don't even have to change your monograms, do you?"

"I can hardly believe we're finally married." She threaded her arms around him while he maneuvered the craft.

Feathering a kiss on her lips, he said, "What a year it has been."

"One year ago today, we met in Naples," Celina said, resting her head on his shoulder and thinking about the year that changed their lives. "As I recall, that wasn't a very friendly welcome."

"How about I try to make it up to you again tonight?"

Celina nibbled his earlobe. "I wish you would."

"Or we could drop anchor in our magical hideaway."

Just the thought of that day, the first time they'd made love, brought a flush to her face. That surreal, watercolor memory—the expression of their love—had sustained her through nearly overwhelming challenges. "Mmm, I love that cove."

Just last week they married in the Duomo, the beautiful Sant'Andrea cathedral in Amalfi, in an intimate ceremony. Under soaring arches of a frescoed, gold-trimmed ceiling and surrounded by ornate, inlaid marble columns, Celina and Lauro exchanged their vows. She couldn't have been happier.

Celina wore Sara's wedding dress of ivory silk and lace, which Adele helped to fit to her. Joining them were Sara and Carmine, Adele and Werner and their children, and Nino, along with some of the extended Savoia family. Even Marge and Lizzie came for the wedding, much to Marco's delight. A baronial spread of delicacies, from the bounty of Campania and fresh seafood to chocolate fantasies that Celina had created especially for the party—including truffles flavored with wine from the vineyards above Amalfi—delighted their guests at the Villa Savoia. At sunrise, Celina and Lauro stood at the stone terrace, welcoming the dawn of their new life together.

Sara and Carmine had promised to look after Marco while they were gone. Thinking about them, Celina smiled and wondered what they were doing right now.

"We have three glorious weeks away," she said, reflecting on their journey with their family and friends.

After returning from Peru, Adele had been so astounded to see Nino again and hear the story of their connection that she rushed right over to see Celina. They renewed their friendship, and since then, their children played together often.

Lauro draped his arm around her and kissed the tip of her nose. "Where do you want to go first? Positano, Capri, Sorrento, Procida, Ischia. Your choice."

The yacht picked up speed, and Celina faced the salty spray, loving the sense of freedom in being on the ocean.

When she didn't answer, Lauro went on. "Or we can hike the Sentiero degli Dei, visit Pompeii or Ravello's gardens, or warm our toes in the hot spring at Baia di Sorgeto. Then there's Praiano, Conca dei Marini, Castiglione, Maiori, and Salerno."

"Too much, too much." Laughing, Celina placed her finger on Lauro's lips. "How about lunch in Positano before heading to Capri. From there, who knows?" For the next few weeks, she wanted as few plans as possible.

"That's a great idea."

"We'll have plenty of time to explore," she said. "Years, I hope." Here along the Amalfi coast, she had learned to enjoy the small moments. *Walking Marco to school. Playing on the beach with him and his cousins. A glass of wine with Lauro in the evening. A new truffle flavor. And now, waking with Lauro in the morning.* Compared to San Francisco, life on the Sorrento peninsula moved at a leisurely pace.

"Positano it is," he said. "What else would you like to do there?"

"Anything, except hike a mountain." She laughed and flung her arms overhead, stretching toward the sky and feeling free. "Though I miss that little tent we had in Marañón Canyon. Someday I'll muck through mud with you again. For now, I want lots of late mornings, breakfast in bed, and sandy beaches."

"Massages?"

"Mmm, by you? My favorite."

"Mine, too." Lauro grinned at her. "I've been thinking, Capri might be a good place for a *cioccolateria.*"

"For Stella di Cioccolato or Cioccolata Savoia?"

"We're strictly wholesale—definitely Stella di Cioccolato."

"Interesting," she said. "Maybe after I open my shop in Naples."

When they returned from their holiday, they were moving into a home in Vomero to be near the *fabbrica di cioccolato* for Lauro. Marco had more cousins his age nearby, so he was thrilled with the move. They would continue to spend holidays and the month of August in Amalfi with his parents at the Villa Savoia. After all that she and Lauro had been through, Celina loved how their life was working out.

"Adele's friend, the journalist, wrote such a glowing review of your *cioccolateria* in the newspaper," Lauro said. "I think you'll do well in Napoli."

Celina wrinkled her nose. "You don't mind sleeping with the competition?"

"I don't even mind fooling around in the test kitchen." He cupped her bottom and drew her closer to him. "Maybe we'll drop anchor and go below."

Laughing, Celina kissed him. "We're only a few minutes out of Amalfi."

As for Stella di Cioccolato, Celina had built up a devoted clientele. Her overseas orders were growing. I. Magnin had sold out of the inventory she'd sent. Based on her success there, she'd contacted buyers from City of Paris in San Francisco, Gimbels in New York, and Harrod's in London. Orders poured in, and it was all she could do to keep up with the business. Karin was working out well, so Celina had trained her to manage the shop in Amalfi. Soon it would be time to increase their artisanal production in a larger facility in Naples.

Celina loved experimenting with new flavors and expanding Stella di Cioccolato. She'd created a spicy chocolate truffle with mild chili peppers and white truffles made from cocoa butter and lemon. But the secret of the *gran blanco*—the rare white beans—would remain a secret of the Andean people until they wished to share it with the world again.

"Nino called this morning," Lauro said, the sun glinting off his sunglasses.

"Good news?" Celina loved the close relationship that Lauro and Nino shared. Not only brothers, but also the closest of friends. They had finally made peace with their past.

"He's starting his lab research next week."

Celina hooked her arm into Lauro's. He stroked her bare arm, which sent tingles through her. She was happy for Nino, who was getting another chance at his dream. He had been accepted to medical school in Rome to complete the study he had started in America before enlisting. As part of his program, he would conduct research on traditional herbal treatments of the Andes and other cultures.

She tented her hand against the sun. "Think Nino will stay in Italy after medical school?"

"He'll go where he feels needed." Lauro kissed her cheek. "Luckily, I feel needed right here."

"So do I, my love."

The salt air breeze tousled their hair as they cruised along the soaring cliffs, admiring the view and enjoying their time together. This was all that Celina had ever dreamed of. To feel at home, to love and to be loved. Had she not made one phone call, none of this would have happened.

As they neared the location of the cove, Celina and Lauro turned to each other and grinned. The memory of their magical cove sent delicious tingles through her. Why pass up such a lovely respite?

"Let's go," she whispered.

"*Quanto ti amo,*" he said, laughing and kissing her. "*Andiamo.*"

The End

Note from the Author: Thank you for reading *The Chocolatier.* You might also enjoy reading my other stories set by the sea. *Summer Beach: Seabreeze Inn* is the contemporary story of two sisters who transform a historic, California beach house into an inn. Find it online or at your favorite bookseller.

Books by Jan Moran

20th Century Historical
The Chocolatier
The Winemakers: A Novel of Wine and Secrets
Scent of Triumph: A Novel of Perfume and Passion

Contemporary
The Summer Beach Series:
Seabreeze Inn
Seabreeze Summer
Seabreeze Sunset

The Love, California Series:
Flawless
Beauty Mark
Runway
Essence
Style
Sparkle

Nonfiction
Vintage Perfumes

To hear about Jan's new books first and get special offers, join Jan's VIP Readers Club at www.JanMoran.com.

Reading Guide & Discussion Questions

1. The desire for family and home represent overarching themes in *The Chocolatier*. Can you think of a time when you longed for your family or a sense of home?

2. In this story, Celina's husband Tony steals an identity in desperation and subsequently covers it up with a lie that has a broadening ripple effect. Have you ever witnessed a deceit that rippled into a larger issue with consequences?

3. Families must often deal with the tragedy of missing members, whether through death or disappearance. Some people create alternate families. Did you suspect that Sara knew of the deception? What did you think of her acceptance of Celina and Marco?

4. *The Chocolatier* follows Celina, who must process the devastating loss of her husband and face starting over in a new home, with a job, in a new neighborhood—even with a new family and in a foreign country. Have you ever had a loss in life and had to change direction? How did this make you feel, and do you think others understood? What did you find challenging? Or did you find it freeing to recreate yourself?

5. Celina is often motivated by the love of her son, Marco, and makes choices based on her desire to give him a better life. Did your ancestors make sacrifices in your family? Have you made changes in your life for your children?

6. The love between Celina and Lauro is forbidden on several levels, yet they persevered. Can you think of an experience of forbidden love that had a happy or unfortunate outcome?

7. At times, Sara, Celina, and Lauro attribute serendipitous occurrences and coincidences to miracles. Have you experienced anything in your life that you attribute to a miracle? Do you believe in miracles, divine guidance, purpose, fate, or destiny?

8. What surprised you most in the story?

9. Think about the scenes centered on chocolate. Which ones were your favorites? Which descriptions of chocolate did you find most compelling?

10. What are your favorite chocolates? Take a poll: Milk, dark, or white chocolate?

11. If you like chocolate, did you discover anything new or interesting about the history or production in this book? What are your favorite chocolates? Do you have memories related to chocolate?

12. Jan's books often take the reader on a journey. Have you ever traveled to San Francisco, Italy, or Peru? Do you have any fond memories to share? Would you like to visit?

Traditional French Wild Truffle Chocolate Confection

Contributed by Chef Michael Antonorsi, Chuao Chocolatier

Ingredients

Filling:

2 ¼ cups (530 ml) of fresh heavy cream
4 oz. (120 ml) corn syrup or honey
1.5 lbs. (680 grams) of dark chocolate (Around 60% cacao content)
1 oz. (28 grams) of softened whipped butter

Dipping/Coating:

4 cups (500 grams) of melted dark chocolate
4 cups (500 grams) of cocoa powder

Procedure

- Boil cream together with the corn syrup.
- Chop the chocolate and put into a bowl.
- Add the hot cream to the chocolate and let sit for half an hour until it cools down to around 95°F (35°C). Mix softly to incorporate into a smooth chocolate ganache.
- When the mixture is cooled down to around 90°F (32°C), add the softened butter and mix in well.
- Leave the mixture to cool down and set overnight.
- With a melon baller, scoop out the individual amounts desired per truffle.
- Using cocoa powder as a nonstick agent in the hands, roll the scooped amount into a small ball.

- Temper 4 cups (500 grams) of melted dark chocolate. (See Notes below.)
- Dip the balls halfway into the chocolate and roll them between the hands to have an even, thin coating all around the truffle. Place the dipped balls on the parchment paper again and let crystallize.
- Dip the balls a second time with an even thinner coating of chocolate. This time roll over the cocoa powder and cover completely. Let set for a few minutes.
- Store the finished product in an airtight container.

Makes about 70 truffles
Shelf life: 2 weeks

Notes

On Tempering the Chocolate:

The simplest way to temper chocolate for truffle making is to use the seeding method. This consists of using a ratio of 75% melted chocolate and 25% solid chips or chopped bar of chocolate.

For this example:

- Melt 3 cups (375 grams) of dark chocolate in a double boiler. Make sure not to heat it too much, but just enough so that all of it is melted.
- Remove from the double boiler and add 1 cup (125 grams) of solid chips or chopped chocolate bar.
- Mix slowly and let the chips melt as much as they can. Do not worry if not all of it melts. The incorporation of the solid chips will slowly seed the melted chocolate and temper it.
- Once most or all of the solid chocolate has melted, proceed with dipping the truffles in the chocolate.
- If the chocolate begins to thicken, then put the bowl back on top of the double boiler and heat slightly. Do not overheat because the temper will be lost.

On Infusing Flavors:

- Wild truffles are very versatile and one can infuse the cream with anything that can infuse it, including tea leaves and rose petals, or herbs such as basil, rosemary, and others.
- Bring the cream to a boil and add the leaves. Let steep for 10 minutes, then strain. Measure the cream and add more cream to return to the initial measure. Bring to a quick boil again and use.

On Using Alcohol as Flavoring:

- Using an alcoholic beverage as flavoring is always a great idea because it extends the shelf life of the truffles.
- Use alcohol that has a distinctive flavor such as Rum, Whisky, Amaretto, Grand Marnier or Kahlua.
- Substitute an amount of cream that is equivalent to the alcohol used. For example, if 2 ounces (60 ml) of cream are required, remove 1 ounce (30 ml) of cream and add 1 ounce (30 ml) of alcohol.
- Always add the alcohol at the end after all ingredients are mixed.
- Boiling alcohol with the cream will boil away the alcohol.

Author's Notes

Researching creative and culinary arts is such a pleasure, and I hope my writing inspires deeper appreciation of the artistry of talented creators. I've always been attracted to nature's gifts that appeal to the senses and add beauty to our lives—and to the creative, strong-willed visionaries that bring these sensory indulgences to life. That said, I have a few notes to add.

In 1916, a devastating hemibiotrophic fungus commonly called Witches' Broom (*Moniliophthora perniciosa*) swept across Ecuador and Peru, obliterating Pure Nacional, a coveted cacao plant that produces white cocoa beans prized for their floral aroma and smooth flavor. After the infestation, Pure Nacional was thought extinct—lost to the world forever.

Yet in 2009, a few hardy Pure Nacional trees were discovered in Marañón Canyon in Peru at a higher elevation than most cacao trees grow, thus these survivors, some of which were more than one hundred years old, avoided the plague of the Witches' Broom. Legend has it that some locals knew of these coveted plants but kept the location secret for their own use, so with that in mind, I included a discovery of these rare cacao trees in the story.

During the research phase, I delved into the magical world of chocolate and soon discovered the complexity of the industry. From farmers to traders and chocolate makers—as well as end chocolate users: chocolatiers, chefs, and consumers—each has a love for this delicacy that descended from Mayan and Aztec civilizations in central and south America. The study of chocolate can fill a lifetime, and I often lost myself in research. While I spoke with numerous professionals in the industry, any mistakes are my own—which I attribute to a happy, chocolate-induced haze. Ditto with historical details.

For more details on chocolate, wine, and perfume, please visit my website at JanMoran.com. Thank you for reading, and I enjoy hearing from readers.

Acknowledgements

In the writing of this book, I had the pleasant task of researching chocolate—how cacao is grown, how cocoa and chocolate are derived, and how chefs and chocolatiers employ this magical ingredient to delight chocolate lovers around the world. Everywhere I turned, providence seemed to intercede.

I chanced upon a Chuao chocolaterie in my neighborhood and fell in love with the spicy Mayan chocolate, Firecracker, and other unique, delicious creations. Chuao's co-founder, Chef Michael Antonorsi, who attended culinary school in Paris and lives in San Diego, invited me into his professional kitchen. He and his business partner, Richard, are brothers descended from Venezuelan cacao growers. Thank you, Chef Michael, for sharing your abundant joy and extensive knowledge of chocolate.

My sincere appreciation to the team at Valrhona, maker of some of the world's finest chocolate for chefs and chocolate aficionados. Thanks to Jennifer Butler, Alex Espiritu, Benjamin Figarede, Danielle Fitzpatrick, Colleen Gibson, and Marine Leman. Great appreciation to Peruvian cacao planters Eduardo Espinoza Tamariz and Albino Riega Vizueta. The tasting, history, and technical details helped me weave in authentic details.

To Bennett Zimmerman, with whom I sampled artisan chocolate in Israel, along with Cheryl Rosenstein, and her friend, Deborah Prinz, whose book, *On the Chocolate Trail,* detailed a wealth of historical research. Chocolate sweetens even the finest friendships.

As for the Italian phrases, *mille grazie* to my dear friend, actor Luca Della Valle, a native of Naples who helped me appreciate the language, culture, and beauty of the Campania region of Naples. Again, any errors are my own, and my only defenses are chocolate and Piedirosso, Campania's superb wine. A special acknowledgment also goes to one of Amalfi's delightful chocolate shops, Cioccolato Andrea Pansa.

My deepest gratitude to Kerstin Schaub, my editor at Goldmann Verlag / Random House in Germany. What a pleasure it is to work together on these delightful stories! And to Erin Bennett, for lending her lovely voice and dramatic talents to the audio narration.

To my treasured family, Eric, Ginna, and Zoë, for their love and unwavering support. And finally, to my readers: Thank you for being part of this delicious, enchanting journey.

Jan Moran
Los Angeles, California

Made in United States
North Haven, CT
02 January 2022

14039721R00226